also by
JESSICA PETERSON

LUCKY RIVER RANCH

Cash

Wyatt

Sawyer

JESSICA PETERSON

Bloom books

Published by Bloom Books, an imprint of Sourcebooks
P.O. Box 4410, Naperville, Illinois 60567–4410
(630) 961-3900
sourcebooks.com

Originally self-published in 2024 by Jessica Peterson.

Cataloging-in-Publication data is on file with the Library of Congress.

Printed and bound in the United States of America.
LSC 10 9 8 7 6 5 4 3 2 1

For the cowgirl in all of us.
Ride hard. Ride often.
Ride free.

CHAPTER 1
Kiss My Ass, Cowboy
Mollie

I'm deep in cowboy country, but I still jam on the brakes when I see an actual cowboy park his actual horse outside an actual saloon.

Have I gone back in time? Or is the whole scene a mirage? My dashboard does say it's 109 degrees outside.

The cloud of dust that's followed me since Belton billows around my SUV, temporarily obscuring the view of a building marked *The Rattler*.

The Hill Country dust clears. Yep, that's definitely a horse. And that's definitely a guy in slim-cut jeans and a cowboy hat sliding off the saddle with an ease that makes my breath catch.

Mom's words echo inside my head: *Hartsville is a one-horse town.* I didn't know she meant that literally.

I feel a whisper of recognition as I take in the building's facade behind the cowboy and his horse. It's two stories, brick, with windows whose uneven panes glint in the hazy afternoon light. A faded green-and-black-striped awning bears the image of a white rattlesnake, its forked tongue protruding from between its fangs.

I was six years old the last time I was in this tiny town, smack-dab in the middle of nowhere. Why would I remember a bar of all places?

"Mollie? Did I lose you?"

My stomach seizes, the sound of Wheeler's voice on the phone yanking me back inside the Range Rover. Without looking, I immediately hit the gas, then send up a silent prayer of thanks that Main Street is deserted. No one to hit, thank God.

Well, except for the cowboy and his horse, who I glimpse in my rearview mirror. I'm less than two hundred miles southwest of Dallas, but I might as well be on another planet for how different this place feels.

I reach for the vent beside the steering wheel and aim a blast of AC at my face. "Sorry, I'm here. I just got to Hartsville and...I think I may have just had an *Outlander* moment? But a Western-themed one, with a saloon and a cowboy."

My best friend and business partner's raspy laugh pours through the speakers. "Bring cowboy Jamie back to Dallas. Tell him city life is better."

"No shit." I peer out my windshield as my GPS tells me I'm approaching my destination. "Mom wasn't joking when she said there was nothing out here."

"Get your money and get the hell out of Dodge. Call me when you're done, okay? I'm thinking of you."

I smile, even as my stomach seizes again. "Thanks, friend. I can't wait for the pop-up."

"Same. I'm so curious to see how it goes."

One of Dallas's better-known boutiques is hosting a

pop-up shop for our cowboy boot company this week. The boutique's clientele is fashion-forward and well-heeled, so we'll hopefully make a decent number of sales. Lord knows we could use the revenue.

Hanging up, I slow down in front of the last building on the left before Main Street continues down a desolate stretch of nothingness ahead. The chalk-colored dirt, dotted sparsely with trees, cacti, and brush, wavers in the midafternoon heat.

A brass placard beside the building's door reads *Goody Gershwin, Attorney at Law, Est. 1993.*

"You have arrived at your destination," my GPS informs me.

I pull into an angled parking spot beside an enormous candy-apple-red pickup truck. It also appears to be from 1993, its windows rolled down to reveal a front bench seat upholstered in faded gray fabric. A box set of Brooks & Dunn's greatest hits sits on the passenger side of the bench.

It's a box set of *cassette tapes.*

Maybe I really have gone back in time.

The heat hits me like a slap to the face the second I hop out of my car. It radiates off the blacktop and singes my bare legs.

At the same time, the sun bears down on my head and shoulders from above. It's like being pressed inside a griddle.

Looping my bag over my shoulder, I wonder why the hell anyone would live out here. What did Dad see in this place?

I can't believe I'm actually here. I can't believe he's actually gone.

Most of all, I can't believe I lost the chance to ever make things right between us.

Grief, mixed with a hefty dose of anger, sits on my chest like an elephant.

A literal bell jangles above the door as I enter the building. It's blessedly cool inside the office. The familiar scent of brewing coffee makes me feel slightly less discombobulated.

A young man with round glasses smiles up at me from a nearby desk. "You must be Mollie Luck. Welcome! I'm Zach, Goody's paralegal." He rounds the desk and holds out his hand. "Can I get you anything? Water? Coffee? I hope the drive wasn't too bad."

I take his hand. "Three hours. Not terrible. Nice to meet you, Zach. And I'm fine, thanks."

He eyes my metallic-pink boots. "Those are *spectacular*."

"Aw, thank you. They're part of my boot company's most recent collection."

"You own a boot company?" A woman with short, dark hair in a light-colored linen suit emerges from a door to my left. She appears to be wearing a bolo—black, silver buckle—without a trace of irony. "How amazing!"

"They're manufactured right here in Texas."

The woman's eyes crinkle as she smiles at me. "Even better. I'm Goody Gershwin. Nice to finally meet you, Mollie. Your dad talked about you often. He was so proud of you."

My eyes burn, and my heart twists. Was Dad proud of me? He never showed it. Definitely never said it. But I'd like to think he'd be a little proud of how I turned out at least.

I paste on a smile. "Nice to meet you too."

"I'm so sorry for your loss. The community here has taken Garrett's death hard, but I can only imagine how tough it's been for y'all."

A piercing ache shoots through my heart and settles in the back of my throat. "The community" must've been a lot closer to Dad than I was. Then again, no one except Mom, Mom's parents, Wheeler, and I showed up to his funeral in Dallas three months ago, so who knows?

"I appreciate that."

"Well, we're glad you're here." Goody drops my hand. "Today should be relatively straightforward. As the executor of your father's will, I'll walk you through his estate and the distribution of his assets, along with his wishes for—"

Goody looks up at the jingle of the bell behind me. The creases at the edges of her eyes deepen.

"Hello, Cash! Always a pleasure seeing you."

Cash. Why is that name familiar?

"Ma'am. Good afternoon."

Something about the deep voice—its scraped-bare sound maybe, or the thick-as-molasses accent—has me glancing over my shoulder.

My heart takes a tumble at the *very* handsome man standing just inside the door. He looks to be in his late twenties, maybe early thirties. Tall—six three, I'd guess—with the kind of build you see on quarterbacks: broad shoulders, thick arms, long legs with thighs that strain against his fitted jeans. Wranglers, if I had to guess.

He's holding a cowboy hat to his chest, like he just swept it off his mass of messy brown hair, which curls out at the ends. Veins crisscross the back of his hand. He's sporting a scruffy beard that's longer along his top lip—I don't normally find mustaches attractive, but somehow, it's downright hot on this guy—and a white-and-blue-striped button-up that complements his cobalt eyes.

Eyes that are so blue, in fact, they seem to glow against his deeply tanned face.

Those eyes lock on mine. My pulse blares inside my ears. One beat. Two.

The intensity of the extended eye contact, the ballsiness of it, makes my stomach drop. His gaze flickers. Why do I get the feeling he's annoyed? Angry even?

The memory hits me: a pair of gangly blue-eyed boys in the bed of a pickup truck. One of them was punching another in the head, the blows increasing in frequency until a voice shouted at them from the cab to quit it.

The Rivers boys.

Despite the obvious prevalence of bodily injury in their family, I was so jealous of those kids. As an only child, all I wanted was a house full of siblings, and here were the Riverses with oodles of them. I distinctly remember seeing Mrs. Rivers in the passenger seat, her hand on her pregnant belly.

Their family owns the ranch next to Dad's property. I remember seeing the boys at the tractor supply store here in town and at the rodeo out in Lubbock once. Not often enough to be friends—their mom homeschooled them on their ranch, so they weren't around a lot—but often enough to know who they were.

Unable to withstand Cash's gaze another second, I look down at his boots. They're square-toed, dark brown. The leather is creased with age but obviously well cared for, the color gleaming from a recent coat of conditioner.

The whisper of vague recognition I felt earlier returns.

Thanks to my job, I know cowboy boots better than anyone. This is a pair of Lucchese: expertly made, expensive, and classic. They're the kind of cowboy boots you pass down from generation to generation.

Dad wore Lucchese. I don't know how I remember this, but the certainty of it sits in my gut like a brick.

"Mollie, allow me to introduce Cash Rivers." Goody extends her arm. "He's been the foreman at your family's ranch for, goodness, has it been—"

"Twelve years."

Cash's clipped reply makes me think he really is annoyed. With me? But why? And he's working on our property now? What happened to his family's ranch? I'm confused.

That does explain why he'd be at the reading of Dad's will, though. As the foreman, maybe he'll be giving me the literal lay of the land?

Not like it matters. The second Lucky Ranch is in my name, I'm putting it up for sale. I have absolutely no interest in running a Hill Country cattle ranch. I've always been more of an indoor girl, and my whole life is in Dallas anyway—my friends, my family. Bellamy Brooks, the cowboy boot company I started with Wheeler, is also based in the area. Business is finally taking off, and the inheritance I'm about to get will definitely bring us to the next level.

"Cash. Wow. I remember you." I extend my hand.

He glances at it, his mouth a hard line. An awkward beat passes before he wordlessly envelops my hand in the warm mitt of his. My pulse skips at the firmness of his handshake. How his heavily calloused palm presses against mine, dry but somehow thrillingly alive at the same time.

I give him a firm handshake back, making a point to look him in the eye again.

"Been a minute," he says at last.

A scent rises off him. Simple soap, cut with something sexier. Aftershave? Whatever it is, it smells fresh and herbal, and it's delicious enough to make my pulse skip a second time.

"Good to see you again," I manage.

I wait for Cash to reply. What kind of name is Cash anyway? His real name? A nickname?

He doesn't say a word.

"Well, now that we're all here"—Goody grabs a file and a small zippered pouch Zach holds out to her—"we can get started. Just follow me to the conference room."

She heads down a hallway. I glance at Cash, who lifts his hat a half inch off his chest. "After you."

I wonder if he's a man of few words or if he's just an asshole.

I want to be back in Dallas so bad, my stomach hurts. Then again, my stomach always hurts, so that's nothing new.

I follow Goody down the hallway, Cash's heavy footfalls behind me.

One hour. Two, max. Then I'll have the money I need to make my dreams come true.

Well, one dream at least.

And maybe using Dad's money to fund Bellamy Brooks will finally make me feel less angry about—well, everything.

Goody takes a seat at the head of the long, shiny

conference table. I grab the chair to her right and watch Cash fold his large body into the chair to Goody's left. He sets his hat on the table upside down so that the brim is facing up. What's that about? A way to protect the hat's shape or something?

Then he reaches up and runs his blunt fingers through his hair, drawing his shirt taut across the well-muscled expanse of his chest.

Looking away, I busy myself pulling my planner out of my bag. I have no idea why I'd need it, but I have to do something with my hands. I'm suddenly nervous.

Which makes no sense. Mom assured me I was Dad's only living child and heir. According to their divorce settlement, I'll get all his property since he never remarried or had other children. Money is the one thing Dad did give me over the years. Anytime I needed it, he'd cut a check.

But anytime I needed him, he'd never show.

I blame my nerves on the glowering cowboy across from me. Who, by the way, is lazily leaning back in his chair, knees spread, forearms slung across the armrests like he's bored.

I feel a surge of anger. *I don't wanna be here either, dickwad.*

Dad and I were not close. But I still wish he hadn't died, even if I am about to get a boatload of his cash and his ranch. In fact, I very much wish he were still here, so I could—I don't know—try one last time.

Maybe call him one last time and say *I love you, I'm sorry, can we start over?*

I always assumed we'd have all the time in the world to mend our relationship. Part of me wanted him to know just how hurt I was by his absence in my daily life after my parents got divorced when I was six, so once I got older, I totally shut him out. I figured once I hit a certain level of success—once I was a real adult, one who didn't hold grudges—we'd iron things out.

Now I'll never get that chance, and it kills me.

Goody sets out several pieces of paper on the table, pushing them around until they line up in rows of three. "I'd like to start by saying emotions can run high during these situations. It's okay to take a break if you need it, all right?"

I uncap a purple felt-tipped pen. "Okay."

"Yes, ma'am." Cash sits up in his chair and rests his elbows on the table.

"Let's dive right in." Goody glances down at the papers. "For simplicity's sake, we'll divide Garrett Randall Luck's assets into two buckets: financial and tangible. The Lucky Ranch comprises two hundred fifty-six thousand acres and fifteen thousand head of cattle, along with twenty-two structures, several pieces of heavy equipment, and an oil operation that produces approximately one thousand barrels a day. As of the signing of this will, the ranch employed fifty people…"

I hear the whisper of denim on denim. Looking across the table, I notice Cash's knee is bouncing. He's anxious too.

Why *is* he here? Is he expecting to get something from Dad?

"…and then we have the financial bucket, consisting of cash and an investment portfolio. Garrett requested this be put in a trust…"

Cash glances up, and our gazes collide. I finally recognize the look in his eyes.

Resentment. *What?* Why? I haven't been in this town for twenty years. What could I have possibly done to him?

"All this is to say"—Goody inhales sharply, and Cash's eyes cut to her—"Garrett last amended his will in April of this year. In that amendment, he stipulated that Lucky Ranch and all its operations be bequeathed to his only living relative, Mary Elizabeth Luck, nicknamed Mollie."

Cash's hands land with a *whack* on the table, making me jump. "With all due respect, Goody, that's incorrect. Garrett said the ranch would go to me."

My head spins. A fist grips my lungs and squeezes. "Excuse me?"

"Garrett promised me the ranch." Cash looks me square in the eye. "Many times, in fact."

Goody frowns. "We don't have that in writing, I'm afraid."

I stare at Cash. "Are you delusional?"

"Are you?" he fires back. "Goody, Garrett said he'd put it in his will. I can have all of Hartsville—every single person—vouch for me. Patsy and John B. The ranch hands. Sally and Tallulah, and, well, everyone heard Garrett say it. Think about it. I know Lucky Ranch better'n anyone. My family's been in Hartsville for generations—"

"He was my dad." *Regardless of the fact that he and I barely spoke over the past decade.* "I'm his daughter. What makes you think you're entitled to his assets? I've barely even heard of you."

Cash's blue eyes burn. "You would have if you'd called or spent any time on the ranch."

Fuck. This guy. For life.

"You know nothing about me." My voice wavers. "And clearly, you know nothing about my family. The ranch belongs to me—"

"Lemme guess. You're gonna sell it."

"That's none of your business."

"Sure as hell is my business. I'll be damned if our operation is sold to one of your idiot trust-fund friends who doesn't know their ass from their elbow when it comes to ranching. You got no idea how much work we've put in—"

"I don't care." I clench my teeth. "Truly, I could care less about you or whatever work you do."

"You couldn't care less."

"Excuse me?"

His eyes bore into mine. "That's the proper expression."

"What the hell is your problem?"

"Where do I begin?" He leans forward.

"All right, y'all." Goody raises her voice. "Let's try and keep it civil, all right? Garrett wouldn't want y'all arguing this way. We have to respect his wishes as he laid them out in his will. It is the law."

"I'm gonna fight this," Cash says.

I purse my lips. "I'd like to see you try."

Goody clears her throat. "May I finish?"

Cash's eyes stay locked on mine. "Go for it."

"The monetary assets—cash and the investment portfolio, which have been placed in a trust—will also go to Mollie."

Dad made a pile of money back in the nineties when oil was discovered on a far corner of our family's property. Mom got some of it in the divorce, and she used it to start a real estate brokerage company in Dallas. Dad divided the rest between the ranch and the stock market. Considering the Dow Jones Industrial Average has increased fourfold since then…yeah, there's a lot of money there.

Cash lets out a dark chuckle. "See, City Girl? You got your money. Let us have the ranch."

I take a page from his book and stay silent. No point honoring that ridiculousness with a response. Although what does he mean when he says *us*?

"However"—Goody flattens her palm on the table beside mine—"there is a stipulation."

I finally break eye contact with Cash to look at Dad's attorney. "A stipulation? Like I have to be a certain age or something to inherit the estate?"

"Sort of." She hesitates. "This stipulation…is unique, I'll say that much. Your father is requiring you to reside on Lucky Ranch for one full calendar year before you can access any of the funds in the trust. He also requests you actively participate in the day-to-day operations as principal of Lucky Ranch Enterprises Incorporated. If you do so, you'll receive a generous monthly stipend from the trust for every month you reside in Hartsville."

I laugh.

I throw back my head and laugh, hard, because if I don't, I'm worried I'll puke.

Surely, Goody is joking. *Surely*, my father, a quiet, practical man, would never ask *me*—the daughter he sent to boarding school and then to college in major cities—to live in the middle of nowhere for a year while running a *cattle ranch*.

But Goody just looks at me and blinks. Totally unfazed.

Oh God. She's serious.

"That can't be right." Cash leans over to glance at the paperwork. "Doesn't sound like Garrett."

At least we can agree on that.

Goody tilts her head. "I was sitting in this very chair when Garrett said exactly those words back in April. We drafted the new will that day."

I blink back tears, my stomach pitching. "But why make me live on the ranch? Is that even legal? How can it be enforced?"

Goody takes a long inhale and then holds out her hands, palms up. "It's what your dad wanted, Mollie. I'm sorry. I know it's not what you hoped to hear."

"What if I don't do it?"

Cash harrumphs. "Shocker."

Ignoring him, I press on. "I have a job. Like I said, I run my company back in Dallas. And I have a condo, and—and my mom lives there, and I—my friends, everything—I can't just—"

"Leave?" Cash raises a brow. "You could try it, right now."

I narrow my eyes at him. "Why don't you take your own advice? My dad clearly didn't leave you anything—"

"That's not exactly true," Goody interjects.

"—so why don't you get the hell out of here already?"

Cash turns to the attorney. "I'm listening."

"Can't you just release the funds, Goody?" I ask, desperate. "Even just a portion of them? At least until I can get Mom's lawyers to look at the will."

She offers me a contrite smile. "Wouldn't be right,

Mollie. I'm sorry. We do this how your dad wanted it done, or we don't do it at all. My hands are tied."

My mind whirls. Pressing my fingertips to my forehead, I close my eyes and try not to panic. I can't make heads or tails of what was my father's dying wish. I haven't stepped foot on the ranch in twenty years. Why bring me back now?

Why make me Lucky Ranch's principal owner?

Why do I care?

Why the hell do I care?

I don't know why. But my heart still feels like it's being passed through a paper shredder.

"As ranch life is"—Goody clears her throat—"clearly not a passion of yours, Mollie, I suggest you establish residency here in Hartsville as soon as possible. The sooner the clock starts, the sooner you'll get your stipends, and the sooner you'll be able to go back to your life in Dallas."

"She won't last a week," Cash mutters.

"You're not going to last another minute if you keep insulting me." I open my eyes to glare at him. "I don't know what my dad saw in you, but it's obvious he was a piss-poor judge of character. Seriously, leave."

"I'm not goin' anywhere until I know Lucky Ranch ends up in the right hands."

Goody rises. "How about we take five?"

Jamming the cap back onto my pen, I throw it into my bag, along with my planner. "I'm done here. Goody, you'll be hearing from my lawyers."

"Don't let the door hit your ass on the way out," I hear Cash say as I stalk out of the conference room.

"Wait, Mollie—Miss Luck—" Zach rises from

behind his desk, but I zoom past him and out into miserable afternoon heat.

I only allow myself to burst into tears when I'm safely ensconced inside my car. Grabbing my phone, I hit Mom's number, the dial tone barely audible over the roar of the air-conditioning.

"Mollie!" Her familiar voice makes my runaway pulse slow ever so slightly. "How are you, sweetheart? How'd everything go?"

I collapse against the steering wheel, burying my face in my forearms. Letting out a sob, I say, "Not great."

CHAPTER 2
Raise Hell
Cash

Pulse thumping, I stare at the empty doorway. A sinking feeling takes root in my gut.

What the hell just happened? And how can I still smell City Girl's perfume, even though she left?

"You're serious." I turn to Goody. "Garrett left the ranch to *her*."

Goody nods as she folds a manila file. "That's what the will says, yes."

"Then we're fucked."

"You don't know that."

"I do, though. If he'd left the ranch to me——" My voice catches. I look away, tapping the bottom of my fist against the table. "I'd take care of it. The people. The land. The animals. She's in charge, all that goes to shit."

"You don't know that," Goody repeats. She opens a zippered pouch on the table beside the folder.

"She wore pink cowboy boots, Goody." I wince. "Shiny ones. *New* ones."

"Be that as it may, let the dust settle, and then we'll see what happens. We have to respect Garrett's wishes."

Pushing up to my feet, I grab my hat. "I respect Garrett more'n anyone. That's why I won't let this stand."

"He did leave you something."

"What's that?"

She digs into the pouch and holds out a key. "A lockbox. It's here at the Lonestar."

The Lonestar Bank & Trust Co. is the only bank that has a branch in Hartsville.

Looking down at the key, my chest twists. What the hell was Garrett smoking when he wrote this will?

"Any idea what's in it? The lockbox?" I ask.

Goody shakes her head. "Only thing he told me is that it was precious to him. He didn't want to risk losing it, so he brought it to the bank."

I screw up my face, more confused than ever. Garrett wasn't warm and fuzzy. He definitely wasn't sentimental. Can't imagine he owned any family heirlooms, much less stowed them safely away in a lockbox.

That mean he put cash in there? Jewelry or guns? But none of that seems right either.

Whatever the case, it's not gonna be what I want—the ranch.

"I'll give it a look." I tuck the key into my pocket. "Thanks, Goody. Tell Tallulah I said hi."

Goody gives me a warm smile. "She misses seeing you at the Rattler, you know."

I was a Friday night regular at Hartsville's infamous dive bar until a line dancing accident sent me to the hospital six years ago. The concussion kept me from working on the ranch for weeks, and shit hit the fan while I was away. Can't risk that happening again.

My knees and feet throb as I head down the hallway and out the door. I've been up since three and was on horseback, working cattle, at half past four. I'm so tired I could fall the fuck over, but I don't have the luxury of collapsing. Especially now that my plans for my family's future just went up in flames.

I draw up short when I see the fancy SUV parked next to my truck. That wasn't there when I ducked into the pharmacy before heading to Goody's office earlier. The vehicle belongs to Mollie, no question. People in Hartsville drive practical cars. Ones that don't have five-hundred-dollar tires and cost an arm and a leg to fix.

The Range Rover is just as shiny and ridiculous as its owner.

Rounding the front of my Ford, I jam my hat onto my head and resist the urge to roll my eyes at the grumble of the Rover's supercharged engine.

Mollie's got the dang AC going full blast at all times, no doubt. A princess like her would wither in the heat.

Did she drive this thing to the funeral? The one none of us—the people who knew Garrett best—were invited to?

The SUV is white. Its paint, tires, and lights are dusty from the drive from Dallas, but the vehicle is obviously brand-new.

It's also enormous, equipped to scale mountains or, in Mollie Luck's case, troll parking decks at malls in ritzy suburbs. Thing must've cost well over a hundred K.

The only six-figure sum I've ever seen was on the first Lonestar Bank & Trust Co. statement I opened after my parents passed. It detailed the amount of the home equity loan they'd taken out to cover the ranch's losses after beef prices took a nosedive in 2010.

I'm still paying that fucking thing off.

Then again, paying that bill means we've managed to hold on to Rivers Ranch for another year. And my brothers and I have been able to pay because of Garrett Luck.

He wasn't perfect, but he was kind to me when no one else was, and he was always a man of his word. It's not like him to say one thing but do another.

Also not like him to leave his life's work in the hands of a spoiled brat with a sense of entitlement as big as her goddamned mouth.

But here we are.

I miss Garrett. So damn much. He was the father figure I needed over the past decade. What in the world do I do without him?

Right now, I just gotta pray the truck my daddy bought used back in '96 makes it through another calving season. I keep my head down as I dig my keys out of my pocket and unlock the driver's-side door. I don't want to see Mollie as much as she don't wanna see me. Even if I couldn't stop staring at her back in Goody's office.

My stomach swoops at the memory of Mollie's eyes. Same as her daddy's, dark brown and deep set. Expressive.

Gripping the chrome door handle, my bones go heavy. This grief—it's gotta get gone already. I have too many people depending on me to keep feeling this busted up.

I'm pressing my thumb into the button that unlatches the door when I hear a low moan.

Glancing over my shoulder, I look through the

Rover's passenger-side window and see City Girl slumped over the steering wheel. My stomach swoops again when I see her back convulsing in time to what appears to be deep, heaving sobs.

They're loud enough that I can hear them over the engine.

For a second, I feel sorry for her. I know what it's like to lose a parent, and I wouldn't wish it on anyone. Even her.

But then I remember she barely knew her daddy. I remember the sad look Garrett would get when he talked about her. I remember attorneys calling the ranch, telling us they were "retrieving" his body so they could transport it to Dallas. Garrett didn't live there a day of his life.

A voice sounds over the sobbing. Bluetooth, coming from the Rover's speakers. Mollie's on the phone.

"Get out of that hellhole and come home," a woman says.

"I don't understand," Mollie replies. "Why make me work for it this way?"

"Your dad...he was always so damn difficult. That money belongs to you, sweet girl, and I'll make sure you get it, come hell or high water."

I climb into the truck and start the engine. I hold the steering wheel in a death grip, my knuckles white. I'm already sweating, my shirt sticking to my back.

Mollie's not upset because she lost a father.

She's upset because she didn't get her money. That's all Garrett was to her—an ATM.

To me, he was everything. The father I lost. The mentor I needed. The friend who kept me sane when I was drowning in grief.

Losing Garrett could very well mean losing every-thing now. Our way of life. The land we've called home for five—no, six generations, since my niece, Ella, was born a few years back.

I just lost everything, but here's this spoiled city girl, sobbing over the millions she has to wait a year to get while calling the man who saved my life and my family "difficult."

Mollie is pretty. Anyone with two eyes and a pulse can see that. But nothing turns me off more than her kind of carelessness. Her sense of entitlement.

Yanking on the gearshift, I put the truck in reverse and whip out of the parking spot. Glancing at the Rover, I see Mollie's head pop up. Even through the tinted glass, I can see how swollen her tearstained face is. My chest twists.

I ignore it and hit the gas. Mollie Luck is not my problem.

Figuring out how I'm going to support my family— and keep all six of us together while honoring Garrett's memory and his work—is.

My truck doesn't have AC, so I roll my window all the way down. Hot, humid air blows into my face. Glancing up at the sky, all I see is haze. We need rain, but it doesn't look like we're going to get it today.

If Garrett were still alive, we'd be in an ATV at this hour. Too hot to be on horseback if you don't need to be. Probably over by the bend in the Colorado River that marks the western boundary of Lucky Ranch. We'd be surveying wildlife, maybe, or casting a line in a shady spot.

Garrett loved the river. Almost as much as he loved hunting, nineties country, and spicy ranch waters.

But he loved nothing more than the daughter he talked about often but who never came to see him.

Why the fuck did he say he was leaving Lucky Ranch to me if his will said something different? We talked constantly about the ranch's future. He was obsessed with the place. Like me, ranching was in his blood. His granddaddy bought the first ten thousand acres that eventually became Lucky Ranch back in the early 1900s. It's been in the Luck family ever since.

Garrett took me under his wing when I was nineteen, right after my parents died. I'd dropped out of college to care for my four younger brothers and run our family's ranch. He helped me set everything to rights. Even if that did mean selling off every last steer and spare tractor tire to pay my parents' debts. I swore I'd restore Rivers Ranch to its former glory one day. But back then, it was about survival.

With nothing left for us on our ranch, Garrett hired my brothers and me to work on his. It was fair pay, plus we got room and board. We couldn't afford the upkeep on our family's house on Rivers Ranch, so being able to live in the cushy bunkhouse Garrett built on his property meant we could rent out our childhood home for some much-needed cash. He helped me teach my brothers everything they needed to know about working cattle. Being on a ranch as established and successful as Garrett's ensured we all got a world-class education.

I often wondered why Garrett was so good to us, a ragtag crew of orphans. He was rich. Successful. He didn't need to be generous. But I think we kept him from feeling lonely. He and his wife, Aubrey—Mollie's mom—divorced long before I was in the picture, and she took Mollie with her back to her hometown of Dallas.

But like my dad, Garrett was a family man at heart. And I think we became his family over the years.

My brothers and I worked hard. We love the land like it's our own. We ate every meal with Garrett, inhaling Patsy's cooking as if it were our last day on earth.

He loved us, same as we loved him.

Still, I never expected Garrett to turn to me one day and ask, "What do you say to taking over when I'm gone? Can't think of anyone better to run the place."

My throat is tight. I slow when I approach Lonestar Bank, ducking my head to look out my passenger-side window at the building's glass doors. The lights are on inside, but there's a sign on the door. I don't need to read it to know the manager, Harley, is "out handling business and will return in the morning."

In other words, business was slow today, so he cut his staff loose and went four-wheeling out by Starrush Creek.

Guess I'll be checking out the lockbox another day, then.

Sweat drips into my eyes as I drive out of town. I swerve to avoid a pothole, then slow when I see a familiar figure ahead, its outline fuzzy in the heat.

Only my brother would ride to and from town when it's this hot. And he'd only do it if he had money to collect from his weekly poker game.

Wiping my eyes on my shirt, I stick my head out the window. "Please tell me you took some rich motherfucker for all he was worth."

Wyatt turns his head and grins down at me from the

saddle. "You're the only rich motherfucker left in these parts. How's it feel, being owner of Lucky Ranch?"

I squint up at my brother. A beat passes.

He frowns, pulling on his horse's reins. "Shit."

"Yep."

"What happened?"

"No idea. Garrett forgot to update his will maybe? I don't think he'd lie to me."

"He'd never lie to anyone."

"Ranch is going to Mollie Luck. She gets everything—the operation, the trust."

Wyatt's eyes bulge. "She ain't ever been out here."

"I know."

"She's gonna sell it."

"I know."

Wyatt looks out over the hills, simmering in the heat. "Cash—"

"I'll figure it out. I got some ideas."

My brother casts me a dubious glance. "No, you don't."

"I can—"

"You can't do everything, Cash. Let us help. We'll come up with something—you, me, the boys. Patsy and John B. There's a poker tournament in Vegas—"

"You know I can't spare you that long when we got hay to bale."

"Ella's in preschool now, three mornings a week. Sawyer will be around more."

Ella is my younger brother Sawyer's three-year-old daughter. She's cute as hell and the apple of everyone's eye on the ranch.

I let out a breath. Sweat rolls down my temples.

The inside of my truck feels like an airless oven. "She's gotta live on the ranch for a year—Mollie. Play pretend as the boss lady. Only way she'll get her money. It's in Garrett's will."

Wyatt stares at me. "That makes zero sense."

"No shit. Garrett and Mollie didn't talk much, sure, but he would've told me if she ever expressed any interest in the ranch. She would've visited, you know? To put her in charge of everything..." I shake my head. "Seems reckless."

"Garrett was not reckless."

"Exactly. Makes me feel like he's sending us a message." So does the whole lockbox thing. I decide not to tell my brother about the key in my pocket. I don't want to get his hopes up. Figure I'll see what I'm working with and go from there.

"Maybe." Wyatt lifts a shoulder. "Or maybe he just wanted to keep the ranch in the family."

We are his family. I'm certain of that.

Before he promised me the ranch, I never assumed I'd get a dime from him, other than the wages he paid me.

I never expect to get anything from anyone. Expectations lead to hope, and hope leads to disappointment.

Maybe that's what pisses me off the most about Mollie—how she feels like the world owes her something.

No way I'm working for her.

Then again, do I have a choice? What am I gonna do if she actually comes to live on the ranch? Yeah, I'm the foreman, which means I call the shots when it comes to pretty much everything that goes on at the property. I oversee a staff of fifty. I manage budgets, repairs, equipment maintenance, our calving operation and veterinary programs, not to mention hundreds of thousands of acres of land.

I get shit done. But ultimately, the person who owns Lucky Ranch is the one who signs my paychecks and those of my staff.

I bite down on the inside of my cheek, hard. We really are fucked if Mollie is that person. Not only will her sense of entitlement make her a nightmare to work with, but she also has no idea what the hell she's doing.

Let's not forget, she's going to sell the ranch the second she can. Where will that leave us? At the mercy of some billionaire asshole with a cowboy fantasy?

"I got eight hundred bucks." Wyatt pats his worn leather saddlebag. "I wasn't planning on taking it to the bank, but I can deposit it if that would help? Should buy us some time—"

"Harley closed the Lonestar early again. But really, Wyatt, you should be careful riding around with that kind of cash."

He glances over his shoulder at the Beretta shotgun tucked behind his saddle. "I'll be just fine."

The shotgun was a gift from Garrett for Wyatt's twentieth birthday. I don't think I've seen my brother without it since. Probably why he's a crack shot. Good thing, considering Wyatt runs an illegal poker ring out of the Rattler's basement.

"Rent from the house should cover our bills this month. Keep the eight hundred for a rainy day."

Wyatt glances up at the sky. "None of those in sight."

The heat is killing me. I let off the brakes. "Were you able to fix the tire on the baler?"

"Duke patched the hole, yeah. It was a nail. Changed the oil in the tractor too."

"And the cutting—"

"Got it done. Also, John B and Sally were just arriving as I left to look at the four cows we were worried about. Sally thinks it's just a virus. I reckon they're about wrapped up with their examination by now."

"Good work. See you at supper, then."

Wyatt smiles. "Patsy's making her cottage pie. See? It don't all suck."

Just mostly, I think as I hit the gas.

The sun-bleached pavement glimmers in the heat. I feel short of breath. Throat tight, pulse drumming.

I hit the knob that turns on the stereo and crank it as loud as it'll go. I'm able to rein in my runaway heartbeat as the opening notes of "My Maria" fill the truck.

I fucking love Brooks & Dunn. Been into them ever since Garrett introduced me to their first album, *Brand New Man*.

I have a lot to do back at the ranch. Chat with John B—short for John Beauregard, his middle name—about those cows. I should check on the fence some ranch hands were supposed to repair in the southeast pasture. I need to call the mechanic to schedule routine maintenance on our feed trucks. Text our farrier to remind him about our appointment tomorrow. Dude always mixes up his dates.

Ryder said his throat hurt this morning. I wonder if he got strep from Ella? We keep passing that shit around.

Maybe it's because I have so much to do that I drive right past the manicured entrance to Lucky Ranch, its gnarled oaks providing much-needed shade to the vibrant green brush below.

28

I need a breather. Time to think. I keep waiting to feel less anxious—less overwhelmed. Garrett passed months ago. I should at least be able to sleep more than a couple of hours at a time by now. But I'm worried that if I stop moving—stop doing all the things for all the people—something bad will happen again.

It's a waste of gas, but I know I'll fall apart if I dive back into the chaos right now. And the last thing everyone needs is a foreman—a brother—who can't do his job.

Music blaring, I drive another ten minutes. A dirt road appears on my left, the land around it blistered and broken, a shade of gray brown that makes my chest hurt. The rusted wrought iron arch above the road reads *Rivers Ranch Est. 1904.*

Once upon a time, this land was well tended to. Granted, it wasn't as green as Lucky Ranch. Few ranches are. Garrett took his role as steward of the land seriously. Together, we worked with conservationists to make the ranch a haven of biodiversity.

I'd love to do the same for Rivers Ranch. But that kind of project takes time. And money. Lots and lots of money. Money I thought I'd have in hand today. Between the cattle and oil operations, Lucky Ranch is a highly profitable enterprise. Even with Mollie receiving Garrett's monetary assets, the ranch generates so much income, I'd have plenty left over to revive Rivers Ranch.

It's a smart investment; combining the two ranches would allow me to add lucrative revenue streams to our portfolio. I could increase the size of our cattle and oil operations. Add a hospitality element, maybe renovate my childhood home into some sort of event venue or bed-and-breakfast. Set up a hunting camp that could be rented out or used by local schools for wildlife projects.

It'd be an enormous undertaking but a worthy one. It would bring revenue to our community, making Hartsville a destination for hunters, weekend travelers, wedding parties.

Instead, that money is going into Mollie's pocket. I can only imagine what she'll spend it on. A newer Range Rover? More shiny cowboy boots that wouldn't last a day on a working ranch?

I turn onto the road, wincing when the truck lurches as I hit a divot. That's new. The empty front pasture stretches out on my left. A fence, long since abandoned to the elements, sags in several places.

I'm hit by a memory: my dad helping me pull on my work gloves before he squatted beside me next to that fence. He was teaching me how to repair it. It was early morning, spring. Lots of sunshine. Warm enough to leave Duke in his car seat in the back seat of this very truck, the windows rolled down. I remember him singing to himself as Dad patiently helped me dig a deep hole in the ground, the dirt softened from all the rain we'd gotten that year.

I will never forget how proud I felt when the post was up, and Dad squeezed my shoulder. "Now that's one fine-looking fence, son. Well done."

Duke had started to fuss, so we climbed back into the truck and headed to the house. Mom fed us a laughably huge lunch: burgers slathered in pimento cheese, homemade sweet potato chips, broccoli casserole. All washed down with toothache-sweet lemonade.

For dessert, there was—what else—Texas sheet cake.

Pretty sure my brothers and I polished off the whole thing. Ryder had so much frosting smeared on his face and arms that Mom had to hose him down in the backyard. Then she hooked up the sprinkler, and we spent the afternoon running around in it like the little lunatics we were.

Those were good times.

The best.

My chest hurts even more knowing they're gone for good, and so is Garrett.

I turn down the music and take a lap around the ranch. House looks okay, but everything else has gone the way of the fence. The hay barn is missing its roof, thanks to a tornado outbreak five years back. The irrigation system quit working ages ago, and now every pasture I pass is barren.

I want to make more memories here so badly. To preserve the memory of my parents and honor all the hard work they put into Rivers Ranch. To create a place where my brothers can thrive and feel safe.

Sometimes, late at night, I even catch myself fantasizing about raising a family of my own here, alongside my brothers and their families. Life wasn't easy on the ranch, but it was a magical place to grow up.

Swallowing hard, I turn around and head back to the main road. I don't know what the hell I'm going to do. But I'll be damned if some stuck-up city girl gets in the way of giving my family the life they deserve.

She wants war, I'll give her war. I still got some fight in me.

Fight's all I got left.

CHAPTER 3
Sweet-Talking Sacks of Shit
Mollie

"Mom? Did you hear me?"

Mom nods, even though she continues to look down at her phone, thumbs flying over the screen. "Yeah. Sorry, honey, you know that huge listing I've been chasing—"

"The one in Highland Park?"

"Yep." Mom smiles at her phone. "An email from the owner just came in. I think I got it!"

"That's amazing. Congrats."

She finally looks up at me, grabbing her unsweet tea. "Biggest listing in the firm's history. Sixty million! Can you believe it?"

"Sixty? Wow. Who owns it?"

"Didn't I tell you? I thought I told you." She frowns when the server sets down her salad. "I'm sorry, but I asked for this with the dressing and the croutons on the side. The cheese too. Oh, look, Mollie, they also left everything on your salad."

I manage a tight grin. "Pretty sure I ordered it that way."

I returned to Dallas from Hartsville several days ago, but Mom's been traveling and only arrived back in town this morning.

"Oh." She turns back to the server. "Well, just to make it easy, why don't you take both salads back and bring them with all that stuff on the side for us? Thank you."

I watch, stomach grumbling, as the server whisks away our plates. "You know if you take off the croutons and the cheese and the dressing, all that's left is lettuce and some radishes?"

"All that dairy and the wheat in the croutons—I'm sure that won't do your tummy any favors," Mom says.

I love my mom dearly. She raised me on her own, and even though she worked full-time, she still showed up to every dance recital, graduation, and tennis match—unlike Dad, who didn't show up to anything. I have nothing but the utmost respect for her.

But goddamn, sometimes I wish she'd let loose a little. I wish she cared a little less about her looks. A little less about keeping up with the Joneses.

"Anyway," she continues, "this guy owns one of the big oil and gas companies. He's moving to the UK with his new wife. Apparently, they're gutting a swanky place in Kensington, right near where Will and Kate live."

"Ah. Good for them." I reach for my tea.

"How'd the pop-up go at Georgana's?" Mom asks, referring to the boutique that hosted Bellamy Brooks's most recent pop-up here in Dallas.

"It went well—a step in the right direction for sure. We didn't sell a ton, but I did make inroads with some big fashion influencers. Wheeler and I set up meetings with them."

Mom grins. "Aren't you glad Dallas is such a fashion-obsessed place?"

"Totally. I'm not sure Bellamy Brooks could really thrive anywhere else."

I really do mean that. Pop-up shops like the one we just had at Georgana's are the lifeblood of our business. Gaining access to their clientele is priceless, and the exposure we get on social media leads to the kind of invaluable brand recognition that will hopefully get Bellamy Brooks out of the red.

It also helps that tons of powerful influencers call Dallas home. These men and women have hundreds of thousands of followers on social media, and if they post about your products, it can significantly boost sales. But you have to get on their radar, and being able to meet them in person here in Dallas has been huge in that aspect.

"I'm proud of y'all," Mom says.

"Thanks. But speaking of staying in Dallas—"

"Ugh, your father and the ranch. Right. My lawyers are working on it, sweetheart. They agree that the stipulation is totally ridiculous, but we need to give them some time to get it in front of a judge. We'll get there." She reaches across the white tablecloth to pat my hand. "Be patient. Focus on Bellamy Brooks in the meantime. You'll get the money."

The restaurant, totally full, hums around us. It's the kind of place where people like Mom do power lunches. And like Mom, everyone is dressed to impress. I love the fashion—lots of long skirts, paired with designer belts and cute tops—and my stomach flips when I think about how great it would all look paired with Bellamy Brooks boots.

That is if Bellamy Brooks doesn't go under before we

release our next collection, which will only happen if we get a major—*major*—cash infusion.

Wheeler and I dreamed up the concept for a women's cowboy boot company when we were seniors at the University of Texas. We wanted to make classic cowboy boots with a girlie, high-fashion twist. Building the company was our side gig for close to five years, until we saved enough money from our corporate jobs to give it a go full-time.

We poured our savings into Bellamy Brooks, and Wheeler contributed some additional money she borrowed from her grandparents.

Mom also made a sizable investment. She's worked incredibly hard over the years to build her business, and it's finally paying off: Brown Real Estate Brokerage (Mom went back to her maiden name of Brown after the divorce) is now one of Dallas's top-tier firms with over twenty agents.

Her making the investment in Bellamy Brooks was amazing, even if she kindly but firmly said that was the extent of her financial involvement.

Altogether, it was enough to launch our first real collection last year. The collection, composed of two boot styles in five different colors, was exceptionally well received. But between manufacturing costs and the marketing campaign we did, Wheeler and I ended up not making a dime in profit.

Thankfully, we had enough extra cash to keep us afloat. That is until recently, as our expenses continue to outrun our income. Our second collection, which we've been working on all year, *has* to do well if we want to stay in business.

Luckily, we're obsessed with the collection, and we feel it really can soar. The designs we've been working on are classic with a bold, edgy twist. Think boots embroidered with hearts, stars, even diamond rings for a pair we're calling the Bride.

We couldn't stop screaming as we sketched everything out. Designing the collection was fun. But we've been burning through cash to pay our bills, to the point that I get a stomachache every time I receive an invoice from our (very expensive) web designer, the email marketing service we use, our accountant, graphic designer…

The list goes on.

But then Dad died suddenly of a heart attack at the age of fifty-six. It was a total shock. When Mom told me I was the sole heir to Dad's estate, everything changed.

Our company is now getting the capital infusion we so desperately need. Just last week, I contacted our manufacturer to place a huge order. The kind of huge that made me want to go down several bottles of wine and cut up my corporate card. But knowing I was about to receive an inheritance meant I could breathe a little easier.

Placing the order is still a huge risk. One that makes me feel like I'm being repeatedly stabbed in the stomach, especially now that I'm not sure when I'll be getting that inheritance. If I'll be getting it at all.

Then again, I've had some stomach ailment or another for close to five years now. I've seen every gastroenterologist in the greater Dallas–Fort Worth area. And everyone says the same thing: they don't know what's wrong, but I should manage my stress better and try a few different diets to see if I have any food-based triggers.

I haven't found any so far. As for managing my stress, well, that's a work in progress.

"Let's go big," Wheeler said when I told her about getting my trust. "If we have the money, we go all out. You don't want to feel like you left anything on the table, do you? Because if we do this right, I really do believe the sky's the limit."

Over the years, we'd eagerly watched other Texas-born brands hit the stratosphere. There was the pair of sisters whose line of hand-painted wallpaper and fabrics ended up on the cover of *Elle Decor.* A jewelry designer, Cate, has made millions, selling gold-plated chain necklaces and bracelets from her studio in Austin. Some guys from college banded together to make canned ranch waters. Now their products are sold in nearly every grocery store in nearly every state, and they just signed a deal to be the "official cocktail provider" for a very famous Dallas sports franchise.

"Why not us?" I replied to Wheeler.

She smiled. "Why not indeed?"

Although when I'm tossing and turning in bed, I sometimes wonder if my thirst for Bellamy Brooks's success comes from a genuine love of the boots we make or if, as my therapist has suggested, there's another reason I push myself so hard.

A reason that may or may not have something to do with finally getting my parents' attention.

It's not rocket science. My mom has a big, busy life, and Dad was so busy with *his* life, he was never really a part of mine after Mom and I left the ranch when I was six.

I think the lonely kid I was—maybe still am—believes

that if I hit the stratosphere, Mom will finally look up from her phone with pride in her eyes. And Dad—well, he might finally want to be a part of my life, and I might finally have the courage to sit down with him and have the conversation we should've had years ago about righting everything we did wrong in our relationship.

Too late now.

It all started nearly twenty-eight years ago, when Mom met Dad at a honky-tonk in Austin. He was in town for the rodeo, and she was there for a friend's bachelorette party. After a whirlwind courtship, they got married six months later and moved onto Dad's family's ranch in Hartsville.

A month after that, Mom got pregnant with me.

The way she tells it, ranch life was isolating and monotonous, especially after I was born. She was alone, caring for a colicky newborn, while Dad was out on the ranch, doing his cowboy thing. Mom is from Dallas, and like me, she's a city girl through and through. She wasn't used to the quiet or the loneliness of life in the country.

She tried her best to assimilate. She learned how to ride horses, and as I got older, we were able to roam around the ranch more often, sometimes with Dad.

Still, she found it difficult to meet people, and she missed the vibrancy of city life. She was depressed and unhappy. She also didn't love the schools in Hartsville, so when it was time for me to go to kindergarten, she gave Dad an ultimatum: move to Dallas or get a divorce.

Really, she begged him to move to Dallas with us. For all her vitriol toward Dad—as long as I can remember, she's never had a nice thing to say about him—I think she was genuinely heartbroken by his choice to stay on the ranch. I remember my grandmother telling me how wildly in love Mom was with Dad when they met.

But he chose to stay in Hartsville. To this day, I still don't understand why. How could anyone choose to live alone in the middle of nowhere instead of being with his family?

How could Dad choose some cows and a desert over us?

Mom's hurt fueled her growing rage. We moved into my grandparents' house in Dallas, and not long after, Mom served Dad divorce papers. Their split was finalized the day I entered first grade.

While Mom and Dad shared custody of me, Dad pretty much disappeared from my life once I moved to Dallas. Granted, I was in school, so it's not like I could visit him at Lucky Ranch whenever I wanted.

Still, he could have tried harder. I was supposed to spend every other weekend with him, but for some reason or another, it never happened. Dad never came to pick me up, and Mom never offered to drive me. She hated the idea of me going back to the ranch. I think she was worried I wouldn't be safe there, as Dad wasn't exactly a hands-on parent. He was always so busy working.

At first, I was crushed Dad didn't push harder to bring me back to Hartsville. Unlike my mother, I didn't hate life on the ranch. I enjoyed riding horses, and I liked being outside around all the animals there.

Dad would call every so often, and although I don't remember what we talked about, I do remember feeling happy to hear his voice.

Eventually, though, I grew to love my new life in

Dallas. As the years passed, Dad told me he didn't want to take me away from the friends and family I had there. That tracked, especially as I got older. I didn't want to miss my friends' sleepovers. I didn't want to miss middle school dances and my ballet classes.

I still missed my Dad, though, and I never stopped wondering why he didn't try harder to see me. As an only child with parents who worked a lot, I was lonely. Once in a blue moon, Dad would show up in Dallas and take me out to lunch or dinner. But that was only when he was in town on ranch business—buying livestock in Fort Worth or meeting with his bankers downtown.

Once I hit my angsty teenage years, the loneliness and the hurt morphed into anger, just like Mom's did. What was wrong with this man, never showing up to my recitals? My graduations? Why didn't he help Mom more? Couldn't he see how hard it was for her to raise me on her own?

I stopped answering Dad's calls, hell-bent on sending him the silent message that I was pissed. He came to Dallas to try to talk things out, but I refused to see him. Mom didn't push the issue. After that, he stopped calling altogether, and our only touch point was the money he'd send for whatever I needed: boarding school tuition, a car, textbooks for my college classes.

As fucked up as it sounds, I felt like money was something he owed me for not showing up more. Mom made it clear that Dad was a very, very wealthy man, so I knew he wouldn't miss it.

He apparently didn't miss me either. I often felt like I was just another problem he would throw money at.

Money was easy for him. Being a part of my life clearly wasn't.

I would give anything to have Dad back. Truly anything to fix the way he and I fucked up our relationship. I have so many regrets and so much anger left over from the things we did and didn't say to each other. He should've pushed to see me more. I should've had the courage to tell him how much I wanted to see him.

The fact that I lost the chance to ever make things right keeps me up at night. I haven't slept well in… months. Since Dad's funeral, really, which took place in a depressingly bland church near Mom's office.

Dad offered to invest in Bellamy Brooks, but I was too angry—too determined to hold my grudge—to give him a chance. Once he became an investor, he and I would have to communicate again, which meant patching up our relationship. I wasn't ready for that yet.

Add that to my growing tally of regrets, along with all the times he sent money for other things and I never called to thank him.

My throat swells. I take another long sip of tea, the bitter taste just making my throat feel worse. Mom is convinced sweet tea gives you kidney stones, so we order ours unsweetened. I should've asked for more lemons.

Really, I wish I'd asked for tequila.

"What if I don't get the money, though?" I ask Mom. "Without living in bumfuck nowhere first?"

Yesterday, I received a packet from Goody, detailing the monthly stipend I'd get if I lived on the ranch. It is definitely generous. Generous enough to keep Bellamy Brooks afloat for several months.

Am I willing to actually live in Hartsville to get that

stipend? With so much on the line…I mean, I could work remotely for a bit. Drive back to Dallas on the weekends. Goody didn't mention anything about travel restrictions, right?

Honestly, I'd consider returning to Hartsville just for the satisfaction of firing that prick Cash. I'd love to see the look on his face when I tell him to get the fuck off my property. Who does he think he is, believing he's entitled to my family's ranch?

I've found myself wondering if part of me is *proud* Dad thought I was up to the task of running his beloved ranch. I didn't know him all that well, but I suddenly can't kick the desire to *want* to know him now that he's gone.

Or maybe I just want to figure out why he never really wanted to know me.

"You'll live on the ranch over my dead body." Mom glances at her phone, which sits screen up beside her silverware. "That place will chew you up and spit you out. I had to go through hell there, and I won't see you go through it too."

I frown. "I just wish I understood why Dad wants me there so badly."

"Lord forgive me for speaking ill of the dead again"— Mom glances around, like Jesus might be eavesdropping at a nearby table—"but nothing could drag your father away from the ranch. I'm not surprised he wants to drag you there too."

The server sets down our salads. *Piles of lettuce* truly is a more apt description.

"Did Dad ever mention the name Cash to you?" I ask.

Mom dips the tines of her fork into her light vinai-grette before she digs into her lettuce. "Sweetheart, it's been a long time since I spoke to your dad. But Cash—wasn't he one of the neighbors' boys? The Rivers, I think. There were so many of those kids, I couldn't keep track. They just kept having them."

"Cash was at the reading of the will."

"Really?" That gets Mom's attention. "Why didn't you tell me this before?"

I lift a shoulder, like my pulse isn't thrumming at the memory of my run-in with the blue-eyed cowboy. "Your admin said you were booked solid this week."

"Ah. Right. So what about this guy Cash?"

"He's Dad's foreman. Apparently, Dad told him he'd inherit the ranch."

Mom laughs, rolling her eyes. "Of course a cowboy would say that. Your dad was an idiot, but not that much of an idiot. I'll give you some advice, Mollie. Don't listen to a word those cowboys say. They're sweet-talking sacks of shit."

My turn to laugh. "Not to put too fine a point on it. Trust me, I have zero interest in cowboys. Least of all Cash. He wasn't a sweet talker anyway. He was an absolute dick."

Mom harrumphs. "Their moods are the worst. I'm sorry you got to witness that firsthand. Trust me, sweet girl, my lawyers will have this all straightened out ASAP. You won't ever have to deal with Cash again."

That's the hope.

But as I valiantly make my way through the roughage that is my lunch, I can't shake the feeling that I haven't seen the last of Cash Rivers.

CHAPTER 4
Attagirl
Mollie

I'm not proud of using a bottle of Opus One to lure Palmer to my apartment later that week. But desperate times call for desperate measures.

The three-hundred-dollar bottle of wine, along with two wineglasses whose bowls are coated with purple residue, sit empty on the coffee table in front of me. Mom gifted me a case of the rare vintage to celebrate the launch of Bellamy Brooks's first collection. I've been saving it for a special occasion ever since.

Or in this case, an emergency.

I prop my feet on the table's ledge and angle my laptop closer to my face. Scanning the spreadsheet, my eyes ache. I need to take out my contacts, but I don't want Palmer to see me in my glasses.

"I thought you said you needed to de-stress?"

I glance up to see Palmer resting a shoulder against the jamb of the bedroom door. He's gotten dressed, his suit jacket hanging over his arm. He bears no sign of the sex we just had, other than his undone collar and slightly swollen lips. They're curved in a smirk.

I grin. "Mission accomplished."

He strides across the room, all commodities-trader cockiness. "But diving back into Excel is going to reverse all those feel-good endorphins I just gave you."

"You can't give me endorphins."

"I gave you something better." Leaning over the couch, he presses a quick, hard kiss to my mouth. "That was good, Mollie."

"But your lines"—I laugh against his lips—"they're pretty bad."

"I deliver where it counts. You're welcome."

I playfully swat his shoulder. "You're the worst."

"You don't have any more of that wine, do you?"

"I'm done for tonight, I think." I lift my laptop. "Got a lot to do."

I don't wait for him to ask about my work or why it has me so stressed out, because I know he won't. His lack of interest isn't malicious. We just don't have the kind of relationship where we check in with each other that way.

Palmer straightens and adjusts his belt. He's tall. Broad. Handsome.

Part of me wishes I felt disappointed he doesn't push harder to stay and hang out, maybe even spend the night. We had a nice enough conversation while we drank the wine, chatting about former classmates and the bar that just opened down the street here in uptown.

Palmer and I ran in the same circles in college, although we were more acquaintances than friends. A couple of months ago, we ran into each other for the first time since graduation. Three hours and one dance floor make-out session later, I asked him to come home with me.

We've been hooking up ever since. It's exactly what I need: good, no-strings sex that requires very little effort on my part. He's not interested in dating me—like most twentysomething guys making Wall Street money, he's not interested in monogamy, period—and I'm definitely not interested in dating him. He's a little too corporate for my taste. A little too full of himself.

Which is why a larger part of me is relieved he's heading out. Looking at the numbers on the spread-sheet, I'm going to have to do some creative math to pay Bellamy Brooks's bills this month. Maybe I'll ask our publicist if I can pay her quarterly going forward?

I yawn. "Wow, I'm tired."

The smirk is back. "Bet you are."

I roll my eyes. "You really need to work on your lines."

"And you really need to go to bed." He digs his keys out of his pocket. "Thanks for the wine. And the orgasm."

"You're welcome," I say, throwing his line back at him. "Drive safe."

He smiles too, handsome as hell. "Safety is my motto."

"Wow. Worst one yet," I tease.

"You like it."

A beat passes. Palmer looks at me.

I don't know if it's because I'm confused, tired, grieving, or what. But suddenly I'm asking, "What would you do if you inherited a ranch?"

Palmer lifts a brow. I didn't tell him about Dad's will.

Come to think of it, I'm pretty sure I never told Palmer Dad even owned a ranch or that he died. My father is not exactly a light topic of conversation, so makes sense that I've never brought him up when I'm with Palmer.

"Why?" he asks. "Did you inherit one?"

"Just play devil's advocate."

"That's really fucking cool if a ranch did fall into your lap. Back in high school, I'd go to my friends' ranches all the time. We'd have the best parties out there."

"I'm talking about a working ranch. Like with cows and stuff."

Palmer screws up his face. "Shoveling shit? No thank you."

"Right? I don't get why *anyone* would choose to do that."

"I mean, to be fair, it would be cool to get out in nature a little." Palmer glances at the condo's floor-to-ceiling windows that overlook uptown Dallas. The city sits beneath a blanket of steamy haze, tinged yellow by the sunset. "Living here, I can go whole weeks without ever being outside. Makes me feel like a vampire. My dad and I hunted a lot when I was a kid. I miss that sometimes."

"It's just as hazy and hot on a ranch as it is in Dallas."

He turns his head to look at me. "I don't know. All this concrete, the buildings, the cars, the pollution—you can't compare that to the wide openness of a ranch."

"Maybe." I glance back down at my laptop. My stomach is killing me. "Thanks for humoring me."

"If you really did inherit a ranch, I'd gladly visit you."

"You use me for my wine, and now you're using me for my ranch too?"

"So you did have a working ranch fall into your lap." He smiles.

I move my fingertips over the keyboard. "Good night, Palmer."

"Night, Mollie. And get your facts straight. I'm using you for the sex. The wine and the ranch are just a bonus."

I laugh, and he laughs, and then he turns to let himself out of my condo. I live on the eighteenth floor of a high-rise, so I can hear the elevator ding outside my door a minute later. I can picture Palmer stepping inside, rolling his head side to side.

He's already stopped thinking about me. And that makes me feel...nothing. No trace of disappointment or embarrassment.

I tell myself that's a good thing, because I really need to focus on what my next steps are. Glancing at my phone, I see Wheeler has texted me three times and called twice. The stomachache I've had all week pulses.

I'm absolutely using sex and wine to avoid her. She just won't leave me alone about the money we were supposed to have by now but don't. I don't blame her.

But even if that stupid stipulation didn't exist, it would take time—several months at least—for the money to actually hit my bank account. I *would* be able to borrow against my inheritance so we'd have enough cash on hand to get our collection off the ground, however.

I just don't think either of us expected to burn through so much cash so quickly. Spending like we have—neglecting our budgets—has turned into our largest rookie mistake to date.

My gut seizes when I read the texts she sent while I was in bed with Palmer.

Wheeler Rankin: *We really need to follow up with Barb. I'm worried we'll lose our spot in production if we don't get the first payment to her ASAP.*

Wheeler Rankin: *You think you should follow up with your dad's lawyer too? I'm sorry to keep bugging you, but I feel like we're losing valuable time.*

Wheeler Rankin: *Are you okay? I know you're going through a lot right now. I'm sorry. We'll figure this out together, I promise. Just let me know where your head's at.*

I wish I knew.

My lawyers—really, Mom's—have instructed me not to contact Goody, as they've been working with her to come up with a solution. So far, no dice.

Meanwhile, I'm sweating bullets.

Usually, sex with Palmer soothes my frayed nerves. But this stomachache will not quit. Setting down my laptop, I grab my phone and stand in front of the windows. Dallas is many things in September, but beautiful isn't one of them.

The whine of the air-conditioning is loud in the otherwise silent room. My laptop screen goes blank.

I head for the condo's spare bedroom, which has become Bellamy Brooks's de facto headquarters. Wheeler affectionately dubbed it "the closet," mostly because it's a tiny jewel box, dedicated to fashion. It's stuffed to the gills with cowgirl boots in a rainbow of colors, patterns, and textures—mostly samples from our first collection and a few prototypes from our second. We hung inspiration boards on one wall, and they're covered in leather swatches, magazine clippings, Pantone color cards, stencils, and more. A tiny desk is squeezed between two boot racks on another wall. It's topped with a jar of Reese's Pieces—Wheeler's favorite—and a box of my favorite sweet treat, chocolate-covered espresso beans.

My heart hurts in the best way, taking it all in. I'm so, so proud of the work we've done. Running a hand over a pair of brown-and-cream boots, I marvel at the leather's buttery softness. The perfectly executed Western pattern, done in coral embroidery on the boot's vamp, still makes my pulse literally skip a beat, months after I sketched the initial design.

I'll never forget the first email we received from a customer, telling us how beautiful she felt in the pair of Bellamy Brooks boots she wore on her wedding day.

I'm in love with our boots. And it kills me to think we may never make another pair.

Heading back to my couch, I try calling Mom. She doesn't pick up.

I find myself scrolling to Dad's number. My eyes burn. I'm haunted by our last conversation, which happened over text several months before he died. I'd asked him for money to help fix my car.

Sure, he texted back. The next morning, I had the cash in my account.

I didn't thank him, and he didn't follow up. Now, I'm so ashamed of how it all went down.

Without thinking, I hit his number and bring the

phone to my ear. It rings and rings until finally, his voicemail picks up.

Goose bumps break out on my arms at the sound of his gravelly timbre.

"You've reached Garrett Luck. Please leave a message, and I'll get back to you as soon as I can. Have a good one, y'all."

My face crumples. His voicemail beeps.

If I'm still so angry, why can't I stop fucking crying? Anger means yelling. It means frosty silences and heated exchanges. It does not mean crying your eyes out every time you think about the person you loved but hated too.

I hang up, wishing all the while I could ask him why he put that stipulation in his will. Maybe I wouldn't hate the idea of living in Hartsville so much if I understood why he wanted me there. He had his chance to bring me back to the ranch—many chances, in fact, over the course of many years—but he never did. Why insist on it now?

The thought comes out of nowhere: *Cash might have the answer to that question.* He said he was close with Dad. Who better to ask than the man who apparently worked side by side with Dad for over a decade?

Too bad Cash is a jackass. I'd rather pry my eyeballs out of my head with a rusty spoon than talk to him again.

I just wish I had other options.

My memories of the first six years of my life on the ranch are, like the city skyline, hazy at best. But they aren't all bad. I remember riding a pony, Dad leading the horse in a slow circle around a corral. I remember Mom in the front seat of an ATV, the breeze catching

51

in her hair as she turned around to smile at me in the back. And I can still smell the leather-and-hay scent of the horse barn.

I jump when my phone chimes. It's a Gmail notification: my business checking account has reached zero dollars.

I think about Goody's email. The one that detailed how much money I'd get at the end of every month if I lived on the ranch.

What *if* I go back to Hartsville? Just for thirty days, only long enough to get paid? Maybe Mom's lawyers will have gotten a judge to strike down the stipulation by then. Wheeler and I crushed an interview with an influencer earlier today, and we only have two more meetings set up this week. Surely, she can handle those while I'm gone?

I jump again when my phone vibrates. Wheeler is calling.

A white-hot flash of pain slices across my middle. Shit.

Shit shit *shit*. She definitely saw the notification from our bank too. We're both on the account.

Wiping my eyes, I move my thumb across my screen.

"Hey, Wheeler. I'm so sorry I keep missing you. I'll handle the negative balance." I take a deep breath. "I'm going back to Hartsville."

"Wait." She pauses. "You're *going*? As in *going* going?"

"I'm done waiting for our lawyers to figure this shit out. I'm going to get us our money."

Another pause.

"Mollie, you don't have to do this."

"I do, though. I don't see any other way to keep us from going under."

"Let me go with you, then. You can't walk onto your dad's ranch by yourself."

My eyes burn at the thought. Still, I say, "We need you here in Dallas for meetings and social media outreach. I can't imagine there are many influencers or boutiques in Hartsville that are up for a collab."

"We could open one," Wheeler replies with a laugh.

"Next to the tractor supply store? Somehow, I don't think Bellamy Brooks will fit in."

"Every woman likes to feel pretty. Even cowgirls."

"Not the kind of cowgirls you'll find there. At least that's what Mom says. I got this, Wheeler. Really. I can do anything for a month."

"Maybe you'll end up doing some cowboys while you're at it."

I scoff. "No thank you."

"I swear, you're the only woman on earth who isn't into dudes in Stetsons with Wrangler butts."

"Have you met my mother? And let's not forget the *lovely* Cash Rivers."

I told Wheeler about what a dick Cash was when I called her a week ago on my drive home from Hartsville.

"Fair point. Although I can't imagine *all* cowboys are like that." She lets out a breath. "Are you sure about this, Mollie? Ranch life and you…well, y'all don't exactly go together like peas and carrots."

"No shit, Sherlock. I don't plan on doing more ranch stuff than I have to." Although if I'm being honest, my heart does a little flip at the prospect of being on horseback again. I don't have many memories of life on the ranch, but riding horses is one thing I do remember. I *loved* it as a kid.

53

"Be careful."

"I will."

"And send pics. Preferably of all the Wrangler butts you'll see."

I laugh. "I'll do what I can."

"Attagirl. Keep me posted. Godspeed, friend."

"Wheeler?"

"Yeah?"

"I know we've talked theoretically about helping each other bury bodies. But would you actually be my accomplice? If I need you?"

I hear the grin in her voice when she says, "You say the word, and we'll ride at dawn, shovels in hand."

CHAPTER 5
Rope and Ride
Cash

There are hundreds of them.

Some are compiled into little green booklets from the pharmacy. Others are stacked together, bound with rubber bands. Still others are loose, tossed into the safety-deposit box, seemingly without order.

The one thing that unites all the pictures: they're of Garrett, Aubrey, Mollie, or some combination of the three.

Who goes through the trouble of actually developing physical photographs anymore? And why lock them away in a bank when they're clearly meant to be enjoyed?

Frowning, I spread them out across my desk in the ranch's office. Garrett converted an old pole barn into a workspace not long after my brothers and I arrived on Lucky Ranch. On hot days like today, you can still smell the fresh, clean scent of hay, which has been baked into the walls over countless decades.

My desk is tidy, empty, save for a laptop and a small

stack of paperbacks. Nonfiction mostly—biographies, histories—with the odd thriller or Stephen King thrown in there. I'm technically off two days a week, but I always come into the office anyway. Usually, I'm busy, but when I'm not, I never want to be without reading material at hand.

Today, though, my books are shoved to the side to make room for Garrett's pictures. Surveying them, my chest tightens. There was nothing else in the box. Just stacks and stacks of four-by-six photographs.

The fact that Garrett, a wildly wealthy man, considered these some of his most prized possessions has me feeling short of breath.

He was a damn good human being.

A flawed one too. I know he regretted letting Aubrey and Mollie go. But far as I know, he never chased after them like he should've.

"The regret is killing you," I told him once. "Go get them."

But the next morning, he still tacked up his horse, Maria, clearly intent on staying in Hartsville. I think so much time had passed that he didn't want to disrupt the new lives Aubrey and Mollie had built in Dallas.

I think, more than anything, he was scared. And stubborn. And he used the excuse of running the ranch to avoid confronting his feelings. His failings too.

Pot, meet kettle.

I glance at the empty desk across from mine. Garrett's. Wyatt and Sawyer cleaned it out a couple of weeks after he passed, even though I said I would do it. I think they knew going through his things would likely destroy me.

Kind of like looking through these photos must've

destroyed Garrett. He clearly loved his ex-wife and daughter, but they never visited, and he never visited them. As far as I know anyway. Is that why he put the photos in the lockbox? So he wouldn't have to face his regret?

I pick up a sun-bleached photo of Mollie. She was really fucking cute as a kid. Blond pigtails. Big smile that showed off the two front teeth she was missing.

There are countless photos of her on horseback. More'n a little shocking to see City Girl cheesing it on top of a gorgeous, spotted Appaloosa. But she looks at ease in the saddle. Happy even.

Wonder if she misses it. The horses, the sunshine. The wide-open spaces of life in Hill Country.

I shove that thought aside in an attempt to ease the ache in my chest.

Garrett also looks happy in these photos. Really happy. I wouldn't say he was unhappy during the time I knew him, but he definitely wasn't lit up the way he is in these pictures.

Families are complicated. I know that better than anyone. But the idea that Garrett died without ever making things right with the people he clearly loved more than anything is downright tragic.

I should've pushed him more. Tried harder to get him to Dallas—or at the very least get him on the phone more often. But he got set in his ways and ended up using his money in a failed attempt to buy his daughter's affection.

Now he's gone.

What if I die before I have a chance to make my dreams come true? What if I'm not able to save Rivers Ranch?

What if I never have a family of my own?

No-strings sex suits me just fine for now. I wanna get laid. I got calls to make.

Sometimes, though, I wish I had someone who slept in my bed for more than a night. I wish I had a person—*the* person—to talk to and take care of. Someone who'd take care of me too. Life is heavy. It'd be nice not to have to face it alone for once.

Not like it matters. I'm too damn busy taking care of everyone else to even think of adding a girlfriend to the mix.

Maybe that's why Garrett stayed single after his divorce. Still, I wonder why the hell he left these pictures to me and not to Mollie or Aubrey. What is he trying to tell me? Is he trying to teach me some kind of lesson? Show me a way to avoid making the same mistakes he did? Or was this some sort of clerical error, a typo in the will that was never fixed?

Looking out the window over my desk, I blink the blurriness from my eyes. Do I share these with Mollie? Send them to her maybe?

She's gotta regret not trying harder with her dad. What the fuck is wrong with her, not visiting even once? The man clearly adored her, but she couldn't be bothered to come see him. She sure enjoyed the fruits of his labor, though. I saw the checks he sent to the University of Texas. Heard him negotiating with real estate agents to buy her the condo she wanted in a ritzy part of Dallas.

Red-hot anger sweeps through me. I'd be thrilled just to *see* my parents again. But nothing, not even the most extravagant gifts, was ever good enough for Mollie.

I startle at the knock on the door. Quickly wiping

my eyes, I gather the photos and carefully place them back in the worn leather bag I used to carry them home from the bank. I have no idea why Garrett gave me these pictures or what he wanted me to do with them. All I know is they were important to him, so they're important to me.

It's my job to keep them safe until I figure out what the fuck this all means—him promising me the ranch but giving me pictures of people I don't know instead.

Clearing my throat, I glance over my shoulder. "Come in."

Goody slips through the door. She glances around the office, her eyes flickering for a beat. She's taking his passing hard too. Goody and Garrett were close, having worked together for decades. She was his legal counsel on all Lucky Ranch Enterprises Incorporated's deals, and now she's a rich woman because of it.

"These were in the safety-deposit box." Digging into the bag, I pull out a picture of Garrett and Aubrey line dancing and hold it up. "Not what I was expecting, but—"

"Garrett was a complicated man, I know." Goody closes the door behind her. "You all right?"

I nod, swallowing. "Yes, ma'am. I'll be just fine."

"How like you to say that." She offers me a soft smile. "Why don't I believe you?"

Ninety-nine percent of the time, I love living in a small town. But right now, I fucking hate how well we all know each other. No getting anything past anyone in these parts. Why can't I brood in peace like a normal person?

"What can I help you with?" I manage.

"I have some news."

My stomach dips. I place the photo in the bag and zip it up. "Good or bad?"

"Depends."

I can't read her expression. Her eyes have this funny, knowing gleam in them.

Turning, I lean the backs of my legs against my desk and cross my arms. "Let's get it over with, then."

"Mollie's coming to the ranch."

You can hear a pin drop in the silence that fills the room.

I run a hand over my face. "To stay?"

Goody takes a sharp, short breath through her nose. "I asked her that when she called this morning, but she just said she wanted to 'get a lay of the land.' I don't know for sure if that means she's staying, but considering what's at stake...yes, I'm guessing she'll be at the ranch for a while."

I grit my teeth, biting down so hard my back molars light up with a flash of pain. "What the hell are we gonna do with her?"

"I reckon we'll figure it out. She owns the place, so..."

My heart flutters in my chest like a trapped bird. "What if she doesn't end up staying the whole year? Who gets the trust then?"

"Garrett did not leave it to you, if that's what you're asking."

"That's not my question."

Goody searches my face for a beat. "He has a plan for the money. We'll cross that bridge if we get there."

"*When*. When we get there. City Girl ain't gonna

last a day. The will said she had to actively manage the ranch, right?"

"Cash." Goody's tone is laced with warning. "I don't need to tell you to play nice, right?"

"I don't play. And I'm not nice."

That soft smile of hers is back. "Horseshit."

Can't help it. I laugh, the heaviness in my chest lifting for half a heartbeat. Maybe that's why I blurt, "Why do you think Garrett told me I'd get the ranch if he never intended for me to have it?"

Goody thinks on this for a minute. "I'm not sure, Cash. Who knows what he intended? It's entirely possible he did want the ranch to go to you, but he didn't think he'd die before he amended his will."

"Maybe." But I don't buy it. There's a tickle in the back of my brain—a feeling that I'm missing a piece of whatever puzzle Garrett put together.

"Whatever the case, it will all work out." Goody claps me on the shoulder. "Mollie arrives tomorrow, midafternoon. I'm going to get the New House ready."

The New House is what we call the six-thousand-square-foot mansion Garrett and Aubrey built right before they divorced. Aubrey apparently hated living in the circa-1920 farmhouse Garrett brought her home to when they married, so after they struck black gold, they built Aubrey's dream house.

That still wasn't enough to keep her around. No one lives there now, but Patsy, Lucky Ranch's resident chef, uses the massive, modern kitchen to turn out breakfast, lunch, and dinner for the entire staff during the week.

After Aubrey left, Garrett moved back to the old

farmhouse. My brothers cleaned out his belongings only last month, and now Wyatt calls it home.

I suck in a long, deep breath. In my gut, I knew Mollie would come to the ranch, but I still hoped there was a small chance she'd chicken out.

Not too late for that. Maybe once she's here, she'll realize she's not up to the task of running a ranch. She's a city girl with soft hands and likely no real physical skills. Can't imagine she knows how to muck a stall or drive a tractor.

I tell myself she'll more than likely run screaming after a day or two.

"Cash!"

I look up to see a tall cowboy stride into the office.

"I been lookin' for you. Weren't we supposed to meet at the horse barn?"

Pasting a smile on my face, I walk over and extend my hand. "Hey, Beck. My apologies. Must've gotten my times mixed up." *That or I had a near miss with a nervous breakdown.* "Thanks for stopping by."

"Horses are ready when you are."

Sally, one of Lucky Ranch's veterinarians and an old family friend, peeks her head into the office. "I took a look, Cash. They are fine animals in perfect health. Beck, y'all have your reputation for a reason."

Beck Wallace heads the horse breeding program on his family's ranch about twenty or so miles from here. They're famous for producing some of the best ranch horses this side of the Rockies, which is why we recently purchased two quarter horses from them. Beck is here to deliver the mares.

He smiles, wrapping an arm around Sally's shoulders

when she steps up beside him. "Why, thank you, Miss Sally. High praise indeed, coming from Hart County's rising star."

Sally grins. "Aw, Beck, stop. You're makin' me blush."

"What's wrong with that? I'm just givin' credit where credit is due."

Sally recently returned to Hartsville after going to college and veterinary school, followed by a years-long stint doing a residency. Her dad, John B, is a hugely talented vet in his own right, but Sally's already giving him a run for his money.

Wonder what he'd think of this little flirtation between his daughter and Beck Wallace. Beck's a good guy, but he and his brothers have a bit of a reputation. They get around, as my mama used to say.

I turn around to open a desk drawer. "I'll bring the checkbook. Meet y'all out at the barn?"

"Sounds good." Beck opens the door and motions Sally through it. "After you, sugar."

Goody chuckles once the door is closed. "Well, that was...something."

"As long as it ain't Wyatt giving her that look, I'm fine with it."

Patsy and John B are like family at this point. Really, the only family we have left. I don't want to risk losing them if Wyatt does what he always does with girls and breaks Sally's heart.

"I feel like everyone still thinks Sally's seventeen. She's a grown woman now. She wants to have some fun, I say let her."

Goody eyes me as she reaches for the door. "Ever thought of taking your own advice?"

"Sure have." I dig a pen out of the drawer and shove that in the back pocket of my jeans, along with the checkbook. "I'm about to have a lot of fun with City Girl."

"I'm serious, Cash. You'd be smart to make Mollie an ally, not an enemy."

Jogging to the door so I can open it for Goody, I hold out my arm. "After you, *sugar.*"

Goody chuckles again. "Allies. Please."

I tell myself I'm only taking Goody's advice as I make plans to give Mollie Luck a *very* warm welcome to Lucky Ranch indeed.

CHAPTER 6
Come on, Snakes. Let's Rattle
Mollie

Green.

It's everywhere. In the canopy of giant oaks that border either side of the ranch's entrance and in the grassy stubble that covers the ground. Green cacti, shaped like enormous ears, spike up from the pale-yellow earth. Even the letters and logo stamped in the massive beam overhead are green: *Lucky Ranch Est. 1902.*

Considering how barren the landscape has been for the past two hundred miles, all this green is a shock to the senses.

A pleasant shock. But a shock nonetheless.

Lucky Ranch is a literal oasis. How? Why? And why does the sight of the simple but lovingly tended entrance, its stone supports weathered with age, cause a strange stirring inside my chest?

I don't remember the ranch being this green or the oaks this grand. Then again, it's been twenty years since I stepped foot on this land. A lot has changed since then.

Taking the right, I pass underneath the arch and continue down an unpaved but tidy road. My tires crunch on the dirt and gravel. This is Hill Country, so the road climbs and dips often. It goes on for longer than I remember, hinting at the grand scope of the property.

It's beautiful. Meadows open up on my left, and I slow when I see a pair of deer there, their ears perking up as I approach. After staring at me for a long beat, they merrily leap off into the trees, light as feathers on their feet. Hooves. Whatever.

Gnarled oaks and sycamores provide a canopy of much-needed shade overhead. I crest a big hill, a canyon yawning into view on my right. The breath leaves my lungs as I take in the vista: pastures, woods, the green glimmer of a distant river.

"Wow," I breathe. I definitely don't remember the ranch being this beautiful. Granted, I was a kid the last time I saw it. I don't think I would've appreciated it then.

Now, though? It's pretty enough to make me stop at the top of the canyon to gawk at the vastness of the property. The unspoiled wildness of it all.

For a split second, I'm gripped by the image of a blue-eyed cowboy on horseback galloping across the meadow below. He's in jeans and a hat, strong arms filling out the sleeves of his Western blue-and-white-striped button-up. He moves gracefully with the horse, his big body undulating in time to her strides.

My pulse skips a beat.

I'm fantasizing about Cash. *Jesus.*

As if my stomach weren't already in knots. I'm back on the ranch my estranged father left me for God knows what reason. I have no idea what—who—I'm going to find here or how long I'm going to have to stay. What if Mom's lawyers don't come through? What if I'm stuck here for *twelve* months instead of one?

It doesn't help that I'm fantasizing about how well asshole cowboys ride things. Cowboys who, in all likelihood, live right here on the ranch.

Cowboys whose help I'm going to need running this place.

Maybe Mom was right to freak out when I told her I was returning to the ranch. "Nothing good happens in Hartsville," she said.

She begged me not to make the trip. But I'm out of options.

Shoving the image of Cash and his stupid hat aside, I continue down the road. About a mile or so in, my heart skips a beat when I see buildings come into view.

I remember the first house we lived in here on Lucky Ranch. It was small and simple—a white clapboard farmhouse my great-grandfather built. Then Dad struck oil, and he built Mom a modern stone mansion with huge windows and a metal roof.

We didn't live there for long. Less than a year after construction wrapped up, my mom and I left Hartsville for Dallas. Little did I know then that I wouldn't lay eyes on this land again for two decades.

I see the stone house first. It's bigger than I remember. More beautiful too. I breathe a silent sigh of relief. At least I'll be comfortable there.

Beyond the house, there's a landscaped yard with a pool. Farther back, I glimpse a pair of barns, a silo, and a corral.

My pulse skips another beat when I see cowboys

on horseback by the corral, kicking up dust in the midmorning heat.

There's a lot of them. Way more than I'd anticipated. Ten cowboys? More?

I know nothing about ranching. Less than nothing about ranching on *this* scale.

I slap my hand to my forehead, feeling sick. I want to fire Cash Rivers the second I see him. But I don't see how I'm going to run this place without the help of Lucky Ranch's foreman. A quick Google search told me that foremen are a ranch's go-to guys (and girls)—the people who oversee pretty much everything.

I glance at my rearview mirror. I can just see the road through the cloud of dust behind me. It's not too late to turn back.

Maybe Mom's lawyers are close to convincing a judge that Dad's stipulation is stupid and ultimately unenforceable.

If not, I could always ask Mom for a loan against my inheritance. But she's already made an investment in Bellamy Brooks, and again, she made it clear that was the only investment she'll make. Being the people pleaser I am, I don't want to overstep or stress her out. I know she's working hard right now, trying to sell her client's estate. I know she has lots of money tied up in other projects too. I don't want to pile on to her problems.

So I park in front of the house and pray like hell my stay here is only temporary.

The front door opens, and Goody emerges onto the front step, waving at me as I climb out of my car.

"Mollie! You made it."

I called her yesterday when I decided I'd be returning

to Hartsville. She said she'd meet me at the ranch "to help smooth the transition."

I didn't tell her I have no intention of living here longer than I have to. Mom employs the best of the best when it comes to lawyers. Surely, they'll have straightened out this whole mess by the end of the month.

"How was the drive?" Goody asks. Her bolo is taupe today. Same as her suit and matching boots.

"Hey, Goody. It was fine."

"I'm so glad you changed your mind about returning to the ranch."

I paste on a smile, already starting to sweat. It's hot as hell out here. "It's what Dad wanted."

"Come on in. Everyone is eager to meet you."

A bloom of anxiety takes root in my center as I climb the limestone steps leading to the front door. The regret I feel over not visiting Dad on the ranch takes on a vicious edge. What must the ranch's employees think of me? I'm Dad's only child, but I rarely called and never visited. They must've known we were estranged. But do they know why?

My cheeks burn. Will they resent me for treating the man they apparently adored so poorly? I sure as hell would.

Nothing I can do about that now, except show them the character I (hopefully) have now that I didn't back then as a hurt, headstrong kid.

I'm hit by the homiest, most delicious smell ever the second I step through the house's massive door. It's sweet, and it's savory, and good *Lord,* am I hungry.

Goody smiles at the audible rumble of my stomach. "I'm glad you arrived early. Patsy's lunch spread is not to be missed."

"Patsy?"

"Lucky Ranch's chef, and dare I say the best cook in Hart County."

The house is cool but not at all quiet. Voices ramble down the long, wide hallway ahead. I follow Goody toward it, taking in the house as we go. It's huge, and it's got Mom's fingerprints all over it. I recognize the twelve-foot ceilings from the house she built in Dallas. The iron light fixtures, exposed stone walls, and enormous windows too. Even the furnishings look like items she would've picked out: antique chairs, neutral upholstery, lots of pillows.

I frown. Everything is in pristine shape. No way Mom picked it all out twenty-plus years ago?

Goody must read my mind, because she says, "Recognize any of this?"

"I'm not sure, to be honest."

"Your dad didn't change a thing after you and your mom left. To be fair, he didn't live here for very long after that either. He preferred your grandparents' place."

"He moved back to the farmhouse?"

Goody dips her head. The voices get louder. "He did."

Huh. Dad must've really hated this house if he preferred a tiny, hundred-year-old clapboard spot instead. Did he hate it because it reminded him of Mom and me?

Or did he hate it because he hated her? She sure as hell did not like him.

My stomach twists. Growing up, all I wanted was a normal family. One where my mom didn't despise my dad. Seeing my friends' parents flirt or kiss or even just sit at the dinner table beside each other always felt so special.

Now that I'm an adult and I understand the complexities of adult relationships, I know there were good reasons why my parents split. But it never stopped hurting like hell when Mom would talk shit about Dad or when I'd convince myself that Dad hated me too because I was on Mom's side, and that was why he never brought me back to the ranch. I didn't mean to pick sides. It just kind of happened. And then years passed, and resentments grew, and…yeah, now I'm here, ready to burst into tears at any moment.

"The kitchen is really the only part of the house people regularly use," Goody continues. "It's the only place big enough for us to sit down and eat. Of course, when your dad entertained guests, they'd stay here. I imagine you'd like to stay here as well? The primary bedroom is lovely."

I nod, pulse drumming as we approach the kitchen. I tell myself not to be nervous. I own the ranch now, which means I own this house and employ all the people I'm about to meet. Maybe they're nervous to meet their new boss too.

I'm still downright nauseous as I follow Goody through a large doorway on our right. I bet Cash isn't the only one who hates me.

Like the rest of the house, the kitchen has generous proportions. There's a massive table at the far end, which is simply but beautifully set with cream plates and light-blue glassware.

A commercial-style range with two ovens and more burners than I can count occupies the center of the room. Mom definitely picked that out, along with the bleached oak cabinets and soapstone countertops. The vibe is luxe rustic, with an enormous island dominating the space.

But it's the spread set out on that island that makes my eyes bulge. I'm not sure I've ever seen so much food. There are several platters of what appear to be chicken-fried steaks, smothered in thick white gravy. Sweating jugs of tea and lemonade sit beside them. There's a huge bowl of green beans and two bowls of the most delicious-looking potato salad. Then a tray of brownies, each one slathered in white frosting and drizzled with more chocolate.

The petite woman behind the counter is pulling another tray of brownies out of the oven when she turns around and sees us.

Her face splits into a smile. "Well, hey there, y'all! Come on in! Mollie, we've been waiting for you to arrive. I'm Patsy. Welcome to the ranch."

I watch her set down the brownies on top of the oven. My stomach grumbles. I wish I could eat that kind of thing and not be in pain afterward.

Patsy is midfifties, if I had to guess, her gray hair neatly parted down the middle and pulled into a low ponytail. She's got a warm smile and bright, curious brown eyes.

I like her immediately. Or maybe it's the delicious smell of just-baked goods that I like.

Whatever the case, Patsy rounds the island and immediately wraps me in a hug, ignoring the hand I extend. "It is so nice to finally meet you, sugar. And those boots! Love the purple."

I don't know how I feel about being called *sugar*. But Patsy's hug is tight and warm, genuine in a way I haven't

72

experienced in a long time. I feel a smidge of relief that she doesn't appear to hate me.

So I just keep my smile pasted on my face and say, "It's nice to meet you too, Patsy. Your food looks delicious and smells even better."

She releases me, putting her hands on my shoulders. "Lordy, you look just like your daddy."

I want to reply with something like *That's what everyone says* or *I get that a lot.* But no one's ever said that to me. No one I know anyway. My life in Dallas was so separate from Dad's on the ranch—our paths crossed so seldomly—that none of my friends or neighbors even knew who he was. They couldn't say whether I looked like him because he was never around.

My throat contracts. *I will not cry.*

Swallowing hard, I look away and nod at the food. "So you cook like this all the time?"

"We have lots of mouths to feed here on the ranch. We fit as many as we can here in the kitchen, but the bulk of the ranch hands will eat the food I bring to the bunkhouse." She nods at the older man standing at an enormous farm sink and a younger one seated at the table with a paint-smeared toddler on his lap. "Mollie, meet my husband, John B, and there at the table is Sawyer Rivers and his daughter, Ella."

My stomach dips at the name *Rivers*. Sawyer looks at me, raising little Ella's hand in a wave, and my stomach dips again at the familiar cobalt-blue shade of his eyes.

No question he's Cash's brother. He's got the same build: big shoulders and broad chest. But unlike Cash, he offers me a friendly smile.

"Nice to meet ya, Mollie. Ella, can you say hi?"

Ella doesn't say anything, but she also smiles, a mirror image of her father's, dimples and all.

I wave at her. "Hi, Sawyer. Hi, Ella. How old are you?"

Sawyer helps her hold up three fingers. "Just had a birthday, didn't we?"

"Ella get more presents?" the little girl replies.

We all laugh.

"Ella, honey, I think you know the answer to that." The older man turns around, resting his hands on the lip of the sink behind him. "You're always getting presents."

Patsy grins. "How could we not spoil you, sugar? Look at that sweet face."

"She is absolutely precious," I say.

"Thank you." Sawyer smooths back Ella's baby-fine blond hair. "But really, y'all, it's becoming a problem. She's got so many toys, we're running out of room."

John B shakes his head. "Good problem to have. Mollie, welcome to Lucky Ranch."

"Are y'all cowboys here or…"

"Sawyer is." John nods at him. "My daughter, Sally, and I provide veterinary care across the county."

"Best vets in Texas," Sawyer adds.

Goody nods. "It's true. The care they provide for the animals is second to none."

A young woman in jeans and boots strides into the kitchen from what appears to be a pantry, a five-pound bag of sugar tucked in the crook of her arm. "Thank you kindly, Goody. I've learned from the OG."

The woman, who I'm assuming is Sally, goes up on her tiptoes to kiss her dad on his whiskered cheek.

"*OG* as in old guy?" John B laughs.

Sally smiles. "That or *original gangster*. Either way, you're the world's best teacher."

"You're a mighty fine student, sweetheart, when you're not being a mighty big pain in the ass."

Patsy scoffs. "Like y'all aren't two peas in a pod. Sally, honey, this is Mollie Luck, Garrett's daughter."

"Mollie! Hey! It's so great to finally meet you. Your dad talked about you often."

My heart clenches. That answers that question. "Hi, Sally. That's kind of you to say. I"—my throat tightens, and I clear it—"miss him."

"Aw, Mollie, I'm so sorry for your loss." Sally sets down the sugar on the island next to the jugs of tea. "We all miss Garrett."

Patsy nods as Sally helps her pour an obscene amount of sugar into the jugs. What I would give to be able to drink that stuff without paying for it with a terrible stomachache later.

"He was so good to all of us."

"Truly the best," Sally says, grabbing a wooden spoon. She stirs the tea while her mom rolls up the mostly empty bag of sugar.

Watching them work together, I'm gripped by the acute need for my own mother. Mom wouldn't be caught dead making her own tea, much less with sugar in it. But she's always been my biggest cheerleader and a constant source of support, even if she is super wrapped up in her work and the Dallas social scene.

That's support I could really, really use right now. I may be twenty-six years old, but in this moment, I feel all of fourteen, awkward and lost and bursting with emotions I can't process and don't understand.

I feel myself tilting into a death spiral of regret and grief. My eyes burn. I can barely breathe around the moon in my throat.

I am in a room full of people who had a closer relationship with my father than I did. And none of them are even *related* to him.

It makes me feel like absolute shit.

But just as I'm about to actually burst into tears, the back door opens. Sunlight floods the kitchen as a man steps inside, sweeping his sweat-stained hat off his head.

"Ooooo-eeee, don't that smell good! Y'all got no *idea* the hurt I'm 'bout to put on this food. Sally, don't tell me you made your buttercream frosting for those brownies."

Sally rolls her eyes, but she's grinning. "Wyatt, you smell atrocious."

"Eau de horse." He waves his scent toward her.

She flaps her hand in front of her nose. "More like BO."

"You're welcome to hose me down out back." He holds out his arms and smirks. "You can undress me and everything."

"Let me get my rubber gloves," Sally deadpans.

The man coming in the door behind Wyatt roars with laughter. "Dang, Sally, we missed having you around. Someone needs to kick this kid's—"

"Children are present," Sawyer warns, covering Ella's ears with his hands.

"Sally recently graduated from a veterinary residency," Goody explains. "She's been shadowing her dad ever since while she decides what she'd like to do with her degrees long term. That's Duke." She points to the other man. "He's Sawyer's younger brother."

"Ah," I say, staring at the door as one cowboy after the next wipes his boots on the mat outside before entering the kitchen. Each one takes off his hat, hair soaked through with sweat. Their faces and hands are deeply tanned, making their blue eyes pop even more.

The men are alarmingly dirty and even more alarmingly handsome, despite the sweat and the dust and the, er, *outdoorsy* smell that rises off them.

My heart pounds. How many Rivers boys were there? Four? Twelve?

And when is Cash going to walk through that door? *Is* he going to walk through it? What do I say to him? So far, everyone's been exceptionally kind to me. I don't want to break the spell. But I also don't want to give him any kind of advantage by playing nice.

The last cowboy to enter the kitchen is the tallest. He's wearing a T-shirt of indeterminate color that's dotted with sweat. It's not soaked through, so I get the impression he must've changed before coming to lunch. But the shirt still clings to his chest and his stomach, revealing a thickly muscled torso.

His jeans—those cling to him too. Add in the cowboy boots and the wide leather belt and the way he holds his hat to his chest—

"Cash!" Ella shouts with delight, holding up her arms. "Ella hold you!"

I watch, head spinning, as Cash aims a wide white smile at the little girl before dropping his hat on the table, crown up, and scooping her into his arms. "Ellie belly boo, I missed you! How was school?"

What in the *world*? I wonder if Cash has a twin brother. One who has the same name. Because this guy?

The one cooing to his niece while he smiles at her like an idiot?

This cannot possibly be the same asshole cowboy I met in Goody's office last week.

"Ella loves school," the little girl replies.

Sawyer grabs a cup from across the table and takes a sip of water. "Probably because she's the teacher's pet."

Cash puts her on his hip, arm slung easily underneath her bottom like he's done this hundreds, thousands of times. "How could she not be? You're the smartest *and* the cutest kid in the class, aren't you?" He tickles her tummy. "Aren't you, Ella?"

She giggles, a high, happy sound that's so sweet, I can't help but smile, even as I continue to stare.

That's when Cash looks up, and our gazes lock.

My stomach bottoms out. His smile fades, his eyes taking on a hard glint. They flick down my body. Back up. His jaw ticks, as if he doesn't like what he sees.

I blush so furiously, I can feel it all the way in the soles of my feet. Still, I look him square in the eye. Screw him for making me feel off-kilter. Embarrassed even. He's the one who should be embarrassed with his sweaty shirt and stupid beard-mustache thing.

Goody smiles at him. "You remember Mollie, Cash?"

"How could I forget?" He says it like a joke. Like *I'm* a joke. "Hello, City Girl."

CHAPTER 7
Giddyup
Cash

Not gonna lie, my heart skips a beat at the fire that ignites in Mollie's brown eyes at the insult.

"I'd prefer you not call me names," she clips, crossing her arms.

Didn't think it was possible, but she's wearing an even more ridiculous outfit than the one she wore to Goody's office last week. Today, it's a very short, very tight dress, huge earrings, and a pair of tall purple boots.

I still can't believe that *this* is the owner of Lucky Ranch. Hundreds of thousands of acres, worth hundreds of millions of dollars.

Her.

Mollie's outfit shows too much leg and not nearly enough judgment. *Way* too much leg.

Or maybe not enough.

Ignoring that thought, I hand Ella back to Sawyer. "I'd prefer you get back in your big, fancy car and go back to your big, fancy city."

"Cash." Patsy gives me a warning glare. "You best mind your manners, cowboy, or you won't be welcome in my kitchen."

It's actually Mollie's kitchen now. But that's the problem, isn't it? Because now that she's here to stake her claim, she's one step closer to selling the place. Which means I'm likely one step closer to being out on my ass, along with my brothers.

Who knows if Lucky Ranch's new owners will want to keep the cattle operation? In all likelihood, they'll split the ranch into parcels, selling them off piece by piece until there's nothing left but the house and the pool.

What will we do then? Far as I know, no one in the area is hiring—at least not five cowboys at once. I refuse to break up our family. But cowboying is all we know. If we can't do that and we can't pay the bills at Rivers Ranch...

We'll have to sell that too.

Despite the panic swirling in my gut, I manage to grunt, "Yes, ma'am."

"Mollie, I apologize," Patsy continues. "Cash sometimes takes a minute to warm up to strangers. These are his brothers. Cash is the oldest, and that there is Wyatt—he's next in the birth order. And then there's Sawyer, who you've already met. Then Ryder and Duke, the twins."

Mollie blinks. I imagine she's doing the math, figuring out exactly how horny my parents were back in the day. "Five of y'all? No girls ever came along?"

"We felt sorry for our mama too." Ryder shakes his head. "But if anyone could handle us, it was her."

"Your mom, she—"

"Passed." Wyatt runs a hand over his face. "Twelve

years ago this October. She and our dad died in a car accident."

Mollie blinks again. She looks up, her eyes catching on mine for a beat before she looks away. "Oh my God, I'm so sorry. Y'all must've been really young."

"Ryder and I were fourteen, yeah," Duke says. "Didn't seem young at the time, but looking back…"

"I can't imagine how awful that must've been," Mollie says. "I don't know what to say."

My heart twists. I don't know why. I hate this woman and her fake sympathy. I hate how the grief is still there. I hate that I don't know what to do next and how that scares the shit out of me, so I ignore it and glare at Mollie while I think of another rude thing to say to her.

When she glares back, I swear she looks just like she did in one of Garrett's pictures. In the photo, she's giving the camera a look that could kill while Garrett squats in the dust beside her, a huge smile on his face in a clear attempt to cheer her up.

Goody glances at me, then at Mollie. "Why don't we have some lunch? I think y'all must be…hungry. Then the three of us can sit down and talk about the transition."

"Is there anyone else I can talk to?" Mollie doesn't break eye contact with me. Girl ain't afraid—I'll give her that. "I get the feeling Cash won't be exactly helpful in showing me the ropes."

I feel my brothers watching us. Duke even has the balls to smile.

Ignoring them, I say, "The help you need ain't the kind of help I can provide, *Mollie*."

"You can call me Miss Luck, *Cash*. And that's too bad, isn't it, considering I'm your boss now?"

Wyatt rubs his hands together. "I like where this is going."

"Shut up." I turn back to Mollie. "Miss Luck, with all due respect—"

"Lord save us, here it comes," John B mutters.

"I really do think it's best you go back to Dallas. You clearly don't belong here—"

"Enough." Patsy's voice cuts through the tension in the room like a warm knife through butter. "Goody is right; let's eat. Maybe with a full belly, Cash will recognize that his mama—God rest her soul—raised him better than this. If he doesn't, well..." She thwacks her wooden spoon against her palm.

"Not the spoon," Ryder whispers.

Wyatt arches a brow and looks at me. "Dude, don't tempt her. I've felt the business end of that thing, and lemme tell you, it ain't an experience you wanna have."

"Mom really beat you with a spoon?" Sally wrinkles her nose.

He grins. "Only once, but I deserved it."

"He was runnin' across the yard, naked as the day he was born," Patsy says. "I was right here, having my coffee, when I looked up and saw a full moon—and not the pretty kind. Only way I could get him back to the bunkhouse was by chasing him down. I just so happened to have a spoon in my hand."

I stare at him. "Jesus Christ, Wyatt."

"Are you surprised?" Sally says with a grin.

"Hey, I was twenty-two and stupid. Drunk off my ass. But I can reenact it for you if you'd like." Wyatt reaches for his belt buckle.

The room erupts all at once.

"No!"

"Please, God, don't."

"Someone get the bleach for my eyes."

Sally's gaze dances when she says, "Tempting, but I'll pass."

"Offer always stands, sunshine," Wyatt says. "Just say the word, and you got all the moon you want."

"Good night, moon," Ella singsongs.

Duke grins. "The nickname is cute, y'all."

"No, it's not," I grunt.

I glance at Mollie and see her watching us, arms still crossed, her lips twitching.

City Girl's loving this, us acting like the idiot cowboys she assumes we are.

I give Wyatt a discreet kick to the shin. Not only do I need him to behave in front of City Girl, but I also need him to cool his jets with Sally.

They've been friends since they were kids, so I don't mind a little flirtation. But ever since she got back from her residency, he can't stop looking at her. I know that gleam in his eyes. It ain't friendly—I'll say that much.

Casanova can have anyone else in Hartsville. Probably has. No wonder he mentioned going to Vegas; he's probably looking for new girls to chase. But he's gonna keep his mitts off Sally. He so much as lays a finger on her, he puts our relationship with her parents, John B and Patsy, at risk. We lose them, we lose very important allies in keeping the ranch afloat. More than that, we'd be losing family, because that's what the three of them have become to us.

Then again, Lucky Ranch may well be in its final days anyway.

Whatever the case, I hope Sally starts hanging out with Beck Wallace a lot more and my brother a lot less.

John B claps his hands. "All right, y'all, dig in. We got a real treat today. Patsy made her famous chicken-fried steak with white gravy. The potato salad's got eggs in it, Ryder, so you wanna stay away from that. Brownies are Sally's recipe. No, Cash, you can't have more than three. I think that covers it?"

I extend my arm, holding my brothers back as I nod at Mollie. My eyes slip to her legs again. They're long. Flawless. Not a freckle or scar in sight. "*Ladies* first."

When I look up, I see her eyes are narrowed.

"Why do I get the feeling you're insulting me?"

"Wouldn't dream of it, Miss Luck. I'm just being polite. That's how my mama raised me." I nod at Patsy, who's shooting daggers at me with her eyes.

There'll be hell to pay after this. But it'll be worth it when Mollie leaves. Someone punches my shoulder. Duke, if I had to guess.

"Excuse my brother." Yep, it's Duke. "He doesn't know how to act around beautiful women. Last girl he was with—"

"Don't." I curl my right hand into a fist. Pray for the patience I need to handle my brothers without committing an act of homicide.

Sally loops her arm through Mollie's and pulls her to the food. "Ignore them. Sometimes, there's a bit of a *Seven Brides for Seven Brothers* vibe going on here." She tosses me a look over her shoulder. "Some people forget how not to be heathens. They'll get better, I promise."

I watch Mollie pick up a plate, which she fills with a big pile of Patsy's green beans and…nothing else. Skips the steak, the potato salad. Even the brownies, which she looks at longingly before turning away.

If I didn't hate Mollie Luck before, I despise her now. She won't even try the brownies? Why the fuck not? Her Pilates instructor threaten to excommunicate her or something if she eats chocolate? And what about Patsy's steak? How rude to not even put one steak on her plate.

I'm starving, so like everyone else, I pile my plate high: two chicken-fried steaks smothered in gravy, three brownies, and plenty of green beans too.

Goody, being the consummate lawyer she is, takes over the conversation at the table. She fills Mollie in on things the owner of a ranch should already know: staff, seasons, equipment we own, equipment we lease. Goody goes around the table and has each of us describe what we do and the tasks we complete on a daily basis.

Mollie nods politely as she chews on her green beans. She doesn't say much. Doesn't ask any questions. A couple of times, I catch her glaring at me over the rim of her water glass.

And a couple of times, I catch myself wondering how far up her legs that little dress of hers rode up when she sat. If I looked under the table, what would I see?

Christ, I need to get laid. Been too long, clearly, if I'm fantasizing about City Girl's legs.

But the fact that they're flawless means she's not used to manual labor. Or being outside, for that matter. My brothers and I, we're beat up and bowlegged from spending most of our time on horseback.

I smirk as the idea takes shape.

Tossing my napkin onto the table beside my empty plate, I clap my hands against my thighs. "Well, Miss

Luck, since you're here to see your ranch, let's get to it. Sawyer, tack up an extra horse."

I bite back a laugh at the flicker of panic in Mollie's eyes.

"A horse? For me?"

"Cash," Wyatt says. "Just take the ATV. It's too hot—"

I hold up a hand. "ATV can't get where we're goin'."

"I don't ride," Mollie says. "Or I haven't ridden in…a really long time."

"You best pick it back up if you wanna run this ranch."

She stares at me, nostrils flaring. That *fire*. Fuck me if it don't make my skin feel two sizes too tight—

I shove the thought aside. Gotta keep my eyes on the prize: chasing this brat off our property before she takes a shine to it. Because that's always what happens when visitors come to Lucky Ranch.

It's what Garrett admitted happened to him as a kid following his daddy around the property.

"What about taking my car?" she asks. "It's got four-wheel drive—"

"Too big." I shake my head. "Ask anyone in here. You wanna get the lay of the land, you gotta do it on horseback."

Mollie glances at Goody, who grimaces.

"He's not wrong. But the tour can wait perhaps? There's some paperwork we should go over—"

"Don't have time. We either go now or we don't go at all." I get up and start grabbing plates, stacking them on my forearm.

I'm shocked when Mollie pops up and starts doing the same, piling her plate with silverware and water glasses. "That was delicious, Patsy. Thank you."

"You sure you got enough to eat?" Patsy asks.

I step around Mollie and head for the sink. "There's no food court on the ranch, Miss Luck. You get hungry, you'll be SOL."

"Oh? So no Auntie Anne's Pretzels, then?" She cocks her head, spearing me with a glare. "Never would have guessed. I'll be fine."

Duke chuckles. "You're a feisty one, ain't you, Miss Luck?"

"I prefer the term *spirited*."

"Self-possessed," Goody adds.

I turn on the faucet. "You know what we do with spirited horses here on the ranch?"

Mollie lets her plate fall with a clatter beside the sink. Leaning her hip into the counter, she crosses her arms. "I'm not a horse."

"We break them."

She gives me a tight smile. She's close enough that I can smell her perfume over the clean-water scent of Ivory dish soap. "And you know what happens to people who are out of a job? They go broke."

Sawyer claps his hands. "Dang, she's clever."

"I told you to tack up the horses."

Mollie purses her lips. "You're really doing this."

"Yes, I'm really taking time out of my day to show you around your ranch. You're welcome."

"Fine."

I feel her looking at me for a beat as I bend down to load the dishwasher.

"I'll ride. But Goody comes with us. Whatever plan you had to ditch me or feed me to a bear or whatever isn't going to happen."

Straightening, I take the dirty silverware she holds out to me and return her smile. "We don't have bears on the ranch. But we do have bobcats. And coyotes. And rattlers big enough to take out you and your horse."

"Won't be the first snake in the grass I've encountered here."

The reply is quick, a slap just firm enough to make my skin tingle.

Sally grins. "I like her."

I don't. But with a little luck and a lot of help from the South Texas heat, this will be my first and only ride with City Girl.

CHAPTER 8
Shit Outta Luck
Cash

"You with the circus?" I ask, looking Mollie up and down as she strides into the horse barn alongside Wyatt. "Even Dolly Parton doesn't dress like Dolly Parton all the time."

"Don't you dare speak ill of Dolly." Mollie slips her thumbs through the belt loops of her skinny jeans. "And the only clown I see is you."

Sawyer's chuckling again, shaking his head as he tightens a saddle on one of the horses in crossties. He's been here for twenty minutes or so, helping me tack up the horses. "I like the burn."

"Don't you have a job to do?" I snap, then turn back to Mollie. "Dolly is a goddamn treasure. I'd never insult her. But she's not out here riding horses and working cattle in her big fancy getups, is she?"

Mollie's eyes go a little wide as they move over the horse. "Working cattle? That mean what I think it does?"

I meet Sawyer's gaze. It's all I can do not to grin. She's gonna *hate* this.

"Means we're handling the cows. Moving them from pasture to pasture. Takin' care of sick cattle, finding lost ones, that kind of thing." Wyatt leans an elbow against the stall. "For the record, Miss Luck, I like the look."

I don't. She's gonna be uncomfortable and hot as hell in her skintight jeans and long-sleeved denim shirt unbuttoned practically to her navel. A lacy purple bra peeks through. It matches her purple boots and the ridiculous feathered band wrapped around her pristine Stetson.

I look away. I honestly can't tell if Mollie is wearing this shit ironically or if she's just that ridiculous. That clueless. It's a hundred fucking degrees out there. She'll melt in this stuff. Never mind how dirty she's going to get.

She smiles. "Thank you, Wyatt. And you know, I was just kidding about the Miss Luck thing. Please call me Mollie."

I drop the mounting block on the ground by her feet. "Time to get on the horse, Mollie."

"Not you, Cash. You can still call me Miss Luck."

Rolling my eyes, I shove my hat onto my head. "Let's get a move on."

"Where's Goody?"

"Out here!" the lawyer calls from the corral. Like a true Texan, Goody keeps spare riding gear in the trunk of her pickup. She'd changed and was in the saddle less than ten minutes after lunch wrapped up. "Y'all take your time."

Mollie dubiously looks up at the brown mare waiting for her. "Please tell me his name is Easy Rider. Or Sweetie. Or Sugar Puff."

Sawyer holds out his hand, still smiling. "This is Maria. She was your daddy's horse."

Mollie goes very still. My chest tightens at the emotion that flickers across her face.

I remind myself that she's here for the money. Said so herself.

But what would Garrett say if he saw her right now? Can't help but feel he'd be happy his daughter finally stepped foot on the ranch, even if she is wearing sparkly purple boots for an afternoon ride.

He'd be proud as hell to see her riding Maria.

I think of all the pictures Garrett saved of Mollie on horseback, which makes me feel a stab of guilt. He wouldn't be happy, knowing I was trying to chase her off. But it's the right move, isn't it? He loved the ranch, same as he loved me and my brothers. He wouldn't want to see our hard work undone.

How they share the same genes, I don't know.

I half expect Mollie to throw up her hands and quit on us before she even gets in the saddle.

Or maybe that's just what I *hope* will happen.

Instead, she's taking Maria's velvety nose in her hand and stroking the white star on her head. "Hi, Maria. I'm Mollie. I get the feeling you took good care of my dad, yeah?"

Maria, being the sweetheart she is, nuzzles Mollie's hand, tucking her head into Mollie's chest.

"Aw, hey, I like you too. Please don't throw me off. And if you wouldn't mind being patient with me, that'd be great. I'm a beginner. Well, I rode when I was younger, but it's been, like, a million and a half years since I got on a horse, and I'm a little nervous." Maria whinnies, and Mollie bites her lip. "Okay, a lot nervous."

Sawyer and I meet eyes again. He arches a brow.

Garrett loved talking to Maria this way. My brothers and I would joke that the horse was our long-lost sister. Mama was so desperate for a girl, she ended up with five boys trying for one.

"Thank God for Patsy," Garrett would joke. "Sometimes, I think she's the only thing standing between y'all and the gates of hell. Or the penitentiary."

Taking a sharp breath through my nose, I turn and stalk toward my horse—a colt I named Kix—and climb into the saddle. My left leg throbs from a run-in with one of our longhorns this morning. Back aches because I'm old and I didn't sleep great last night.

Glancing at Mollie, I wonder if she's losing any sleep over her daddy passing. Looks rested enough. Then again, she didn't see it happen.

She didn't miss the signs the way I did. Garrett complaining about shooting pains in his arm that week. How he'd kept a hand on his chest that morning, clearly hurting. He blamed it on heartburn, saying he'd overindulged in Patsy's ribs and jalapeño cornbread the night before.

She wasn't here to see him collapse inside a working pen, calves streaming around his lifeless body like he was a boulder parting a river.

My shoulders slump beneath the weight of my exhaustion. Glancing behind me, I watch Sawyer and Wyatt help Mollie onto the horse. It takes three attempts and several *oh sweet Jesus*es to get her into the saddle.

"You got this." Wyatt slips her feet into the stirrups. "We all gotta start somewhere."

He gives her a quick lesson in riding. Shows her how

to steer the horse, how to get Maria to go, to stop, to pick up pace.

Mollie gasps when Maria shuffles to the side. "And how far away is the nearest hospital?"

"Eh"—Sawyer hands her the reins—"you'll be fine."

"That far, then?"

"Well—"

I gather my own reins in my hand. Check that my rifle is secured with the other. "John B will get you right as rain should you need medical attention."

Mollie scrunches her brow. "Isn't he a veterinarian?"

"We're all animals at the end of the day. Let's go."

Wyatt gives me a look. *Be patient. Go easy on her.*

Thing is I got no patience when it comes to saving my family from ruin.

When it comes to preserving the land and the life Garrett Luck loved so much.

"Forgot to mention," Sawyer says. "We got that fundraiser at Ella's school tomorrow night. Gonna need the truck."

"It's yours. Just make sure to gas it up on your way back home."

"Speaking of trucks"—Wyatt takes off his hat and scratches his head—"what about that mishap with the liquid feed? The pickup still stinks."

"I got Tyler coming to disinfect the upholstery tomorrow at eight."

The sun slices through my shirt the second I'm out of the barn, searing my skin. It's gotten hotter every year, the heat increasing in intensity and duration, to the point where summer lasts until the beginning of October.

I'm over it. Same as I'm over the purple princess riding behind me.

"Good *Lord*," Mollie says. "This heat is unreal. How is it so much hotter here than it is in Dallas?"

"It's actually about the same." I slow my horse so I fall in beside Mollie. "You're just never outside in Dallas."

"I play pickleball." She sniffs.

"Drinking games don't count."

She laughs. The high, clear sound sends a jolt through me. "It's not a drinking game. It's a legitimate workout."

"Sure it is. Right up there with shopping and tanning by the pool."

"Okay then." Goody trots over to join us. "What's on the agenda, Cash?"

Light Mollie Luck's hair on fire so she runs from the ranch screaming.

"See a pasture or two. Take a lap down by the river. Give our honored guest here an understanding of the size and scope of our operation."

I wait for Mollie to correct me. She's not a guest. She's our new owner.

But she doesn't say a word. My heart skips a beat. Maybe that means she's not planning on staying. Why come at all, then?

I keep an eye on Mollie as we head toward the first pasture. She actually does all right. I can see traces of the decent form she had as a kid: straight back, rolling hips.

A hawk circles overhead, startling Maria when it swoops low to the ground. Mollie yelps. I veer to the right and grab her reins, giving them a tug.

At the same time, Mollie's hand darts out and grabs on to my forearm.

"Whoa, girl. Easy. Easy," I say.

"Trust me, I'd rather die than touch you—"

"I was talking to the horse." My lips twitch.

Maria slows her roll.

"Oh." Mollie's still holding my arm in a death grip. "Sorry. But I actually don't want to die, so…"

"You're not gonna die. Not on my watch."

She glances at me from underneath the brim of her ridiculous hat. Sunlight slants across her face, her irises crystal clear, the color of whiskey. "Oh? I thought maybe that's how you were going to get rid of me?"

"Nah, Miss Luck. I was gonna let the land do the dirty work." I nod at the pasture ahead of us. "Like I said, plenty of things out there that'll get the job done for me."

She laughs again. It strikes me that maybe I made her do it on purpose this time.

"Ah, manslaughter. Isn't it hilarious?" Mollie squeezes my arm before letting me go. "You're a funny guy, Cash."

"Manslaughter is, in fact, quite the opposite of hilarious," Goody says.

My heart dips at the loss of Mollie's touch. "Y'all keep up. We got a good ride ahead of us."

Same as during lunch, I let Goody do most of the talking. She knows the ins and outs of Lucky Ranch's operations almost as well as I do. The way she and Garrett worked so closely together over the years, I'd have thought for sure the two of them had a thing going on if Goody wasn't married to Tallulah Smith, Hartsville's largest landlord. Tallulah also moonlights as a bartender at the Rattler, which she owns.

Goody talks. I keep one eye on Mollie and the other on the pastures we pass through. She doesn't look comfortable in the saddle, but she stays in it. Doesn't complain. I gotta give her credit for that.

The ride doesn't turn out to be a total waste of time. We run into a pair of heifers that went missing yesterday. I radio in their location—a little island in the creek by the southeast pasture. Duke and John B say they're on their way with a trailer and medical supplies. One of the heifers was hanging at the back of the feeding pen earlier this week, so Doc wants to take a look at her.

Mollie sits up in her saddle. "Where are the rest of the cows?"

"Long ways away. You gotta move 'em around so they don't overgraze the pastures. A herd this size, we're movin' 'em often. They're about four miles that way." I point into the distance.

Mollie's eyes go wide. "Four miles?"

"That's nothin'." I turn my horse and head for the river. "Lucky Ranch is big, but it ain't nearly as big as some of the famous ranches. Some of the older ones that have been around a while, they're the size of Rhode Island."

Goody smiles. "You don't appreciate just how big Texas is until you're out here, do you, Mollie?"

"I really had no idea." Mollie puts a hand on her head. "Wow."

I point in the other direction. "The river was Garrett's favorite part of the ranch. You should see it."

It also happens to be a hilly ride from here. Figure the longer City Girl's in the saddle, the higher the chance she'll be so sore and tired tomorrow, she'll hate everything.

Me. The ranch. This life.

What if she doesn't, though? No way I'll stick around if she decides to stay. Either she'll fire me or I'll have to quit, no question. But then what?

Realistically, my hands are tied, whether Mollie stays or not.

I catch her looking at me a couple of times. Maybe because she knows I'm looking at her? But I don't see ire or annoyance in her eyes when they catch on my face.

Or more often, my body. She checking me out? Or is she watching me ride, trying to pick up some pointers?

I'm sweating bullets by the time we crest the final ridge that rises above the mighty Colorado River. I can smell the water before I see it: earthy petrichor, the smell of rain on land that's gone too long without it.

Glancing at Mollie, I wonder what she'd do if I pulled off my shirt and went for a swim to cool down. Would she fire me on the spot? Or would she just keep staring?

The river's quiet rush fills the silence.

I stop a little before the edge of the cliff and dismount. "Safer to walk the horses. There's a twenty-foot drop at the edge there."

"Um, okay." Mollie glances at the ground. Glances at me. "You made getting off your horse look easy, but somehow, I don't think it is."

Goody dismounts, too, pulling off her gloves. "You need help, Mollie?"

"I got her." Sidling up beside Maria, I loosen my grip on my reins but keep them in hand. I hold up my arms. "Come on, then."

Mollie turns her head to look at me from the corner of her eye. "I keep thinking about manslaughter."

The heat presses down on my neck and back as I squint up at her. "I'm not gonna drop you. Even if I did, at worst, you'd break an arm."

"I don't trust you."

"You don't have a choice. Put your hands on my shoulders, and I'll handle the rest."

She looks at me for another beat. Then she does as I tell her, placing her palms on the tops of my shoulders. Ignoring the twist of heat in my center, I keep my eyes level with the saddle and circle her waist with my hands. I lift at the same time that she drops, pressing her weight into my torso.

I glance up to make sure she's okay. Our eyes lock. Another twist of heat. Now that her face is inches from mine, I can see just how pretty she is. There's a smattering of freckles across her nose and cheeks, constellations of tiny brown dots that are a shade lighter than her eyes. Straight nose, full at the tip. And lips that are expressive and soft-looking.

I hate that I'm noticing all this shit.

I fucking *hate* that I can't stop staring.

"Oh!" Mollie gasps, her eyes going wide as she lurches forward all at once. I lock my hands around her waist and manage to stop her fall before she takes us both out. She lands with a small thud on the ground, her hands still on my shoulders as she breathes, "My boot slipped. I'm so sorry."

I'm out of breath too when I say, "Those boots aren't doing you any favors."

"Yeah, well, I didn't make them for riding."

I meet eyes with her again. "You really own a boot company?"

"I really own a boot company, yes." Her gaze flicks to her hands, and she blinks, dropping them. "My friend and I came up with the idea back in college."

As someone who owns one business outright—Rivers Ranch Incorporated—and runs another, Lucky Ranch Enterprises Incorporated, I know the kind of elbow grease that requires.

Surely, she has other people do the heavy lifting for her, though?

"What?" she asks.

I shake my head. "Nothing. Didn't believe you were actually employed."

Her eyes narrow to slits. "Because you thought I spent my time getting tan and going shopping?"

"And playing pickleball. Don't forget that."

Her lips twitch.

Am I flirting with Mollie?

Why the fuck am I flirting with Mollie?

"Y'all—oh! Oh my *goodness.*"

I turn at the sound of Goody's voice, just in time to see Maria take off at a gallop, back the way we came.

"You didn't hold the reins?" I bite out, looking at Mollie.

She throws up her hands. "You didn't tell me to!"

"Jesus Christ." I take off running. "Maria! Come here, girl. Maria!"

But because the universe is apparently out to fuck me over, the mare just picks up pace as she sprints farther and farther away.

"I got Maria." Goody gets back up on her horse.

"Y'all stay here. I'll be back in a jiff."

"Goody—"

"Y'all stay, really. Don't let a little mishap interrupt the tour."

Before I can protest, Goody digs her heels into her horse's sides and sets off after Maria.

I'm left stranded at the edge of a cliff with only one horse and the city girl from hell.

CHAPTER 9
Hump Day
Mollie

Is he going to push me?

That's my first thought as I peer over the edge of the cliff.

My second: *Should I push him first?*

The drop looks bigger than twenty feet. My vision wavers, heart going wild inside my chest.

I venture a glance at Cash. He's frowning at his old-school walkie-talkie, his horse's reins in his free hand.

I look back over the cliff. The river meanders quietly below. It's beautiful, bigger, and more impressive than I'd imagined. It winds like a thick, rippling rope through the rugged countryside, cutting a path lined with gently rolling hills in some spots, sheer cliffs like this one in others. Its surface glints in the sun, so bright I have to hold up a hand to shade my eyes against the glare.

It's like something out of a movie.

Something that's not quite as picturesque? The look on Cash's face. Forget manslaughter. The angry, liquid gleam in his eyes, the hard set of his scruffy jaw—that's pure murder right there.

Even now, a handful of minutes after I accidentally let Maria loose, I wince at my stupidity. Cash is so *cool* and *calm* and, yeah, fucking *hot* doing cowboy-type things.

Meanwhile, I'm a hot freaking mess. Literally. I think I've sweated through every article of clothing on my body. Socks and bra included.

I know Maria getting loose is not my fault. Not really. I didn't know to hold her reins. But I'm mortified nonetheless. Cash has spent the last few minutes hollering into that walkie-talkie, clearly stressed.

Goody and Maria have yet to resurface.

Taking a deep breath, I move closer to the edge. Try to think about Dad instead of the idiot mistake I just made.

But my relationship with Dad—wasn't that another idiot mistake of mine?

"Too close," Cash barks, making me startle. "So help me God, if I have to go down there after you—"

"Sorry, sorry." I step back, arms crossed. "This is beautiful. I get why Dad liked it out here."

That makes Cash's expression soften ever so slightly. "The water comes down from the mountains, so it's cold. He liked to fish after the day was done. Great way to cool down. Get your head screwed on straight."

I remember Dad and me taking off our shoes on the bank and putting our toes in the water. It *was* cold. He laughed as I screamed about it while splashing around in the water anyway. After a while, I watched him show me how to hook bait and cast a line in the river. I remember feeling…giddy. Happy. Like there was nowhere else on earth I'd rather be.

Usually, it's my stomach that hurts. But right now, my chest aches more than anything. The kind of ache that spreads upward, making my throat tight.

I'm angry at Dad for not making more memories like that with me. I'm angry at myself for not opening up to him more. For not asking for what I needed from him, other than money.

So much freaking *anger*. Predictably, my eyes well with tears.

The crackle of the walkie-talkie yanks me back into the heat and the humiliation of the present.

"Goody just called in." The voice sounds like it belongs to Sally. "She's got Maria, and everyone is peachy keen. But she had something come up at work, so she had to run. Y'all are gonna have to get back on your own."

Cash's head falls back, baring the thick sinews of his neck. His Adam's apple bobs on a swallow.

The man can be a grade-A asshole, but right now, I feel kinda bad for him. From my limited observation, Cash really is the go-to guy here on the ranch. People come to him with problems, and he always has a solution. I imagine that kind of responsibility—the constant barrage of interruptions—is a heavy weight to carry.

Last thing he needs is one more problem. But here I am, one gigantic pain in the ass wrapped up in a purple bow.

You're human. You're allowed to make mistakes. I repeat my therapist's refrain in my head.

And then I remind myself that pain in the ass or not,

I'm the one Dad left the ranch to. I need this money to keep the company I've poured my heart and soul into in business. I have every right to be here.

Just like Cash has every right to be pissed off.

After a beat, he lifts his head and brings the walkie-talkie to his mouth. "No one can come get us?"

"We're tied up. Ella refused to nap, so Sawyer had to go back to the house. We're one cowboy short and can't spare another."

Cash shakes his head. "Of course we are. All right, we'll head back now."

My stomach flips. What does this mean? Are we walking back? Glancing across the hills, I don't see the barn or the house. We're *far* out.

Cash shoves the walkie-talkie back into his saddle-bag. Then he checks the thick leather strap that goes around the horse's belly.

My stomach flips again. Oh no.

No, no, no.

"Tour's cut short," he says. "With two of us on one horse, it's gonna take us a while to get back. Let's go."

My heart pings around my chest like a panicked pinball. "The horse can carry both of us?"

Cash isn't wearing sunglasses, so I can see the skin crinkle at the edges of his eyes when he squints at me and says, "He doesn't have much choice, does he?"

"I'll walk."

"You won't make it a quarter mile in those boots." He holds out a hand. "Don't forget the snakes."

"Exactly how many fanged animals are out here? How are any of y'all still alive?"

His lips twitch, curling into a handsome smirk that

makes my stomach flip for an entirely different reason. "Decades of experience. Dumb luck. Let's go."

Turning my head, I get one last glimpse of the river. *Dad, if you're out there, please help me survive this.*

I take a deep breath and head for Cash and his waiting horse. "You pick a black horse to match your soul?"

"You wanna know if I ride like the devil?" He shifts, angling his hips toward me. "Get in the saddle and find out. Grab the reins in your left hand, then put that hand on the pommel."

"I don't have much choice, do I?" Rolling my eyes, I do as he tells me. "Something tells me Satan's got nothing on you."

"Aren't you lucky, then? Now put your other hand on the back of the saddle, and bend your left knee."

Cash squats and grabs my leg, one hand on my knee, the other on my ankle. I'm suddenly aware of my body, how hot I am, the bloom of electricity inside my skin. His grip is gentle but firm. Confident.

"I'm gonna give you a leg up. When I lift you, swing your other leg over the saddle. I got the rest. On the count of three, I'll lift."

My brain is short-circuiting. Maybe that's why I can only stand there, frozen with one knee bent, as Cash counts to three.

I yelp when he lifts my leg, using it as a springboard to launch my body onto the horse. I manage to toss my other leg over the horse's side, and then I land with a thump in the saddle.

It's almost like I've done this before.

I *have* done this before. But it's been twenty years. No way muscle memory lasts that long, right?

I feel very, very high up. Cash's horse is taller than Maria. He nickers softly beneath me.

Cash's hand is on my calf now, guiding my boot into the stirrup with brute efficiency.

I'm on fire. Help. "You can't manhandle me like this."

"Watch me, City Girl. Scoot forward. Even more. Jesus, Mollie." He puts his hands on my hips and yanks me toward the pommel. "There."

Then he's somehow climbing onto the horse behind me without any assistance at all. He doesn't even use a stirrup.

Only when he lands on the horse's back behind the saddle do I realize just how close we're going to be on this ride.

Very, *very* close.

I can't breathe. Can't think. I can only feel the press of his chest against my back. His thighs bracket mine, my backside tucked neatly into the cradle of his pelvis. He wraps his arms around me, reins in hand.

Cash is literally plastered against me from shoulders to shoes.

He doesn't hesitate as he clicks his tongue, urging the horse forward. Doesn't attempt gentleness. He is pure practicality, all firmness and confidence. If I'm being honest, his lack of pretense is…obscenely sexy.

It does not help that the center seam of my pants presses against the pommel with the horse's every step, hitting me *right* where I don't want it to.

I stiffen, squeezing my eyes shut. I really hope I don't burst into flames. Or faint. Or have dreams tonight about fucking the inconveniently gorgeous cowboy behind me who also happens to be an absolute jerk-off.

"You gotta move with the horse." Cash nudges my backside with his pelvis. "Otherwise, you're gonna end up getting hurt."

It's all I can do not to sputter as he rolls his hips, urging me to roll mine too. My scalp prickles as a wave of unwelcome desire moves through me. "Um. Ahem. I... feel like I'm humping the horse while you're humping me."

"No humping. Only riding."

I hear the smirk in his voice. He rolls his hips again.

I roll mine too, if only to lessen the intensity of the contact. "You know you're a walking, talking sexual harassment suit."

"I'm the guy keeping you in the saddle. Best mind your mouth." He clicks his tongue again, and the horse picks up pace.

I don't know who I'm riding anymore—the horse or the cowboy.

"You'd better mind your...your..."

"My what, City Girl?"

"Don't call me—oooh!" I tilt to the side when the horse hits a divot.

Cash immediately rights me, grabbing my hand and putting it on the pommel. "Hold on tight. Tighter. Both hands. Squeeze, Mollie. Come on."

"Do you not hear yourself?" I'm starting to panic. We're moving so fast, and I'm so uncomfortably hot and flustered, I'm worried I really will faint.

"You're not gonna fall."

"Famous last words."

Cash pulls on the reins, and the horse slows. "You all right?"

"Nope." I swallow. "But this is better."

"That's because you're doing better. Look, you're moving with the horse now."

I didn't realize it was happening until I look down and see my body undulating in time to the horse's stride.

"Maybe you are Garrett's daughter after all," Cash says with a chuckle. "Man could ride like nobody's business."

My heart spasms. Cash saw a piece of Dad that I never truly got the chance to know. The guilt I've been carrying around for the past three months—the regret—presses down on my breastbone.

At the same time, my pulse flutters at the fact that Cash is actually complimenting me. In a backhanded way, sure. But my chest hurts a little less at the idea I'm at all like the man I came from.

I'm undulating in time to Cash's body too. Maybe that's why, desperate for a distraction, I blurt, "Y'all were close. You and my dad."

"We were."

"Twelve years y'all worked together?"

"Yes."

"What was that like?"

Cash's chest presses into my shoulder blades as he inhales. "Garrett was a great boss. Great friend. Treated us fairly and with more kindness than we deserved. Most of what I know, I learned from him."

I swallow the sudden thickness in my throat. I like hearing that Dad was good to his people. But that makes me wonder why he wasn't all that good to me.

"How'd you end up on Lucky Ranch anyway?" I ask.

Another inhale. "After my parents died, we didn't have the money to maintain Rivers Ranch. I was nineteen with four brothers to look after. Garrett took us under his wing, offered us jobs and a place to stay so we could rent out the house on my family's land for extra income. Been here ever since."

"Wow." I swallow again, my eyes burning. "That must've been a lot for you."

"Wasn't fun. My parents were hell-bent on me being the first Rivers to go to college, but I had to drop out my sophomore year."

My chest clenches. "That sucks."

"We made out all right."

I don't know whether to laugh or cry. Is Grumpy Cowboy here a secret optimist? And really, how *did* he survive losing his parents? How did he not crumple when, at nineteen, he was faced with the huge responsibility of raising his brothers?

How did he feel, having to give up on his parents' dreams? What about *his* dreams?

Why the hell do I care about any of this?

"Your dad"—Cash urges the horse into a trot—"he was a huge help. The five of us kept him busy."

Too busy to take an interest in his daughter?

I blink, hard, and look out over the hills. The light has taken on an orange tinge. Nighttime, and the cooler temperatures it brings, is blessedly within sight.

This has been the longest day ever.

My insides feel mushy and sore. And my outsides—ugh, why am I not more grossed out by the way my sweaty shirt sticks to Cash's?

"That's why he'd theoretically leave you the ranch." Anger feels safe. These mushy things do not. "Because you were like a son to him."

Cash goes rigid behind me. "I don't know what I was to Garrett. But he was a father figure to me. Showed up when I really needed one." A pause. "I loved him."

More anger. The burn in my eyes becomes unbearable. "I loved him too."

Another pause. "Losing a parent—I think that's the suckiest thing of all the sucky shit I've been through."

Cash would know. If what he's saying is true, he's lost every parent he's ever known.

Doesn't make my pain any less real. But it does put it in perspective. This guy has been *through it*. How can a person withstand so much and not collapse?

"It is pretty sucky, yeah." I lift my shoulder to wipe my eyes on my shirt. "To be fair, I don't have any siblings to worry about."

"I wish I could say it got better. The grief."

I laugh, the sound mirthless. "Aren't you a barrel of monkeys?"

"You want me to lie to you?"

"No. Well, maybe. I don't know." I look down at his feet, my chest clenching. "Those are Dad's boots, aren't they?"

"How'd you know?"

"I remember them. He kept his things forever."

And Cash is forever wearing these boots. Does he wear them to honor Dad? Keep his memory alive?

If I'm being honest, I don't hate either of those ideas.

Cash chuckles. "Never met someone who hated shopping more."

"No wonder he and my mom didn't make it."

Cash doesn't say anything. My face burns. I don't know why I'm sharing so much. Maybe the steady

110

motion of the horse, combined with being wrapped up in Cash's big body, has lulled me into a false sense of safety.

"Garrett gave the boots to me for my thirtieth birthday. Said they were a present from your mom for his thirtieth," Cash says after several uncomfortable beats of silence.

"That's something she'd buy him, yeah."

"Relationships ain't easy. Your dad—he had a lot of regrets."

My pulse lurches. Cash keeps throwing me bones, and I'm not sure why. Is it some kind of distraction tactic? Or is he making me trust him so he can strike while my guard is down?

"And he shared those regrets with you?"

"Sometimes. Days are long on the ranch. Gets lonely. As I got older, Garrett opened up. You and your mama, y'all were a big part of his story."

I scoff, mostly because I'm worried I'll burst into tears if I don't. "Didn't feel that way to me."

"He talked about you." Cash shifts in the saddle. "A lot."

"Now you're lying."

"I'm many things, City Girl, but a liar ain't one of 'em."

"Stop with the City Girl."

"Then stop with the City Girl bullshit. You wanna be a rancher, act like one."

I whip my head around, the brim of my hat catching on his. "I don't want to be a rancher. This life—it was never *ever* on my radar. I'm just here—"

"For the money." His blue eyes bore into mine.

It takes every ounce of self-possession I have not to look away, our faces inches apart.

"Now tell me I'm lying."

Why not tell him the truth? So what if it makes him hate me more than he already does? Maybe he'll quit and solve that conundrum for me. Or at least keep his distance.

"The money's part of it, yeah. But since you're all about honesty, tell me *I'm* lying when I say that's why you want the ranch too. For the money."

His nostrils flare. His eyes flick to my mouth, and for a second, I'm gripped by the wild notion that he's going to shut me up by kissing me.

Part of me hopes he'll actually do it. How satisfying would it be to slap him right across the face?

"You not listen to what I just told you?" He's staring me down again. "All the shit I had to give up? Of course I want the money. I want the money because I'm going to make Rivers Ranch look like this." He tips his chin at the land around us. "Bringing my family's land back to life has always been the goal. Your daddy knew that."

I open my mouth. Close it.

Of course Grumpy Cowboy would have a noble reason for wanting ownership of Lucky Ranch. And of course it makes the mushiness in my chest spread to my stomach.

Maybe Cash isn't an asshole just to be an asshole. Maybe he's grumpy because he's been carrying the weight of the world on his shoulders for over a decade. He's lost his parents. Raised his brothers.

Lost my dad.

"I didn't know that," I say at last.

His jaw ticks. "You would've if you'd asked."

"Like you've asked a damn question about me."

"Me, me, me. That's you in a nutshell, isn't it?"

I narrow my eyes. "You know, I was just starting to feel sorry for you."

"I don't need your sympathy."

"I don't need your judgment." I turn my head and straighten my spine, face burning all over again.

I should fire him. Right now.

But that would make me the asshole, wouldn't it? And let's be real; I'm way, *way* out of my element. I know how important a foreman is to the ranch's operation, and I have no idea where I could find another go-to guy on such short notice.

One thing I do know? Cash makes this little world go round, much as I hate to admit it. If I'm going to be on the ranch—if I'm going to manage it in a way that would make Dad proud for the little while I'm here—I need Cash Rivers's help.

"Why would Dad tell you the ranch was yours but not change it in his will?" I ask.

I feel Cash shrug. The motion has him pressing his belly flush against my back. My pulse spikes. I ignore it.

"I don't know."

"But you said he and Goody worked closely together? Wouldn't she have urged him to put that in the will?"

"Goody was always at the ranch, yeah. Why do you think she was able to tack up a horse so quickly? She's ridden that filly so often, it's practically hers at this point."

"Ah. Right."

"But yeah, I imagine he thought he'd get around to

changing the will, and then…who plans to drop dead at fifty-six?"

That's one thing I do know about Dad. "He was always in such great shape."

"You have to be if you wanna keep cowboyin'," Cash replies.

I scoff. "I think my dad loved being a cowboy more than he loved anything else."

"That's not true."

"You don't know that," I snap.

Cash yanks on the reins, pulling the horse to a stop. I turn my head a little so I can just glimpse Cash in my peripheral vision.

I furrow my brow. "What?"

"You resent me for knowing him better than you did, don't you, City Girl?"

I turn away, my eyes welling with tears. I'm more angry than sad, but I cry anytime I'm upset.

Usually, I'll try to hide it. Keep everyone else comfortable. At the very least, keep me from embarrassing myself. But fuck that. Cash wants brutal honesty, that's what he'll get.

"I do, yeah." I wipe my eyes with my sleeve. "Maybe that makes me petty, but whatever. Dad was so good to y'all…goddamn, I wish he'd been that good to me."

Cash is quiet for a beat. "I didn't mean to upset you."

"I *couldn't care less* about your intentions. Take me back to the house, Cash."

"Mollie—"

"This conversation is over."

CHAPTER 10
Texas Pete
Cash

I can't sleep.

Usually, it's because a wave of grief hits me, and I'm unable to turn off my mind.

Tonight, it's because I haven't been able to stop thinking about Mollie, even though it's been three fucking days since I saw her last.

I made her cry. Took it way too far and made the daughter of the man I respected more than anyone else in the world fucking *cry*.

To be honest, I didn't think she cared enough about Garrett or the ranch to cry. She never visited us. She and her daddy weren't close. But that doesn't mean his death wasn't a knife through the heart for her.

I would know. I'm embarrassed I assumed losing a parent wouldn't deeply affect her. *I wish he'd been that good to me.* Lord, how that must've hurt, me throwing in her face proof of how well Garrett cared for my brothers and me. I didn't do it intentionally, but still. Doesn't sit right, knowing I reminded her of a past she'd rather forget.

When we got back to the house, Mollie disappeared inside without a word. She didn't come to supper. I weathered Patsy's judgmental looks, Wyatt's not-so-subtle questions, best as I could.

I haven't seen Mollie since. Patsy mentioned she spoke with Mollie a few times when she emerged from her room for a late breakfast or lunch, and Wyatt told me he ran into her before supper last night. She said she'd been tied up, working on her company, but I have a feeling she's been avoiding us for other reasons.

Avoiding me in particular, because I crossed every line imaginable and was a total prick to her.

This is exactly what I wanted—to put Mollie on the run. But my victory doesn't feel nearly as satisfying as I'd hoped.

In fact, it feels pretty fucking awful.

Lying awake in bed, I stare at the ceiling as the drone of the air conditioner outside my window fills the silence.

Like her father, maybe Mollie has regrets too. Things she wishes she'd said or done differently.

Maybe she isn't as careless or self-centered as I thought. The look in her eyes when she turned her head to meet my gaze—the vulnerability I saw there, the flicker of intelligence, interest—

She's a fucking stunner. Decent on horseback too. Pickleball must actually be a good workout—you gotta have strong legs and a decent amount of stamina to stay in the saddle that long, even with me behind her. We were both sweating, but it just made her prettier. Her skin glowed in the afternoon sun. And the way she moved on

116

the horse with me, hesitant at first but more confident as time went on, makes me think she'd be a good rider if she put her mind to it. That tight little body of hers is surprisingly limber.

I wince when the sheets catch on my dick as I kick them to the bottom of my bed. I'm sweating. The half chub I've had all night is suddenly rock-hard.

Reaching down, I suck in a breath. I'm already leaking.

Jesus *Christ*. I need to masturbate while thinking about City Girl like I need a goddamn hole in my head.

Yeah, she's a knockout, and she tells it like it is. And she didn't quit on me the other day, despite the overwhelming experience of being back on her daddy's ranch for the first time in decades.

But Mollie's also greedy and stuck-up. And the shit she wears. Riding behind her, I could almost see down her purple shirt. The thing was *this close* to coming totally unbuttoned all the way to her navel, which allowed me a glimpse of the soft swell of her tits as she rolled her hips in time to mine.

I fist my dick in a tight grip and pull. Tell myself I'm only taking care of it because I won't be able to sleep if I don't.

Tell myself I'm only this hard, this needy, because it's been too long since I got laid.

The whole thing is ugly and quick. Hard pulls. Images of Mollie bent over a fence. Bent over a chair. Bent over the edge of my bed. I fuck her with the greediness I saw in her the other day. But she takes it.

Lord, she *takes*. I'm shoving inside her mouth now.

She plays with herself as she sucks my dick. I try to slap away her hand, but she ignores me, running the pads of her fingers over her clit again and again and again.

Her playfulness, her refusal to be pushed around, has me coming in hard, hot spurts into my hand.

———

I still can't sleep. At three thirty, I shower. Pull on jeans and a shirt. A belt and Garrett's boots.

I'll always want to make him proud. Which means I gotta talk to Mollie. I can't afford to get fired right now. And maybe…

I mean, what if Garrett wanted us to work together? I have no fucking idea why he'd want that, but I do know he was torn up about the mistakes he'd made with his daughter.

Even if he didn't want Mollie and me working together—even if he did really just forget to update the will—I still have to iron this out.

And yeah, maybe if I establish some kind of functional working relationship with Mollie, there'll be rewards for my brothers and me down the road.

Maybe, if I play nice, she'll eventually get bored and spend all her time making more sparkly cowboy boots, leaving the ranch to me and the boys. And Ella, of course.

A year is nothing.

I can do anything for a year. Keep four brothers and a niece alive. Tend to fifteen thousand head of cattle.

Surely, I can work with Mollie Luck without one or both of our lifeless bodies ending up in a ditch?

At four, I'm at the house. Through the open window above the sink, I can see Patsy is already in the kitchen, the velvety smell of coffee filling my head as I step up to the door.

I draw up short when I see Mollie standing at the stove.

Wait a second.

Wait.

She's finally showing her face? What's changed?

I'm shocked—relieved—to see her. I'm also shocked she's up this early. But the most shocking thing of all? She appears to be actively helping Patsy cook breakfast, stirring something in a pan while our chef chops some veggies by the sink.

"I went on this stupid diet once where all I could have was egg whites, green peppers, and mezcal," Mollie tells Patsy as she sips a mug of coffee. "Now I'm an expert at making omelets. And mezcal margaritas."

Patsy laughs. "What kind of diet was that?"

"I get really bad stomachaches all the time. No one can really figure out what the problem is, so I've been put on all these different diets to see if anything makes me feel better."

"Have you had any luck?"

Mollie shrugs. "Not yet."

She gets stomachaches? Is that why she only ate green beans the other day?

Also, why the fuck do I care?

Sweet Jesus, *why* does she have to look so damn cute so early in the morning? My eyes rove up her legs and back. For the first time, she's wearing something semi-normal: a pair of jeans and a white T-shirt. Her hair is pulled back in a ponytail.

She's also wearing glasses. I step closer to the entrance and peer through the open screen door.

Fuck, since when am I attracted to girls who wear glasses?

"I'm so glad you decided to join us today," Patsy says. "I hope you're feeling better?"

Mollie is quiet for a beat. "I am. I think I needed a little time to...process. Work's also been busy, so that didn't help. I've been chained to my laptop all day, every day."

"But I hope exciting things are in store?"

Mollie smiles. "I hope so, yes. Would you like hot sauce on your omelet?"

City Girl is actually doing something nice for someone else? I'm confused.

Patsy slides a tray of sweet potato hash browns into the oven. "I'd love some, thanks. I keep it there in that cabinet to the right of the range. We go through it like you wouldn't believe. The cowboys dowse everything in Texas Pete."

Mollie reaches up, her shirt lifting to reveal a tanned slice of stomach and side. That's when I see the words, embroidered in sequins because *of course*, on the front of her shirt: *I AM A LUXURY.*

I don't wanna smile, but I do. Shirt's ridiculous, but I'm starting to wonder if that's the point when it comes to Mollie's clothes.

"I don't see the hot sauce," Mollie says.

Patsy straightens. "We must've run out again. There's a few more bottles on the top shelf there, I think. Here, I'll get the step stool..."

I open the door. "I got it."

The women whip around at the sound of my voice.

Mollie's hand immediately flies to her glasses. "Jesus, Cash."

"Good mornin' to you too."

"Shoulda known you were coming. Always the first up." Patsy crosses the kitchen to press a kiss to my cheek. "Sleep okay?"

"Not really. You?"

"I did all right."

I head for the range. Mollie moves out of the way, her hand still on her glasses. She embarrassed about them?

"How many bottles of hot sauce do you want?" I ask.

Mollie clears her throat. She's barefoot, and I tower over her.

"Just one."

I grab a bottle of Texas Pete and hold it out to her.

She looks at it. Looks up at me. "Thanks."

"Want me to open it?"

"I got it." She takes the bottle.

"Smells good. Whatcha making?"

Mollie peels off the green plastic sleeve that covers the bottle cap. "Egg white omelets. I'd offer you one, but you're kind of a dick, so no."

Laughter rumbles in my chest. "I was a dick the other day. I'm sorry."

"You should be."

"Y'all need a minute?" Patsy asks.

"No," Mollie replies.

I smile at Patsy. "That'd be great, Patsy, thank you."

"I'll be in the pantry. Holler if you need me."

Mollie twists the cap off the Texas Pete. Tries to anyway.

"You always up this early?" I ask.

She doesn't look up when she replies, "Sometimes, when I have a lot to do."

I nod at the Texas Pete. "Can I help you with that?"

121

"No."

"I really am sorry."

"I really don't care."

"Let me make it up to you."

She grits her teeth, twisting the cap. "I'd rather you not."

"We had a new foal hit the ground last week. Ella's preschool class is coming to the ranch to see it today. The baby goats too."

That gets Mollie's attention. She looks at me. "Y'all have baby goats?"

"Of course we have baby goats. They eat the stuff on the ground cows won't, so we use the pastures more efficiently. Sally's also got a side gig, making goat cheese."

"Freaking yum."

"It's delicious. Can I count you in? Ella seemed to take a shine to you the other day."

Mollie looks back down at the hot sauce, twisting the cap so hard her knuckles turn white. "Maybe. If I have time."

"I hope you do. Jesus, Mollie, give me that." I grab the bottle and crack it open. "See? Easier when you let people help you."

She narrows her eyes at me. "Why do I get the feeling you need to take your own advice?"

"That's my business. Speaking of business, you said you had a lot to do today."

"Goody is coming over to walk me through a bunch of nuts-and-bolts stuff this morning. I have a few calls to make for Bellamy Brooks after that."

"Bellamy Brooks?"

"My company."

"Ah. Right." I make a mental note to google the name. Wonder if they have a website.

"Patsy!" Mollie turns off the burner. "Omelets are ready."

I put a hand on the counter. "We're meeting at ten o'clock at the barn. I hope to see you there."

"I hope you get bitten by a snake."

"Well!" Patsy claps her hands. "That seemed to go... well."

Mollie scoops an omelet onto a plate and shakes a couple of dashes of Texas Pete onto it. She holds out the plate. "Patsy, you're a saint for not poisoning him."

"Aw, he's a good man underneath all that gruffness." Patsy eyes me. "Although I'd be lying if I said I wasn't tempted to knock some sense into that thick skull of his sometimes."

I shrug. "I've been knocked around plenty. Three concussions. Three that were diagnosed anyway."

"Really?" Mollie scrunches her brow. "Occupational hazard?"

Patsy laughs. "Two of them were. The third he got when he fell on a dance floor, trying to do the Cotton Eye Joe."

Mollie blinks. "*You* dance?"

"Used to, until the concussion." I lean my backside against the counter and cross my arms. I don't miss the way Mollie's eyes flick over my torso, stopping to linger on my forearms. "Made a rookie mistake and wore new boots to the Rattler. Hadn't scuffed up the soles enough to get traction."

Patsy's face lights up. "Oh! Speaking of the Rattler!

123

We're playing there tomorrow night. Mollie, you have to come. We're pretty darn awesome, if I do say so myself."

"You're playing?" Mollie scrunches her brow. "Are you a guitarist or…?"

"Patsy and Sally are in a band called Frisky Whiskey," I explain. "And they are really, really good."

Mollie smiles at Patsy. "As if I couldn't adore you more. How cool! I'll be there." She looks at me. "As long as you're not going."

Patsy gently elbows me. "Cash hasn't been to the Rattler in a while."

"Don't mean I ain't itchin' to go back." I mean that. Sort of. I don't miss the hangovers, but I do miss the live music. And the dancing. And the ice-cold beer.

"Hmm." Mollie taps a finger against her chin. "Maybe I'll pass, then."

I hold up my hands. "Then I won't go."

Mollie grins. I'm gripped by the urge to grab her face and—

Hell no. No more fantasies about Mollie's mouth.

No more fantasies about Mollie, period.

"Then I will," she says. "I love live music. Thanks for the invite, Patsy."

Jesus, Mollie is *such* a brat.

I wish I hated that about her as much as I did three days ago.

CHAPTER 11
Baby Goats and Bad Decisions
Cash

I'm soaked through with sweat when I walk through the kitchen door at the New House later that morning.

Usually, I'd change my shirt or grab a quick shower. But I'm running late, thanks to Duke falling flat on his back after attempting a dumbass trick earlier.

He basically tried to ride his horse right into the trailer, the plan being he'd grab the top of the trailer just as the horse was entering it. He'd lift himself off the horse and do some fancy thing where he'd drop to his feet on the ground.

"It'll make a great reel," he said.

I looked at him. "What the fuck is a reel?"

Instead of "creating content," Duke ended up on his back in the dirt, mewling like a baby because he got the wind knocked out of him. Luckily, he's all right. But the whole episode ate up half an hour I didn't have.

That trailer getting not one but two flat tires a mile from the barn ate up another half hour. Now here I am, covered in sweat and dirt and cursing like a sailor because I'm running around, trying to get everything done.

Ella's class will be arriving at any minute. The bottle needs to be prepared for the foal. Snacks and juice boxes need to be transported to the barn, along with those picnic blankets we have around here *somewhere*.

Ordinarily, Sawyer would help me out with this stuff. Patsy too. But Sawyer's leading the caravan from preschool to the ranch. Patsy is out at the barn, putting the finishing touches on the goody bags she made for the kids.

Whole thing was my idea anyway. Ella comes home every day from school chatting about the animals they've learned about. Last week, it was polar bears. The week before, it was butterflies. I figured why not make this week about horses and visit some real ones while we're at it?

Sawyer reached out to Ella's teachers, and they were thrilled by the idea. Not exactly novel, considering we're in small-town Texas. Classes visit ranches all the time. But with the new foal's arrival, this feels special.

I'm starving and thirsty as hell, but I don't have time to fix that. I stalk into the pantry and nearly run face-first into City Girl.

She startles, Goldfish tumbling from the open packet she's got in her hand. "God*damn* it, Cash. You keep doing that!"

"Doing what?" I glance at her pink dress and brown boots. The boots have red and pink hearts on them.

Ridiculous, but cute.

Bending down, she picks up the Goldfish. "Barging into rooms and scaring the shit out of people."

"I'm in a bit of a rush." Pulling up my shirt, I use it to wipe my face as I point to the juice boxes behind her. "Can I grab those?"

Mollie is staring at me as she straightens.

Specifically, she's staring at my naked stomach, eyes raking over my skin.

My body pulses. I try to ignore it, but the prickling awareness in my thighs and groin won't quit.

"You…need a new shirt." She licks her lips.

I look away, smoothing my shirt back over my belly. It sticks to me like a second skin. "Don't got time. The juice boxes, please. Kids'll be here any minute."

"You're going to scare those kids off with that stink. You smell like poop. And horses."

"Dealt with a lot of both this morning. Kids need their snacks."

"The juice boxes and the Goldfish?" She holds up her packet. "There were, like, seventy packs of these, so I figured it was all right if I stole one."

"Ella's obsessed. So are Duke and Ryder. The juice boxes, please."

Mollie sets down her Goldfish and wipes her hands. "How about you grab a new shirt—or better yet, a shower? I'll take the snacks over to the barn."

I put a hand on my hip. "I got it."

"You're always saying that. Trust me, you want a new shirt. I'll meet you at the barn." She tucks the carton of juice boxes underneath her arm. "Anything else you want me to bring?"

For a second, I just stare at her. Stuck-up City Girl is actually offering me help? She's being *thoughtful?* Kind even? Same as she was with Patsy this morning in the kitchen and the other day with Wyatt and Sawyer in the barn?

"There are some picnic blankets I was hoping to find," I say.

"I'll poke around."

I turn my head. "What's the catch?"

"No catch. I just wanna see some babies of the human and goat varieties. Go shower, Cash. Now."

"You sure you got that?" I nod at the juice and the Goldfish.

Rolling her eyes, she steps around me. "Jesus, that *smell*."

I hop in an ATV and hit the gas. Ten minutes later, I'm back in the ATV, showered and pulling a fresh shirt over my head.

The barn is a hive of activity when I pull up. My chest swells at the sight of ten tiny three-year-olds crowded around the nearby corral, where Wyatt put the goats and their babies. Parents stand nearby, sipping on glasses of Patsy's lemonade.

Lemonade that—holy shit—Mollie appears to be pouring for our guests. She scoops ice into glasses and then fills them, handing them out to parents and ranch hands while she chats them up.

"What are you doing?" I ask her.

She glances up at me as she dumps ice into a glass. "You showered. Good. You smell better."

To be honest, I feel better too. The perpetual grit I have in my eyes from not sleeping feels slightly less sandpapery after a quick rinse.

"What are you doing?" I repeat.

Mollie's eyebrows snap together. "What does it look like I'm doing? I'm bartending."

"You got booze back there?"

"No drinking and riding allowed." Her lips curl into a smirk as she pours lemonade into the glass. "Kids are having a ball." She holds out the glass. Like me, it's already sweating in the morning heat.

"Did you poison it?" I eye the lemonade.

"Take a sip and find out."

"Would that be murder or manslaughter?"

Mollie lifts a shoulder, her eyes on mine. "Neither. I cover my tracks."

"You're gonna miss me when I'm gone." I take the lemonade, the cold pressing into my hand.

"Nice Brooks and Dunn reference. But no, I most certainly will *not* miss you."

I sip my lemonade. Just the right balance of tart and sweet and cold enough to make me feel a shade short of overheating. "You like Brooks and Dunn?"

"I fu—" She glances at the kids nearby. "I freaking love Brooks and Dunn. They were my first concert. My parents took me."

I search her eyes over the rim of my glass. "Your dad said it was a thrill, dancing with you to 'Boot Scootin' Boogie.' He got y'all first-row tickets, didn't he?"

That gives her pause. She blinks, swallowing. "My dad told you about that?"

"He was so proud you liked country music as much as he did. Man had tunes on day and night."

She blinks again, lips twitching into a tiny smile. My pulse skips. I'm not sure why I'm sharing this with Mollie. I still think Garrett deserved better from his only daughter.

Then again, no one deserves to lose a parent.

129

No one deserves to see their parents go through a divorce. Can't imagine how much that must've sucked for Mollie. My friends whose parents split, their lives were totally upended. For her to go through that so young—

"I also brought you this."

I stare at the foil-wrapped item she holds out. "More poison?"

"Ha. No. It's a fried chicken sandwich. Found it in the fridge."

My pulse skips again. "How'd you know I was hungry?"

"Gave you the benefit of the doubt and assumed you were hangry back at the house."

I take the sandwich. "Thank you?"

"Oh, please." She rolls her eyes. "If I wanted you dead, you'd be in the ground already. Except for your head. And your hands. I'd toss those in the river."

Laughing, I unwrap the sandwich and take a giant bite. *Dang, that's good.* "Exactly how much *Yellowstone* have you watched?"

"Enough to know my way around dismemberment."

"This sounds fun." Wyatt appears at my elbow, empty lemonade glass in hand. "He hangry again?"

Mollie eyes me as I go to town on my sandwich. "I'm starting to think he's always hangry."

"That's because I don't have time to eat," I reply, mouth full.

Wyatt rolls his eyes. "I don't see you wasting away."

"I don't see you helping out with the kids." I nod at the corral. "Where's the foal?"

"Up your—"

"I'll help." Mollie loops her arm through Wyatt's. "I'm terrible with adult animals, clearly, so maybe I'll have more luck with the baby ones."

Wyatt grins. Are they gonna be buddy-buddy now? And why does that piss me off so much?

"To be fair, Maria's been skittish since your daddy passed," my brother says.

A shadow flickers across Mollie's face. "Sounds like a lot of us miss him."

"He was a legend." Wyatt pats the hand she's got on his forearm. "You got a good name, Mollie."

Ignoring the now-familiar twist inside my chest, I crumple the empty foil and shove it in my back pocket. After the shower, the lemonade, and the sandwich, I feel like a new man.

I also feel like punching my brother. But that's nothing new.

Following Wyatt and Mollie out to the corral, I nearly fall the fuck over when I see Mollie head right for my niece. Mollie crouches beside her, smiling as she shows Ella how to straighten her fingers so the goats can nibble at the carrots in her palm.

Mollie smiles. A bright, happy thing that makes an entirely different sensation bloom in my center.

I will myself to ignore it.

"Great job!" she says, holding up her hand for a high five.

Ella slaps it, giggling like the adorable lunatic she is. "More! Ella need more!"

Sawyer turns from his conversation with Ella's teacher. "How do we ask?"

"Please!" Ella says.

Mollie laughs, glancing up at my brother. "How can I resist when she asks so nicely?"

"Ella use her manners," my niece replies. "You loves her." Then she body-slams Mollie in her approximation of a hug.

Sawyer and I both lunge forward at the same time. "Ella, gentle!"

But Mollie just laughs, wrapping her arms around my niece. "She's fine. I needed a hug, Ella. Thank you."

I will not dwell on why Mollie would say that.

I will not keep staring as she and Ella become fast friends.

I also will not stare at Mollie's breasts, which look like they're about to spill out of the deep neckline of her dress.

But desire—familiar, achy—grips my heart and squeezes. It's not sexual desire. Well, not entirely. It's... deeper than that.

I loved growing up in a big family. Loved being surrounded by people, despite the chaos. Most of all, I loved the feeling of belonging I'd get when the seven of us were together.

I felt safe. Seen. Happy.

Even when I was young, before my parents died, I knew I wanted a family of my own. I always thought I'd raise a bunch of kids on Rivers Ranch, same way I was raised: surrounded by nature, community, and a real sense of home.

But then life happened. And, well, I'm too fucking busy taking care of *this* family to think about starting my own. Especially now that we're back to square one in terms of our future. I can barely keep my head above the water as it is. Emotionally. Financially. Physically. Adding a wife and babies to the mix...

Yeah, that ain't gonna happen.

Most days, I'm okay with that. Too busy to dwell on shit I can't change. But sometimes, it really fucking hurts.

Mollie looks up, her eyes catching on mine. There's a flutter just inside my breastbone.

I should look away.

I have a million very good reasons why I need to look the fuck away.

But there's a spark in her eyes I haven't seen before. Or—wait—I have seen it, only in pictures.

Garrett's pictures of a five- or six-year-old girl, giddy to be playing cowgirl beside her daddy.

Crouching in the dirt, a three-year-old Velcroed to her side, Mollie looks...lit up, like she does in Garrett's pictures.

Is it the baby goats? All the toddlers? Wyatt's shameless flirting?

Or is it something else that's making her happy?

Shoving those questions aside, I tear my gaze from Mollie's and glance up at the sky. Still no sign of rain.

That hand is still around my heart, its grip fierce.

Lifting my hat off my head, I smooth back my hair. It's already damp with sweat again. If this heat doesn't kill me, Mollie Luck surely will.

I put my hat back on and clear my throat. "All right, y'all, who wants to feed the baby horse?"

CHAPTER 12
Happy
Mollie

It's the shock of the century.

Well, I imagine it wouldn't be shocking at all to see ordinary cowboys—ones that aren't growly grumps—patiently bottle-feed a tiny baby horse.

But it is a shock to see Cash Rivers doing it, and doing it well. Just like the LL Cool J song, it's really fucking hot.

Like, *really* fucking hot.

My mouth literally goes dry as I watch Cash patiently feed the foal, his hat tipped back so I can see his face. He's got one enormous hand on the bottle, the other on the foal's glossy brown coat.

I need to leave. Now. Turn around and walk out of the barn, because if I don't, I'm worried I'll combust. Watching Cash is making me *feel* things.

Things that are inappropriate and inconvenient and just plain wrong.

"Happy's mama couldn't feed her, so we're going to

do it," Cash says, slowly running that hand up and down the horse's back as she nurses. "Happy is doing so well, isn't she?"

Ella, who took my hand as we walked over from the corral and hasn't let go since, buries her head in my leg.

"Neigh," she says softly.

Cash looks up, a smile creasing his face. "That's right, Ella. That's the sound horses make. Can y'all do it too?" He glances at her classmates.

Most kids are too shy to say anything. But a few, along with Ella, let out quiet *neighs*, making my chest swell with laughter.

If that isn't the cutest thing ever, I don't know what is.

Also, when was the last time I laughed at twelve o'clock on a Thursday afternoon?

When was the last time I was *outside* on a Thursday? With other people? I honestly can't remember.

The sound of the kids neighing startles Happy. She pulls back from the bottle, kicking her hooves. Someone gasps.

Cash doesn't flinch. He continues to gently run his hand over the horse's back, murmuring, "It's all right, Happy. They're just here to say hello. It's all right. Can you take the bottle again for me? There we go. That's it. Great job, Happy. I can already see you growing big and strong."

"Horse whisperer," John B says, smiling as he shakes his head.

The veterinarian is not wrong. I just…don't get it. This show of tenderness is at odds with the rough way Cash practically tossed me up into the saddle the other day.

The rough way he *spoke* to me. Makes me think he's trying really hard to be an asshole when I'm around.

Also makes me think he has a softer, gentler side. One that would make him excellent in bed.

Squashing that thought, I wonder instead if Cash is just plain exhausted. Maybe he's fed up, being saddled with so much responsibility.

And yeah, maybe he's a little scared. He just lost his mentor. Lost the ranch he thought he'd inherit. I imagine Cash is the kind of guy to always have a plan, same as he always has an answer for every question and problem that comes up.

What's his plan now that he's not going to inherit Lucky Ranch? And the brothers who depend on him, what are they going to do?

Not my problem.

But I feel bad enough for Cash that I want to help him out. He showed his ass the other day, but he did apologize to me this morning.

He did love my dad. As much as it hurts knowing they were closer than Dad and I ever were, that's not Cash's fault. It's mine. And Dad's. Cash Rivers shouldn't have to pay for that.

Watching him nurse this sweet little foal, I wonder why he feels like he needs to pay for what happened to him and his brothers. I get that they needed a father figure when they were younger, but now that they're all grown—I mean, Sawyer has a kid of his own—why is Cash still lighting himself on fire to keep everyone else warm?

Why doesn't he let anyone give him the help he so clearly needs? No wonder he's grumpy.

It's why I offered to bring the snacks for the kids. It's

also why I grabbed Cash that extra sandwich from the fridge. He was so soaked in sweat earlier, it looked like he'd been caught in a rainstorm. I imagine that kind of physical labor makes you hungry, especially when breakfast is at four thirty in the morning.

I turn to Wyatt. We're just far enough away that Cash can't hear us if we keep our voices low. That's what I hope anyway. "Is Cash always like this? With the horses?"

"He's like this with every living thing. Except humans. Adult ones anyway."

"What's that about?"

Wyatt twists his lips to the side. "Your guess is as good as mine, Miss Luck."

"Mollie."

"Right." Wyatt smiles. "Day going okay so far?"

I look at Cash. Look down at Ella. "Honestly? It's going way better than I anticipated. Life on the ranch isn't...as isolating as I thought it would be?"

"It's not always like this, you know." His eyes twinkle. "Hot cowboys in the vicinity, cute babies everywhere, homemade lemonade available by the gallon to cool you off..."

My turn to smile. "You forget I was stranded on top of a cliff the other day with that guy and only one horse to get us the, like, eight miles home." I tip my head toward Cash. "I'm well aware today is special."

"It was more like a mile. But I get your point."

"It sure as hell felt like eight. More than that."

Wyatt's smile fades as he looks at his older brother. "Can I show you around today? Make up for it? I can introduce you to our ranch hands."

I owe Wheeler a call. Mom too, and my good friend

Jen, who recently shared the news that she's expecting her first baby with her husband, Abel. Goody also made me promise I'd take a look at the payroll documents she left with me this morning.

Long story short, I really should go back to the house and get shit done.

But the thought of being inside again, alone, with only my laptop for company makes me want to crawl out of my skin.

Yes, it's hot as hell out here, and it smells like manure.

Yes, I'm not going to be of any help in the horse barn or outside in the pastures. Best-case scenario, I don't get anyone else hurt. Worst-case scenario, I *do* get someone hurt, and I hurt myself too in the process. What happened the other day is a case in point.

But I still want to stay. And that's a problem for... God, so many reasons.

"You don't have anything to make up for," I say. "I know Cash has a lot on his plate."

"I'm happy to show you around, Mollie."

"You sure? I don't want to be a pain—"

"This is your ranch now." He looks me in the eye. "Whether you're a pain or not, if I were you, I'd want to learn my way around. You'll be fine. We'll all be fine, I promise."

But glancing at Cash, who's nuzzling Happy's sweet little nose now that she's finished her bottle, I'm not at all sure I'll be okay.

Yet I still find myself saying, "All right. Thanks, Wyatt."

———

Wyatt is an excellent tour guide, showing me around first in an ATV and then in a huge Lucky Ranch–branded pickup when we move farther away from what everyone around here calls the New House.

I thought he was being flirty with me before, but now I see that he flirts with everyone. He's *that* guy—charismatic, witty, with a wickedly handsome smile that wins you over every time. I feel comfortable enough to ask him about a hundred questions, which he patiently answers. I meet a hundred people—from the owners of the local feed store to wildlife experts hired to keep food chains intact to the landscapers who maintain Lucky Ranch's green spaces.

The ranch is one hell of an operation. It started out purely as a place to raise cattle, most of which end up as beef on American dinner tables. The cowboys who live here care for the herd, often accompanying the cows on horseback to move them to new pastures in pursuit of fresh sources of food. Cows eat a lot. Like, *a lot* a lot, which means they need to move often so pastures don't get overgrazed. The cowboys also make sure the cows stay healthy, which is a full-time job in and of itself. The horses too are a big part of the operation. The ranch owns a stable of them, and Cash is apparently always looking for new horses to replace retiring ones.

Dad got involved in some oil prospecting too. Once he made a big strike, he had the money to turn the ranch into more than just a place for cattle drives. Now it's a magnet for bird-watchers, hunters, and fishermen.

My feet hurt, and my head is spinning. But time flies by. Being surrounded by so many people—so much action—is a refreshing change of pace from working solo or just with one or two other people.

It's also a really great distraction from thinking about Cash.

Wyatt drops me off back at the New House later that afternoon. It's only four, but I am beat.

He laughs when I yawn. "You'll get used to the hours. It's an early start, but if you can make it past two p.m., you'll be fine through supper. Drinking lots of water helps."

"I'll keep that in mind. Thanks for the tour. I had an awesome time, and I really appreciate you being so kind."

Wyatt lifts his fingers off the steering wheel. "Anytime. Sorry my brother's being a punk. He's taking Garrett's death really hard."

Scoffing, I look down at my lap. "Yeah, well, he can join the club."

"We all loved Garrett. But he and Cash had a special bond. I think…" Wyatt shakes his head. "He's struggling to come to terms with all this. Losing Garrett. The ranch going to you, and now you being here. It's a big change for him, and if there's one thing Cash doesn't handle well, it's shit not going to plan."

A familiar ache rises in my throat. "I didn't plan on this happening either."

"You're doing great, Mollie. Just keep showing up. Cash'll come around. And if he doesn't, I'll take him down a notch. Gladly."

Laughing, I look at Wyatt. He's handsome in a rugged way: shaggy blond hair, overgrown scruff, earnest, piercingly blue eyes. So different from Cash's dark intensity yet so similar too.

"That a promise?" I ask.

His face creases in a grin. "Promise. See you at supper."

The inside of the house feels blessedly cool after a day spent in the blazing heat. I strip off my clothes, which are soaked with sweat and caked in dirt, grime, and God knows what else, and take a long, cool shower.

It's still not time for dinner—or supper, as they call it here—after I get dressed, so I decide to give my friend Jen a quick call.

She answers on the first ring. "Hey, cowgirl!"

Hearing her familiar Carolina drawl, I'm hit by a wave of homesickness. Which makes no sense, because Jen lives on a tiny island off the coast of North Carolina a thousand-some-odd miles from here that I've only visited once.

Maybe there's a certain kind of homesickness for familiar faces—Jen and I went to college together. If that does exist, I have it. Bad.

"Hey, friend."

Jen picks up right away on the emotion in my voice. "Aw, Mollie. Things not going well on the ranch?"

I've filled her in on my situation via text and a few phone calls. Jen has been my rock since Dad passed. We talk and text often, so it's no surprise she immediately knows something's wrong.

"It's going well. And not well at all."

"Oh boy. Is that cowboy you told me about giving you a hard time?"

No use lying. As embarrassed as I am to admit it, my feelings for Cash have morphed from hatred to strong dislike with a twinge of something else.

Something that's the opposite of hatred.

And then there's the fact that I kinda sorta enjoyed my time on the ranch today.

"Life here is different than I thought it would be. Everything is different, including Cash. He was such an asshole when we first met. But this morning, he looked me in the eye and apologized, and then today, I watched him be sweet as pie with his three-year-old niece. So I was nice to him, and now I'm wondering if I'm being smart and building a relationship with my foreman or if I'm being a total chump."

Jen chuckles. "He's hot, right?"

"Well, yeah. Even if he didn't have the whole cowboy thing going on, he'd turn heads."

"But he does have the whole cowboy thing going on. I can't say that I know many of them myself—"

"I imagine there aren't a lot of cattle on the coast," I say with a smile.

"But he lives in a different world than you do. Which leads me to believe he's going to be different from the guys you know back in Dallas. I feel like the guys you've dated have been assholes because they're, well, assholes. But maybe Cash just came off that way. Maybe deep down, he's a good guy who's really scared about the changes happening in his life."

Glancing up at the ceiling fan, my throat tightens all over again. "Maybe."

"I say give him a chance. If it ends up biting you in the ass, well, at least you got to hang with hot cowboys for a little bit. That'll make a great story at cocktail parties."

I laugh, feeling slightly better. "How are you feeling? Ultrasound go okay?"

"It went great. Baby is measuring right on time. And I'm feeling all right. I have good days and bad days. I'm definitely looking forward to the second trimester. Everyone says you feel a lot more like yourself then."

"I'm so excited for you."

I can hear the warm happiness in her voice when she says, "Thanks. We're excited too. Abel says hi, by the way."

"Tell him I said hi back." I draw a breath through my nose. "Do you like it? Living in a quiet place? Like, do you miss Wilmington at all?"

When Jen and Abel got together, she moved from the small city of Wilmington, North Carolina, to Bald Head Island, which is about as quiet and small as it gets at five square miles. Wild to think Lucky Ranch is several times that size. Bald Head is accessible only by ferry, and cars aren't permitted on the island; the only modes of transportation are boats, golf carts, and bicycles.

"I do miss the city," Jen replies. "You know I love to shop, and I miss being able to just pop into coffee shops or restaurants. But Wilmington isn't all that far from Bald Head, so whenever I get the itch, I hop on the ferry and take a day trip. I will say I'm always glad to get back on the ferry to the beach at the end of the day. The island has a way of permeating your bones. Like you crave it."

"I think you just crave your gorgeous husband."

"Him too, yes." She laughs. "I do wonder if I'd feel the same if I didn't have my own little family of sorts on the island. Maybe that's what gets into your bones— the people more than anything. I feel connected to the community here in a way I never did in Wilmington.

Life didn't necessarily get bigger or smaller when I moved to a small town. But it did become more vibrant."

My heart pings faster and faster, the way parking sensors do in a car when you get too close to something. "I like that idea."

"Something to think about. I imagine life on the ranch is similar?"

"There are lots of people around. Like, all the time. And everyone knows everybody. I get the sense that they're all close, but I'm obviously the outsider, so..."

"Do they treat you like an outsider?"

I lift a shoulder, thinking about Patsy's invitation to the Rattler. "Not always. But I think people don't know what to do with me."

"You're figuring out your place, Mollie. That's up to you to decide. It's like you're feeling your way through the dark right now. You've never done any of this before. I say you try it all on and see what feels right."

Try it all. The advice circles around my brain.

"I like that idea too."

"Good. And who knows? Maybe you'll end up having some fun with that hot cowboy while you're at it."

"No, thank you."

But my reply is half-hearted at best.

CHAPTER 13
Red Flags
Mollie

The smell of stale beer and cigarettes permeates the air.

The floor is sticky enough that my boots make a crackling sound every time I take a step.

The only light comes from the neon beer signs hung haphazardly across the walls. On the far side of the space, there's a stage where Sally, Patsy, and—ha!—Goody's paralegal, Zach, are setting up for Frisky Whiskey's show.

The Rattler is, in other words, the perfect dive bar.

Stepping through the door, three Rivers boys hot on my heels, the bone-deep exhaustion I've felt all day lifts.

I love it.

I also know it somehow. A vague memory takes shape inside my head. I was on the dance floor with Mom and Dad, the three of us lined up together in front of the stage.

"Hey, Wyatt?" I ask.

He turns to look at me. "What's up?"

"Do they host line dancing lessons here?"

"As a matter of fact, they do." He grins. "Every Wednesday, once in the afternoon and once in the early evening."

That's why I recognized the Rattler when I first drove into town. My parents took me here to learn how to line dance.

How cute. My heart somersaults at the idea that Mom and Dad liked each other enough to do something fun together like that. Makes me feel warm and fuzzy inside that they included me too.

I follow Wyatt and the other cowboys to the bar. I wondered where the hell everyone got the energy to go out on a Friday night after a long-ass week on the ranch. But when the bartender, a woman with a shock of bright blond hair and dancing blue eyes, looks up from emptying a dishwasher and smiles at us, I get it.

The vibe, the band, the sense of anticipation in the air—you just know you're about to have a good time.

And yeah, considering the multiple bombs that've been dropped on me lately, I could really use a drink. I can't stop thinking about what Jen said—the stuff about Cash being scared and life becoming more vibrant in a small town in a way she wasn't expecting.

Is that what's happening to me?

"Whatcha drinking?" Wyatt settles his elbows on the bar beside me.

He drove Duke, Ryder, and me to town in one of Lucky Ranch's pickups. Sally and Patsy drove separately so they could get here early to set up. Sawyer's back at the ranch, putting Ella to bed, and Cash is...I don't know where.

I tell myself I don't care.

I dig my credit card out of my crossbody. "Honestly, I could go for a cold beer. Let me buy you one or three for letting me tag along again today."

I was able to get away from my laptop and Bellamy Brooks for a couple of hours this morning, so Wyatt took me under his wing for a second time and showed me the ranch office, introduced me to the farrier—a guy who takes care of the horses' legs and hooves—and then took me to the equipment barn, where he explained what each of the enormous machines parked there did.

It wasn't physically taxing work, but it was important, and I feel like I learned a lot. This beer is well deserved.

"You don't have to buy me a drink," Wyatt says. "It was my pleasure."

"I insist."

Wyatt smiles at the bartender when she heads our way. "Hey, Tallulah. How you been? Ankle any better?"

"They took the boot off on Tuesday. It's still a little sore, but worlds better than it was. Only what I deserve for attempting the Cupid Shuffle four whiskey sours deep." Tallulah smiles, then glances at me. "This Mollie Luck? My wife has told me all about you."

"Tallulah is married to Goody," Wyatt explains. "They tied the knot, what, three years ago now? John B officiated the ceremony right here at the Rattler."

"Three years and three months of wedded bliss, yeah." Tallulah extends her hand. "Welcome to my bar, Mollie. We're happy you're here. What can I get you?"

A bubbly warmth rises in the back of my throat. I don't know this woman, who married a lawyer in a bar in a ceremony officiated by a veterinarian, but I already like her.

I take her hand and give it a firm shake. "Thank you so damn much for having me. I adore your place. I'll have a Shiner Bock, please."

"Make that two."

My heart takes a swan dive at the sound of the gravelly voice behind me.

I glance over my shoulder, and my heart falls to the goddamn *floor* when I see him.

Cash.

He stands a few feet away, one hand tucked into the front pocket of his jeans. He's wearing a baseball hat.

A *backward* baseball hat. Add to that his broken-in Wranglers and the clean white tee that stretches across his chest and shoulders in the most mind-bogglingly sexy way imaginable, and you have one very tall glass of water.

Cash is a smokeshow when he's doing his cowboy thing, no denying that.

But in these neon lights, in *that* hat and *those* jeans, he is...epically, obscenely hot. My pulse riots, a bloom of pure, unadulterated desire spreading between my legs.

Squeezing them together in an effort to cut that shit off at the pass, I blurt, "I thought you weren't coming."

He comes to stand beside me at the bar and meets my eyes. "Changed my mind. You gonna leave now, City Girl?"

"I will if you keep calling me that."

He smells like he just got out of the shower, the clean, simple scent of soap rising off his skin. I detect a hint of something subtly minty and herbal too.

I do my best to ignore it. But this man would get eaten *alive* at the bars I go to in Dallas. I mean that literally. Men and women would be all over him. Looking around the Rattler, people seem to notice Cash, but no one's approaching us. Why not?

Maybe, like me, they've witnessed his less than friendly side.

Or maybe he's already slept with them. Does Cash get around? And why does that thought make my chest cramp?

I need to stop thinking about this shit.

"You drink Shiner Bock," he says, forehead creased in disbelief.

Looking away, I put my card on the bar's gleaming wooden surface. "Of course I do. It's delicious. I was just about to buy Wyatt and myself a round as a matter of fact."

Cash pushes my card aside. "Your money's no good here. Tallulah, put it on the tab."

"You have a tab?"

"Of course we have a tab."

Tallulah grins as she pops the tops off three longnecks. "The boys are here...often."

"What she means is"—Cash takes a beer from Tallulah and hands it to me—"Wyatt may or may not host an illegal poker game here every so often. The people who play with him may or may not lose enough money to pay our tab many times over."

Wyatt nods, sipping his beer. "Tallulah gets a cut of my winnings."

"What if you lose?"

"I don't. Someone's gotta put money into Ella's college fund."

Cash meets my eyes again, his longneck at his lips. "Come hell or high water, a Rivers is gonna get a degree."

Tipping back my beer, I look away. I have to. I might literally melt if I keep looking at this indecently handsome man who's apparently hell-bent on sending his niece to college.

It's a dream he couldn't make come true for himself. But he'll be damned if it doesn't come true for his loved ones.

For a second, I get this weird, floaty feeling, like the ground is literally shifting beneath my feet. Cash is continually taking me off guard. He's continually surprising me, and I'm not quite sure what to do with myself when he does. Hating him is easy.

But if I don't hate him...then what?

I startle at the sound of a snare drum. Glancing at the stage, I see Patsy twirling a drumstick in her hand before the band launches into its first song.

Watching Patsy play the drums, a smile splits my face. *Of course* she plays the drums. And *of course* she absolutely rocks it, pounding away like she wasn't up long before the sun, making the first of many meals to feed many mouths.

Zach is on the steel guitar while Sally is a backup singer at a microphone, a violin on her shoulder. I don't recognize the lead vocalist or the gal playing the acoustic guitar, but I'm sure they're somehow connected to Lucky Ranch.

I'm learning that everyone around here is.

The song they play is a George Strait cover. One of my favorites—"It Just Comes Natural." Maybe that's why the ground suddenly steadies and I'm tapping the toe of my boot in time to the beat.

This I know.

This I love.

Live music. Classic country. A bar where no one gives a fuck who you are or what you're wearing. We're all just here to have a good time.

We're all here to forget life for a little while.

I'm not the only one in need of an escape. People immediately move from the bar to the dance floor. I smile harder when I see John B leading the pack.

Turning back to Cash and Wyatt, I catch Cash looking at me. Checking me out, more like it. His eyes rove up the length of my body, a slow, steady perusal that feels like a physical caress.

It should piss me off. Offend me at the very least.

Instead, his attention makes me feel...definitely *not* offended.

Is Cash into me? Am I into him?

No. Definitely not. Although I'd be lying if I said I wasn't the tiniest bit flattered by the idea that he's physically attracted to me.

Then again, that makes the fact that I'm attracted to him that much more dangerous.

Let's be real, though. There's zero chance we'll hook up. I don't want to stay on the ranch, but I also don't want to be reckless with its future. The more I learn about the place, the more I recognize how essential Cash is to its operation. I lose him, I lose the ranch. Period, end of sentence.

I sip my beer. "Frisky Whiskey is really good."

"Best cover band in South Texas, no question." Cash's eyes reflect the red and blue lights of a nearby Bud Light sign. "That's how I got that concussion, dancing to their cover of 'Cotton Eye Joe.'"

"Back when you were fun," Wyatt says wistfully. "I miss those days."

I screw up my face. "Cash was fun?"

Wyatt sips his Shiner Bock. "Hard to believe, I know."

"I'm still fun." Cash crosses his arms, beer dangling over his taut stomach. The pose makes his biceps strain against the sleeves of his T-shirt. "I'm here, aren't I?"

Maybe it's the biceps. The beer. The band.

The nagging question in the back of my mind— *Why* is *Cash here?* Did he come to blow off some steam? Or did he come to keep an eye on me?

For whatever reason, I feel like egging him on, even though I shouldn't.

I really, really shouldn't.

"But you're not dancing," I say.

"Running the ranch without me because I'm in the hospital with another head injury is not a risk you wanna take, City Girl."

"Worth the risk to see you shake it for me, Country Boy."

Cash's turn to screw up his face. "I hate that."

"See? Stupid nicknames suck."

His lips twitch. "Fine. You got me there, *Mollie*."

"Told you, *Cash*." Heart thumping, I loop my arm through his. "Now let's go dance."

CHAPTER 14
Worst Way
Cash

Fuck me if Mollie ain't fine as hell.

She's tan from a day spent outside.

She's drinking Shiner Bock at my favorite bar in the world.

She's wearing a tiny skirt and crop top. Legs for days. Bare arms, bare shoulders. Big smile.

She's singing the words to my favorite George Strait song.

Maybe that's why I let her lead me to the stage. The music is loud enough that I feel the beat reverberate inside my breastbone. Patsy's really going for it on the drums. Don't blame her. Looking after us all, she's got a lot of tension to work out.

Glancing over my shoulder, I see Wyatt watching Mollie and me. He tilts his head the tiniest bit.

Don't be a dick.

Tallulah also sends a look my way, a knowing smile on her face as she fills a frosty glass at the tap.

I haven't taken someone home in a while. With everything that happened first with Garrett and then with Mollie, I've been too tied up—too beat up—to make the effort.

Probably why I feel so keyed up with Mollie on my arm. She smells good, the perfume she's wearing somehow sweet *and* sexy. Hint of vanilla. Another hint of something floral and pretty.

This was a bad idea.

Coming to the Rattler and having a beer with Mollie was a really bad fucking idea.

I need to leave. Immediately.

But then the song ends, and Mollie throws up her arms. She lets out a loud holler that puts a big old smile on Sally's face.

It also captures the attention of every guy in a twenty-foot vicinity. Several shamelessly stare at Mollie, a few of the bolder ones even moving closer. I see the Wallace boys in the mix. Wonder if anything ever happened between Beck and Sally. And where the hell is their sister, Billie? She's good at keeping them in line.

My grip on my beer tightens. *This* is why I'm here. Last thing I felt like doing after a long day on the ranch was getting dressed and going out. But I didn't like the idea of Mollie getting hit on left and right by local drunks who get a little too handsy after a couple of drinks.

Wyatt is too distracted by, well, everyone to watch over Mollie. Sawyer's back home, putting Ella to bed. And Duke and Ryder, they're too busy trying to get laid to keep tabs on our new owner.

As usual, it's up to me to keep everyone safe.

"Thanks, y'all," Patsy says into the mic. "Always fun to cover the king himself."

"You're a rock star!" Mollie says.

John B holds up his hand. "Ain't she, though?"

"I'm already a fan for life." Mollie gives him a high five. "Your girls are so talented."

He beams. "I'm the luckiest man alive."

"This next one is for Cash Rivers." Sally glances at me before taking a swig of her margarita. "Since we haven't seen him for a minute here at the Rattler, figure we'll welcome him with one of his favorites. Y'all enjoy."

My chest stirs as the opening notes of "Neon Moon" fill the bar.

Mollie glances at me, her smile in her eyes now. "This is one of my favorite Brooks and Dunn songs too."

Seems too simple for a girl like her—the pleasure of a great song being played by a great band in a bar as old as we are. I would've thought only a trip on a private jet or a Rolex for her birthday would light her up like this.

But here we are. My heart thumps as people pair off around us. Watching couples move across the dance floor, her gaze flickers.

Mollie doesn't have a ring on her finger. I imagine if she had a boyfriend, he'd be here right now. No way I'd let my girl walk into this bar alone. Much less walk onto the ranch she just inherited by herself.

She's single, then.

Or maybe I just hope she's single. Which is plain stupid. Mollie Luck is gorgeous, sure. She's got more grit than I gave her credit for. But I can't get involved.

I don't want to get involved, my thumping pulse notwithstanding.

But then Roddy Oldman, a cowboy from one of the smaller ranches across town with a crooked smile and wandering hands, holds out his arm to Mollie. "Can I have this dance?"

Turning away from me, Mollie grins. "Aren't you a gentleman? I'd love—"

"Nope." Aw shit. Now I'm curling an arm around Mollie's waist. I'm pulling her against me, my body lighting up like a firecracker at the contact. My hand finds her side, and I hold her there, my grip firm.

I don't miss the way her tits rise on a sharp inhale.

I tell myself I'm just looking out for her. I'm just keeping her safe. If I'm here, there's no chance Roddy will put his dirty paws on her.

"Wait, wait." Mollie looks up at me, eyebrows pinched together. "Are you—"

"Dancing? Yes."

She blinks. "I'm confused."

"It's simple. The band plays a song, and we dance to it."

"Together?"

"That's how the two-step works, yeah."

She blinks again, cheeks flushing pink, and nods at Roddy. "I'd like to dance with him."

Keeping my arm around her waist, I set my beer down on the edge of the stage. "You're dancing with me."

"What the hell, Cash?" Roddy says.

I offer him a tight smile. "Over my dead body, Roddy."

"You're rude," Mollie says.

"Yep." Grabbing Mollie's beer, I set it down beside mine. "Watch the boots. I just cleaned them."

156

She glances down at my feet. "Do you ever take Dad's boots off?"

"Not if I can help it." I grab her hand and put my other hand on the small of her back, my pinkie meeting with bare skin thanks to her crop top. My pulse blares. The heat of her skin seeps into my own.

I can't two-step with this girl and not lose my goddamn mind.

I also can't leave her to the likes of Roddy Oldman.

Leaning in, I manage, "I'm doing you a favor. Once he starts drinking, he won't stop pawing at you."

She looks up at me, an uncertain—but not unhappy—gleam in her eyes. "Oh. Okay. Thanks, I guess?"

I really do almost lose my mind when Mollie puts her hand on my shoulder. I imagine that hand gliding up to my neck. She'd play with the hair at my nape, pulling me close. Her mouth an inch from mine, soft and hot and—

Hell no. *No, no, no.* That fantasy isn't going any further.

Tearing my gaze from Mollie's lush mouth, I step forward at the same time as she does, our bodies colliding. The heaviness gathering in my core pulses, a searing shock of heat ripping through me at the feel of her tits pressed against my chest.

"What are you doing?" She looks up at me.

I look down, clenching my teeth. Her skin glows in the red and yellow stage lights. "I'm leading. Let me."

"No one leads a dance anymore—"

"I do." I search her eyes. "Let me."

"Or what?"

"Or we're gonna miss the rest of this song."

She blinks. A funny expression comes over her face, like she wants to smile but won't let it happen. "Oh. Good point. Okay."

I step forward again. This time, Mollie steps back. She's half a beat too late on that step and the next one, but at least she's letting me guide her, her gaze locked on our feet.

She steps on my toe and recoils, the hand she's got on my shoulder fisting in my shirt. "Shit, sorry."

"You're all right. Follow my lead. It's quick, quick"—I make the steps, firming my hold on her back so that she's pressed against me—"slow, slow. There you go. Simple two-step."

I wait for Mollie to pull back. Create some space between us.

She doesn't.

Trouble.

"I feel like I'm Happy, the baby horse." Mollie glances up at me, my heart skipping at the playful gleam in her eyes. "I don't know how to use my legs yet, so you have to help me out."

"You know how to use your legs."

She finally does smile, this time a closed-mouth thing that makes me think she's holding back laughter. "That sounded wrong."

"Only because you're a pervert."

"You're the one who said the pervy thing."

"You're the one who pointed it out!"

I don't realize I'm smiling until Mollie says, "Aha. Maybe you are still fun."

You don't know how fun I can be, sweetheart. You want me to teach you how to use those legs? Let me get between 'em, and I'll show you exactly how it's done.

"You okay?"

I blink at the sound of Mollie's voice. "What? Yeah. Why?"

"You just got this look on your face. Like you wanted to punch someone."

Fuck someone, more like it.

Glancing over my shoulder, I see Roddy staring us down. The second I let this girl go, he's gonna make his move. We don't get many visitors here in Hartsville, so you gotta act fast if you want to stake your claim on someone new.

Ain't happening tonight for Roddy. Or ever.

The chorus rises. I try to focus on anything but the beautiful woman in my arms, the one who's picked up the two-step in less than a minute. Fast learner, I guess. Good for her.

Bad for me.

I think about all the times I listened to this song in my truck with Garrett. "Neon Moon" is a classic country song, the kind where the guy loses the girl and goes to a bar to drown his regret in whiskey.

Listening to it, Garrett would get quiet, rolling down the window to let his arm hang out the side of the truck. Sometimes, he'd sing the lyrics. Other times, he'd just stare out the window, lost in his thoughts.

I know he was thinking about Aubrey, his ex-wife. I'm sure he was thinking about Mollie too. I'm surprised she believes her dad *didn't* think or talk about her.

Then again, Garrett rarely left the ranch. Yeah, he was busy looking after my brothers and me. But we could've held our own if he went to see his daughter back in Dallas.

I called him out on this, of course.

But Garrett would just wave me away. "It's complicated. Mollie needed to live with her mama. They don't want me around."

"A kid always wants her parents around," I replied. "Trust me on that."

But Garrett and I agreed to disagree on that point. You can lead a horse to water, but you sure as hell can't make him drink.

Looking down at Mollie, I wonder why *she* didn't push Garrett more. Maybe she did. I only know one side of this story. And maybe, after putting in so much effort without any reward, she just stopped trying.

She's comfortable enough with the steps that she's singing now, lost in the song.

She's also swaying her hips, getting a little saucy on the turns as I lead us across the dance floor. I hadn't realized there'd been a permanent divot between her eyebrows until now, when the skin there is smooth.

Relaxed.

It's like she's finally let loose. Her lips are curled into a smile, the long waves of her hair moving over her shoulders as she turns her head in time to the beat.

She catches me watching her. Instead of calling me out, she smiles harder, bigger, the kind of smile that touches her eyes.

There's a sudden, sharp drop in my chest. God*damn*, the joy I see in her face—it's infectious.

Before I know what's happening, I'm lifting my arm and twirling her around. She laughs, the sound loud and real, so I twirl her again and again.

On the third twirl, she slows the pace, spinning slowly

while she pops her cute little ass in time to the beat. Someone hollers. I look up and see it's Patsy, smiling down at us from the stage as she pounds on the drums.

Mollie holds up a hand, wiggling her fingers at Patsy. Then she lets me pull her back into my arms. The way we move now, it's easier, more fluid. Mollie doesn't look at our feet and instead looks up at me, sinking her teeth into her bottom lip.

I wanna bite that lip.

The song ends. Everyone goes wild, like they usually do. But unlike usual—Sally loves to talk to the crowd between songs—Frisky Whiskey dives right into another song.

Another *slow* song.

It's like they know I'm about to pop a woody dancing with my new boss, and they wanna push me right over the fucking edge.

Roddy drinks his beer in a far corner, waiting for his chance to pounce.

I look down at Mollie and see she's still looking up at me. My heart dips at the question I see in her eyes. She really wanna dance with me again?

Hell yeah, she does. Apparently, I still got it, despite not having danced for—wow, how long has it been now?

I step forward, starting the dance all over again, and this time, Mollie moves right into the two-step without hesitating.

Don't know why this makes me smile, but it does.

Maybe because she's at ease with me? She's singing her heart out now, making the dance her own while somehow letting me lead at the same time.

She's a *fucking* knockout.

When the chorus hits, she presses against me, going up on her toes to say in my ear, "Your turn."

Despite almost blacking out at having her plastered against me, I ask, "My turn?"

"To spin. Give the ladies what they want." She pulls back, lifting our joined hands.

"What's that?"

"A show." Her other hand curls around the ball of my shoulder. Then she pulls.

I pull back. "I don't spin."

"Yes, you do."

"No, I don't. That's how concussions happen."

"C'mon. You gotta show me how legs work, remember?"

I let out a bark of laughter. Hard, genuinely surprised laughter that hits me in the sides and makes me feel light on my feet.

"Do it!" Ryder shouts above the music.

I didn't realize he was so close; he's just to our right, dancing with Billie Wallace. Thank God that girl showed.

I arch a brow at Mollie. "You gonna be the one to take me to the hospital if I fall?"

"You're not going to fall." She parrots my line back to me with such precise, steady wickedness, I laugh again. "You twirl. I'll take care of the rest."

"You have some fucking memory."

"You have some fucking nerve, not giving your dance partner what she wants. C'mon, cowboy."

"Do it! Do it!" Ryder and Duke are chanting it now.

Glancing at the bar, I see Wyatt with a shot of whiskey in his hand and a big, stupid smile on his face.

Save me, I mouth to him.

He just holds up the whiskey and then downs it.

I am going to kill him later.

Turning back to Mollie, I sigh. Then I lift up our arms as high as they'll go. I still have to duck, but I manage to twirl, my boots sliding a little too easily on the floor. Had 'em resoled recently, so I have to be extra careful.

Then I'm facing Mollie again, her smile bright. Genuine. Around us, scattered applause breaks out.

She laughs, a sound that sends a rush up the back of my throat. "See how much they loved it?"

Did you?

Apparently so, because when the band plays the chorus again a minute later, Mollie is holding up her arm. This time, all she has to do is bite that bottom lip again to get me to twirl.

She hollers. Because I have a death wish, I find myself egged on by her attention, rolling my hips to the beat.

I fucking love to dance. Makes me forget how tired I am. How overwhelmed. All the shit I have to do, the never-ending list of tasks that floats around in my head day and night, evaporates as I move.

Only I must roll my hips a little too hard, because suddenly my left foot slips out from under me. My stomach lurches as I stumble and lose my balance. *Shit, not again—*

But I'm yanked upright by a hand wrapped around my arm.

Mollie's hand.

I immediately grab on to her, the two of us hanging on to the other's forearm like we're doing some kind of secret handshake.

She looks at me with wide eyes. "You okay?"

"I am." My pulse pounds in my temples. "Thanks."

That smile. "Told you I wouldn't let you fall."

"I shouldn't be out here in the first place." I nod at the floor. "Dancing."

"Yeah, you should." She gestures at the bar, which is getting more crowded by the minute. Everyone's watching us, smiles on their faces. "Told you they wanted a show."

The song ends. Again, the crowd hoots and hollers and claps. But I just stare at Mollie, trying—failing—to ignore the weird, buzzy feeling that rises inside my chest.

First the lemonade. Then the shower break and sandwich. Now the dance-floor rescue.

Mollie's looking out for me, isn't she?

The spoiled, self-centered trust-fund brat is paying attention to me in a way no one else has in...a while.

Maybe she's not such a brat.

Or maybe she's got an ulterior motive. Really, *why* would she look out for me if not to trick me into trusting her?

Only my gut tells me otherwise.

My knees wobble. Mollie keeps her hand on my arm, grip firm. I got several inches and a hundred pounds on her, but she's stronger than she looks.

Who the fuck *is* this girl?

And why do I want to suddenly commit unspeakably violent acts against every guy who so much as glances at her?

I gotta get gone. Now. Climb in my truck and peel out of here like the building's on fire. That'd be the smart thing to do.

But Mollie's the smart one, isn't she? And I don't see her going anywhere.

Curling an arm around her waist, I pull her against me. "Then let's give 'em a show."

CHAPTER 15
Let Go and Let God
Mollie

I can't stop smiling.

Just like I can't stop dancing. I have no idea how much time has passed, only that I'm covered in sweat and my feet hurt.

"This one isn't a country song," Sally says into the mic, "but you can't not dance to it, so we figured we'd play it for y'all."

Patsy counts out the beat with her drumsticks, and then Frisky Whiskey bursts into a twangy version of "Wobble."

People go *nuts*. I shout. Cash puts his fingers into his mouth and lets out an earsplitting whistle.

The dance floor is packed now. Who knew so many people lived in such a tiny town?

Who knew they could all wobble like a boss?

I'm downright giddy as I join the front line of dancers beside Cash. His face shines with sweat, his cheeks pink, shirt sticking to his chest and stomach.

When he shakes his ass, bending his legs in time to the beat, I can only stare. Laughter bubbles up inside my chest.

"You laughin' at my wobble?" he shouts over the music.

Nope, I'm checking out your delicious Wrangler butt like every other person in this bar. "I would never!"

"Good luck keepin' up."

"Watch me."

I let go and let God. I dance my heart out, smiling like an idiot while sneaking glances in Cash's direction.

He looks *so* damn hot in his jeans and backward hat. I should've known he was a good dancer by the easy rhythm he finds whenever he's on horseback. But to see those long legs and that perfect butt in action like this—witnessing him letting loose in a way I never imagined he was capable of?

I'm so turned on I could scream.

My body pulses at the memory of how Cash manhandled me the other day. At the time, I found it offensive. Now I'm wondering if he'd manhandle me that way in bed. He's got the muscle to toss someone around—that's for damn sure. But would he have the balls?

I close my eyes and will the thought to evaporate. Sure, I'm having the time of my life dancing with Cash. And the way he told that guy who asked me to dance to fuck off?

Not gonna lie, being spoken for like that—protected—was hot as hell. Guys back in Dallas are sexy in their own way, but they're never territorial.

They never speak so plainly or act so quickly.

They also don't dance the way Cash is dancing.

Despite all that, I can't touch this cowboy with a ten-foot pole. I'm realizing just how important it is to establish a solid working relationship with him and his brothers. I feel like Dad and I let each other down in so many things.

I'm not going to let him down again by doing something stupid with the guy who runs our family's ranch.

Even if that guy is turning out to be a decent human being.

A decent, thoughtful, incredibly sexy human being who can wobble with the best of them.

On any other night at any other bar, I'd be taking him home.

Tonight, the only thing I can do is take him to task on the dance floor.

We dance, and we laugh, the bar a blur as we move. Cash keeps tabs on me during every song, not so much as glancing at other people.

I never ever want to stop.

But I finally hit a wall when Frisky Whiskey moves into another slow song. My feet throb. My eyes burn, knees and back on fire.

I'm suddenly so tired, I could fall asleep standing up.

Cash must notice, because he puts a hand on my back. "Ready to get outta here?"

"I'm beat." I glance around the bar. "Shoot, where did Wyatt go? He's my ride home."

"I'll give you a ride."

I arch a brow at Cash. We've been too busy dancing to drink much—two beers each, the last one finished several songs ago—so I know he's okay to drive.

I just don't know if I'm okay to drive with him. Just the thought of riding shotgun beside Cash already has me thinking about a different kind of riding.

The naked kind.

I've enjoyed more than a few back-seat make-out sessions in my day. But making out with a cowboy like Cash in the back of his pickup? Those big hands roving slowly over every inch of my body?

That'd take the experience to a whole new level.

I wish I could ignore the tight, buzzy energy between us. I wish I could stop leaning into it. But it just feels too damn good to be touched this way.

I'm just having too much fun.

Even now, sparks erupt inside my skin from the place where his fingers find the gap between my top and skirt on my back. There's no chance we'll actually get naked together. But the idea of it—the tease—there's something to be said for that kind of anticipation.

Hooking up with Palmer is very straightforward. There's no buildup. No flirtation. Just a knock on the door and then, well, we get to it. Sometimes, we'll have a glass of wine beforehand, but I always, always know how it's going to end.

Honestly, that's why our situationship works so well. I don't have the time or the bandwidth to play guessing games. But being out with Cash makes me realize just how sterile my interactions with Palmer are. The sex is fine, sure.

Bet the sex with Cash would be better.

Clearing my throat, I ask, "So you can dispose of my body on the side of the road?"

Cash grins. My pulse skips. "That'd be plain stupid. I'd feed you to the cows, obviously."

"Obviously."

"Do y'all always joke about dismemberment like this?" John B asks. "It's a little…dark."

"Only when we're together." Cash pushes me toward the exit. "We'll see you in the mornin', John B."

"Y'all be good." John B chuckles. "No body parts in the feed, all right?"

Stepping out into the night, I'm hit by a blast of still, humid air.

"How the hell is it still so hot out?" I fan myself with my hand.

Cash is still grinning as he digs a set of keys out of his pocket. "Lucky for you, my truck doesn't have AC."

"They make cars that don't have AC?"

"Yes, ma'am, they do." Dropping his hand from my back, he yanks open the passenger-side door of the same enormous red pickup I saw parked outside Goody's office that fateful day we read Dad's will. "I'm among the lucky few to own one."

I climb into the truck. "How do you not die?"

"I drive naked a lot."

"No, you don't!"

He laughs, the sound making my stomach flip in the most delicious way. "I don't. Your butt sticks to the seat too much. Gives you this, like, terrible rug burn."

Hesitating, I glance at the upholstery. "Ew."

"Aw, c'mon, Mollie. I've never had my bare ass on the seats. Not the front ones anyway. I like to keep a clean car."

My nipples pebble to tight, sensitive points. Can Cash actually read my mind?

What would he say to all the dirty shit he sees there? The stuff about back seats and big hands?

And how does he keep a clean car on a ranch? He must spend a good amount of time taking care of it. I don't know why that makes my heart beat faster, but it does.

Cash closes the door behind me. The window is already partially rolled down, so it's not totally stifling inside the truck.

Glancing around, my stomach flips again at how *neat* the interior is. Cash wasn't joking when he said he likes to keep it clean.

The pickup is old, but the gray upholstery looks new. A little worn, sure, but very well maintained. There's a cassette deck in the dash. The front seats are actually one large bench that's surprisingly comfortable.

The truck smells like sun-warmed cotton and clean air. Hint of lemon on account of the faded air freshener hanging from the rearview mirror.

Buckling my seat belt, I try not to stare as Cash climbs in beside me and puts the key in the ignition. The muscles in his forearm bunch against his skin as he turns the key.

The truck rumbles to life, sending a vibration up the backs of my thighs that lands right in my clit.

I suck in a breath.

Cash freezes, his hand on the gearshift. "You all right?"

"Yep. Yes. Fine." *Just about to burst into flames, no big deal.*

He uses one hand on the top of the wheel to guide the truck out of the parking lot. The crunch of tires on gravel fills the cab.

Then we're moving smoothly through the night on a road so dark, it's like being out in space. Cash cranks his window all the way down, and I do too. The breeze sends my hair flying. He glances at me, the red light of the dash catching on the slope of his nose, the fullness of his lips.

"Too much?"

I hang my arm out the window, surfing my palm on the breeze. "Just right."

"Music?"

"Sure."

He punches a button on the dash, and a Brooks & Dunn song starts playing from the middle. It's just loud enough to hear over the roar of the open windows.

"Cassette tapes," Cash explains with a shrug.

This old-school approach to driving is actually kind of charming. I hum along to the music as the breeze cools my skin and blows the hair back from my face.

Turning, I catch Cash looking at me.

"What?" I hold my hair back with my other hand.

He shakes his head, focusing his gaze on the windshield. "Nothing. You just look like your daddy, sitting like that."

My heart squeezes. "I do? How?"

"He'd hang his arm out the window too. Although he'd sing a lot louder."

I grin. "I inherited my mom's voice. You do not want to hear me sing."

"I heard you plenty back at the Rattler."

"You didn't run."

"Don't mean I didn't want to." He's smiling, eyes liquid, and my *God*, how does someone so handsome exist? "Your daddy did have a nice voice."

"I remember that, yeah. He *loved* music."

"You do too. Y'all are alike—I can see that now."

It's a compliment. One that makes my chest hurt.

Cash is throwing me bones again. Glancing at him, I want to know why.

I want to ask the question that's been banging around inside my head since we met.

"Why didn't you come to the funeral?" I ask. "You say you and Dad and everyone else on the ranch were tight. But no one from Hartsville showed up."

Cash's chest rises on a sharp inhale. "We weren't invited."

My stomach lurches. "What? That's not possible. Mom said she invited everyone Dad knew."

"She didn't invite us."

"You sure? Maybe y'all missed it in the mail—"

"No one got an invitation of any kind, Mollie." He adjusts his hand on the top of the wheel. "I know, because I reached out to your mama after she sent those men to bring your dad's body to Dallas."

"You called my mom?"

"Garrett never lived in Dallas. He only mentioned it because it was where you and your mama lived. I knew he wouldn't want to be buried there, so I reached out to Aubrey to tell her that."

The saliva thickens inside my mouth. "What did she say?"

"Nothing nice." He chuckles darkly. "When it became clear she wasn't gonna budge on the location of the burial, I asked her to send me the details so we could attend. She said the service was for family only and to please stop calling her."

Yep, now I definitely feel like I'm going to vomit.

I want to fight Cash on what he's telling me. Call him out for lying. But if I'm being honest, this sounds like something Mom would do. Maybe to protect me? To stick it to Dad one final time?

Whatever her reasons, it was a shithead move on Mom's part. She hurt these people. I see that now, because Cash's Adam's apple bobs on a hard swallow.

"That must've truly sucked for y'all," I manage. "I'm really sorry, Cash. I wondered why no one from the ranch came. Mom said she sent word to Dad's friends, but…"

He lifts a shoulder. "We did our own thing here. Little ceremony, nothing fancy. But I think everyone needed a sense of closure, so I put something together."

Always a leader.

Always thoughtful.

The lump in my throat is the size of the moon. "How are you not angrier about this?"

"I am angry." He glances out his window. "Really fucking angry, Mollie. But at some point, I gotta let it go, or it'll eat me alive."

I feel that.

God, do I feel that.

"I'm angry too. At myself mostly."

That gets his attention. He glances at me with this *look* in his eyes—softness, pain, all of it raw and real— that makes my stomach dip. "Why's that?"

I look down at my lap while I pick at a loose thread in my skirt. "I should've known Mom was up to something. I feel like I should've—I don't know—followed up or double-checked the guest list or something."

"You didn't know, Mollie."

"I think part of me did, though." My turn to swallow. "Mom never had nice things to say about Dad. And I'm sure you noticed, but my father and I didn't exactly get along. I think…maybe I was so angry at everyone, myself included, that I let shit slide. I'm sad Dad is gone. But I was—am—mostly angry."

That's one hell of a confession.

A pause.

Then Cash says, "I had a therapist tell me once that for some people, sadness manifests as anger."

I laugh, if only so I don't burst into tears. "You've been to therapy?"

"Of course I've been to therapy. Why do you think I'm such a charming, well-adjusted beacon of contentment and emotional maturity?"

I laugh again, this time for real. "You're full of surprises, I'll say that much."

"Can I ask what happened?" Cash does that thing where he adjusts his hand on the wheel. "Between you and Garrett?"

Letting out a long, low breath, I fall back against my seat. "Long story short? My parents had a nasty divorce. Not because anyone cheated or anything. But I think my mom was really hurt by the fact that my dad didn't follow us to Dallas. He didn't choose her, you know? And he didn't choose me either. They were supposed to split custody, but Dad never brought me back to the ranch, and he never really came to see me in Dallas."

"That'll break anyone's heart."

I swallow, hard. "Broke mine, yeah."

"I'm sorry, Mollie."

"Thanks." I manage a tight smile. "Dad loved life on

the ranch, but Mom really struggled with it. She said she felt like she was living on a deserted island. I think she missed her family and friends back in Dallas."

Cash nods. "That's fair. Ranch life isn't for everyone. Takes a special kind of person to weather the ups and downs."

"She begged him to move with us to Dallas. But I guess he loved the ranch too much to leave it behind, so he stayed. Mom says she's not angry anymore, but sometimes, I think she'll always hate my Dad for not chasing her. For a while, I hated him for not chasing me."

Cash takes a minute to absorb this. I appreciate the fact that he's not filling the silence with empty platitudes about grief or relationships. If there's one thing Cash doesn't do, it's small talk.

"Did you and your dad talk or see each other much when you were little?" he asks.

I tilt my head back and forth. "Here and there, yeah. Every so often, he'd visit, usually when he had business meetings. He'd take me to dinner or whatever, but that was it. I know Mom didn't want me going back to the ranch alone with him. I think after a while…" I shrug. "He just stopped trying maybe? Who knows? But it pissed me off, and my mom, she didn't help me feel any better about it because she was pissed too. I hated him because she hated him, you know? I felt bad for her."

"Not easy, raising a kid on your own."

"Exactly. So when I started feeling some teenage angst on top of all that, I think I snapped. I stopped answering Dad's calls. When he came to visit, I refused to talk to him. Our relationship never really recovered."

"That's tough," Cash says gruffly.

I blink back tears. "I really regret it now. By the time I was in high school, Dad and I were strangers."

"How old are you now?"

"Twenty-six. Why?"

Cash glances at me. "When your dad stopped calling, that was right around the time he took my brothers and me under his wing. Not that that's an excuse, but...yeah, we kept him busy. Real busy."

I blink again, a mixture of emotions unfurling in my center. Do I feel relief that Dad disappeared not because of what I did but because he took in five orphaned boys and had his hands full?

Or do I feel hurt that he chose those boys over me? Because, God, knowing he loved them day in and day out—knowing he showed up for them in a way he never did for me—sends a knife through my heart.

No wonder I've been so angry all this time. What I'm really feeling is sadness over the fact that Dad made me feel unwanted for most of my life. It wasn't intentional on his part; I get that now. But that's how I felt, and it still hurts like hell to hear how wanted—how loved—he made other people feel.

"I know that's a lot to chew on," Cash continues, reading my thoughts once again, "but it's something to consider."

I nod, the breeze blowing my tears across my temples. "I'm glad he was good to y'all. I really am."

"But?"

"But what?"

"Be honest."

I cut him a glance. "Why? So you can hate me even more?"

"So you can get it off your chest. Whatever it is, Mollie, don't let it eat you alive."

My heart somersaults. I look him in the eye.

One, am I imagining it, or does Cash keep saying my name? My *actual* name? I like it more than I should.

And two, why not tell him the truth? Chances are I'll be back in Dallas sooner rather than later, and I'll never have to face Cash Rivers again. So what if he thinks less of me? I really do have nothing to lose.

Maybe that's why I blurt, "But I wish Dad had been good to me too. I wish I'd been good to him when I had the chance. I wish...well, my mother is clearly a piece of work. I wish I hadn't let her sway my opinion of Dad so much."

Cash's eyes move to the windshield. We're quiet for a long beat. My cheeks burn, even as the lump in my throat begins to dissolve.

Go figure. Telling the truth really does make you feel better.

"Your mom is your mom," he says at last. "She's the one who raised you. Of course you were going to side with her. Cut yourself some slack."

"Would you? Cut yourself some slack after you irreparably damaged your relationship with your dad?"

He thinks on this for a minute. "I got on your dad once or twice about this. More'n that, actually. All the things I wish I'd said to my parents that I never got to..." He takes a deep breath. "I told him he'd regret not making more of an effort with you."

My stomach seizes. "You did?"

"Hell yeah, I did. Maybe you messed up, but he was the parent. He was an adult. He should've known better.

I loved Garrett—don't get me wrong. But he could be so stubborn. The regrets I have, I knew he'd have them too, so I said something."

"And what did he say?"

Cash takes a breath. Lets it out. "He said it was too late to right all his wrongs. From all accounts, he was wrecked after y'all left, and he didn't know what to do. He knew your mom was unhappy. He said he thought it wasn't just the ranch that made her miserable—it was being with him. He didn't want to cause her more pain by following her to her new life."

"But he caused so much more pain by not doing anything," I reply thickly.

"I hear you. As far as you were concerned, he said he didn't want to take you away from your mom. He knew Aubrey needed you, and you needed her."

"I needed him too."

"I told him so. I think he finally came to that realization, but he felt like he'd done too much damage at that point to ever fix it. I'm not making excuses for him—"

"I know."

"But he was sick over it, Mollie. I swear on my life that Garrett died loving you more than anything."

I can only stare, eyes welling. "Cash."

"Yeah?"

"Can I hug you?"

He laughs. "I thought you wanted to murder me?"

"I can do that too. But…thanks? For sticking up for me."

"If I'da known you, I wouldn't have done it," he replies with a smirk.

I give his shoulder a shove. "Just when I was starting to like you."

"See?" He meets my eyes, a grin on his lips. "Charming and well-adjusted as fuck. You're welcome."

It's then that I realize my stomach has stopped hurting.

CHAPTER 16
Keeping Up
Cash

"Feeling full of ourselves because we did some twirls tonight on the dance floor, I see." Mollie's eyes shine. "Don't get ahead of yourself, cowboy."

"I thought we said no more nicknames."

"*Cowboy* isn't a nickname. It's more of a…vibe."

"A vibe you like?"

"A vibe I can tolerate, yeah."

I hang a right, my tires meeting with the dirt road that announces our arrival on Lucky Ranch.

Thank God we're home, or I might be tempted to do something stupid. Like reach across the cab to grab Mollie's face and kiss her.

I got no clue what the fuck is wrong with me. How'd I go from wanting this girl gone to wanting to taste her mouth in less than, what, a week?

Why can't I stop flirting with her?

Why won't she stop flirting with me?

I pull up in front of the New House, my headlights

flashing across the windows. Putting the truck in park, I turn off the ignition.

Mollie goes still. "What are you doing?"

"What do you think I'm doing?" I grab the handle. "I'm walking you to your door."

"Why?"

"Because," I say slowly, "it's dark, there are animals around, and I want to make sure you get inside okay. You forgot to turn on the outside lights."

She looks so fucking cute when she's perplexed like this, nose scrunched up and lips pursed. "Is this part of the cowboy vibe?"

"Sure."

"I'm fine. To walk alone, I mean. It's only, like, thirty feet."

I grin, shoving my door open. "Exactly. It's only thirty feet, so let me walk you in."

"I'm not inviting you inside!" she calls as she opens her door.

I jog around the hood to hold the door open. "Never said I wanted to come inside."

"Perv alert." She takes the hand I hold out to her and hops to the ground, flashing me a whole lot of leg in the process.

Laughing, I say, "I wouldn't've caught that if you didn't say something. Get your mind out of the gutter."

"I'd prefer not to, thanks."

If Mollie Luck is as quick and self-assured and shamelessly filthy-minded in bed as she is outside it—

Heaven *help* me.

Discreetly adjusting my jeans, I reply, "You're trouble."

"I know." Offering me a smile, she looks up, and her breath catches. "Oh my God, the stars. They're beautiful out here."

Tilting back my head, I take in the wide-open sky. Because the house lights aren't on, I can see everything with startling clarity: the half-moon, the bright stars, even the tiny, not-so-bright stars that look like specks of dust.

"Spectacular, isn't it?" I say.

"They sure as hell don't look like this in Dallas. There's so much light pollution and haze, you can barely see the moon most nights." Mollie crosses her arms. "This almost looks fake it's so pretty. Does it ever get old? The stars, the night sky?"

"No." I step closer to her. "It doesn't."

Her swallow is audible in the quiet. "I really can see why Dad loved it out here."

I look at her. Drink in her thoughtful expression, the soft, slender lines of her neck. "Those of us who love it—"

"Really, truly love it." Her eyes move to meet mine. "How could you not? If I wasn't about to fall over, I'd stay out here forever."

I nod at the front door. "The stars'll be here tomorrow. And the next night. Let's get you inside."

"That mean you want me to stay?" Her eyes glitter in the darkness. "Be honest. I know you were trying to scare me off the other day."

Smiling, I kick at the gravel. "You're Garrett's daughter. If you're as good of a boss as he was…"

She's smiling too as she turns and heads for the house. I shove my hands in my pockets and follow her, my footsteps sounding a hard, steady beat on the steps up to the door.

Do. Not. Touch her.

But. I. Want to.

When she's on the top step, she turns around. I draw up short, heart lurching.

"Thanks for listening," she says. "I don't usually confide in strangers—"

"I'm not a stranger."

Our gazes lock. The space between us tightens, sparking with electricity that works its way into my skin as her eyes slip to my mouth.

Holy fuck, is *Mollie* going to kiss *me*?

"No," she says. "You're not."

Then she goes up on her toes and wraps me in a hug.

I'm so taken aback that I just stand there for a second like an idiot.

I know this kind of hug. Her arms circling my neck, chest and belly pressed against mine.

She likes the contact. The feel of my body touching hers.

She wants more of it.

Need roars inside me, my blood crackling with the desire to give this girl exactly what she's asking for. Without thinking, I wrap my arms around her waist and pull her even closer, burying my face in her neck.

Even after a night spent dancing at the Rattler, she smells real fucking good. Sweet, like girlie shampoo and that sexy perfume of hers.

"Let's not murder each other, okay?" Her voice is different. Barely above a whisper.

My voice is different too when I reply, "I make no promises."

"You're difficult, you know that?"

"Wouldn't be fun if I made things easy."

She scoffs, her breath ruffling the hair on the nape of my neck. "You're anything but easy, Cash."

Honey, you kiss me, and you'll see just how easy I can be.

All she has to do is ask. Make the move. And I'll have her on her back with my face between her legs in two seconds flat.

My dick perks up at the thought of her being wet. If I put my hand up her skirt, what would I find? Ridiculous silk panties, probably.

And a hot, tight pussy, swollen from a night of dancing and touching and flirting.

My pulse blares at the same moment as Mollie releases me, falling back just enough that our eyes meet again.

She looks at me.

I look back.

I'm acutely aware of the way my heartbeat has migrated to my lips. Hers part, revealing a glimpse of white teeth just inside the pink seam of her mouth.

My hands are on her waist. Hers are on my chest.

I try very hard to remember all the reasons why kissing Mollie Luck is a terrible idea.

I try, and I fail.

But just when I'm about to go in for the kill, she steps back and turns toward the door, offering me a little wave over her shoulder. "Good night, Cash."

I have the presence of mind to yell after her, "Lock the door."

185

"Of course I'm locking the door. I don't want you getting in."

Brat.

But apparently, I'm one hundred percent into that now. I'm hard. And wide awake. And supremely annoyed that I'm hard and wide-awake at midnight on a Friday.

Running a hand over my face, I wait until I hear the bolt slide home in the lock. Then I climb inside my truck and head home.

Not gonna lie, I wish Mollie were coming home with me.

————

Mollie is in the kitchen when I arrive at four o'clock sharp the next morning. Smells good, like something's being sautéed in a shit ton of butter.

I'm technically off on Saturdays and Sundays, but I always end up working anyway, which is why I'm up. Patsy's off weekends too, so she'll stock the fridge on Friday with all kinds of stuff for us to pick on until Monday.

Nice change of pace to have a hot breakfast made by none other than Mollie Luck.

She's at the range again, stirring that pan. Pieces of bread are lined up in a nearby toaster. I draw up short when I notice she's wearing riding clothes. Cowboy clothes, more like it. T-shirt, jeans, boots that aren't sparkly and pink.

She want to work with us today?

That fact shouldn't put a smile on my face, but it does. Maybe seeing the stars last night made her realize the magic of being out here. And yeah, I like that she's taking an interest in the ranch.

I like that she cares.

She's got her hair in a ponytail. She's wearing the glasses again.

I fucking love her in glasses.

I resist the impulse to sidle up behind her. Wrap my arms around her and kiss her neck.

My right hand clearly ain't doing it for me anymore.

I watch Mollie open the cabinet beside the stove and reach for a new bottle of hot sauce. We killed the other one at dinner last night. Texas Pete takes Patsy's white chicken chili to the next level.

Wordlessly, I cross the kitchen and grab it for her. Today, she smells like sunscreen. So she *is* planning to work with us.

Falling back on her heels, her arm brushes my side as she smiles up at me. "Thank you."

"Mornin'. Smells good." I peel off the plastic and twist off the cap before handing her the bottle. "What are you doing up so early on a Saturday?"

She lifts a shoulder. "Wyatt invited me to join y'all today. And you're up early too. Want an omelet?"

"I'd love one." Turning around, I lean my backside against the countertop and cross my arms so that I'm facing Mollie. She's got bags underneath her eyes. But her eyes themselves? They're lit up, same as they were last night. "How're you feeling?"

"Okay. I don't know how y'all stay out so late and then get up at the ass crack of dawn."

I nod at the coffeepot. "Why do you think we make it so strong? Appreciate you makin' some food for us this morning."

"I imagine everyone will be more than a little hungover this morning. Carbs and cheese are the answer."

I get that buzzy feeling in the back of my throat again. Like my heart's plugged into an electrical socket and its vibrations echo up and down my spinal column.

"Kind of you," I say.

Mollie flips the pair of omelets sizzling in the skillet. "Don't call the devil. I've never made breakfast for twenty people before, so I really may end up poisoning y'all. Although this time, it won't be intentional."

"Look at us, making progress. No more threats of manslaughter."

She smiles. "You're getting ahead of yourself, cowboy. How are you feeling? You were working up a sweat on that dance floor."

Drawing a breath, I have to think about that. When was the last time someone asked about me? How I'm doing?

When was the last time I felt *decent* after getting less than four hours of sleep?

"I'm...all right, actually. Tired, but not?"

"Me too." She's still smiling as she flips the omelets one last time. "I forgot how much I love to dance."

I grab a pair of plates and hold them out, giving her a wink. "That's because you've never danced with me before."

"You're not half bad." She uses a spatula to slide an omelet onto each plate. "Not as good as I am, granted."

"Hey. It's been a minute. What do you want with this?" I hold up a plate. "Salsa? Sour cream?"

She blinks. "Both, please. And Texas Pete."

"Got it."

"Should I start on some more?" Mollie glances at the door. "I don't know when to expect everyone else."

"Like you said, people will be moving slow this morning. We can eat." I set us up at the corner of the table, then head for the coffeepot. "You have any yet?"

"Not yet, no."

"How do you like it?"

She blinks, like her mind went right into the gutter, just like mine. Is she blushing?

Aw, yeah, I like making Mollie blush.

"Black, please."

Hand on the carafe, I frown. "Really?"

She hesitates. "Actually, can you make it light and sweet?"

"Yes, ma'am, I can. How I like it too."

We sit and dig in. I love this time of day. The quiet. The hot coffee and cool air. Well, it's not exactly cool, but it's cool*er* than it was last night.

"This is delicious." I wipe my mouth on my napkin.

Mollie sips her coffee. "So is this. Thank you."

"Drink up. You're gonna need that energy if you're coming out with us today."

She hesitates again, coffee still in hand. "Is that an invitation?"

"You're coming whether I invite you or not."

Her lips twitch. "What gave me away?"

"The fact that you're not wearing a single sequin. And the Ariats."

"Just taking notes." Mollie glances at my own Ariats under the table. I wear them every so often to keep Garrett's boots from getting too banged up. "I thought I'd ask you to return the favor. I got you dancing last night, so I was hoping you'd get me riding today."

My turn to blush. Jesus Christ, my brain is back to horny-fifteen-year-old-boy mode.

"I can do that," I manage, scalding my tongue when I take a big sip of coffee. "So you're really gonna stay. On the ranch."

Mollie uses the edge of her fork to cut her omelet. "Honestly? I don't know yet. My whole life is back in Dallas. My business partner is there. Mom, my grandparents. I'm hoping Mom's lawyers figure out a way around that stipulation so I at least have a choice as to whether I stay."

My heart twists.

I nearly drop my mug. Whoa, whoa, *whoa*. Am I actually…a little bummed Mollie isn't sure about staying? Since when? I don't *want* her to stay. But I guess I also don't want her to leave?

Lord above.

"You can always leave the ranch to me," I joke. Only it's not a joke.

I expect Mollie to roll her eyes. Call me out on being shameless.

Instead, she lifts a shoulder and says, "You're really fucking good at running it. I have a lot to learn from you."

I open my mouth. Close it. Open it again. "And you want to learn?"

She meets my eyes. "I am my father's daughter."

"You are." I'm smiling like an idiot again.

I'm also gripped by the idea that now would be a good time to share Garrett's photos with her. He left them to me—supposedly—but really, they belong to Mollie. I wonder why he didn't send some of them to

190

her. Was he planning to send them to Mollie or Aubrey later on? And when did he put everything in the safety-deposit box? Did he ever go to the bank to look at the photos?

My stomach clenches. I still have so many questions, and I can't imagine what Mollie would say. I don't wanna fuck with her head or send her into a tailspin of renewed grief. We're all barely keeping our heads above water as it is. Would the photographs make her day? Or pull her under?

That's a risk I'm not willing to take. Not yet.

"Now I wanna know exactly how much he rubbed off on you," I say.

This time, she does roll her eyes. "Can I ride with y'all or what?"

"You can ride. But you gotta keep up."

"I can keep up."

"Prove it. Maybe then I'll stop calling you City Girl."

Grinning, she kicks me underneath the table. "You're the worst."

I am.

But I'd be lying if I said this wasn't the best morning I've had in a long-ass time.

CHAPTER 17
Long Live Cowgirls
Mollie

Sunrise.

It breaks over the hills in shades of peach, neon pink, and bright, shimmery yellow. In front of me, an enormous herd of cattle is spread out over a pasture that stretches as far as the eye can see.

Taking it all in from the saddle, I feel a similar rise in my chest. A warmth that spreads through my bones and fills me with a sense of calm so deep, I close my eyes to savor it.

My stomach feels settled. Calm. No pain to speak of.

I breathe steadily, evenly, aware of the way the fresh morning air hits the bottom of my lungs. The sun's heat pours over my skin.

Maria nickers beneath me as she quietly munches on the grass. Cowboys laugh somewhere nearby.

I know this feeling. The sun, the calm.

The sense of amazement.

I remember feeling it, riding with Mom and Dad

when I was little. Dad rode a brown filly, but Mom had this gorgeous gray Andalusian she named Storm.

We were up early back then because, well, ranch life. Sometimes, I'd stay back at the house with Mom. Other times, when Mom felt like riding, she'd take me out to watch Dad work cattle with the other cowboys.

More than anything, I remember feeling this incandescent sense of happiness. I loved being with both my parents. Made me feel special.

I also loved being outside, on the ranch, on a horse. Made me feel like I was part of something bigger. The action was exciting. And the attention I got from my parents was...everything.

"Pretty, ain't it?"

I open my eyes to see Cash on his horse beside me. He's wearing gloves, his forearms already glistening with sweat.

He's also wearing chaps today.

Honest-to-goodness *chaps*. They're brown leather and held together by a clasp that's placed distractingly front and center over his crotch.

Words can't adequately describe how delicious he looks in those things. And the easy, confident way he handles his horse? The hopeful way he asked at breakfast if I was staying on the ranch?

I roll my hips, hoping to alleviate the insistent pressure between my legs. The motion just makes it worse. The seam of my jeans glides roughly over my center, making me want...more.

It makes me want Cash there instead. But that's not happening, so thank God for vibrators, I guess?

Cash and I rode mostly in silence in his pickup truck

to this pasture a little while ago, towing a trailer full of horses behind us. He said we're about five miles from the barn. Now we're on horseback—I'm riding Maria, and Cash is on his big black horse, Kix—and his brothers and the other ranch hands are arriving in several Lucky Ranch Dodge Rams behind us. We're about to start the day's work.

I smile. "Last time I saw the sunrise, I was walking home from a bar. I was too hungover to appreciate it then. This is...something else."

"You dirty stayout," he teases.

"Hell yeah, I was a dirty stayout. Where do you think I learned to dance?"

"I was hoping at cotillion or your dance recitals or some shit."

I laugh, even as my pulse blares. Cash remembered that I took dance. "I learned there too."

"You gonna be okay?" Cash nods at Maria. "Holler if you need help."

I shift in the saddle. "It's like riding a bike, right? Just need to practice, and it'll all come back to me."

"If you say so."

I reach over to give him a shove. "Thanks for the vote of confidence."

"Mollie Luck, if there's one thing you don't need, it's someone telling you what you can't do. You know what you're capable of." Looking at me, he screws one eye shut against the brightening sun. "So get out there and do the damn thing."

Smiling, I sit up straighter. "That was a surprisingly great little speech, Cash."

"Thank you kindly." He touches his fingers to the

front of his hat, looking so much like Brad Pitt from *Legends of the Fall* that I can only stare, heart lodging itself somewhere in my throat. I half expect Anthony Hopkins to show up and chastise me about ogling his best-looking son.

Are there really no bears out here?

This whole thing would be a lot easier if Cash wasn't so fucking gorgeous.

"Thanks for letting me tag along," I manage.

He smirks, sliding a pair of gold-rimmed aviators onto his face. "You're welcome. Now watch how it's done."

And Lord, do I watch. Guiding Maria toward the fringes of the herd, I watch Cash round up the cowboys and head toward the action. It may be the weekend, but all the Rivers brothers, save Sawyer, are here—Ella doesn't have preschool, so he's on Dad duty—along with ten or so other ranch hands.

Their dedication is impressive.

They're all on horseback. The way they work is like a dance: Cash always in the lead on his big black horse, everyone working around him in coordinated steps to move the herd toward another pasture.

Dust fills the air, along with the earthy smells of grass, sweat, and manure. The lowing of cows echoes through a nearby canyon.

It's not long before the heat arrives, but that doesn't slow the guys down. I watch, body lighting up, as Cash urges his horse into an all-out gallop to chase down a rogue longhorn. He leans forward in the saddle, one hand on the reins, the other on the rope tied to his saddle.

The graceful, athletic way he and the horse move

together is hypnotic. Long strides, sweat flying, singularity of purpose. There's no hesitation. No concern for how they might look or whether they might stumble.

They just do the damn thing.

They do it very, very well, Cash managing to move the longhorn back toward the herd after a little showdown near the crest of a small hill.

I feel the beat of his horse's hooves in my chest as Cash thunders my way. He has a big old smile on his face.

"Yeeeee*haw*," he yells.

His joy—his confidence—spreads through the pasture like wildfire, the cowboys returning his shout with yells of their own.

My pulse thrums. This is…fun.

Really fucking fun.

Laughing, I draw a quick breath and let out a yell of my own. "Hot *dayum*."

Wyatt, who's nearby, whistles. "Dang, girl, you got a set of lungs on you, don't ya?"

Cash draws his horse to a stop a few feet away. He and the horse are both heaving, a cloud of dust billowing around them. "Were you catcalling me?"

"I was congratulating you."

Wyatt lifts a brow. "Sounded like a catcall to me."

Cash grins. "You like what you see, then, City Girl."

"You still haven't stopped with that?" Wyatt asks.

"He's about to." I click my tongue and give Maria a tap with my heels. She starts walking, head bobbing in time to her steps. I feel Cash's eyes on me, Wyatt's too, but I try not to think about that as I ride.

And ride.

And keep riding.

Wyatt told me to squeeze the horse with my legs to stay on, so that's what I do. I roll my hips, flexing my thighs so I move more easily with the horse.

Half an hour in, I feel a twinge in the small of my back. Nothing too bad, but I know I'm going to be sore tonight.

An hour in, I'm sweating bullets, and so is Maria, but I feel more confident in the saddle. I even attempt a couple of turns that take me closer to the herd.

What would Dad think if he saw me? What would he have said if he were here?

"Lookin' good," Wyatt says. "You feel all right?"

"This is a workout, but I'm okay."

Cash trots over, his shirt plastered to his chest and stomach. "Take a break if you need one. Drink lots of water. More'n you think you need."

"Who made you boss?" I say with a smirk.

"Your daddy did. You best listen."

I wag my eyebrows. "Yes, *sir*."

Wyatt eyes us. "Is this some kinda weird foreplay y'all got going on?"

"Nah." I sip water from the thermos Cash dropped into my saddlebag earlier. Bless him, he put ice in it. "Just your brother pretending to be in charge."

Cash's forearm flexes as he guides his horse closer. "That a challenge?"

"Just a fact," I clip.

Wyatt throws back his head and laughs. "She's got more Garrett in her than I gave her credit for."

I expect Cash to scowl. Say something underhanded and mean at the very least.

Instead, he just looks at me from under the brim of his hat. "Surprisin' us all, ain't she?"

My back hurts from riding. My face hurts from smiling. Having Wyatt and Cash compare me to Dad makes my chest swell.

I really, really wish I'd made more of an effort to see Dad. To get to know him.

I'm really, really proud of the fact that I inherited some of his traits.

Loving this land just might be one of them.

Loving this *life*, more like it.

My phone vibrates in my saddlebag. By the time I manage to pull it out, there's no service, so I don't get to call Mom back.

Honestly, it's a relief. I doubt she'd have nice things to say about the fact that I'm on a cattle drive with fifteen cowboys in the middle of nowhere.

Really, she wouldn't have nice things to say about the fact that I'm enjoying it.

But my heart does this funny little somersault when I wonder if she has news from her lawyers. Of course I want to go back to Dallas. I want access to my inheritance so I can make my dreams for Bellamy Brooks come true. That can't happen soon enough.

The thought of going back to my quiet condo alone, though…I don't love it. And I don't know what to think about that.

I chalk that up to the newness of all this. Of course I want to stay on the ranch right now. It's exciting and fun because it's new. And there are hot cowboys here. The shine will wear off eventually. Let's be real; that'll happen sooner rather than later. I set my alarm for three thirty this morning. I can't wake up that early forever.

I'm ravenous by the time we load up the trailers and head back to the house for lunch. I inhale one of Patsy's pulled pork sandwiches from the fridge, which I piled high with homemade slaw and the tangiest, most delicious barbecue sauce on earth. I wash it down with lemonade and one of Sally's brownies, which Cash begs me to try.

I end up having two. I'm amazed my stomach can handle all this food. It's kind of a miracle. And I figure I'm burning the calories anyway. It's nice not to deny myself for once.

It's nice to use my body in such a physical way. Although my hamstrings *sing* when I get up from the kitchen table. No wonder these cowboys are bowlegged. A few hours in the saddle, and I'm already waddling around, back screaming, feet aching.

"You need some ibuprofen." Cash joins me at the sink, taking my empty plate out of my hands. "And a rest."

I shake my head, determined to make it through a whole day of cowboying. If I'm going to take the literal and proverbial reins here, I'm going to give it my all. "I'll be fine. Where to next?"

He eyes me. "You sure? I don't want you hurtin' yourself."

"I'm sure," I say, heart doing that swelling thing again at his concern.

Who knows how much longer I'll be here?

Who knows when I'll get to be outside again? The heat is awful, sure. But looking at the negative balance in my business checking account is worse.

I like the fresh air. The sense of purpose I feel when I'm with the cowboys. One thing I'm learning about life on a ranch is that there are always people around, and I think it's keeping me from getting in my head too much.

Makes me think about how often I'm working alone back home. Am I doing this all wrong? My career? My dreams? My life?

Or am I just suffering from a bad case of grief, mixed with Cash-flavored sexual frustration?

Whatever the case, half an hour later, I'm mucking stalls in the horse barn alongside Cash and Duke. John B joins us after checking in on Happy.

The heat inside the barn is unreal.

Around two o'clock, I start to fade fast. My back is screaming. My hamstrings feel like rocks in the backs of my legs, and I'm so soaked in sweat, it's left a gritty, salty residue on my skin. But I don't want to be the weak link, so I push myself to keep going.

I can collapse into bed right after dinner. Six o'clock bedtime if I eat quickly. Six thirty at the latest.

Cash is busy—no fewer than seven people approach him with questions or problems—but I still catch him watching me from the corner of his eye. I'm nearly delirious with exhaustion, so I could be imagining it. But I think I see a glimmer of admiration in those baby blues.

I may have been born into enormous privilege, but I want to show him that I still work my ass off. Come hell or high water, I'm going to be the last man—woman—standing.

Dad was that guy, even after he made piles of money.

Now I'm going to be that girl.

But man, does this work hurt. Badly. I took the

ibuprofen Cash suggested, but I think I'm beyond help at this point.

A whimper escapes my lips as I straighten after helping Cash give Happy her afternoon bottle, a sharp pain slicing through my lower back.

His expression darkens. "You're hurting, aren't you?"

"No." I put my hand on my back, biting back a wince.

I'm glad John B and Duke aren't here to witness this. They're out in the corral, tending to some horses that need medical attention.

"Time to call it a day, Mollie."

I shake my head. I'll be damned if I disappoint Dad. What would he think of his daughter, the one who can't make it through a single day on the ranch he loved with all his heart?

My throat closes in. "I'm good."

"Are you crying?"

Shit, I am crying. The exhaustion, the pain, the wonderfulness of this day—it's finally getting the better of me.

I won't let it.

I can't fall apart now.

I press the back of my wrist to my eyes and blink, hard. "I'm not crying. There's no crying in cowboying."

"Cute *League of Their Own* reference," Cash says, even as his nostrils flare. "But cowboys do cry, Mollie."

"Tom Hanks was so good in that movie."

"Madonna was better."

My heart dips. Of course he'd say that. Goddamn it, this man is *relentless* today.

Makes me cry harder. I'm overwhelmed.

I'm so sore, it hurts to breathe.

"I love Madonna." I wipe my nose on my sleeve.

"Of course you do." He ducks his head to look me in the eye. Lowers his voice when he says, "You crushed it today, Mollie. No shame in calling it quits. I'll be doing the same in an hour. Less."

My heart full on plummets. "You really think I did okay?"

"I really do. Go home, Mollie."

"But you need help."

"You need to rest."

"You sure?"

"I'm sure. Let me drive you back to the house in the ATV."

I shake my head. "Don't be ridiculous. I can walk."

"You're a stubborn motherfucker, aren't you?"

I can't tell if his words are a dig or a compliment.

I shuffle toward the stall's door. "So are you!"

"I'll walk you home, then."

"Stop." I wave him away. "See you in the morning."

But when I reach for the latch on the door, a muscle in the middle of my back cramps. I cry out, heat flooding my face as my knees buckle. How embarrassing to go down like a sack of potatoes like this.

There's a shout behind me. "Mollie! Jesus fuck."

Then I'm scooped into huge, hard arms, Cash literally sweeping me off my feet as he cradles me against him.

I look up at him, and my pulse seizes. His eyes are dark. Hard and soft and hot, all at once.

Oh God. Now I really can't breathe.

"Cash—"

202

"Enough," he snaps. "You're coming with me. Put your arms around my neck. Don't make me ask twice, or so help me God, I'll get really angry."

His steady, rock-hard tone brooks no argument. It also draws my nipples to tight, aching points.

Go figure. My body is broken, but Cash Rivers can still turn me on like nobody's business.

Help, I say to the universe.

"Okay," I say to Cash and loop my arms around his neck.

I've never been carried damsel-in-distress style before, and I have to say, I don't hate it. Cash is barely out of breath as he brings me outside and sets me gingerly in the passenger seat of the nearest ATV.

I startle when he grabs my seat belt and buckles me in, his hand brushing the side of my breast.

"Sorry," he grunts.

I'm not. "I can do that myself."

"Don't move."

"Okay, okay."

I'm confused when Cash hangs a left when we should be making a right to go back to my house. "Where are we going?"

A muscle in his jaw ticks. "My place."

"If you're planning to have your way with me—"

"The supplies we need are there."

"See? Kinky."

He cuts me a look. "Mollie."

"Cash."

"Stop."

"What supplies are you talking about?"

"You'll see."

My chest contracts when we pull up in front of a small log cabin ten minutes later. It looks old, the chinks between the weathered logs thick and uneven, but it appears to have been recently—lovingly—restored. It's got a sloping tin roof and a wide front porch, stone chimneys standing proudly on either side of the structure. The windows have hand-blown panes that waver in the late afternoon sun. There's not a smudge or speck of dirt in sight.

It's romantic and pretty and so very *him*.

"Cash," I breathe. "This is yours?"

He dips his head. "Was the original log cabin your great-granddaddy built when he claimed this land. It was abandoned after the farmhouse was built in the twenties. Total wreck when Garrett took over, but he wanted to restore it."

"Let me guess." My heart drums an uneven beat inside my chest. "You helped."

"I did. When he offered it to me as the new foreman's cabin—hell, that was one of the best days of my life." Cash climbs out of the ATV. "Probably because I got to move out of the bunkhouse."

I unbuckle myself, but Cash doesn't even let me try to stand. Instead, he bends down and reaches for me, pulling me into his arms.

This time, I don't protest. I just wrap my arms around his neck and allow myself to revel in the luxury of being carried around by a scruffy, foul-mouthed cowboy.

Maybe there really is a heaven, and this is it.

He carries me up the stairs and through the front door. I'm just able to glimpse how clean and neat the interior is before Cash is setting me down inside an absolutely gorgeous bathroom.

It's rustic; the floor, ceiling, and walls are covered in wood, but the fixtures are all modern. There's a glass-walled shower, a marble-topped vanity, and a huge, freestanding copper tub that gleams in the low light.

"My one request," Cash says as he digs a couple of bags out of a cabinet underneath the sink. "The tub. Nothing helps sore muscles like a long, hot soak."

Scoffing, I look away, my eyes burning. I don't know why the fact that Cash loves a soak makes me want to cry. Maybe because Dad probably took a lot of pride in restoring this house exactly how Cash wanted it? In being there for this poor guy who lost his parents, dropped out of school, and raised his brothers on his own?

Maybe Dad wasn't a bad person. Maybe I'm not either. Maybe we were both just hurt people, and we did the best we could with what we had.

Just because we weren't good to each other doesn't mean we haven't been good to the people who are in our lives.

Cash turns on the tap that fills the bathtub. Glancing at the bags he set on the counter, I see that they're Epsom salts.

Holy God. This cowboy is drawing me a bath. *With Epsom salts.* Because I'm sore and sad and he's apparently a thoughtful, stand-up guy.

Would he climb in with me if I asked him?

I clear my throat. "So the supplies you were talking about—"

"The salt. And the privacy. Wasn't sure if you had them at the New House."

"I don't think I do."

After pouring several cups of salt into the water, he

straightens, drawing to his full height. The cabin has low ceilings, and Cash looks *huge* in here. And broad. And sweaty.

"Soak for at least twenty minutes." He points at the water. "An hour is better, though, so take your time." He turns, opening a cabinet beside the shower to grab a pair of towels. "I'll set these on the counter here. Anything else you need?"

I blink, speechless. The herbal, almost minty scent of eucalyptus blooms inside the room, making my heart skip a beat.

That's what I'm always smelling on Cash's skin. He must bathe often in this stuff.

Taking his hat off his head, he spears a hand through his hair. "What?"

"Who the fuck are you?"

His lips twitch. "Your foreman. Now get in the tub."

Then he walks past me and closes the door.

CHAPTER 18
Stuck
Cash

What's that thing British people say? "Keep calm and carry on?"

I try my best to do exactly that as I head for the kitchen. Steady, even steps.

Steady, even heartbeat.

Only it's not steady. It sure as hell ain't even. My pulse pounds through my body like a shock wave, every beat a reminder that Mollie Luck is getting naked in my bathroom right now.

I pour myself a glass of water and down it. Sweat rolls down my neck and back. I startle when I hear a *thump*.

"Sorry!" Mollie calls. "Just my boots."

Glancing at the bottle of añejo tequila beside the fridge, I wonder if I should take a shot. Or three. It's almost four o'clock. Close enough to five, right?

It's wrong to think about what Mollie looks like, taking off her clothes. Totally wrong to imagine her shimmying out of her jeans, the denim falling to the floor along with her panties.

She was just crying in the barn, for fuck's sake. Poor thing is a mess. I need to make sure she's okay.

I don't need to fantasize about grabbing that tequila and opening the bathroom door and—

No. Nope. Can't—won't—go there.

So I chug my water, and I wait for the tight feeling in my skin to dissipate.

Mollie worked hard today. Too hard. I shouldn't have let her come out to the barn after lunch. But I did, and I feel terrible about not noticing sooner how much she was hurting.

It's why I brought her here. Sure, I could've dropped her off at the New House. Mollie's a grown woman. She can take care of herself.

What if I want to take care of her, though?

Even seasoned ranch hands like me get sore on occasion. Never fun. Mollie is *really* sore, and I know it's going to take more than a couple Advil to make her feel better.

Was I wrong to run her a bath? Part of me feels like I'm crossing a boundary. An *intimate* boundary. Normal people don't invite their bosses into their homes for a soak.

Then again, my relationship with Mollie is anything but normal. How can I be normal around the girl I love to hate?

Thing is I don't hate her anymore. I...don't know how I feel, but I do know I'm not about to leave this girl crying alone in a bathtub.

I could go. I probably should go. Still stuff to do at

the horse barn. Have a couple of calls to return that I missed throughout the day.

But my feet don't move. Instead, I hang my hat on the hook by the door and grab my phone—having Wi-Fi at the cabin means I don't have to use my walkie-talkie—and call Duke, who I know will be at the New House right now, grabbing a snack.

"I'm on it," he says when I give him instructions. "Sawyer and Ella stopped by, so I'll get their help."

"Give that baby a kiss for me. I'll see y'all at dinner."

"You all right?" Duke pauses. "I saw you leaving with Mollie."

"I literally had to carry her out of the barn to stop her from working. Her body's wrecked."

Duke chuckles. "Something tells me you didn't mind carrying her one bit."

"Shut up."

"She okay?"

"I'm handling it."

"I bet you are."

"I'm hanging up now."

"Y'all would make a cute couple."

"Goodbye, Duke."

"Go easy on her, would you? We like Mollie. She's got questionable taste in men—"

"Why? Because she ain't into you?"

My brother chuckles. "Because she's into *you.*"

"Shut up," I repeat, even as my heart skips a beat. "She's not into me. We're just...we work together."

This time, Duke flat out laughs. "Your voice sounded funny when you said you had to stop her from working."

"I wasn't expecting her to bust her ass like that is all."

"Garrett's daughter? Really? The one who's been up at four a.m. almost every damn day she's been here?"

I groan. "She's not who I thought she was."

"Aw, yeah. The plot thickens."

"There is no plot. I'll have you shoveling shit all day tomorrow if you don't quit your talking."

"You're the one who hasn't hung up."

"I'm hanging up!"

"You have condoms at the cabin, right?"

"Fuck off." I glance down the hall at the bathroom door. *Shit, do I have condoms?*

It doesn't matter if I do, because I'm not going to fuck Mollie. Even if my dick does perk *right* up at the idea.

"Safety first," Duke singsongs. "Y'all get to it. We got it handled here."

"Don't forget to check the front irrigation system."

"Don't forget to have fun. Judging by the way y'all were dancing—"

My thumb trembles as I hit the red button on my screen, ending the call. Tossing the phone on the counter, I let out a breath. Remind myself that my job is to make everyone on the ranch feel safe, Mollie included.

The clock above the sink ticks. I'm not sure I've ever been home this early. My end-of-day routine usually consists of me taking a cold shower and trying to stay awake past six o'clock.

I can't shower with Mollie in the bathroom. And I'm way too keyed up to rest.

I hear her turn off the water. There's a small splash, probably her climbing into the tub.

Naked.

The words inside my head ram together in a panicked collision. *This was a bad idea. What was I thinking? What do her tits look like wet? You are a pervert. She needs comfort, not an orgasm.*

But don't orgasms make you feel better?

I shove the thought from my head. Girl's hurt. Last thing she needs is an orgasm. Unless I gave it to her gently...

I could be gentle.

I'm opening the refrigerator and diving for a beer before I know what's happening. I may need some of that tequila too, depending on how well I can control my thoughts.

Sitting down at the tiny kitchen table, I start answering emails on my phone, knee bouncing all the while. The beer cools me down, but it doesn't do jack shit for the inconvenient thoughts that loop through my head.

Sniff.

I look up from the text I'm typing out to a local mechanic. Did I just hear something? The cabin is quiet.

Sniff, sob, sniff.

My pulse stutters, chest clenching. "Mollie?"

A beat.

Then, "You're still here?" Her voice sounds thick. She's definitely crying.

I'm out of my chair and at the door in two seconds flat, beer still in hand. "Of course I'm still here. Are you all right?"

"You didn't have to stay."

"I wanted to stay. Are you okay?"

Another beat.

"No." *Sob.* "Really, I can find my way back to the house if you need to—"

"I'm not going anywhere. What's wrong?" I put my other hand on the knob. "Answer me."

I hear her sigh. "I know this sounds stupid, because I didn't see Dad much. But I miss him."

My heart crumples. Leaning my forehead against the door, a moon rises in my throat. "Not stupid. He was your dad. I miss him too. So fucking much, I...can't even tell you."

"Being back here—working with y'all—I just—I missed out on so much. If I had known what life was really like here...I mean, I would've *loved* to be out working on the ranch with Dad. I think I'm starting to understand..."

I suck in a breath. "What?"

"Why he never wanted to leave."

She sounds so sad that for a second, my grip tightens on the doorknob. Do I go in there? Comfort her?

I can comfort her from here, best as I can.

"I know you have regrets, Mollie. But seeing you today—" I swallow. "You're doing the right thing."

She scoffs, the sound echoing inside the bathroom. "Maybe. But whether it's right or wrong, I'm too late."

"It's never too late to start over. Take the lessons you learned, and try to do better with the people who are still around." I let go of the doorknob. A wave of grief moves through me, filling my legs with a familiar heaviness. "What else can you do?"

"Not be an asshole, for starters."

I grin, despite the sting in my eyes. "I'm working on it."

"I'm talking about me. I was an asshole to my dad. I mean, you were an asshole to me, don't get me wrong—"

"Past tense."

"What?"

"You said I *was* an asshole. That mean you think I'm not anymore?"

A pause.

Somehow, I know she's grinning too when she replies, "You're growing on me."

There's a flutter in my stomach.

A stupid, inconvenient fucking flutter that simultaneously brings a smile to my face and brings my grief that much closer to the surface.

"You can cry too, you know," Mollie says, reading my mind. "I can't even see you, so it'll be like it never happened."

I wipe away a tear. "I'm fine with crying."

"But you're just too busy to do it."

I chuckle. "Something like that."

Everything about this is weird. Us having a conversation through a door while Mollie's naked in my bathtub. Mollie being here at all.

The weirdest part? I feel strangely *safe* in this moment. Maybe it's the privacy the door affords us, or maybe it's because I'm just too damn tired to keep my guard up and my feelings buried. Whatever the reason, I'm not scared to bare my heart.

Warning bells go off inside my head. I'm not like this. I don't do this.

But here I am, doing it.

Here I am, turning around and sinking to the floor, my back to the door. Sipping my beer, I try to breathe despite the elephant sitting on my chest.

"You still there?" Mollie asks.

"I'm still here."

"Tell me about your parents."

"What about them?" I push my ragged thumbnail underneath the damp label on my beer bottle.

"I don't know. How did they make you *you*?"

I laugh, even as I wipe my eyes on my sleeve. "You mean how'd they raise me to be so damn excellent?"

"Ha."

Thinking about it, I land on a specific memory. "My parents were always around. They worked nonstop—as you're seein', that's just life on a ranch—but they made sure we tagged along. Even if it meant adding a shit ton of aggravation to their day. I remember this one day, I was throwing a tantrum over God knows what. I was five, maybe six? My mom was pregnant with the twins, and she'd had it with me. So Dad scooped me up and put me in the saddle with him for the day." I smile. "I was about as sore as you are after that. But I loved every fucking minute of it."

I can hear the smile in Mollie's voice when she replies, "I loved it too. That feeling of working together, being a part of something."

"Exactly." *Exactly*. "That's one of the things Mom and Dad were best at. Giving us a real sense of belonging. Of purpose. Our family was—is—tight. Had no other option, really. We either helped each other out or it all fell apart."

Mollie sighs. "Having each other's backs that way sounds nice."

"You're really close with your mom."

"I mean, yeah." A pause. "But it's not like the bond you have with your brothers. Being an only child has its perks, but, well…I'll say it this way: I want more than one kid if I'm lucky enough to have a family of my own."

My heart leaps. I drain my beer. "You want kids?"

"I do. Being on the ranch is showing me that I really love having people around. My life in Dallas feels pretty damn small in comparison." She scoffs. "Do you? Want kids?"

Loaded question. I consider not answering. Changing the topic.

But that feels bullshitty and wrong right now. And yeah, maybe I want to get Mollie's thoughts on my predicament.

Maybe I want her to play devil's advocate. Why? I don't know. But I like the way her mind works.

"I do. Not sure I'll ever have 'em, though. In some ways, I've already got four sons. Plus a daughter."

"Ah. I get that. You've been the man of the house for a while now."

"Yep."

Another pause.

"You do know your brothers are grown now, right? Sure, they say and do stupid things sometimes. But who in their twenties doesn't? They seem to be perfectly capable of holding their own. Wyatt gets shit done. And look at Sawyer. He's a great dad."

"A *single* dad. He's a good example of why I haven't started my own family. Don't have the bandwidth. He needs help."

"Lucky for him, there's plenty of people willing to give it. Many hands make light work. Having that many hands also means you can take a break when you need it, because others will be there to pick up the slack."

She has a point. I've left everyone to their own devices this afternoon, and there hasn't been an issue. Far as I can tell anyway. No explosions, no panicked requests for help on the walkie-talkie or phone.

Go figure. My brothers are doing just fine without me.

And I'm doing just fine without them.

"It'd be a shame, you know," Mollie continues, "if you didn't have a family. Sounds like you got a world-class education in making one. A happy one. A whole one."

My heart twists at the sadness in her voice. Here I thought this girl had everything. Her parents were divorced, yeah, but they were both alive until recently. She's got money, an education. Her own company.

She doesn't have anyone to take care of other than herself.

Family is great, but it's also a burden.

"I'm jealous of you," I say. "Your freedom."

She scoffs again, this one louder, harsher. "I'm jealous of you. Your support system. Your sense of conviction. You know who you are. You're chasing the right things. You love the right things."

"You don't?"

"Honestly?" I hear her let out a breath. "I'm not sure. All I do know..." Her voice trails off.

"What?" I ask softly.

"I wish I had what you do. The chaos is real, sure, but so is the joy."

I chuckle. "Take some for yourself, then. You're welcome to it."

"You mean that?" Her voice is soft now too.

"I mean that, Mollie."

Scary part is I really *do* mean it. She's welcome to stay. Welcome to take whatever she wants. She's lonely, and I know how awful loneliness is.

Right now, though, I don't feel lonely at all.

I like the idea that she doesn't either.

"Tell me about your mom," I say, clearing my throat.

"Oh, my mother. I admire her for raising me on her own while building a hugely successful real estate brokerage empire. There's not a person in Dallas she doesn't know. She's got tons of friends, she plays golf, she gambles. True Renaissance woman."

"She and Wyatt would get along."

"She'd take Wyatt for a ride. I'm serious. She wins every round of poker she plays."

"I like her already."

"I love her. Dearly. But being the only child of divorced parents—I don't think she meant to do this, but she kinda put me in the middle of her and Dad."

"How so?"

"She wasn't shy about sharing her less than stellar opinions of him with me. And it was from a young age too. I clearly remember her calling my dad a dickweed for the first time."

I chuckle. "Dickweed?"

"She gets an A-plus for curse-word creativity. But I was ten at that point, so—"

"Not cool. Explains why you'd cut off contact with him. You only had your mom's side of the story. She was the one raising you."

"Right. I could see how stressed out she was, trying to juggle being a parent with everything else. She did it

217

on her own, and that's not fucking easy."

"Sawyer will always say he's never worked harder in his life than he has as a single parent."

"So yeah, I sympathized with Mom. I trusted her judgment, so I knew there had to be a good reason why she felt the way she did about Dad. She thought he was an asshole, so I thought he was an asshole too. And some of the things he did really were shitty. As I've gotten older, though—now that I'm here—"

"You're seeing the other side of the story."

"Exactly." Her voice gets thick again. "I'm seeing *your* story. And it's making me really rethink things."

I let my head fall back against the door and look at the ceiling beams that run the length of the hall.

My chest feels full. So full, it aches.

But the feeling is somehow light too; the elephant on my sternum disappeared somewhere around the time Mollie asked me about my parents.

Why does Mollie have to be so fucking sweet? So open-minded? So quick, so intelligent, so open and honest and *real*?

Can't remember the last time someone asked me about my past.

Can't remember the last time I wanted to ask about someone else's.

The hardwood floor bites into my sit bones. Don't care. I could talk to Mollie like this forever.

"See?" I sit up a little straighter. "You're doing the right thing, deciding for yourself how you feel about Garrett. He'd be proud. It was one of the things I loved most about him—how unafraid he was to do his own thing, even if it didn't make sense to anyone else."

"Only had to make sense to him," Mollie replies slowly. "There's a certain kind of integrity in that. I'm taking notes."

"Of course you are," I sputter.

"What's that supposed to mean?"

Means I like you. More than I should.

"Nothing." I spear a hand through my hair. I need another beer.

The quiet sound of moving water fills the silence. I'm seized by the image of Mollie sinking deeper into my tub. She's relaxed, hair in a knot at the top of her head. Her tits are round and perfect, pink nipples breaking the surface of the water. Cheeks and chest flushed the same shade of pink. And her pussy—with her legs spread, it'd be spread too—

"Hey, Cash?"

I clear my throat for the hundredth time. "Yeah?"

"The water is getting cold. I think I'm ready to get out. Could I ask a favor, though? My clothes are disgusting. Any chance I could borrow something? Just to wear back to the house? I'll wash it and give it back to you as soon as I'm done."

Dear. *God.*

Jesus, Lord and savior, why you gotta test me like this? Mollie, in my shirt? What if she doesn't wear a bra under it?

What if she doesn't wear panties? What I'd give to slide a hand up her bare leg. I'd use my fingers to part her. Stroke her, gathering wetness on my fingertip so I could circle her clit. Mollie, being Mollie, wouldn't be shy about showing her pleasure. She'd moan, hand fisting in my shirt to pull me closer.

"Don't fuck with me, Cash," she'd breathe. *"Give me more."*

I shove up to standing, willing the image to disappear. "Course. Gimme a minute."

"Take your time."

Only the image doesn't disappear.

The longer it stays, the more I'm not sure I want it to go anywhere. Same way I feel about Mollie.

CHAPTER 19
Backsliding
Mollie

Cash is weirdly quiet on the drive home.

And I am weirdly turned on wearing his green Hatton's Tractor Supply & More T-shirt and a pair of red basketball shorts.

They're old clothes. Soft and nubby from countless days in the sun, countless cycles through the washing machine. But wearing them still gives me a sense of intimacy with Cash that's at odds with our budding friendship.

Can I even call it that? We're coworkers, technically. But after everything we just shared—after he scooped me up, carried me to his house, and ran me a bath, complete with an absurd amount of Epsom salts in it—I'm not sure where we stand.

More than coworkers, less than friends?

More than friends, less than...what?

Is he weirded out by the intense conversation we had through his bathroom door? Even now, my stomach flips at the thought that he *stayed*. Not only that, but he sat outside the door and made sure I was okay.

I cried, and I think he cried too, and I'm so overwhelmed that he opened up to me that my heart won't quit pinging around my chest like a pinball.

Glancing at him, I take in his handsome profile. He ditched his cowboy hat and is wearing the backward baseball cap again. His scruff is darker and thicker than it was this morning.

A wave of desire hits me, hard, landing in the backs of my knees with this hot, tingly rush that makes me want to giggle and scream all at once. I hold the handle on the ATV's frame in a death grip.

My heart takes a nosedive when the New House comes into view. I'm not ready for whatever this is to end.

Guess there's no use fighting these feelings anymore. They're clearly here to stay. I just can't act on them.

I unbuckle my seat belt when Cash parks at the back door. "Thanks for the therapy session. And the tub."

"Feel any better?"

"I do, yeah."

Our eyes meet. The air between us vibrates.

Kiss me, you stupid bastard.

I want him to kiss me more than I've wanted something in a long, long time.

Scratch that. I wanted him to join me in the tub even more. I kept thinking about how hot it would be, literally and figuratively, if Cash slipped in behind me. Cradled me between those big thighs and then reached between mine.

"Well…" His Adam's apple bobs.

222

I lick my lips, laughing nervously. "I'll get these clothes back to you."

"Keep 'em." His eyes flick over me, one side of his mouth tipping up. "They look good on you."

"Fishing for compliments now?" I grin. "Waiting for me to say they look better on you?"

He splays the hand he's got on top of the wheel. "Well, yeah."

You're hot as fuck, and you know it. I don't need to tell you that.

"Keep dreaming, cowboy."

He laughs. "Get some rest. And keep taking that Advil."

"Yes, *sir*."

His eyes flash. "I like it when you call me sir."

Must.

Get.

Inside.

Immediately. Or I'll combust. Or do something really stupid and lean in and kiss him myself.

"Don't get used to it." I sniff, and then I make a mad dash for the house.

———

The next morning, I wake up sore but not as sore as I thought I'd be. I worried I'd be pretty close to dead when my alarm went off at three thirty, even though Cash told me to take the day off. I don't bound out of bed, but I'm able to walk to the bathroom without wanting to die.

My pulse leaps. Good. That means I get to do my cowgirl thing again today. Which means I get to see

Cash. And all the other cowboys. Because I like cowboys in general, not *one* cowboy specifically.

At least that's what I tell myself as I brush my teeth and braid my hair.

But I'd be lying if I said I wasn't downright giddy as I open my bedroom door at five till four. Will Cash want another omelet?

Will he do that obscenely sexy thing where he opens another bottle of hot sauce for me?

I draw up short when I see several shopping bags on the floor in the hall outside my door. Leaning down to open one, I see that they're filled with bags of Epsom salts.

Eucalyptus scented.

There's no note, but I don't need one.

Barely able to breathe, I grab a bag and scurry to the kitchen. Cash is at the coffeepot, pouring coffee into a pair of mugs. He tops each one off with milk and sugar and then lifts them, turning.

He grins when he sees me.

"What's this?" I hold up the Epsom salts.

Cash casually sips his coffee, like he didn't just perform a gesture that's not exactly grand but not exactly small either. Because I'm not sure I've ever received such a thoughtful gift. Sure, I've gotten elaborate gifts. Ridiculous ones. But gifts that are thoughtful and sweet, given out of kindness, not obligation?

Never.

"You need to be in that tub every night, Mollie."

"Your tub?"

His grin twitches. "If you want."

"I don't know what to say."

224

"*Thank you* is a good start."

I only set down the bag when Cash holds out a mug of coffee to me. "Thank you. I really mean that." Crossing the kitchen, I take the mug. "And thank you for this too."

Am I imagining it, or did Cash intentionally brush his fingers against mine? Electricity zips up my arm, awareness blooming inside my skin.

"The salt makes a difference, doesn't it?" Cash's eyes are locked on mine. "You seem to be moving around pretty well this morning."

He noticed how I'm moving?

Why does that make me blush? And smile? And want to tackle him?

Where the hell is Patsy? Oh right. She has weekends off.

"You were right," I manage. "It helps."

"Bet it kills you to say those words."

I hold up my fingers, pinching them together. "Only a little."

He watches me sip my coffee. I watch him sip his. Fire streaks through me at the satisfied rumble that sounds inside his chest.

"Do you work every weekend?" I ask.

He shakes his head. "I actually have them off, but I work anyway."

"Of course you do."

His lips twitch as his eyes lock on mine over the rim of his coffee mug. "Don't know what I love more. My morning coffee or my afternoon beer."

"Depends on who you're having it with, I think."

His hair is still wet from the shower. The smell of his soap is intoxicating.

I am *this close* to jumping the man's bones.

Especially when he says, "Then I think I like my coffee more."

Don't flirt back.

Do. Not. Flirt.

"Or your evening Shiner Bocks at the Rattler," I say.

That rumble of laughter. That smile. That happy, playful gleam in his blue eyes. "I like that too."

Oh Lord, am I falling for this guy?

That would be a disaster—a risk I can't take. Especially now that I'm getting involved in the ranch's day-to-day operations.

Especially now that I'm starting to like the place.

I've learned Lucky Ranch is what it is because of Cash. I lose him, there's a very good chance I lose my family's legacy. I want to do Dad proud.

Which means I absolutely cannot do Cash.

Even if he is kind. Thoughtful. And so hot it hurts sometimes.

Maybe I just need to get laid. Surely, this is just sexual frustration rearing its ugly head? I bet some good sex with someone other than Cash will cure me of any inconvenient attraction I may feel for my foreman.

But who the hell do I sleep with in Hartsville? I can't pick up any of the other cowboys or ranch hands. I don't have the time—or the energy—to hang at the Rattler by myself and meet people there. Could I possibly shoot back to Dallas next weekend? Then again, Goody and I haven't discussed my ability to come and go from the ranch like that.

The answer comes the next morning, on Monday.

Or really, later that night. Guess Palmer was having

Sunday Funday and stayed out late, because he sent a text at 11:45 p.m.: *U up?*

My pulse thuds. I could ignore him. I probably should.

But I need to do *something* to keep my feelings for Cash in check. Otherwise, I think I'll go lose my mind—or worse, give in to those feelings.

I move my thumbs over the screen before I can think better of it. *How far are you willing to drive for a hookup?*

He replies a few hours later. *You're on that ranch, aren't you? The one you inherited.*

Three hours from Dallas, I text back.

Palmer: *I think I can swing that.*
Mollie: *Next weekend?*
Palmer: *I'm in.*

It works out perfectly. Well, kind of. I don't want to make Cash jealous or anything. But chances are Palmer and I won't even leave my bedroom. Cash doesn't have to know he's here. No one has to know, really. I can always say I'm tied up with boot business.

I'm being stupid. I know I am. But I don't know what else to do.

I didn't come to Hartsville for a roll in the literal and proverbial hay with the man who runs my dad's ranch.

I definitely didn't come here to fall in love.

I came to get my money and keep Bellamy Brooks in business. Learning how to cowgirl from cute cowboys is just an added bonus.

Nothing more, nothing less.

———

"I have a bone to pick with you."

Mom scoffs. "Oh? Do tell."

I tuck my wet hair behind my ears. I just got out of the shower after spending the entire day outside on the ranch. It was a good day.

A really good day. Mostly because I kept catching Cash looking at me, which made me feel hot and bothered and wonderful.

More than that, he looked *out* for me. When I started to sag in the saddle, he reminded me to drink some water. When Wyatt asked if I wanted to help muck stalls, Cash swiftly intervened and took me inside with him to the ranch office. We answered emails pertaining to the upcoming winter calving, and he explained in detail how the whole thing worked.

Even now, my heart flutters at how patient he was with me. The way he took his time made me feel like he actually enjoyed us being together.

I sure as hell did.

But now I have to have a super awkward conversation with my mother, which I've been putting off for as long as I can.

"Dad's funeral," I say carefully. "You told me you invited all his friends and family."

A telling pause.

"You're judging me for not inviting some random ranch hands to your father's funeral, aren't you?"

"These people aren't random, Mom." My heart is a furnace inside my chest. "They're his family. Maybe they're not related by blood, but he loved them, and it was wrong not to give them a chance to say goodbye."

"Sweetheart, I don't know those people from Adam. I wouldn't even know where to begin with the invitations. The church was small, and your father wouldn't have wanted a big to-do anyway."

I bite my tongue to keep myself from saying something I'll regret. "You could've begun by talking to the people Dad worked with every day for decades. I imagine Goody reached out to you. She would've told you who he was close with."

Mom clears her throat. "What's done is done. I'm sorry you're upset—"

"I am upset. I'm also embarrassed. This makes us look mean and coldhearted. Everyone here is grieving. They're good people, Mom. They deserve better."

Another pause.

"I'm sorry."

My heart clenches at the sadness in Mom's voice. I cover my face with my hand.

"We need to do better, Mom. I'm trying. You need to try too."

Mom's swallow is audible through the phone. "I'll do my best. So things are okay there?"

"Things are good. Mostly because the people are wonderful."

"Oh." Mom's never one to be caught speechless, so I know I must be getting through to her. "I'm relieved to hear they're treating you well. I miss you, sweetheart. So damn much."

My turn to swallow hard. Unless Mom is traveling or super busy, she and I talk on a regular basis multiple times a week.

"I miss you too. But I'm starting to think…" My eyes

burn. I squeeze them shut. "I like it here. A lot. I know you didn't, and I understand why. But I can't let that keep me from giving Lucky Ranch a chance."

"Oh. Well, okay. Just as long as you come back to Dallas."

I'd roll my eyes if they didn't hurt so much. "I should go. Supper will be ready in a few minutes."

"Be careful with the food. I don't want your stomach becoming more of an issue."

"My stomach has actually felt so much better since I've been here."

"Really?"

I laugh, the sound hollow. "Don't sound so surprised."

"I'm happy for you. Wonder what it is that agrees with you."

Fresh air? Less stress? Hot cowboys?

All of the above?

"I'm not sure what it is, but I want more of it."

Awkward silence.

"Remember, you said you'd do your best," I say at last.

"I will. And remember, you're coming home. Good night, sweetheart."

"Bye, Mom."

———

I cowgirl most of the week.

The weather is cooling off ever so slightly now that we're approaching October. One morning is even close to crisp. I can't get enough of it. The sun, the action, the way the cowboys rib each other while tossing lassos and caring for injured cows.

Maria and I finally bond. I'm more confident in the saddle with each passing day.

We're so in tune, I even eat like a horse, devouring Patsy's excellent cooking. One night, she makes these melt-in-your-mouth ribs, slathered in sweet, tangy barbecue sauce that's so good, I practically finish a rack of ribs myself. I can't get enough of the cheesy grits she makes one morning or the homemade chicken salad she pairs with croissants she bakes from scratch for lunch.

My stomach hasn't hurt in...wow, a week now. Makes me think my problem isn't food or any kind of allergy. It's something else entirely. *Can* fresh air cure stomach pain? Was there something in the water in Dallas that was killing me?

Or do I just like life on a ranch more than life in the city?

I try not to dwell too much on that last question, because the implications are...alarming, to say the least. I'm not staying on Lucky Ranch. Not for the long haul anyway.

But I do love how wrung out my body feels at the end of each day. I dutifully take my Epsom salt baths and then fall into bed.

I've never slept so well in my life.

I've also been struggling to juggle my responsibilities. I'll squeeze in some Bellamy Brooks stuff after supper in the evenings, but needless to say, I don't last long before I'm nodding off.

By the time Friday rolls around, I've missed so many calls and have so many emails and invoices to catch up on, I decide to take the whole day off from doing my cowgirl thing to do my cowboy-boot-designer thing instead. Palmer is arriving this afternoon too, and I want to take a long shower so I can shave everything and wash my hair.

Cash blinks when I inform him at breakfast that I won't be joining him and the other cowboys today. "Oh."

My heart somersaults. "If y'all need me——"

"Do your thing. We got it handled."

"You sure?"

He sips his coffee. "I'm sure."

"You're gonna miss me, aren't you?"

"Maria will. She likes you."

I smile, even as my heart does another flip. Why do I get the feeling Cash is disappointed? Does he actually want me out there with him?

Is he actually going to miss me?

"Enough with the guilt trip," I say.

His eyes glitter. "Passive-aggressive ain't my style, Mollie. But you're the one who's gotta share the news with your horse. She cries, that's on you."

"She's Dad's horse." I shove Cash's shoulder. "And horses don't actually cry, do they?"

He shrugs. "You're about to find out, aren't you?"

I don't want to laugh, but I do.

I don't want to think about Cash and Maria and the other cowboys as I clear out my inbox later that morning in the soaring, silent office at the front of the New House, but I do.

Wheeler picks right up when I call her. "Hey, hey."

"Good morning," I singsong. "How's it going?"

"Don't you sound chipper! Please tell me it's because you got railed by a cowboy with a rock-hard——"

232

"Only railing I've dealt with this week was the kind that makes a fence."

Wheeler chuckles. "Look at you, doing authentic ranch shit! I'm proud of you. But I'd be prouder if you did the other kind of railing too."

Trust me, I've thought about it. A lot.

"So my stipend's about to hit our account."

"You're not very smooth at changing the subject. Wait, wait. You didn't get railed, but you're getting close. Oh my God!" She's squealing now. "Yay for you! There's a reason they say cowboys do it better and faster and harder and all the things."

"Actually, I invited Palmer to the ranch."

Dead silence.

Then, "You're telling me you're surrounded by hot cowboys, but you're going to have sex with Gordon Gekko instead?"

"Oh stop. Just because Palmer's not your cup of tea—"

"He's fine, Mollie. But that's all he is. Fine. And not in the sexy sense of the word either."

Wheeler's hung out with Palmer and me a few times, usually at the tail end of a night out when Palmer or I send each other the proverbial *U up?* text. If he's close by, he'll usually meet me at whatever bar I'm at, and then we'll head to my place or to his.

"He gets the job done," I say diplomatically.

"That's a job someone else can do better. How's Cash?"

Clicking on an email, I roll my eyes. "He's fine. So once we have the money, let's firm up our completion dates with—"

"You're cute."

"What? C'mon, Wheeler, focus. I have a lot to catch up on."

"I know you have a crush on him."

I scan the email. "Crush or not, it's never happening. We work together."

"Perfect. You can get busy in the barn, and no one will blink an eye."

"Real-life barns aren't nearly as picturesque as *Yellowstone* makes them look."

"Who cares? It'd be so hot. He could use, like, the reins from a horse to tie you up, and then he could bend you over a saddle—"

"Wheeler."

"Sorry, sorry," she says, laughing. "I'm just having too much fun living out my cowboy fantasies through you. The money is coming, Mollie. Thank you for that. I'm not saying it isn't a huge deal, because it is. But we're going to be fine. No, we're going to be better than that. Bellamy Brooks is going to crush it. Which means you're free to…have fun with reins and saddles."

I roll my eyes again, even as my heart skips a beat. "I still have to finalize the stitching design on the Brittney boot. And I love the pebbled leather we chose for the Keira boot, but I'm not sure if I *love* love it. Then there's all those invoices that are past due…"

"They'll get paid on Thursday, when the money hits. We got this. *I* got this."

"You shouldn't have to deal with all this on your own. That's not fair."

"Who knows? Maybe I'll have my own cowboy romance keeping me busy one day, and you can cover for me then. In the meantime, take me up on my offer to do the bulk of the work you're talking about and go enjoy your time on your dad's ranch. Sounds like the place is surprising you in all the best ways."

My heart's skipped several beats at this point. Lucky Ranch *is* surprising me. I *am* being kept busy and by a kind of romance too. Maybe I don't only have a crush on Cash. Maybe I'm crushing on Hartsville too, and Patsy and Happy and Ella and Maria.

I'm already head over heels in love with mornings on the ranch. And the sunsets, the stars—those are spectacular too.

"What I'm saying is, 'Please run off with a cowboy,'" Wheeler continues.

"Ha."

Truth is, though, I'm more than a little tempted to do just that.

Which is why I feel a swoop of relief when, a couple of hours later, I hear the sound of tires on gravel. Glancing out the window, I see a big, shiny GMC pickup pull up to the house.

Funny, but even though Palmer's car is a truck, it still looks out of place on the ranch. The shiny wheels maybe? Platinum grill?

Like I care. I asked Palmer to come for the weekend for one reason and one reason only.

Distraction. Nothing like some solid sex to clear cute cowboys from my head. Palmer is a good reminder that my stay on Lucky Ranch is temporary. My life is still in Dallas.

It will always be in Dallas. And Cash will always be in Hartsville.

Not like I'm looking for anything long-term anyway. But if I were—

I'd want to end up with someone like him.

Slamming my laptop shut, I dash to the bathroom. I yank off my glasses and put in my contacts, and then I'm at the front door to greet Palmer.

He looks better than ever as he smirks at me, pulling me in for a hug. "And you thought I wouldn't come."

"You always come."

"Good one." He squeezes me. "You're welcome."

I scoff. "You always say that."

"I always mean it. What do you smell like?" He sniffs at my skin. "That's new."

"Eucalyptus. I take Epsom salt baths every night. Helps with the soreness."

He grins. "You're turning into a bona fide cowgirl, aren't you? C'mon, then, Annie Oakley. Show me around your ranch. This place is sick."

"You—wait, you actually want to see the ranch?" I furrow my brow. "I thought we'd, you know, just hang here."

Palmer arches a brow. "We have plenty of time to *hang*. C'mon. I drove all the way out here, Mollie. I wanna do some country shit. See some horses, ride some four-wheelers. Go out and have beers at a dive bar."

My stomach pitches when I think about the possibility of us running into Cash. Or any of the Rivers boys, really, because they'll definitely tell their older brother about my visitor.

Why does the idea of Cash meeting Palmer—the idea of Cash knowing I invited the guy I hook up with to the ranch—make me feel queasy? Again, my intention in bringing Palmer here isn't to make Cash jealous or anything. It's to keep my feelings for that cowboy in check. I figure if I release some pent-up sexual energy, I'll stop thinking about Cash's Wrangler butt all the time.

I'll stop wanting him so much.

I also don't want to be a total dick to Palmer. He did just drive two hundred miles to see me. And so what if we run into Cash? His opinion of my friends—my hookups—doesn't matter.

At least that's what I tell myself when I paste on a smile and say, "Okay. Sure."

CHAPTER 20
Hell Is a Dance Floor
Cash

Driving past the New House, I hit the brakes when I see an unfamiliar truck parked out front.

Taking in the pristine chrome wheels and king cab, my stomach dips. "Who does the pavement princess belong to?"

In the passenger seat, Ryder shrugs. "No clue. Just seeing it now too. Maybe Mollie has a visitor? Fancy truck. Looks like someone from Dallas."

"Why did no one tell me we had a visitor? I'm supposed to know these things."

"Because we were out all day with you, jackass."

I'm gripped by a sense of unease. The truck is a Denali. Current model, like Mollie's Range Rover. And like the Rover, this is a six-figure vehicle.

One that's clearly never seen a day's work outside. I'd bet my life savings that the guy who owns it either parks it in his deck at work or at his country club in the suburbs.

Maybe I was wrong. Maybe Mollie does have a boyfriend.

Maybe he's the kind of douche who spends his money on a truck he absolutely doesn't need.

Why would he come now, though, long after Mollie left Dallas? She were my girl, I doubt I'd be able to go a single night without her in my bed. Nothing could keep me away from her.

Nothing.

What excuse does this asshat have? And why did Mollie buy it? I fucking hate the guy already.

"We should get goin'." Duke yawns in the back seat. "Band starts soon, and I ain't got much gas left in the tank."

It's Friday night. End of another long, hot week. Clouds rolled in earlier this morning, giving the boys and me a much-needed break from the sun. Still waiting on the rain, though.

The herd kept us busy well past lunch today. I'm beat.

But here I am, driving my brothers and me the fifteen minutes into town for some cold beers and live music.

I tell myself I got a second wind because the weather's turning and fall is my favorite season on the ranch. It has nothing to do with the fact that Mollie might be out tonight, which means I might get to dance with her again.

Absolutely nothing. I couldn't care less where she is. Hell, I don't even have her number. Not like I could text her, ask her if she's coming. If her boyfriend's here, she probably wants to hang out with him at the house anyway.

I don't realize I'm holding the wheel in a death grip until Ryder clears his throat. "Don't break it, man."

"It's probably just a friend of Mollie's," Wyatt says from beside Duke in the back. "She's been away from home for a bit."

"Yeah." Duke glances at Wyatt. "Girls can drive pickups too. Maybe she, like, borrowed it from her parents or something? You know, for the drive to the country."

Wyatt nods. "Exactly."

I meet his eyes in the rearview mirror. They gleam, kindness and understanding written all over his expression.

But there's nothing to understand, I want to yell. I'm fine. So what if it's her boyfriend? I don't care.

I don't want to fucking care. Because caring—

That's how you get your heart ripped out.

That's how you get hurt. And I've had enough hurt to last a lifetime.

Wouldn't Mollie tell me if she had a boyfriend? But why would she? We've had intimate conversations about dreams and family and grief, but we've never talked about our romantic lives. Seems strange now that I think about it.

And not strange at all, because she's my boss. Garrett's daughter. I need to show them both the respect they deserve.

I also need my brothers to stop looking at me like I have two heads.

Hitting the gas, I turn up the radio. The breeze blowing through the windows is refreshingly cool. "Just wanna make sure it ain't her lawyers or some shit. Or a buyer."

Because that's what Mollie said she would eventually do—sell Lucky Ranch to the highest bidder. She could be starting that process already.

Although there's a tug in my gut that tells me that's not it. Mollie's been with me all week, and not once has she mentioned a potential buyer. When would she have the time to find one? She's as tuckered out as the rest of us at the end of the day.

"Maybe." Ryder hangs his arm out the window.

"If it's not a buyer," Wyatt says slowly, "and if she's out tonight with this friend of hers, you're gonna be all right at the Rattler, right, Cash? I just rode into town today to collect my winnings. Best week I've ever had. I'd hate to lose that income if there's, er, trouble and Tallulah decides her feelings on us Riverses are lukewarm at best."

I yank my baseball cap off my head and put it on backward. "Why wouldn't I be all right?"

Duke chuckles. "No reason."

"You got somethin' you wanna say, brother?"

"Not at all, *brother*. Just haven't seen you this keyed up about a girl in a while."

"It ain't about a girl."

Wyatt's turn to snicker. "Sure it isn't."

"Y'all want me to turn around? Because I will."

Ryder holds up his hands. "Let's just go get some drinks, all right? Nothing is gonna happen."

"Thank you," I reply, even as I have the very distinct feeling that something is, in fact, going to happen tonight.

Or maybe I just want it to happen, because I'm sick of feeling so...tight. Wound up. *Hopeful.*

I hold my breath every time I turn a corner now,

hoping I'll run into Mollie. I can hardly sleep because I want to know what witty, pervy things she'll say to me over coffee the next morning. And at night, after supper, I think about her in the tub. The one in the New House has a Jacuzzi setting. She turn it on, get herself off?

She think about me while she does it? Or she think about the prick who drives the Denali instead?

I'm vibrating by the time we roll up to the Rattler. I stalk inside and look around. Mollie is nowhere in sight.

I tell myself I'm relieved as I belly up to the bar. Tallulah pops the top off a Shiner Bock and slides it across the counter.

"Thank you," I say. "Can I get a shot of tequila too?"

Tallulah raises a brow. "Bad day?"

"No." I tip back the longneck. "Yes. Kind of."

She wordlessly pours me a shot of Casamigos Añejo, which I swallow in a single gulp.

The burn feels good.

The band starts. A Johnny Cash cover, which has the already crowded bar hollering and stomping their feet. Everyone is smiling. Everyone is dancing, having a good time.

Except me.

"Wanna talk about it?"

I glance to my right and see Wyatt standing at the bar. "Talk about what?"

"Dude, don't play dumb with me. You like Mollie."

I could deny it. I should deny it.

Instead, I sip my beer. Most people are on the dance floor anyway. No one's paying us any mind.

"Something happen between y'all when you took her to your cabin earlier this week?"

242

I run a hand over the back of my neck. "How do you know about that?"

"Duke can't keep a secret to save his life."

"I didn't sleep with her."

"That's good."

"Trust me, no one knows better than I do how bad me sleeping with Mollie would be."

"But something did happen."

"We talked."

"About?"

I tilt back my head, the tequila making my skin feel buzzy and warm. "Nothing. Everything. Garrett, mostly. Mom and Dad."

His eyebrows pop up. "You talked about Mom and Dad with Mollie?"

"What? She asked, so I told her."

"*You* opened up to *her*. The girl you hated so much, you could barely stand to look at her."

I glance toward the door. "I did, yeah."

Wyatt leans his elbows on the bar. "I take back what I said. I kinda like this for you. You've been in an awful good mood lately, and now I know why."

Shaking my head, I hold up my hand for another beer. "Doesn't matter. She's Garrett's daughter. Our boss."

"Bet she wants you to boss her around, don't she?"

I slam my beer down on the bar. "Wyatt."

"Fine, fine." He holds up his hands. "But now that I'm thinkin' about it, would it be so bad if y'all joined forces? If things worked out between the two of you, that could be good for us, brother."

"Or it could mean losing everything we've worked so hard for."

Wyatt tilts his head. "I think you need to give yourself more credit. You're not young anymore—"

"Shut up."

"You know what I mean. You're not stupid. Or reckless. I don't know." He shrugs, drinking his beer. "Maybe it's your time."

"My time?"

"To settle down. Find your person. Be happy, for Christ's sake."

The idea sends a burst of something...not unpleasant through my bloodstream.

What if Wyatt's right? It's wild, yeah. But wilder shit's happened.

"Didn't Tim McGraw and Faith Hill first meet because they were working together?" he continues. "Now look at 'em. They've built a goddamn empire together. Could be you and Mollie."

I smile, unable to help myself. "But I'm better-looking than Tim, right?"

"Dude, no one's better-looking than Tim. Have you seen him lately? The man is a fuckin' ripped, music-making machine. My point is, maybe...well, who knows what the future holds? But it'd be a cool thing if you and Mollie got together and made some—"

"Wyatt."

"—good business decisions." He flashes me a wolfish smile. "That's what I was gonna say."

"Sure you were." I glance toward the door again. My heart dips when it opens.

My heart full on falls a hundred stories when Mollie walks in, followed by a guy with slicked-back hair. He's wearing dark jeans and a button-up shirt.

Fucker is way overdressed for the Rattler. He sticks out like a sore thumb. But Mollie—

Christ, Mollie looks hot as all get-out. She's wearing a sequined shirt and the tiniest denim skirt I think I've ever seen, along with a pair of cowboy boots. She has her hair in a ponytail, and she's wearing big-ass earrings that are ridiculous but somehow work on her.

My blood pumps overtime when her eyes catch on mine. She immediately smiles. "Cash! Hey!"

The band's bass line vibrates inside my chest as she and Slick approach. I notice he doesn't touch her. No hand on her waist, her back. Her nape.

She were mine, I'd have my hands all over her. Everyone would know she was taken. And she'd know just how much I wanted her.

Fuck.

Fuck *me*, I don't just have a crush on Mollie. I don't just want to sleep with her.

I want all of her. And I can't deny anymore that I want to be *that* guy for her. The one she dances with. Who protects her from scumbags like Roddy and Slick here.

The one who shows her what a true partner could and should be.

I can be that man, Mollie, if you'd let me.

I can't shake the feeling that she and this guy are more than friends. Maybe it's the way his beady little eyes lock on me and narrow.

Pushing off the bar, I grab my beer and paste on a smile. "Hey, Mollie."

"I was hoping y'all would be here. Cash, Wyatt, meet Palmer. Cash is the cowboy I was telling you about—our foreman. Wyatt's his brother." She gestures to Slick. "Palmer is visiting from Dallas."

Wyatt cuts me a glance before he holds out his hand. "Welcome to Hartsville, Palmer."

"Happy to be here." Palmer takes my brother's hand. "Quite the operation y'all got over at the ranch. Mollie gave me a little tour this afternoon."

That all she give you?

I don't realize I'm holding my beer in a death grip until Palmer is holding his hand out to me. I let an awkward beat of silence pass before I finally take it.

"You here for the weekend?" I ask. I don't wanna engage this douche in conversation, but my curiosity gets the better of me. I suddenly need to know who Palmer is to Mollie exactly and how long he plans to stay.

Palmer glances at Mollie. "For a day or two, yeah."

A day or two? And is that disappointment I see flicker across Mollie's face?

I fucking *hate* this guy.

Wyatt was wrong. I can still be stupid. I'm being stupid right now, hating someone I don't even know.

But when I try to rein in that hatred, all I feel is, well, more hatred. So I let it ride.

"Y'all are friends," I say slowly.

Mollie smiles at Tallulah as she takes two longnecks out of the bartender's hands. "Thank you, Tallulah. And yeah, Palmer and I met back in college. Then we ran into each other a few years later in Dallas and…reconnected."

I flick my eyes over his clothes. "What do you do there?"

"I'm a trader." He sips his beer and looks over at the

dance floor, apparently oblivious to my seething hatred and Mollie's presence. "Commodities."

"So you bet on the shit we grow out here in the country to go down in price."

Palmer shrugs. "Sometimes, sure."

Mollie looks at me. I look back. *Him, really?*

In reply, she loops her arm through his, sending a spasm of rage—jealousy, more like it—through my middle.

"Palmer, let's go check out the band. They're awesome. The drummer is our cook, and the backup singer is our vet."

"Cute," Palmer says. "Let's do it."

I pretend to busy myself with my beer, but I can't stop sneaking glances at the two of them on the dance floor. He's got his hands on her now, Mollie swaying in time to a Chris Stapleton cover. She turns to Palmer, and he spins her around. She smiles.

An ache takes root in the pit of my stomach.

This time last week, I was the guy twirling her around the dance floor.

I was the guy she was smiling at.

I do not like seeing her smile at someone else. Not one fucking bit.

They dance, and I drink.

Then Slick bumps into the girls dancing behind them. Instead of continuing to dance with Mollie, he turns around and starts talking to them. They're the Hager girls, a pair of award-winning barrel racers.

They're pretty—a fact Palmer seems to take note of.

The ache in my center builds as I watch Mollie politely engage them in conversation alongside Palmer.

The band is between songs, so I can just barely hear them talking.

A new song starts, and Mollie tries to pull Palmer away.

He doesn't budge. He's smiling at the Hagers, babbling on like he isn't making the most beautiful woman on earth wait. A shadow moves across Mollie's eyes.

I've never wanted to burn anything down, but I'd burn down this whole town if it meant never seeing that look in her eyes again.

Are she and Slick together? Maybe it's a friends-with-benefits situation. Maybe their relationship is new, and they haven't put a label on it yet.

Doesn't fucking matter. He's talking to other girls, and it's upsetting her, and he doesn't seem to give a shit. Tells me everything I need to know.

"Maybe we should go," Wyatt says. "I'm...tired."

"You're fine."

"Cash, she's allowed—"

"I don't care."

"Then why do you look like you want to punch him?"

I don't have an answer for that, so I don't give one. I just sit and glower, watching as Slick finally turns back to Mollie. He doesn't dance, though. He leans down to say something in her ear, and then he's heading back toward us.

Mollie stays on the dance floor, looking annoyed. A little disappointed even.

I bite the inside of my cheek and taste blood.

Wyatt repeats, "We should go."

He's right. But my boots don't budge. Slick saunters over, hands in the pockets of his jeans, and scans the wall behind the bar. Almost like he's looking for a menu.

I laugh.

"What?" He eyes me.

"Nothing. Just—"

"Tallulah will make you anything you want," Wyatt interrupts. "She knows her shit backward and forward."

"Bet you don't have Willett bourbon back there, do you?" Palmer asks Tallulah.

The bartender gives him a tight smile as she wipes her hands on a towel. "You lookin' for the Family Estate Rye or the Johnny Drum?"

Palmer blinks. "Y'all have Johnny Drum?"

"We do."

"I'll take that, then. Ice, splash of ginger."

This guy *deserves* to be punched.

"No ginger," I grunt. "Or ice."

Palmer's eyebrows snap together. "Excuse me?"

"Whiskey that good, you don't add anything to it."

"I'll drink it how I damn well please." He takes a step closer. "You got a problem, son?"

It's the *son* that gets me.

And the slicked-back hair.

And the drink order and the way he flirted with other women in front of Mollie and that dumb fucking Denali truck.

I got several inches on the guy. He doesn't flinch, though, when I step closer too. "I do have a problem, actually. You calling me *son* for starters. You hurtin' Mollie's feelings, though—that's what really bothers me."

"Cash." The warning is clear in Wyatt's voice. "Cool it."

Holding up my hands, I keep my eyes locked on

Slick's. "I was raised better'n than to throw the first punch. Were you, *son*?"

His gaze flashes. "What's your deal?"

"My deal is you treat your date with respect."

"Mollie's just a friend."

I laugh again. "You're an idiot, then."

It happens quick. One second, I'm staring down Slick. The next, his fist rams into my jaw.

Pain blooms inside my face. I taste blood. My heart beats loudly inside my ears. Wyatt shouts. But before he can grab me to hold me back, I'm coiling my right arm and hitting Slick in the mouth.

He falls back with a howl. Suddenly, the entire bar's on its feet, the music going dead just in time for me to hear Mollie scream my name.

"Cash! Palmer! What the hell, y'all? *Stop!*"

She's making a mad dash toward us from the dance floor.

Palmer regroups, the hand holding his mouth falling away.

It's covered in blood. A white-hot sense of satisfaction shoots through my veins.

Wyatt is finally able to grab me by the arms and pull me back. Ryder and Duke appear at my side, Ryder standing between Slick and me.

"Easy." He glowers at Slick. "You're outnumbered, so whatever you're thinkin' about doing, don't."

Tallulah throws her towel over her shoulder. "No fights in the bar. Y'all wanna go at it, head outside."

Mollie is here now, breathless. Her eyes are—well, I can't tell what she's feeling, but it sure as hell ain't disappointment or hurt anymore.

Ryder has the good sense to move closer to Mollie, standing between her and Palmer. I taught him well.

I try to yank my arms free, but Wyatt doesn't let me go.

Slick eyes me. "What the fuck is your problem?"

"Already told you. You upset Mollie."

"What?" Mollie's eyes bulge, a divot appearing on her forehead. "How did you—he didn't—"

"I can't believe that's why you're being such a dick," Palmer says.

I glare at him. "That not a good enough reason?"

"You're crazy, bro. All y'all"—he glances around our little half circle of Riverses—"are crazy."

I give my arms a vicious yank, finally pulling out of Wyatt's grasp. I jab my finger into Palmer's chest, my mouth an inch from his face. "Good. Then you won't ever come back to Hartsville, you hear me? I so much as see that pussy-ass truck again, you'll be in for a world of hurt. Got me?"

He narrows his eyes. "Who the hell do you think you are?"

"Cash"—I push him—"Rivers."

"Fuck you," he says, and then he charges.

I'm bigger than him, and I have my brothers. It ain't a fair fight. That doesn't stop me from locking my arm around his head in a half nelson. I hold him there while he tries to jab me in the side.

I squeeze his neck. "Stop."

"Fuck you."

"I'm telling you, stop before you hurt yourself."

Wyatt's pulling me back again, saying, "Let him go, Cash. He ain't worth it."

"Let him go, my God," Mollie repeats. "Right now. Please."

I meet her eyes. They're alive, gleaming in the neon light of a Pabst Blue Ribbon sign. I see anger there, sure. A little fear.

And a flame that ignites a fire inside my skin.

I release my hold on Palmer. He straightens, spits on the floor.

"Get gone." I put my hands on my hips, breathing hard. "Don't ever—*ever*—come back. While you're at it, stop toyin' with women, yeah?"

I half expect him to lunge for me again. If he leaves now, he's running with his tail between his legs. But like the coward he is, he looks at me. Looks toward the door.

Doesn't even look at Mollie before making a beeline for the exit.

A beat later, the roar of tires on gravel fills the silence inside the bar.

"That escalated quickly." Ryder passes me a bar napkin. I use it to wipe my hands. "Care to explain what happened?"

Mollie stays rooted to the spot. She's staring at me.

"What?" I crumple the napkin and toss it into the trash can behind the counter. "Guy was showin' his ass. I gave him the attitude adjustment he needed."

"An attitude adjustment?" Mollie stares at me. "Cash, you punched him in the face."

"Only after he punched me."

"It—I—seriously, it doesn't matter. There's never a good reason to punch someone."

"I beg to differ."

Her eyes toggle between mine. Searching. For what?

252

She looks as mixed up as I feel.

Why are you messing around with clowns like that?

Why does that fact make me lose my ever-loving mind?

"What is *wrong* with you?" she asks.

Wish I knew. "I was sticking up for you."

She squares those shoulders. "You know what? I'm—I should—" She throws up her hands. "I need a minute."

"Mollie—"

"Don't." She moves past me. I resist the urge to grab her. "Nothing you can say right now will make this better."

"Let me explain what happened."

"Violence is never the answer!" she hollers over her shoulder, then disappears into the hallway that leads to the bathrooms.

It's only then that I realize the entire bar is staring at us.

Well, everyone's staring at me now that Mollie is gone, their gazes bright with curiosity.

"Aw, your first lovers' quarrel," Duke says.

I grit my teeth. "You best mind your mouth before I punch you too."

He gives me a shit-eating grin. "Meant no harm. Just...not like you to, you know, be *that* guy."

"What guy?"

"The one punching other guys over a girl."

It ain't like me.

Also ain't like me to chase what I can't have.

But that's exactly what I do as I make a beeline for the bathrooms, ignoring the stares that follow me.

My heart's going apeshit inside my chest. I don't

know what I'm gonna say or how I'm gonna make this right.

All I know is Mollie's been disappointed for the last time.

She's been hurt by some idiot dickhead for the last fucking time.

CHAPTER 21
Dirty Looks
Mollie

I'm shaking as I push through the bathroom door.

Cash punched Palmer because he upset me.

Not only did Cash punch Palmer, he also knew somehow that Palmer hurt my feelings when he flirted with those cute girls in the cowboy hats. Yeah, I don't want anything serious with him, but it still sucked to see him on the prowl when he's supposed to be here with me.

Cash was paying attention. To *me*. In a bar crowded with pretty women, I was the one he was watching. And when he saw something he didn't like—

Well, he took action.

Stepping up to the sink, I look in the mirror and put a hand on my face. I'm bright red, my skin hot to the touch.

Is Palmer okay? Should I call him? He *was* being kind of a dick. And he did start the fight, although I'm sure Cash had a hand in egging him on.

Honestly, I feel...relieved that Palmer left. Which means what exactly?

Pondering the answer, my legs turn to Jell-O. My heart elbows against my breastbone, its urgent jabs making it difficult to breathe.

Holy shit, Cash was watching me. He cares about how I feel. Who I'm with. What does *that* mean?

I have feelings for Cash. No denying that. But I think I might've just been presented with incontrovertible evidence that he has feelings for me too.

Cash pays attention to me in a way no one has. Ever.

My eyes burn. I cover them, throat locking up with the sudden urge to weep.

I whirl around at a loud *bang*. Cash stands in the doorway, looking so good—so angry—my right knee literally gives out. I grab at the lip of the sink behind me, steadying myself.

"You can't—you shouldn't be in here," I stammer.

The door swings shut behind him as he stalks into the room. His scent—eucalyptus, skin kissed with sweat— fills my head.

My heart lurches as he begins to push open each stall door. "Everybody out. Now."

The third and final stall is locked. The girl inside immediately scurries out when Cash bangs on the door, glancing at me before she loops her purse across her chest. "You okay, Cash?"

"Mind giving us a minute, Lucy?"

"You got it."

When Lucy exits, Cash crosses the room and bolts the door that leads to the bar, the lock sliding home with a definitive *thump* I feel between my legs.

Then Cash turns to me. My pulse leaps, feeling like a fist slamming against the back of my throat.

He looks downright furious. Jaw ticking, nostrils flaring. Eyes on fire.

The hungry, barely contained *something* I see in them turns me inside out. I hold on to the sink for dear life, falling back against it as he approaches.

He closes the space between us in three huge, angry strides. He's enormous. Even in my boots, Cash towers over me, the air vibrating with emotion as he stops six inches from me. Way too close.

Not close enough.

Is he angry with me? Why?

My body pulses at his nearness, sparks of desire catching up and down my spine. My nipples are hard. Pulse is frantic.

"Him?" Cash finally says.

I blink. "What?"

"Palmetto. Palmston. You want *him*?"

"We're not—I'm not—we're friends who—wait. My relationship with Palmer is none of your business, Cash."

His chest barrels out on a sharp inhale. "Answer me."

"We're friends." My voice shakes. "And yeah, we hook up sometimes."

"Did y'all hook up today?"

"I'm not answering that."

He leans in, eyes flicking to my mouth. "Did. You. Hook. Up. Today?"

"We didn't, all right?" I put my hands on Cash's chest and give him a shove. "Why do you care so much anyway?"

257

Cash grabs my wrist, stepping forward so my hands are on his chest again. The firmness of his grip makes my pulse riot. "He's an idiot. You can do better. So much better, Mollie."

"Again, who I'm with—"

"That's really what you want?" He searches my eyes. "Someone who has no clue how fuckin' amazing you are?"

My heart must explode into a million pieces, because I feel its ardent beat everywhere: in my lips, my skin, my stomach.

I'm hit again by the urge to cry.

"Don't," I whisper.

"Don't what? Tell you that I was wrong? That you're everything I thought you weren't? Bighearted and generous and smart as hell and, yeah, fuckin' beautiful? Sexy as hell?" Cash's eyes graze my face. "Tell me to go, then. Tell me to let you go, and I will. But you gotta say the words, honey, or—"

"Or what?" I blame him calling me *honey* for this sudden burst of bravery. "You'll give me what Palmer couldn't?"

His eyes flicker. "You're such a brat."

"Yeah, well, you're a brute."

"I am." His gaze is pleading. "Tell me to go."

But I don't. I look down at my hands, which are still on his chest. He's a solid wall of warm muscle. I can feel his heart beating against my palms.

"You're the center of everyone's universe, you know," I manage. "Everyone on the ranch. Everyone in your family. They all look to you, and you never ever let them down."

He breathes in. Out. "They're everything to me."

God, how have I not gone up in a fireball yet? Because truly, there is nothing sexier than a man who shows up for the people he loves.

He's showing up for me.

"You being here." I swallow. "Sticking up for me. Helping me. Filling me in on everything I missed with Dad. That's everything to me, Cash. You're a good man, and I…"

The edges of his eyes crinkle. "What, honey?"

"At first, I couldn't fucking stand you." I scoff. "And now I can't fucking stand how much I want you."

His eyes look positively feral. "Ask me."

"Ask what?"

"Ask me to give you what you want."

I stare at him. "I can't—"

"But you can." He steps closer, melting his hips into mine. "Because you gotta know by now, I can't deny you anything, Mollie. Not a fuckin' thing."

I thought swooning was something that only happened in books. I can now affirm it is an actual thing that happens to actual people, because it's happening to me.

I go weak in the knees; the only thing holding me up is the solid weight of Cash's body pressing me against the sink.

Reading me like—ha—a book, Cash curls an arm around my middle. The throb between my legs blares hotter at the onslaught of contact. I *love* it. Love the feel of him pressed against me. So much so that I feel my eyes rolling to the back of my head.

I bite my lip. "Be the brute," I breathe. "Leave the good man—"

"Hello?" There's a knock on the door. "Hello?! Y'all, I have to use the bathroom—"

"Get fucked," Cash shouts.

Then he glides his hand onto my face and leans in and kisses me.

Cash Rivers *kisses me*, his scruff catching on my skin as he presses his mouth to mine.

It's the kind of kiss that immediately has my toes curling inside my boots. It's urgent and hot and hard, weeks of pent-up frustration finally let loose. I close my eyes and move with him. His lips are soft but eager as he drinks me in, hard, thirsty pulls that demand surrender.

And oh, am I all too happy to surrender. The soft, slick feel of his mouth gliding over mine draws a moan from the back of my throat. My hands fist in his shirt. His other hand moves from the small of my back to my side, his thumb brushing the underside of my breast. A bolt of lust cracks down my middle, fast and loud as lightning.

He opens his mouth and licks into my own, urging my lips apart. I rise into the kiss and taste him. My hand moves up to his neck. He groans when I dig my fingertips into the hair at his nape. I give it a tug.

He bites my bottom lip. Scrapes his beard against my cheek. I'm definitely going to have beard burn tomorrow, but I don't care.

The hunger I saw in his eyes is very much alive in his kiss. I *love* it.

Bursts of neon light streak across the backs of my closed eyelids. My pulse thunders, my entire being lighting up as he firms his grip on my waist. His thumb arcs over the swell of my breast and moves across my nipple.

At the same time, he ducks his head and kisses my neck—
God, I love neck kisses—and I gasp, arching into his touch.

He lets out a low, sinister chuckle, his breath hot on
my skin. "How much of a brute you want me to be,
honey?"

"We're in a bathroom." I give his hair another tug.
"At a bar."

He sinks his teeth into my jaw. "No one's comin' in."

"Everyone knows we're in here. Everyone knows
what we're doing."

"We better do it quick, then."

Before I know what's happening, he's sliding his
hands down my sides. He's roughly pulling up my skirt.
It bunches around my waist as he lifts me onto the sink,
the porcelain cold against the backs of my bare thighs.

He shoves my knees apart and steps between them.
His crotch meets with my center, and I roll my hips,
my body starving for the friction. He's doing that thing
where he takes my face in his hand and he leans in,
tilting his head. The sinews in his thick neck pop against
his skin.

And then another kiss. He tastes clean, a hint of tequila
on his breath. His tongue finds mine, and suddenly we're
a frenzied tangle of mouths, breaths, bodies.

The feel of him between my legs is everything.

"Can you be quiet?" he grunts.

"Why don't you find out?"

I slide a hand inside his shirt. His stomach caves,
abdominal muscles contracting into hard ridges beneath
my palm.

Can't help it. I laugh.

"What?" He's nipping at my earlobe now.

"Your body." I bite his neck, opening my eyes. "It's laughably hot."

Cash meets my gaze and runs a hand up my thigh. "Could say the same about yours. Only I ain't laughin'."

"What're you gonna do instead?"

In reply, he lifts his hand and turns his head and spits onto his fingertips.

I jump at the sound. It's rude, the gesture even ruder.

It might also be the hottest thing I've ever witnessed.

Now he's reaching between us, reaching between my legs. He presses the pad of his thumb against my underwear.

Another dark chuckle. "May not even need this, huh, honey?"

"Maybe no—*oh*."

He hooks his thumb into my underwear and tugs them aside. Then he's using those spit-covered fingertips to part me.

His spit feels warm on my pussy. His kiss is even warmer, his tongue stroking into my mouth as he strokes me between my legs. I want to howl when he dips a blunt fingertip into my entrance, gathering more moisture there before spreading it upward.

My hips punch forward when he hits my clit. I'm already *this close* to coming.

"Cash," I breathe. "Oh my *God*."

He grunts. "No shit, honey. You're soaked. For me."

"For you."

I bite back a cry when his fingers fall away from where I want him most. But then he's tearing off my underwear and sinking to his knees, and *holy Christ, he's going down on me.*

"Look at this pretty pussy," he says. "Perfect. So fucking perfect, Mollie. I fuckin' hate that you kept this from me for so long."

I don't have time to protest. I don't want to protest. I just knock off his hat and grab his hair and pull him against me.

His turn to laugh. The sound vibrates through my pussy as he grabs my thighs and leans in. I nearly convulse when he gathers my clit in his lips and sucks, the pressure there coiling tight to the point of pain.

His mustache tickles me *just* where I want him.

He kisses my slit. A deep, ardent caress of tongue and lips that's worlds different from Palmer's half-hearted ministrations. It's like Cash is actually enjoying this.

It's like he's savoring me, taking his time. My chest clenches. Is he going slow because this is the first and last time we'll do this? Or is he going slow because, well, that's Cash, isn't it? Going all in on the things he cares about.

He's dropping everything to be here. He doesn't hesitate. Doesn't give a shit what people hear or think. He just gives me what I want, what I need, because that's more important to him than anything.

I close my eyes. A thought circles wildly inside my head. It's not easy to break your way through Cash's defenses. But once you're in—heavens, he's the kind of man who's *so* easy to fall for.

He is so fucking good at eating pussy.

The pressure in my core becomes unbearable. I roll my hips against his mouth, legs beginning to shake.

"Play with yourself," he growls, shoving up my shirt with his hand before pulling down my bra. "Touch your tits."

But he's already doing that, eyes locked on my bare breast as he thumbs my nipple. The pad of his thumb is rough, calloused, but his touch is gentle. The juxtaposition is mind-blowingly hot.

I cover his hand with mine. My orgasm rises, rises, a growing, thunderous throb that has me biting my lip to keep from yelling. Cash licks my pussy, deep strokes that go back to front, back to front. He circles my clit, sucks on it. Plays with my nipple all the while.

My heart flatlines, then bursts into vibrant, ardent life as the orgasm finally slams into me. The release is brutal, and I curl my fingers into Cash's thick hair, searching for relief. Support.

Sympathy.

And I get it. Cash slips a finger inside me, the pressure just what I didn't know I needed. I look down and see him watching me.

"I gotta feel you comin', honey." His Adam's apple bobs. "You gonna come this hard on my dick?"

I can only nod.

"You'd best be tellin' the truth. 'Cause you feel so fucking good. Tight and wet and hot. Imma fuck you here, and you're gonna love it, ain't you, honey?"

I nod again.

Cash presses one last kiss to my clit before straightening. Then it's my mouth he's kissing, keeping that finger inside me. This kiss is soft, sweet, and he wraps an arm around my waist and holds me against him as wave after wave of sensation crashes through me.

"Wow," I say when I'm finally able to breathe.

He pulls his finger out. I wince.

"Shit, that hurt?"

"No. Yes. That orgasm—it was the kind that's so good, it hurts. I think it was that."

"What can I do?"

I rest my cheek against his chest. His heart thunders in my ear.

There's a bulge in the front of his jeans.

"You can do that again," I say, and a sharp, searing sense of light fills my chest when Cash laughs.

A big, booming belly laugh that I'm sure the entire bar can hear. Far as I can tell, the band still hasn't started playing again.

"Happily." He leans down and thumbs my chin. Tilts my face up and kisses me. "Better now?"

"Much." I reach down and cup his bulge in my hand. "But you—"

"I ain't nearly as quiet as you are. C'mon." He yanks down my skirt. "I'm takin' you home, honey."

He bends down and grabs his hat and my underwear. I reach for the underwear, but he shakes his head.

"These are mine now." Tucking them into his back pocket, he helps me off the sink and laces his fingers through mine.

"How do I look?" I ask.

His eyes flick over my face. "Like you just came hard on my face."

"Oh God, Cash—"

"Let them see." He gives my hand a tug. "Who the fuck cares? No one's gonna say a word, I promise."

I shouldn't believe him. But I do.

I shouldn't follow him out the door. But I do that too.

I follow him, and I fight back a smile the whole time.

CHAPTER 22
God Bless Texas
Cash

The band starts playing again, but people still stare as I lead Mollie by the hand out of the Rattler.

I couldn't give two fucks. Maybe they heard us. Maybe they didn't. Maybe they thought we were just clearing the air with some good old conflict resolution back there in the bathroom.

Whatever the case, I know no one is going to fuck with Mollie Luck ever again.

No one's going to touch her. No one but me. And that suits me just fine.

Wyatt eyes me as we pass. "Y'all good?"

"Fine," I grunt. "Get everyone home safe, you hear?"

He holds up two fingers. "Sally said she'd give us a ride."

"Good."

"Y'all behave!" Duke calls after us.

The bar erupts in laughter. My own lips twitch.

Behaving is exactly what I plan on not doing tonight.

I can still taste Mollie's pussy on my lips as I open the passenger-side door of my truck and help her inside.

Her cheeks are bright pink, eyes hazy—that look girls get when they've been well taken care of.

You don't see it often enough.

I already don't want this ride to end. Who knows what will happen after tonight? She said she wants to fool around, sure. But that's no commitment.

If I'm being honest, commitment is what I'm looking for. Maybe it's being around Mollie. Maybe it's losing Garrett. Or maybe it was Wyatt's little speech earlier at the bar. But something's got me wanting to make a change.

Or maybe something is changing the way I think. The way my family needs me—that hasn't changed. Neither have my responsibilities on the ranch. But I'm starting to understand that those commitments shouldn't hold me back from commitments I want to make to *myself.*

For myself. That's the only way I'm ever gonna have a life of my own.

I've missed out on so much trying to be everything to everybody else. No one asked me to be the hero. The savior. And maybe—hell, maybe they don't need me to be their savior. Maybe it's time they learned to save themselves.

Laughing with Mollie, dancing with her—I've missed out on that shit, and I want more of how it makes me feel. Free. Happy. Glad to be alive.

I notice Mollie's hand shakes a little as she buckles her seat belt.

"You all right?" My voice is husky. Probably because my dick is hard enough to hammer nails.

Her eyes flick to meet mine. "I just witnessed my first bar fight, and then you made me come on a bathroom sink. Of course I'm not all right. I'm fucking awesome."

I laugh, even as the pain in my hand and face pulses. "Maybe you really are a cowgirl at heart."

She smiles. I smile.

Lord *above*, I'm in trouble.

I close the door and jog around the front of the truck. Don't got time to waste. If I don't get Mollie home and in my bed soon, I'm gonna come in my pants like a fucking teenager.

Wrong. Right. Sleeping with Mollie is one of those things. But too late to go back now. She needs to be shown how a real man does it.

How a real man treats her.

Fuck, but I feel lucky I'm that man tonight.

I'm glad Palmer is out of the picture and on his way back to Dallas with a fat lip. Hopefully, he knows better than to come back.

Hopefully, he knows better than to ever, *ever* touch Mollie again.

I peel out of the parking lot and head home. It's dark now. No stars, though, on account of the clouds.

When is the rain gonna come?

We're just passing Goody's office when Mollie reaches across and puts her hand on my leg. My dick jumps. She smirks.

Her hand moves to my crotch. She cups my erection and gives it a squeeze.

"Jesus fuck," I sputter.

"Road head gonna be too much of a distraction for you?"

I draw a deep, slightly panicked breath. "But I wanna be inside you."

"We can do that later. It's Friday night, Cash, and we live in the middle of nowhere." She nods at the vast darkness outside the windshield. "What the hell else are we gonna do except fool around?"

I chuckle. "Good point."

Scooting closer, she starts unbuckling my belt. "You give good head. Bet I give better."

"Brat." I look at her.

She looks back. Unzips my fly and reaches inside my jeans. "I'm the worst, aren't I?"

I nearly jump out the window when she wraps her hand around me and gives me a slow, hard tug through my briefs. She circles her thumb over my head, and I feel my underwear go damp as I start to leak.

My balls are in agony.

Still, I drive slowly. I don't want to lose control. I want to enjoy every minute of my time with Mollie.

Up until this point, life's been about survival. It had to be when I was in the trenches after my parents died. But now that my brothers are grown and the ranch is thriving, I see that maybe being in survival mode is a choice I've made.

Which means I can choose a different way of living.

What about Rivers Ranch, though? My plans for my family's land were destroyed when Mollie inherited Lucky Ranch. I still don't know how to fix that. What our next step should be. Which means it's a bad time to be reckless. To choose freedom over safety.

Then again, I thought if I played by the rules and did everything right, life would work out. What a crock of shit that's turned out to be. If anything, losing out to Mollie is teaching me I don't have much control over what does and doesn't happen. And if that's the case…

Why not have a little fun?

Why not try something new, whether it's road head or the idea of starting a life of my own?

I watch Mollie tuck stray strands of hair out of her face. Then she pulls my dick through the gap in my briefs. Gives me another tug, this one harder, faster, my whole body clenching.

She looks me in the eye. Smirks and says, "Eyes on the road. Don't kill us."

Goddamn, girl, you're the one killing me.

One hand on the wheel, I put the other on the back of her head. "Little less talkin', honey."

"I hate being told what to do."

"Then you're gonna hate me."

I push her head down, her shoulders shaking with laughter. I'm being lewd, obscene even, handling her this way. But Mollie doesn't seem to mind. I see stars when she opens her mouth and licks my tip, lapping up my precum with eager strokes of her tongue.

"Aw, *honey*," I groan.

Thank God the road is empty. God bless Texas and her wide-open spaces.

Mollie sucks my head into her mouth. I slam the heel of my hand against the wheel.

She sucks harder. Takes me deeper.

My head falls back against the headrest as heat rips through my bloodstream. Heaviness gathers between my legs as Mollie bobs her head, her hand tugging my shaft in time to her movements.

"You suck my dick like you love it," I breathe. "I love watchin' you like this, honey. You're beautiful. You're fucking—"

She takes me deep. My head hits the back of her throat, and my hips jerk.

"You got me so fucking keyed up. I'm not gonna last long. Look at me."

But Mollie, being Mollie, doesn't listen. She bobs up, down.

So I grab her chin. "*Look at me.*"

Her brown eyes gleam in the light of the dash when they meet mine. She turns her head a little so my dick slips out from between her lips.

"You came in my mouth, I wanna come in yours. If that's gonna be a problem, stop now."

I should've known Mollie doesn't play. She turns back to my dick and swallows me deep, so deep that I'm in her throat, and I thrust my hips. She gags but doesn't stop.

Her willingness to approach the point of pain.

Her adventurousness.

Her magic fucking tongue.

It all does me in. My balls contract, and heat streaks through my dick. Mollie moans when my cum hits her mouth.

And, Christ, do I come. You'd think I hadn't orgasmed in years for how long and hard I come. The release pounds through me, drawing a shout from my lips. My stomach caves, knees go numb.

I fucking love every second of it.

"Show me how good you can swallow it," I manage. "Every last drop, Mollie. Don't you fucking stop."

I have no idea how I manage to keep us on the road, but we're still safe and sound when Mollie straightens. Licks her lips.

"Did my swallowing meet your standards?"

I can't breathe.

Can't think.

I just grab her neck and pull her in for a kiss. One eye on the road the whole time.

"Yeah, honey. You're…really fucking good at that."

She grins. "Thank you."

She tries to scoot back to the passenger side, but I grab her knee. "Nope. You're stayin' right there. Need anything at the New House?"

Mollie blinks. "What? Why?"

"You think after you gave me head like that, I'm lettin' you outta my sight? You're sleeping at the cabin tonight."

She blinks again, a small smile curling at the edges of her lips. "Yes, sir."

I groan.

"You really do like that, don't you?" she asks. "Being called *sir*."

"When you do it, yeah."

"Noted."

Her doing the things I like on purpose—her noticing my likes and dislikes, wanting to please me—it makes my chest swell.

I wanna please her too.

I *like* this girl. This ain't gonna be some stupid half-in, half-out hookup. Not for me.

Her saying that mean this'll be the kind of sex that sticks for her too?

I turn into the ranch. The breeze blows through the window, sending Mollie's ponytail flying. She reaches for the knob on the stereo and turns up the radio. Trisha Yearwood now.

Mollie sings along. And seeing her smile, close her eyes, and lose herself in one of my favorite songs, I feel short of breath. She sinks her teeth into her bottom lip after the chorus ends and shimmies her hips in time to the beat. Her long, bare legs seem to go on forever in the dark.

I grab one, curling my hand around her thigh. She cuts me a look, and I move my hand up, slipping my ring finger and pinkie underneath her skirt.

Her bare pussy is soft to the touch. Her breath hitches. I hit the gas. We bump over the dirt road as Trisha sings.

Mollie says she needs to grab some contact solution at the New House. After making her promise not to grab anything else—specifically any extra clothes—I pull up to the front door. Long as she's at my place, she's either naked or wearing my shit.

She darts inside and emerges a few minutes later with a small cosmetics case. She jumps in the truck, and I peel out of the driveway.

After a small eternity, I pull into my parking spot in the grass beside the cabin and cut the ignition. The night sounds of the ranch fill the silence: crickets, trees moving in a breeze.

"Cash?" Mollie asks.

I shove open the door. "Yeah?"

"What's everyone going to say when they find out I slept here?"

Everyone meaning the people who live and work on Lucky Ranch. She's worried they'll think less of her. Maybe they'll think she slept with me to get something.

Or I slept with her to get something. Namely the ranch.

"They say anything, I'll take care of 'em." I hop out of the truck and hold out my hand.

She tilts her head and pins me with a stare. "Easy for you to say. Everyone respects the hell out of you."

"They respect the hell out of you too. You've earned it this week, working your ass off like you have."

"And now I'm going to lose that respect by fucking my foreman."

My lips twitch. "I promise I'm worth the risk."

"You would say that."

"Look, I get why you're worried. There's a double standard when it comes to this stuff. But people around here—I wouldn't say they mind their own business, but they know better than to meddle in other people's lives. I'll have you home before sunrise. That a deal? No one'll see you."

"And if they do?"

"That's what a shotgun is for. C'mon." I bend my fingers, motioning her out of the car.

"No shotguns." Mollie takes my hand. "But I'll take the early ride home."

"Consider it done."

I don't let go of her hand as we walk up the steps. My heart beats a little harder when Mollie doesn't let go of mine either.

The door is unlocked. Tonight will be the first time in an age that I'll bolt it. Don't want any interruptions.

I open the door for Mollie, and the old floorboards creak as she steps inside the cabin.

"I'm not sure I appreciated how pretty your place was before," she says, taking in the tiny kitchen to our right and the living room to our left. The front of the cabin is all one big room, the floors, walls, and ceiling crafted of salvaged oak. "You're an excellent caretaker."

"Workin' in the dirt all day, it's nice to come home to a place that's clean." I take off my hat and toss it onto the counter. "What can I get you? A beer? Water? I have tequila too."

Mollie arches a brow. "What do you make with that tequila?"

"I'm famous for my spicy ranch waters."

"No, you're not."

I laugh, swiping my hand across the counter. "Lemme make you one. I'll change your mind."

"Who the hell are you making spicy ranch waters for?"

"They were a favorite of Garrett's, for starters."

Mollie's expression softens. Only it's not sadness I see in her eyes. It's more like interest. Curiosity.

She didn't know her daddy all that well. It hits me that in a way, she's learning him through me.

Considering Garrett was one of my favorite people, I'm more than happy to teach her.

"I'd love one," she says. "Thank you."

I nod at the table and chairs. "Sit. Prepare to be amazed."

"Can I snoop around instead?" She glances across the cabin. "I'm not sure if I'll ever be invited back."

"Because you're a terrible houseguest?" I open the

fridge and pull out a bottle of Topo Chico—Mexican sparkling mineral water.

"Because I'm about to break some furniture with you," she replies with a smirk.

Letting out a bark of laughter, I grab a jalapeño from a bowl on the counter and wash it at the sink. "You're funny."

"I know." She's in the living room now, looking at my bookshelves. "This is impressive, Cash. I didn't know you were a reader."

"Have been my whole life. Guess it's my way of staying connected to that part of me—the part that likes ideas. Stories."

She glances at me over her shoulder. "That's hot."

"I know."

Rolling her eyes, she smiles as she moves to the silver picture frames on the mantel. "So you and Dad would drink these spicy ranch waters together?"

"When it was hot like it is now, yeah." I slice up the jalapeño and put it in a glass, pouring several fingers of tequila over it. I give the slices a quick muddle with the back of a spoon. "At quittin' time, Garrett would join us at the bunkhouse for beers. It was lonely at his place, you know?"

"I imagine it was, yeah."

"So one day, we ran out of Shiner Bock. All we had was tequila and Topo Chico, which Patsy buys in bulk. I'd had a ranch water at the rodeo a few times, so I decided to look for some limes and make my own. Your daddy was the one who requested the spicy tequila."

Mollie smiles, arms crossed over her chest. "He loved

his spice. He'd beg me to try it when I was little, but I didn't start to love it until I was a teenager. Now I can't get enough of it."

"So you're the reason we're going through hot sauce like there's no tomorrow." I fill a pair of glasses with ice.

"You and your brothers are the reason. How much y'all eat—I've never seen anything like it."

"Patsy's cooking is hard to resist."

"No kidding. Best food I've had in my life. It's so satisfying, you know, eating real food like that after working your body as hard as we do? Well, as hard as y'all do anyway."

I look up from the lime I'm juicing. "That a request? To work your body hard?"

"Hell yeah, it's a request." Her eyes dance.

"Don't have to ask me twice. But really, you work hard too, Mollie. Give yourself more credit."

"I work hard watching y'all work hard." She crosses into the kitchen. "I work especially hard watching you."

I pour tequila over the lime juice. Then I top off each glass with a good pour of Topo Chico and a slice of lime. "Then why're you messin' around with that jackass from Dallas?"

"Because!" Mollie takes the glass I hold out to her, eyes wide. "I was…frustrated, okay? It's like the world's worst best tease, being around you and your chaps and your fucking mustache all day, every day."

My dick twitches at the idea that I turn Mollie on so much—so often—she had to call a friend for relief.

Aw, honey, you know you're only gonna find relief if it's with me.

"So you like the 'stache," I manage.

277

"On everyone else, I hate it. On you?" Mollie's nostrils flare. "It's like the second coming of Tom Selleck."

I can't stop laughing when this girl is around. "What a stud that man is."

"Stone-cold fox," Mollie says with a solemn shake of her head.

"To Mr. Selleck." I hold out my glass. "And to Garrett."

"To Dad." Mollie clinks her cocktail against mine. "May we make him proud."

"I think we're doing better in that department now." I sip my drink. Cold, crisp, delicious. Hint of citrus and spice. It's the perfect cocktail after a long, hot day.

Mollie smacks her lips after a sip. "That's so, so good, Cash. Wow." She sips again. "You really think Dad would be proud of us?"

"I do." I drink, the tequila hitting my bloodstream. "A homicide hasn't happened yet. You're looking mighty fine on horseback. You and the cowboys get along, and Patsy and John B just adore you." I meet her eyes. "You're tryin', Mollie. I think maybe that's all he wanted when he gave you the ranch and said you had to live here for a bit. He wanted you to try it on."

She blinks. "Why would he want that, though?"

"Not sure." I shrug. "He knew you took after your mama. Could be he thought you might take after him too."

"You think so?"

I set my glass down and lean my backside against the countertop. "I know so, honey."

Her throat works as she swallows. "I like when you call me that. Sounds…so fucking good when you say it, Cash. By the way, is Cash your real name? Or is it a nickname?"

"It's my real name." My lips twitch. "My parents were obsessed with Johnny and June Carter Cash. The first song they danced to the night they met was 'I Walk the Line.'"

"Cute."

"Right? Anyway, when they found out I was a boy, they knew right away they'd name me Cash Robert Rivers. Cash after Johnny, of course, and Robert after my grandfather."

She grins. "That's a good, strong name."

"Thank you. Now get over here."

Sipping her drink, she raises a brow. "Okay. Maybe I also like it a little bit when you tell me what to do."

"You like it a lot. Get over here, honey."

Mollie saunters toward me like I'm not about to yell from wanting her so bad. When she's close enough, I reach out and grab her, yanking her against me so our hips are flush.

She lets out this startled, happy sound when I roll my erection against her.

"Already?" she pants.

"Already."

"Let me finish this, then." She drains most of her ranch water before setting it on the countertop beside mine. "Need some hydration before—"

"I work you hard?" I bend down, wrap my arms around her knees, and toss her over my shoulder. "Good idea. You're gonna need it."

She laughs, and I make a beeline for the bedroom.

CHAPTER 23
Bare
Cash

I toss Mollie onto my bed and immediately get to work on my belt.

I can't fucking believe she's here.

I can't believe this beautiful woman is mine. For tonight at least. How'd I get so damn lucky?

Breathless from laughter, Mollie watches me, brown eyes going hazy as I rip the belt through my belt loops. I left the lamp on the bedside table on, so I can see her expression flicker.

"Wrong that I find that *so* hot?" she asks.

"Not wrong at all." I wrap the belt around my fist. "You like what you like."

The bed is high off the ground, a four-poster I built with the master carpenter who restored the cabin. So I'm able to pull Mollie to the edge of the mattress and step between her legs. Bending at the waist, I run the hand wrapped in my belt up her side before capturing her mouth in a kiss.

My blood jumps when she doesn't hesitate kissing me back. Our lips move in tandem, opening so I can lick into her mouth at the same time as she licks into mine. She's a deep kisser, passionate. Playful and vulnerable.

A few weeks ago, when we first met, I would've been surprised by this. How unlike the stuck-up, snobby city girl to be so sweetly soft. So unabashedly fierce in her hunger.

Now, though, I'm not surprised at all. Mollie ain't afraid to let go, let loose. And something inside me loosens at the idea that I make her feel safe enough to do that.

Bet that dickhead from Dallas didn't see this side of her.

I grab one of her wrists and guide her arm over her head. Do the same with the other arm. Then I take both wrists in one hand and pin them to the mattress.

My cock surges when she sucks on my bottom lip, languidly tugging it between her teeth before arching her back when I reach inside her shirt with my free hand and cup her breast.

Her nipple hardens to a sweet little point when I pluck it through her bra. I shove up her shirt and kiss my way down her throat. She moans when I sink my teeth into her neck. She likes that.

She rocks her hips, guiding the bulge of my erection up and down her center. I growl.

I like that.

I like that she *knows* that I like it. She rolls her hips again and again, and *goddamn* I'm about to lose my mind at just the thought of being inside her.

At the thought that she cares enough to learn me so thoroughly.

I suck on her nipple through her bra. Nick it with my teeth before moving to the other nipple.

"Cash," she breathes. "This is torture. The sweetest torture."

"Just you wait."

Giving her nipple one last bite, I turn my attention to her hands. I watch her eyes as I wrap my belt around her wrists once, twice, buckling it tightly.

"Too tight?" I ask, slipping a finger inside the buckle to check.

"No." She bites her lip. "I like it tight like this."

"You sure?"

"I'm sure, Cash."

"Tell me if it starts to hurt too much. And keep your arms above your head. Understood?"

"Yes."

"Yes, *sir*."

Her swollen lips curl into a smirk. "Yes, *sir*."

"That's better."

Then I'm trailing my hands down her body, and I'm pulling off her skirt. I'm unfastening her bra and shoving that up by her shirt.

Then I straighten, standing at the edge of the bed. Immediately, she bends her legs and pulls them together.

"Nuh-uh." I reach behind my head to grasp the back collar of my shirt. "Open your legs. Right now, Mollie. I wanna see you. All of you."

I yank off my shirt and toss it on a nearby chair. I'm pleased to see Mollie obey me, her knees falling apart on the mattress.

My heart thumps at the sight of her swollen pink

slit. Her pubic hair is neatly trimmed, a little lusher on the top.

I run my thumb over it. "I'm glad you left this."

"I'm glad you took your shirt off. Jesus Christ, Cash."

She laughs when I run a hand over my chest, my fingers catching in the thick, wiry hair there. "You like hair too?"

"I love it. Can I really not touch you?" She wiggles her fingers.

Shaking my head, it's my turn to smirk. "Not this round. Next one maybe. If you listen."

"I think I've proved I'm coachable."

I unbutton my jeans and push them down, along with my briefs. Stepping out of my boots, I shove everything aside so I'm standing in front of Mollie, naked as the day I was born.

Mollie's eyes catch on my cock. Her mouth forms a neat little O. "Of course you'd have a beautiful dick."

"Why didn't you say so in the truck?" I fist myself in my hand and tug. A lazy, indulgent pull that makes my balls contract.

"I couldn't see it this well in the truck. You're—it's not fair, Cash. God pulled out all the stops when he made you. Shoulda left some pretty pieces for the rest of us."

I laugh, reaching for her pussy with my other hand. "You got lots of pretty pieces, honey." Stroking my thumb up her length, I suck in a breath when I feel just how wet she is.

Her body jerks when I circle my thumb over her clit.

Her smirk fades. "Please, Cash. I want you there. Inside me. Please."

I stroke myself again and again, the pressure inside me sharp-edged as I continue to pleasure her too. My mouth goes dry as I rake my eyes over her body. She looks gorgeous with her tits thrust up high, her arms pulled over her head. She's all long legs and soft curves. Luscious hips. Full, pouty mouth.

Her hips rise to meet my touch. I dip my thumb inside her. Curse at how small and sweet and perfect she is.

The thought grips me: *No one else.*

I don't want anyone else knowing what she feels like here.

I don't want her learning anyone else the way she's learning me.

Fuck, I'm in deep. If punching a guy because he hurt her feelings wasn't a sign, me blurting, "We gotta use condoms?" certainly is.

Mollie's eyelashes flutter. Her eyes go dark. I can't tell if that darkness is arousal or disgust.

Rolling my thumb over her clit, I continue, "I never ask that because the answer should always be yes."

Breathless, Mollie nods. "It should be, yeah."

"But the thought of usin' 'em with you, having something between us…" I pump my hips into my hand. "I fuckin' hate it, Mollie. Got my test results from my physical a couple of weeks back, and I'm negative across the board. Haven't been with anyone since."

She raises a brow, eyes flicking over my torso. "With that body, you haven't been with anyone?"

"Been busy with other things." I chuckle. "But this is the kinda busy I like."

Her head falls back when I gather her clit between my thumb and forefinger and give it a gentle tug. "*Cash.*"

"I'll wear a condom if you want me to. No questions asked. But I wanna feel you. All of you." *And yeah, maybe the fantasy of knocking you up turns me on in a way it shouldn't.*

Maybe I wanna have her in a way that's not casual. This isn't a throwaway fuck. I don't know what I am to Mollie, but I sure as hell ain't gonna be a friend she sometimes hooks up with.

The darkness in her eyes deepens. They're practically black now, all pupil. "Results are same as yours. And I'm on the pill. And I know where you live if something happens, so..."

My hips jerk, cock surging in my hand. "You really think I'd run if I got you pregnant?"

It's a weird fucking question. One I absolutely should not be asking Garrett Luck's daughter.

But Mollie, being the perfect human she is, just takes it in stride with a sly little smile. "No, Cash, you wouldn't run. But I don't think you'd let me ride horses anymore."

I laugh, the light, soft feeling in my chest so big and broad it cracks me half. "You're a cowgirl now, honey. And cowgirls can't be tamed. Wouldn't dare to try."

Now she's laughing, and I'm practically choking on the feeling inside me.

"I like you, Cash Rivers," she says, expression softening.

I gather her wetness on my first two fingers. Stroke her clit one, two more times before I reach up and slather the moisture on her nipple. "You're about to like me a lot more, Mollie Luck."

"Awful"—she yelps when I bend down to circle that

285

nipple with my tongue—"full of yourself, aren't you, cowboy?"

"Naw, honey. Just honest."

Then I shape her waist with my hands and toss her farther up on the bed. She gasps. I climb on top of her, my dick hanging heavily between us as I capture her mouth in a hard, hot kiss. I hold her bound wrists in one hand. With the other, I reach down and hook my palm around the back of her knee. I push her leg up and over, spreading her wide.

We look down at the same time. Her pussy glistens in the light of the lamp.

"Beautiful." I look up to meet her eyes. "That pretty pussy's gonna come on my dick, you hear me? I wanna feel it."

Mollie pulls her eyebrows together. They curve upward, like she's in pain. "I wanna feel it when you come inside me."

I stare at her. My dick throbs. I don't think I've ever been harder in my life.

Mollie's eyes toggle between mine. She just admitted something—something I get the feeling she hasn't told anyone else—and she wants to know what I think.

Ducking my head, I draw my nose up the slope of her neck. Stop to suck on the hollow just beneath her ear. "Yes, ma'am." My voice sounds husky against her skin.

She moans.

I reach down and take myself in my hand. I'm hot to the touch. Shaking. But I still manage to glide my head over her clit. I curse through gritted teeth at the soft, slick feel of her bareness.

Mollie rocks her hips, asking for more.

"Remember what I said," I bite out. "You come on my dick."

Then I notch myself at her center. She rolls forward at the same time as I do, her pussy swallowing my crown.

"Oh, Cash." Her eyes are on the place where our bodies are joined. "You feel so fucking good."

I'm only an inch, maybe two, inside her, but her pussy's viselike grip already has me gasping for air. Leaning in to kiss her mouth, I slowly sink the rest of the way inside her. "You're perfect, honey."

She makes a high, soft noise against my lips. Keeping my hand on her wrists, I lower my weight onto her, using the muscles in my core to hold myself up just enough not to crush her.

The feel of her nipples pressing into my chest sends my pulse into a tailspin. She's so fucking *soft* everywhere. Soft but unafraid to share that softness with me.

I lose it.

I draw back my hips and lift my head. Look Mollie in the eye and roll my hips forward, a hard, deep, unhurried stroke that has both of us gasping. My balls make a lewd slapping noise against her pussy as I bury myself to the hilt.

The heat of her swallowing me whole makes my blood riot. I pull back, slam forward. Mollie cries out, a cry I capture in a messy, wet kiss as I fuck her. Hard. Mercilessly. Stroke after stroke of gutting thrusts that have my stomach caving and my heart flying.

I want to fuck away her sadness. Her regret over what she did and didn't do in the past.

Fuck her until she feels it too—the certainty that

she's not so much as looking at anyone else while she's here.

Fuck her so well and so thoroughly that she *stays*.

I take my time, but I go deep, the headboard thumping against the wall in time to my movements.

Mollie is at my mercy with her hands bound, my body pinning hers to the mattress. But she still manages to move with me, her body rolling athletically in time to my strokes. She tilts her head and runs her tongue up my neck, making goose bumps break out on my arms and legs.

At the same time, I start to sweat. Heat creeps up my dick and gathers in my head.

No way Mollie ain't coming first.

Breaking our kiss, I toss her leg over my shoulder. Shove aside her shirt and nip *her* shoulder as I fuck her at a new, deeper angle, her cries becoming yells.

I reach between us. Feel her pussy spread around my girth. I play with her clit, pressing my fingers against it while I increase the speed of my thrusts.

"Lemme feel it, cowgirl." I roughly glide my fingers over her clit.

Her pussy flutters around my cock just as I'm leaning down to kiss her mouth. Our tongues work in a frenzied dance as I bring her closer. Her hips punch forward, pushing me *so fucking close* to the edge of my own orgasm.

Her legs are shaking.

"Now," I growl. "Come now, Mollie. I feel you. Let go, honey. Let fucking go."

Two wild heartbeats later, she does.

Her pussy clamps down on me. She moans my name. I shout, an explosion of stars racing down my spine at the feel of her pulsing around me. Bare. Raw. I can feel myself already leaking inside her as her leg falls off my shoulder.

Our fit is so tight when she's coming, it's almost painful. The pressure makes my head spin. She fights my grip on her wrists, arching against me. Her moaning takes on a pleading edge, her eyes squeezed shut.

Wrong that I take pride in making her come this hard?

I keep kissing her. Keep rocking into her as steadily as I'm able to. But I'm the one shaking now.

"Your turn," she breathes against my lips. "Go, Cash. Please."

She's anything but polite outside the bedroom. But when I get her underneath me, she's so desperate for more, she uses her manners to beg me for what she wants.

I feel like the desperate one, though, as I jerk my hips back and forth. Fucking her hard enough to make her tits bounce against my chest.

"You don't want me to come inside you, speak now," I manage, "or forever hold your peace."

In reply, she nips at the corner of my mouth.

A searing, white-hot pressure gathers in my balls. It shoots up my dick, and I come in hard, hot spurts. The intensity of the release is unreal. I'm surprised I don't bite off my own tongue as I grit my teeth and hang on to Mollie. My hips spasm. My heart crawls up the back of my throat and throbs there, eager for escape.

Mollie sighs into my mouth. I feel her lips pull into a smile against my own.

"You feel so good." She lifts her legs to gently cradle

my hips between them. "Cash, this feels so fucking good."

My chest twists at her tenderness. I feel safe here, even though the things Mollie makes me feel aren't safe at all. Life's crushed me so many times, I've lost count. Yet here I am, opening myself up to total destruction like I don't have everything to lose.

My back aches from holding myself up. I lean a little more of my weight into Mollie. I need her warmth. The scent of her skin and the clean taste of her mouth.

We're silent for several beats, both of us breathing hard.

"Cash?" she finally asks.

"Yeah?"

"Can you untie my wrists? My arms are asleep."

My chest twists again. "I'm sorry."

"Don't be. I liked it."

I do as she asks, unwinding my belt from her wrists. I curse when I see red welts in her skin. I carefully massage her there. "This hurt?"

"A little. But you're making it feel better."

"You shoulda said something."

"I didn't want to say anything because *I liked it*." She wraps her arms around my neck and pulls me down for a kiss. "That was perfect."

You're perfect. I'm falling for you, and I wanna know what I can do to make you stay.

I'm way too close to confessing things I shouldn't. Not here. Not now, while I'm still inside her.

So I pull out a little. A rush of cum follows, coating both of us in warm stickiness. Can't remember the last time I didn't use a condom. I forgot how messy raw sex is.

How hot.

"I'll clean this up. Hang tight."

When I push up to my knees and straighten, I see Mollie's thighs glistening with my release. It leaks out of her pussy in a pearlescent stream.

She's covered in me, her pretty tits rising and falling as she looks at me looking at her.

Something feral takes hold inside me. A desire to possess this woman. Claim her in some fucked-up, caveman way.

So instead of doing what I should—head to the bathroom for a warm washcloth—I reach down and gather my cum on my first two fingers. Then I look Mollie in the eye and use those fingers to push my cum back inside her.

Her eyes go heavy-lidded as I finger her, stretching her past the point of comfort. Her breath catches, eyebrows curving upward.

"Tell me to stop," I grunt.

But she just shakes her head and rolls her hips into my touch. Her hand finds my wrist, and I let her guide me in and out, in and out.

She bites her lip, her pussy fluttering around my fingers.

"You gonna come again?"

"I don't—I never come twice in a row. But this is... getting me close."

What the fuck are we doing? What sick game are we playing at?

I love it.

I want it to be like this every night.

I want her in my bed every night, my cum in her mouth, between her legs, on her skin.

After a minute, she shivers.

I run a hand up her side. "Aw, baby, you cold?"

"A little."

"Any interest in a shower?"

Her eyes light up. "Only if you're in it with me."

———

Later, after we've cleaned up and we're back in bed, it starts to rain.

It's quiet at first. A drizzle. Then it comes down harder on the tin roof, the sound like a steady, rolling thunder that's somehow soothing.

"It's like a lullaby," Mollie says sleepily. She's naked, the little spoon to my big one.

We're on our sides. My arm is locked around her waist. Her ass is pressed into my lap. I nose the back of her neck, inhaling the scent of her skin. I could go for another round—easily—but I know Mollie needs her rest.

"Go to sleep, honey." I kiss her nape.

She grabs the forearm I've got on her waist and gives it a squeeze. "Night, Cash."

"Night, cowgirl."

I hear the smile in her voice when she says, "I like that nickname better."

"Let's sleep in a little, yeah?" I find myself asking. "I know I said I'd take you home early, but if I'm being honest, I'd really like you to stay."

Mollie goes still. "Cash Rivers wants to *sleep in*?"

"Just a little," I say with a chuckle. "I won't set an alarm. Fair warning: I'll probably be up early anyway."

CHAPTER 24
Breakfast in Bed
Mollie

I wake up sore and smelling like Cash.

The scent of his body wash rises off my skin. Burying my face in the pillow, I smell his detergent too.

For such a filthy-minded guy who has a very dirty job, Cash keeps a very clean house. Because he's not delicious enough with his hats and his thoughtfulness and his big, athletic, obscenely gorgeous body, he also lives like a real human. One who has real interests and whose house feels like a real home. I've been to Palmer's place a few times, and while it's in a nice building in a nice part of uptown Dallas, it's sterile—from the expensive but bland furniture no one ever uses to the empty shelves in the living room.

Cash's place is cozy. Comfortable. Lived in.

I love it.

The window across the room is open. It's early, the light barely gray. The rain has stopped, and now a cool, crisp breeze blows into the room. My heart leaps at the thought that autumn has finally arrived.

Somehow, Cash and I are still spooning.

Somehow, I'm still turned on, despite the pair of epic orgasms he gave me last night.

Ordinarily, I'd feel a flare of panic. I make it a point to never overstay my welcome at a guy's place. Mornings can be awkward, and no one is a fan of the walk of shame. Usually, I prefer to get laid and get gone.

But Cash made it crystal clear he wanted me to stay. And yeah, the fact that he got in a fistfight over me makes me feel...

Wanted. Adored. *Safe*, as messed up as that sounds.

And really, what did I have to lose by spending the night at Cash's cabin? If things get awkward, the pain will be temporary. I'm not staying in Hartsville longer than I have to. Definitely not long term.

But listening to Cash's deep, even breathing behind me—feeling his warm, hard body wrapped around me—kinda makes me wish I were.

Oh my God, do I want to stay on the ranch?

Even if I did, could I? What about Mom? And Bellamy Brooks? Wheeler can't do the heavy lifting forever. My whole life is in Dallas.

Except I suddenly, unexpectedly have a life here too. And as much as I love the city...

I think I'm totally falling in love with the country too.

Then again, that could very well have something to do with the incredible sex I had with the incredibly attractive man beside me. But is Cash just part and parcel of why I'm enjoying life on the ranch so much?

There are always people around. People who care, who give a shit about the right things: family, being outdoors, looking after each other and the land.

I like my life in Dallas. But even though it's a huge city and there are technically always people around there too, I don't feel the same sense of connection to those people that I do to Patsy or Wyatt or even Ella. In Dallas, everyone's always in such a rush.

Here, we gather around a table three times a day. We eat real food. We use our bodies instead of sitting in front of a screen all day. The heat is brutal, but seeing the sun rise over the Hill Country makes all the sweat worth it. Feeling that connection with nature is life-giving.

I get what Jen was talking about when she said her life is more vibrant in a small town. There's just a real sense of community here, of family, that I feel like I've been missing in Dallas.

I miss Mom. I miss shopping. I miss sleeping in my own bed.

But I wonder if I'd miss *this* more? Sleeping in this man's bed, a man who knows what he wants? A man who puts the people he loves above everything else? Windows open, homemade breakfast imminent?

Speaking of breakfast, although Patsy will have stocked the fridge with oodles of leftovers from the week, I like the idea of making breakfast in bed for Cash. We were up late last night. And yeah, I feel like making him an omelet is the least I can do after he defended my honor like some old-timey Clint Eastwood character in a Western.

Maybe—*maybe*—if I make Cash breakfast, I'll be able to convince him to stay in bed with me all morning. I definitely want to have sex again. And I definitely think Cash could use a day off.

He turns his head on the pillow so that he's facing me. I hold my breath, hoping I didn't wake him, but he continues to breathe deeply, evenly, his face expressionless with sleep.

I can't believe I'm up before him. Yet I totally can. The man is beyond exhausted. Honestly, when was the last time he slept in?

Seeing him this close in the morning light, I notice all the freckles he has. They dot his nose and cheeks, and a few darker ones are spread out over his neck.

I resist the urge to reach out and trace the little maps they make with my finger.

My pulse panics. I can't remember the last time I wanted to linger in a man's bed, much less the last time I wanted to linger over a man. But here I am, my fingers itching to express the achy tenderness inside my chest.

Is that such a bad thing?

The question has me thinking about Dad. He turned away from this kind of vulnerability.

That had to be one of his biggest regrets.

There's a whisper in the back of my head. A catch, like pieces of a puzzle coming together.

I imagine it's a regret Dad wouldn't want me to have. And the person who's opened me up the most over the past few weeks, who's encouraged me to turn *toward* vulnerability, has been none other than Cash Rivers.

No way Dad intentionally brought us together, knowing we'd end up being good for each other.

No fucking way, right?

Shoving the ridiculous idea aside, I slip out of bed

and head to the bathroom. I turn on the light and nearly gasp when I see the bruises on my wrists.

Cash tied me up last night. With *his belt*. It hurt, and it was awesome.

I brush my teeth using the toothbrush I brought with me from the New House. I forgot to take out my contacts last night, and my eyes burn a little. Idiot move, but really, how could I not have fallen asleep with Cash wrapped around me, the rain making music on the tin roof?

I creep back out to the bedroom and dig a clean white T-shirt out of the dresser by the door.

It smells like Cash. I pull it over my head and then spend a minute or two hunting for my underwear. I remember Cash putting them in the back pocket of his jeans, but I can't find them in the semidarkness. Luckily, his shirt covers my butt, so I tiptoe out of the room, closing the door carefully behind me.

Because Cash is a real human being, *of course* he has real food in his fridge. Kinda surprising, considering he has Patsy to cook for him all week. I find eggs, cheese, and a jar of salsa, along with half-and-half and butter. I get the coffeepot going first, and then I find a pan and get to work on some spicy omelets.

I watch the sky brighten the window above the sink, filling the cabin with soft amber light. The coffeepot gurgles, making the room smell delicious. I open the front door and keep it open when I find a screened door in front of it, allowing that lovely breeze in.

Melting far too much butter in a battered cast iron pan, I wonder if I've ever been happier or if I'm just basking in some kind of postsex glow. I'm tired, and there's a twinge between my legs anytime I move. A reminder of how…thorough Cash was.

I blush when I think about him touching me there after we had sex. What he did was obscene. A little weird.

And so fucking hot, I'm squeezing my thighs together thinking about it. I've never been with someone who… marked me like that, I guess. Are all cowboys so wildly possessive? Or is it just Cash?

Is it Cash, but only when he's with me?

My stomach flips along with the omelet I turn over in the pan. This man is turning me inside out. He's turning me into someone I never thought I was. Or maybe I've always been this woman; she's just been buried underneath old resentments and untrue stories she's made up to bury her own hurt.

The chatter and chirp of birds drift through the screen door. I'm sliding the first omelet onto a plate when a voice sounds behind me.

"Nice shirt."

Glancing over my shoulder, my heart stutters, then stops altogether.

Cash is standing at the threshold, holding on to one of the wooden beams that span the length of the kitchen's low ceiling. He's wearing a pair of brown Carhartt sweats and nothing else. His scruff is especially thick, and his hair is tucked behind his ears.

With his arms extended above his head like this, the sides of his torso bulge outward, making him look *huge*.

Also, how did I not appreciate how lush his chest hair was last night? And that thick, unapologetically furry happy trail—it's like a dark arrow that leads my eyes exactly where they shouldn't be.

I can see the outline of his cock through his sweats. He's not hard, but he's thick enough that I can see it as he drops his arms and saunters across the kitchen.

His eyes are piercingly blue in the early morning light.

"H-hey," I sputter. "Thanks. Thank you?"

His lips twitch as he wraps his arms around my waist and melts his front to my back. I nearly pass out from pleasure when he presses a scruffy kiss to my nape.

"Whatcha makin'?" His accent is thicker in the morning. And his voice—the deep, sleepy rumble of it—makes my nipples hard.

"Eggs. What else?"

His mouth moves up my neck, heat blooming to life between my legs. "You didn't have to do that."

"I wanted to." My breath catches when he nips at my jaw. "I also wanted to bring it to you in bed."

His hand is on the outside of my leg now, moving up. "I wanted to do something else in bed first."

"How are you not starving?"

"I am. For you." He rocks his hips, and that's when I feel his growing erection press into my backside. *That was quick.* "Turn off the burner."

"But the omelet—"

"Can be reheated." He hisses when he discovers I'm not wearing underwear, his hand on my hip. "Fuck, honey."

"You stole them, remember? My panties?"

He chuckles, a dark, masculine sound. "You ain't ever gettin' those back."

His fingers dive south. I drop the spatula when he finds me, parting me with his first and second fingers.

Then he slips one of those fingers inside, moving easily through my slickness.

He grunts. "Wet already. You gotta let me take care of this."

I turn off the burner. Let out a little moan when his other hand slips inside my shirt and he kneads my breast, flicking my nipple with his thumb. Arousal slices through my center. He circles his finger over my clit.

My legs begin to shake.

"You sore?" he asks against my neck.

I nod. "A little. But not enough to—"

Before I know what's happening, he's spinning me around and lifting me onto the countertop beside the stove. The motion scatters the pair of plates and silverware I set out, sending them across the counter, but Cash doesn't seem to mind.

Instead, he lifts his shirt over my head and tosses it aside. His gaze darkens as it trails over my naked body, stopping to linger on my tits. He reaches out and takes one in his hand.

He frowns when he glances at my wrists. "Aw, honey, I'm so sorry." He takes them in his hands. "This hurt? I feel fucking awful—"

"I'm fine. I liked it."

His eyes flicker. "Course you did."

"Seriously, Cash, I'm okay."

In reply, he brings one wrist to his lips and kisses the bruises there. Does the same with the other wrist.

When he's done, he steps forward, settling himself between my legs. Then he tilts his head and leans in.

His kiss is soft but hot. It's the kind of kiss you can't help but fall into. One that makes your head spin and your heart sing, a poignant reminder of the sweetness of being alive and being here. Right now. In this kitchen, with this man.

I glide my hands up his chest before wrapping my arms around his neck and bracketing his hips with my knees, pulling him closer. He tastes like toothpaste and smells like him, that clean, crisp soap. Hint of detergent, probably from the sheets.

Need thumps inside my skin, a growing beat that gathers between my legs. Cash reaches down to gently stroke my clit with his thumb. Desire streaks through my core, and I roll my hips into his touch.

I need him. Now. I don't know if this is the first and last time I'll get to have morning sex with Cash, and I'm not about to waste any time.

I glide my hands down his sides, marveling at the thick bulges and slopes of his body.

He growls into my mouth when I hook my fingers into the waistband of his sweats. I pull them down, his cock jutting against my hand. I wrap my fingers around him, firming my grip how he likes before giving him a tug.

He's enormous and hot, heavy with need. I use my thumb to swirl his precum over his tip. He growls again. His thumb works faster over my clit, his tongue licking into my mouth.

A blinding, beautiful pressure fills me, the need for release making me short of breath. I dig my other hand into the hair at Cash's nape and hold on, squeezing my eyes shut as I'm overcome by searing sensation.

I come. Cash's name is on my lips as I whimper, powerless against the onslaught. Then he's taking himself in his hand and he's putting himself inside me, the pressure enormous as his thick head pushes forward.

I'm still coming when he glides inside me on a smooth, deep thrust. All the sensation—the pressure, the pain, the release, the tenderness—it's overwhelming. I grab at Cash, my legs shaking, and he responds by hooking an arm around my waist and pulling me to him, holding me up while he rocks into me. He holds me *close*, close enough that I'm able to bury my head in his neck.

His warmth, his strength, is the comfort I didn't know I needed.

"I got you, honey," he murmurs against my cheek. "You're gonna be okay."

Cash kisses my nose, my chin. My lips and my forehead.

Emotion clogs my windpipe. I have never felt...less *used* or more cared for in my entire life.

My orgasm lingers, stoked to continuous life by Cash's thrusts. He keeps an even, steady pace. The soreness between my legs dissipates, pleasure rising in its wake.

Cash and I are having sex on the kitchen counter, too needy to make it to the bed. But somehow, the sex is slow and gentle. Deep. The way morning sex should be.

Then again, I haven't *had* a ton of morning sex, so I'm far from an expert. But this is nice.

Really, really nice.

Cash jerks his hips, and then I feel a hot rush inside me. The smell of sex blooms between us as he sinks his teeth into my shoulder, biting back a howl.

It hurts, and I know it'll leave a mark. But that just

turns me on more. I love how unafraid Cash is to just go for it. His passion is so unlike Palmer's impersonal ministrations. Cash has this earthiness about him—maybe it comes from being out in nature and working with animals twenty-four seven, I don't know—but he's at home with his body and with mine too.

Sex may be natural, but there's plenty about it that can be gross. Not for Cash, though. He relishes all of it. The mess, the intensity. The aftermath.

None of it scares him. Maybe I shouldn't let it scare me either.

At last, when Cash is able to speak, he kisses my mouth and says, "Mornin', honey."

I throw back my head and laugh, silliness mingling with the bigger, deeper feelings inside my chest. "Good morning, cowboy. Can I finish making you breakfast in bed now?"

He pulls back to look at me. "You really like takin' care of people, don't you?"

"Learned from the best." I touch a finger to his chest. "So let me take care of you. I know you probably have a million things to do this morning on the ranch, but I propose you don't do any of them and stay in bed with me instead."

The edges of his eyes crinkle as he searches my face. "I do have a million things to do."

"Make me all of them."

He laughs, a deep rumble in his chest. "You're bad."

"You're tempted."

"Hell yeah, I'm tempted." Reaching up, he swipes his thumb over my lips. "This is just...new territory for me. Ain't easy to let go."

There's a catch in my chest at his earnestness. "The ranch did just fine the other day when you quit early to take care of me. How many times do I have to catch you before you learn I'll never ever let you fall on your face?" I hold up my littlest finger. "You said you got me. Pinkie promise I got you."

He looks down at my pinkie and blinks. For a second, I worry I've crossed some kind of line. I'm being *too* cheesy. *Too* vulnerable.

I'm asking for too much.

But then Cash hooks his broad pinkie through mine. "All right."

Two simple words, but they feel momentous. For someone as tirelessly responsible and careful as Cash, it's a big step to play hooky. Even bigger step to play hooky with me.

The thought makes my chest swell.

"What do I say when people ask where we are?" He puts his hands on my hips and pulls out of me carefully. "I know you're worried about what they'll think."

I watch him put his sweats back on before he reaches for my shirt and pulls it over my head. "I am worried. But I guess I'm slightly less worried knowing we're in this together now. Maybe we just say we're spending time together and leave it at that. Could always play it like we're working on ranch stuff. Logistics. Big-picture planning."

He eyes me. "I actually would like to talk about that."

My stomach clenches. I want to talk about it too. But truth is I don't know what my plans for Lucky Ranch are anymore. When I got here, all I wanted was to get my money and get the hell out of Hartsville. I planned to sell the ranch as soon as I was able to.

Now, though, that idea doesn't sit right. At all. Which leaves me…where exactly? If I wanted to keep the ranch, my life would have to change completely. I suppose I could live in Dallas and let Cash run operations here. But that also doesn't sit right.

Maybe because I want to run things too. Not in Cash's place but beside him. We do make a shockingly great team.

But that team could easily be torn apart by the sex we just had. What if things get awkward? What if it inevitably doesn't work out, and Cash quits on me?

What if he breaks my heart?

"We got time," Cash says softly. "All day, as a matter of fact."

Swallowing, I manage a scoff. "You're really good at that."

"Good at what?"

"Reading my mind." I put my hands on his shoulders.

He helps me get down from the counter, hands still on my hips. "I pay attention."

Stickiness runs down the inside of my leg. My eyes catch on my bruised wrists. The bite on my shoulder smarts.

This man is wrecking me. Claiming me so that every time I move—every breath I take—I think of him.

I'm hit by the urge to cry. Not because I'm sad but because I'm just so overwhelmed by Cash's ardent attention. The things he makes me feel are big and loud, and it's terrifying to think I've stepped over some kind of boundary, walked off some kind of cliff, without even realizing it.

And I know it's too late to go back, because the last

thing I want to do is the sane thing—the safe thing—and leave.

I turn back to the stove and light the burner. I don't have to ask Cash if he wants cheese in his omelet or hot sauce on the side. He doesn't have to ask me if I want cream and sugar in my coffee.

We know each other now.

I *like* knowing Cash this way.

I manage a smile. "I love it."

CHAPTER 25
Beautiful Mess
Cash

We're in the bathtub a week later when I fall in love with Mollie.

It happens all of a sudden. Or maybe it's been happening all along, and it only takes some bubbles and a good, hard laugh for the realization to finally crystallize.

She's on my lap, facing me. The water is hot. Small mountains of bubbles float on its surface, slicking her skin with bits of foam. Mollie insisted on the bubbles, and my girl gets what she wants.

But being an adult male, I don't have bubble bath. I ended up squeezing some of my body wash underneath the running faucet while the tub filled up. It worked a little too well, and now we're surrounded by bubbles.

So many fucking bubbles.

I swat them away. "I feel like I'm five again."

"That's a problem because?"

"Because they're messy." I glance at the floor, which is also covered in bubbles. "And ridiculous."

Grinning, Mollie loops her arms around my neck and presses her tits against my chest. "Shame you don't like messy and ridiculous things, because I am one."

We've fucked five thousand times this week, our last round being twenty minutes ago in bed (we skipped Frisky Whiskey's Friday night set at the Rattler). But my dick still twitches.

Touching this girl, fucking her, only seems to deepen my hunger for her. Because that's what this feels like—physical hunger I can only satiate by being inside her, near her. With her.

What if she doesn't want to stay the night again? Granted, she's slept here every night since I brought her home from the Rattler last Friday. We've worked out a great little system: I sneak her over an hour after supper wraps up. Lucky for us, it's getting dark earlier now, and far as I can tell, no one has seen us.

The second we're through the door, we're ripping each other's clothes off. Then we'll either take a bath or hang in bed, where Mollie often pulls out her laptop and works while I try not to hump her leg like the horny dog she's turned me into.

I love watching her work. She's thoughtful, thorough, and wildly talented. I love watching her work on the design of her boots the most. I also love when she asks for my input on things—from a possible collection of more functional boots for riding and working on a ranch to the design of Bellamy Brooks's website. Makes me feel like she appreciates me for something other than my Stetsons.

Although she appreciates that part of me plenty.

I grab her hips, which bracket my legs, and give them a

squeeze. I'm smiling hard enough for it to hurt, and I don't care. "I stand corrected. Maybe the mess ain't so bad."

"I like the mess. It's real." She leans in to nip at my mouth. "And the bubbles make it fun." Leaning back, she scoops some bubbles into her hand. Gently starts putting them on my face, like she's applying shaving cream. "You know, if you'd've told me that first day you brought me to your place that I'd end up in this tub again, only this time with you, I would've laughed in your face."

I love watching her concentrate. There's a tiny crease between her brows. Her lips are all pouty, eyes alive with interest. Laughter.

Despite how hot the water is, the tenderness of her touch makes my arms break out in goose bumps.

"Why? You like the bath. I like the bath. I like you."

She pulls her lips to the side in a sly grin. "You have a funny way of showing it."

"I've shown you plenty." I rock my hips, my cock meeting with her center.

Her breath catches, eyes going dark. "How are you not dead yet?"

"I work on a ranch. I got stamina."

Although this level of stamina is new, even for me. Since last Friday night, I haven't slept more than three hours at a time. My hunger for Mollie is so fierce, it wakes me in the middle of the night. I can't go back to sleep until I get my fill.

Thankfully, I'm able to nap on the weekends for the first time in…forever. Last Saturday, I fell asleep fast and hard after our breakfast and sex in bed. I woke up in the middle of the afternoon with Mollie asleep on my chest.

When I checked my phone, I didn't have a single

missed call or text message. I called Wyatt while I had my coffee that morning and told him he was in charge that day.

He was silent for a full minute before asking, "Who is this, and what have you done with my brother?"

I laughed and hung up on him.

Shit must've gone sideways at some point. Always does on the ranch. But whatever went down, our crew apparently was able to handle it without me.

Feels…nice. And weird.

And really fucking nice. Despite my lack of sleep, the mental weight of carrying the world on my shoulders is gone. I feel like I can think clearly—breathe deeply—for the first time in fucking forever.

The one thing that rings clear as a bell? I want this girl to stay. I want more lazy evenings like this. I want to do what I *want* to do. Not what I should do.

Not what everybody else needs me to do.

This time is my own. Feels like I'm finally taking it back. Taking what should've been mine all along.

Mollie dabs bubbles onto my mustache. She pulls back to examine her work. My heart turns upside down when she smiles, the kind that touches her brown eyes. "You make a cute Santa Claus."

"Santa Claus?" Laughing, I run my hands up her sides, my thumbs finding her nipples. "I was hoping it was more of a handsome Dos Equis guy look."

She wags her eyebrows. "Say it. Ho, ho, ho."

We're both laughing now. The silliness of this moment, the lightness of it, is completely foreign to me.

It's fucking lovely.

I swipe the bubbles off my face and smear them

310

across hers. She tries to dodge my hand, but I grab her, tickling her side while I scoop more bubbles onto her face. She silently heaves with laughter, and the fact that I can make someone this happy—laugh this hard—has a steady kind of certainty taking root in my gut.

I need to lighten the fuck up.

Nothing bad has happened while I've been away from the cowboys. And nothing bad is happening now that I'm letting myself have a little fun.

I don't feel dread right now or guilt. I feel...fine.

So much fucking better than *fine*.

Mollie is attempting to shove bubbles up my nose. When I try to duck, she pushes my head underneath the water. Coming up for air, I'm the one laughing too hard to make a sound.

"On Dasher," Mollie gasps. "On Dancer and Vixen. Say it!"

Can I say I'm in love with you instead?

The words materialize inside my head, fully formed. The desire to say them aloud is urgent. This is too much to feel alone.

I am too happy not to tell my favorite person about it.

But I can't, and that kills me.

Hooking an arm around her waist, I yank her roughly against me and kiss her. It's way too soon to say shit like that. And I don't want to ruin the lightness of the moment. Definitely don't want to scare her off.

She tastes like my toothpaste and smells like my soap, and our laughter morphs into hungry gasps as our bodies melt together underneath the water.

I'm screwed. But I couldn't stop kissing this girl if you paid me.

311

Her hands find my hair, and she smooths it back from my face. Her fingertips trail ribbons of sensation across my scalp. She kisses me deeply, fiercely, our lips finding an easy rhythm like we've been at this for months, years.

We make out until I'm fully hard again. She sighs when I slip inside her. Holds on to the edges of the tub as she rides my dick, water sloshing onto the floor when she comes with a happy yell.

What a mess.

What a beautiful fucking mess we're making.

———

Later, I watch Mollie work in bed. She's using a graphic design program on her laptop to test new colors on the Nana boot—a shorter style with a pointed toe and metallic details along the heel and shaft.

I absently trail my fingers along her bare thigh underneath the covers. "I like that. The yellow."

"Really? I think I like the red."

I chuckle. "Red it is, then. I like how opinionated you are. Y'all are gonna crush this launch."

"The more you say that"—she smiles, then leans down to kiss me—"the more likely it is that it'll happen. At least that's what the internet tells me about manifesting shit."

I kiss her back, warmth settling inside my skin. "Honey, you work harder than anyone I know. Of course you're gonna manifest that shit."

She looks at me then. "Thank you for saying that. I do work hard. Probably a little too hard."

"Join the club."

Mollie offers me a fist bump.

I give her one, then twine our fingers. "I'm trying to learn how to work less. Ain't easy."

"I know what you mean. I've always been a hard worker. As I get older, though, I've realized that yeah, my drive can be a good thing. But it also might come from a fucked-up place. Like it comes from a wound or something."

"What do you think your wound is?"

She thinks on this a minute. I love that about her—how thoughtful she can be. No filling the silence with empty bullshit.

"I think I always believed that by being super success-ful, I could fix something that was broken."

"What's broken?"

"Me, I guess? Like if I'm perfect, then I'll be loved."

My heart twists at the naked hurt in her eyes.

It's a big deal that Mollie Luck is sharing this with me. She *is* successful. She *is* a hard worker. Those can be good things.

They're also things that keep people—feelings—at arm's length.

They're things I can certainly relate to.

Mollie trusts me. She sees me too, same as I see her.

I need to show her Garrett's pictures. Just gotta figure out the right time and place. I can't help but feel sharing them with her will be a declaration on Garrett's part and mine too.

Lord, we are in it.

"Close the laptop."

Her eyebrows pop up. "Cash—"

"Don't make me ask again. Close it and come here, honey."

Her lips twitch as she does as I tell her. Then I wrap her in my arms and pull her against me, guiding her head into the crook of my neck. My body jumps at the feel of her tits pressed to my chest, her nipples getting hard at the contact.

I do my best to ignore it. I just hold Mollie as I murmur in her ear, "Just because you're not perfect doesn't mean you're broken."

Her fingers trail through my chest hair. She's quiet.

"I don't need perfect. Your parents didn't need it. World doesn't need you to be perfect either. We just need *you*. You and your messes. You light up a room just by being in it, honey."

She swallows audibly. "You're just saying that because you have a hard-on."

I laugh. "I'm always hard when you're around. But even if that wasn't the case, I'd be saying the same thing." I tip up her chin so she meets my eyes. "There's nothing about you that needs fixing. Anyone that makes you feel otherwise, they ain't meant for you."

She searches my gaze, her eyes wide and wet. "You make it sound so simple."

"Nothing's simple unless you make it simple."

She gives me a watery grin. "So I make it simple."

"I'm here to help you try, honey."

CHAPTER 26
Down Bad
Cash

September turns into October. Mornings are gloriously chilly, even if the afternoons are still hot.

Mollie is still intent on learning the ropes of being a true cowgirl. She's with us and the herd almost every day. And every night, she sits in my bed with her computer on her lap, fingers flying over the keyboard as she works on Bellamy Brooks's approaching launch.

We fuck before and after that, of course. First thing in the morning too. But I'm doggone impressed by how hard this woman works. At the end of the day, I'm beat. Mollie, though, seems to get a second wind when we untack the horses.

I admire her tenacity. Even as part of me knows her cowboy boot company is a big part of what's ultimately keeping her in Dallas. We talk about everything but the future. I don't ask, and she doesn't offer any answers. We just live in the moment.

I try to make my peace with that. I know we get

along well. I know she enjoys my company. And the sex is…Jesus, something else.

But that doesn't mean she's in love with me. Definitely doesn't mean she's thinking about moving to the ranch forever. It'd be weird, right, if I brought that up after a few weeks of…well, are we dating? Because we haven't been on any actual dates. We're fucking, but our connection is so much more than just physical.

I tie myself in knots trying to figure it out.

I need to take my own damn advice and lighten up. Maybe this time is meant to be enjoyed, plain and simple. Why do I need answers if I have Mollie in my bed every night?

Because the more I let her in, the more it's gonna hurt when she goes.

Like I can help it.

Like I can stop falling harder for her each fucking day.

Only solution to that would be to get gone myself. But I can't just up and leave. I don't want to.

Leaving isn't in my nature. But I'm not sure staying is in hers.

What the fuck do I do?

I ask myself that question for the thousandth time while I'm helping John B and Sally administer vaccinations to a handful of heifers on Friday afternoon. We've got a cow in the chute, head safely restrained in the neck extender. Sally is giving her a vaccination in her neck, smoothly and quickly inserting the gun-like multidose tool a few inches behind and below the heifer's ear.

The heifer rattles the bars of the chute, but after a second or two, she calms right down.

"That's a good girl," Sally coos.

"So you give the same dose to every one of these cows." Mollie glances at the cows lined up behind this one. "And you use the same needle and gun and everything."

Eyes twinkling, Sally nods. "Yes, and yes. Obviously, we'll change out the needle if it breaks or there's an issue, but the whole point of the gun here"—she holds up the scary-looking contraption—"is to make things easier on everyone. Fewer needles means fewer chances of accidents happening, and you can set up the gun so each animal gets the same dose. The quicker we get this done, the quicker the cows can go back to doing their thing out in the pastures."

John B straightens from examining the cow behind this one. "You wanna give it a try, Mollie?"

Because Mollie is clearly out to make me one heart-sick motherfucker, she smiles and says, "If you think that's all right, I'd love to. Here, I'll go wash my hands."

Sally waves her over after Mollie's done at the nearby sink. "There's a bit of an art to finding the right spot for the needle. But once you get that, we're good to go."

I release the heifer and line up the other in the neck extender so that the cow's head is secured between two metal panels. Sally shows Mollie how to feel for the correct spot on the cow's neck—away from bone and tendon—and together, they use their fingers to feel for the perfect "squishy" spot.

Instead of being grossed out, Mollie appears to be rapt. She takes the gun and lets Sally show her how to insert it at a forty-five-degree angle.

"You're doing great," Sally says. "Right there. You got it! Go, Mollie."

Mollie's face breaks out in a huge smile when she pulls the "trigger" and administers the vaccine. Again, the cow rustles for a bit, but then she calms down.

John B nods his head approvingly. "You didn't flinch, Mollie. Well done."

Handing the gun back to Sally, Mollie turns that smile on me. Holding up a hand, she walks over and says, "Yee-fucking-haw, y'all. I vaccinated my first cow!"

Heart beating a little too fast, I give Mollie the high five she's looking for. Without thinking, I curl my fingers through hers and draw our palms flush. Her eyes go soft, and so does the stuff inside my chest.

We're both covered in dirt and stink to high heaven. But I'm not sure she's ever been more beautiful than she is right now. Lit up. Proud.

At home.

You belong here, cowgirl.

Hill Country is in her blood. And now Mollie Luck is in my blood, and I can't imagine this place without her.

"You did good, Mollie." My voice sounds different.

Glancing over Mollie's shoulder, I see Sally and John B quickly look away. They were watching us. Can't blame 'em—my girl and I are putting on a goddamn show.

I hear Mollie's phone vibrating in her back pocket. She ignores it.

Clearing my throat, I try again. "Practice makes perfect. Do it again."

Mollie's lips twitch. "Yes, sir."

"Is he making you call him *sir*?" Sally furrows her brow.

Mollie sends a wicked little glance my way. "Isn't he such an asshole?"

My body pulses. "Don't make me pull rank, y'all. Get this done."

They do. Mollie's confidence grows with every cow until they're all done and she's still smiling like an idiot.

Or maybe I'm the one who's the idiot, because I can't even pretend not to stare at her as she digs her phone out of her pocket. She frowns when she sees the screen.

My heart dips. Something happen? Something wrong? It's close to four o'clock, which means it's time to turn in. By *turn in,* I mean sneak Mollie away in an ATV so we can shower together at the cabin before supper.

"I need to return this call." Mollie glances at me. "I'll see you at dinner. Sally, John B, thanks again for the hands-on coaching. I really appreciate it, y'all."

"Anytime, Mollie. You're an excellent student," John B says, waving goodbye as Mollie scurries out of the barn.

Sally ducks out too, saying she's going to clean up.

Then it's just John B and me and the knowing look he gives me as I pretend to tidy up the shovels by the door.

"Mollie's turned out to be a lot more interested in the ranch than we initially thought," he says after a beat of pregnant silence. "Y'all seem to be getting along a lot better."

Straightening, I draw in a slow, deep breath. Put my hands on my hips. My body is tired, but my blood is anything but. It races through my veins, thrumming with excitement at the prospect of spending the evening with Mollie.

There's a good bit of trepidation there too.

I swallow. "She's not who I thought she was."

"I can see that."

My face burns. Meeting John's eyes, I see a knowing gleam there.

Aw, shit. He's onto me. Might as well be honest.

"You and Patsy—I know y'all met in high school. But how did you"—I ponder my words carefully—"You know, keep her? Get her to stay?"

John B's face creases pleasantly as he tucks his hands into the front pockets of his jeans. "I kept her by letting her go."

"That makes no sense."

"It does, though. Patsy's a dreamer. I knew she had plans for her life. Whether I fit into those plans or not, that was her call. Relationships are about compromise, sure. But no one should have to compromise on the big stuff. The big dreams."

I kick at the dirt on the floor. "I don't disagree."

"Patsy and I were together in high school, but we went to different colleges, and obviously, I went to veterinary school after that. Throughout that time, I always made sure she knew how much I loved her. That I'd work my fingers to the bone to make her happy."

My heart bangs against my breastbone. "Right."

"So first, you tell her how you feel."

Literal gulp. "Mm-hmm."

John chuckles. "Telling Patsy I loved her for the first time might've been the most terrifying moment of my life. And I've been gored by a bull. Twice."

"Jesus, John."

"Occupational hazard. Anyway, the risk was worth

the reward." He sweeps out his arm. I know what he's referring to—the life he's built alongside Patsy. "I think because I was unafraid of telling her how I felt, telling her what I wanted, she did the same. We always knew where we stood with each other."

"That does make sense."

"And second, y'all gotta have fun with each other. What's the point of bein' together if you can't laugh and have a good time? That's the glue. Get the fun right, and chances are she'll stick around."

Rolling my shoulders, I let my head fall back. "I'm not great at fun."

"You said it yourself. Practice makes perfect."

"The part about letting her go. What's that about?"

John thinks on this for a beat. "Means you let her chase her dreams while you're chasing yours. Be honest about what you want, of course. But don't guilt her into anything. Don't make her feel any pressure to make her life fit around yours. I knew Patsy wanted to go to a different college than I did. It was a better fit for her. Yeah, I was scared shitless she'd find someone new and forget about me. But…" His mouth curves into a small, secret smile. "I made sure I was unforgettable."

My turn to chuckle. "Do I wanna know?"

"Son, a man doesn't kiss and tell." His eyes dance as they lock on mine. "From the way Mollie looks at you, I'd say you're hard to forget too. Keep doing what you're doing. Trust yourself. The rest will fall into place."

I hesitate. "And if it doesn't?"

John's chest rises on an inhale. "Then it wasn't meant to be. Awful thing to hear, I know. But you can't hold on too tightly. If you let her go and she doesn't come back, then we pick up the pieces and do the best we can to help you move on."

My throat feels thick as I swallow. Much as I feel alone in my responsibilities sometimes, I know at the end of the day, my family—both real and found—really will be there to pick me up if I fall.

"Appreciate that," I reply gruffly.

John walks over to clap me on the shoulder. "I got a feeling, though, that Mollie's comin' back."

I hope he's right.

And when she does, I hope she stays.

CHAPTER 27
When It Rains, It Pours
Mollie

"Goodness, Mollie, you're nearly impossible to get on the phone these days."

I hear the *click, click, click* of Mom's blinker on the other end of the line.

"Answer when I call, honey! Otherwise, I worry."

Ducking into the New House's primary bedroom, I close the door behind me. "I'm sorry, Mom. I've been so freaking busy, I haven't had a second to catch my breath."

A pause.

"Not busy with any cowboys, I hope?"

My stomach flips as I force out a nervous laugh. "I know how you feel about cowboys."

Looking around, my stomach flips again at the disaster before me. There are clothes everywhere. Shoes litter the carpet while stacks of paperwork sit on every available surface. The only semi-neat area is the bed itself. I made it up, gah, when? Last Thursday? Thursday before that? Whatever day was the last time I slept here before I ended up at Cash's.

I've stayed at the cabin ever since, only coming back to take my birth control and grab what I need before supper every day. Which is why this room is such a mess. Between working on the ranch, then working on Bellamy Brooks at night, *then* working out my stress between the sheets with Cash, I don't have time to pick up. I told the cleaning service that comes every week to just leave the room alone. Why clean it if it's not actually being used?

On the opposite end of the spectrum, I blush when I think about how often we're changing Cash's sheets. Even now, bone-tired from a day working cattle along-side the cowboys, my body heats at the thought of messing up those sheets again.

"Hello? Mollie? Are you still there?"

Blinking, I put a hand on my face. My skin is hot. "Yes. Sorry. How are things in Dallas?"

"I'm happy to report that I have news." She singsongs the last word.

Maybe that's why my heart takes a swan dive into my stomach.

I know—I *know*—her lawyers have figured out a way around the stipulation in Dad's will. Which means my mandatory stay on the ranch is about to officially end.

I can go back to Dallas. Meet Wheeler in cute coffee shops to work on the new collection's rollout. Money hit my account at 9 a.m. sharp the first of the month. It was enough to not only pay our overdue bills but also to pay for the manufacture of the first batch of boots from our second collection.

It's why I've been glued to my laptop at night. Our manufacturer has been wonderful about keeping us updated on any progress, and it's been such a thrill to see our vision finally brought to life.

Why, then, do I have a brick in my gut?

"And?" I lick my lips and look out the window.

A deer is nosing at a patch of grass beside the gravel driveway. I like how unhurried she is. Nowhere to be but here.

"And you get to leave that hellhole! A judge ruled that the stipulation in your father's will is essentially unenforceable. I don't remember all the legal jargon, but now that we're wrapping up the probate process, you'll get your trust as soon as next week. What a win for us, huh?"

The saliva in my mouth thickens. "Yes. Totally. Wow. I...don't know what to say."

"Don't sound so excited that my lawyers worked day and night on this. The bill's going to be huge, you know."

"Right. Of course. I really appreciate all the work you've done, Mom. Thank you. Sincerely. It's only...a lot to process. This feels so sudden."

"This feels sudden?" Her hurt is palpable through the phone. My chest clenches. "Sweetheart, this is what you wanted, right?"

"It is what I wanted," I say on an exhale. Only when I think about leaving Lucky Ranch, I feel like dying.

I hadn't realized how much had changed since my arrival a month ago until this very moment. Because really, *everything* is different. How I feel about Hartsville, life on the ranch, working cattle, and the heat and the animals and the cowboys and Cash.

I'm falling in love with everything about this place.

I also love my job and my friends and family back in Dallas.

I don't want to abandon my life there. I also don't want to leave the ranch.

My mind whirls. I could split my time between Hartsville and Dallas. Do weeks here, weekends there? But that would leave Wheeler on her own for the large majority of our working hours. And I need to be on the ground in the city when our collection launches. Do events at local boutiques, host pop-ups at friends' homes.

I could split weeks maybe? But Cash couldn't be away from the ranch that much. And at some point, he's going to start work on restoring Rivers Ranch, which means his free time will be essentially zero.

Holy shit, I'm making plans for the future with Cash.

We haven't talked about the future. At all. Our complete silence on the topic leads me to believe we're both avoiding it.

I have no idea what Cash is thinking. He hasn't asked me to be his girlfriend. But he also won't let me out of his sight. I catch him looking at me all day long. And the one time I tried to shower at the New House so I could save some time, he immediately put the kibosh on the idea.

"You shower with me at the cabin," he'd said. "It's the best part of my day."

How could I not melt? I haven't showered alone since.

I catch his brothers watching us. Wyatt has said a few things to me about the change in Cash. How he hasn't been this pleasant in years and how he seems to have some extra pep in his step.

I haven't told Wyatt about what Cash and I do after hours. It's not my news to share. But Wyatt knows.

Everyone knows. And go figure, Cash was right—people seem to be quietly happy for us. There's no ribbing. No sideways glances.

I just keep showing up to work, and everyone keeps respecting me for it. Simple as that.

The alarm goes off on my phone, yanking me back to the present. I drop my phone from my ear to turn it off.

"That your alarm for your birth control?" Mom asks. "You're still taking birth control, right?"

Furrowing my brow, I head for the bathroom. "Of course I'm still taking birth control. What kind of question is that?"

"Just making sure some idiot cowboy isn't putting idiot thoughts in your head."

No, that's not what my cowboy's been doing.

What would Mom think of Cash? She's clearly biased against cowboys. I understand why she feels the way she does. But Cash is different. He's not an idiot, and he's definitely not full of shit.

He's kinder and more capable and more intelligent than any guy I've dated. Ever.

But he is still a cowboy. And being with him means being in Hartsville, something Mom doesn't understand and wouldn't approve of. She believes there's no opportunity here, especially when it comes to a career outside ranching.

Would she hate me if I stayed? Resent me even, for making a different choice than she did? I'm right around the age Mom was when she packed up our things and drove off the ranch for the last time.

How do I make her see that Cash is different? *I'm* different? Mom and I are alike, sure. But we're also opposites in so many ways. Ranch life wasn't for her, and that's fine. For so long, I assumed it wouldn't be for me either. Her story was the only one I knew.

But now that I've started my own story, I'm questioning everything.

My stomach starts to hurt. It's the first time it's done that in weeks.

"Not all cowboys are shitheads, you know." I dig my birth control packet out of the vanity's top drawer. "The people out here are different, yes. But in a good way."

Mom is silent for a full beat. "You're coming back to Dallas, Mollie."

The way she says it is matter-of-fact. A statement. But I hear the question in her tone. The hint of vulnerability.

She's scared. *Join the club.*

"Don't I have to sign some paperwork for the will? I'll be back."

"My lawyers are ready to meet as early as tomorrow."

"Um, well, I'm not sure I can get there so quickly. But I'll try."

"Good. And then you'll sell the ranch."

I press my thumb against one of the pills on the bottom row of the blister packet. I'm going to get my period any day now, which is a bummer. I have a feeling it won't keep Cash away, but it will definitely make things messy. I don't exactly feel sexy while I'm on my period either.

"Listen, Mom, I haven't made any decisions yet—"

"What the hell are you going to do with a ranch, Mollie? This isn't like you. I haven't had a real conversation with you in two weeks. More than that."

328

Has it really been that long? Looking down at my birth control, it hits me that yes, it has been more than two weeks.

Also, I'm on day three of the last row of pills. I usually get my period on day one. Day two at the latest.

An icy blast of panic bolts through me as I blink. Count. Blink and count again.

"I miss you, sweetheart," Mom is saying. "We all do. I ran into Wheeler the other day, and she said the same thing."

Oh God. My period is late.

It is never, ever late.

Memories flash through my mind: Cash coming inside me in bed. In the shower. In the tub. In the kitchen.

Yes, I'm religious about taking my birth control every day, usually at the same time. But since I've been on the ranch, my schedule's less predictable. I'll take my pill an hour early here, a couple of hours late there. Is that enough of a change to make it less effective?

Holy God, did Cash get me pregnant?

I'm shaking. But weirdly enough, the panic I felt a second ago is fading. I don't know what rises in its place, but the emotion isn't nearly as icy. In fact, it feels kinda warm. Nice.

Which is *wild*. And wrong. I've known Cash for all of a month. I'm not ready for a baby, and neither is he. I have no idea where we stand in terms of our relationship. We're exclusive, but we're also really busy. It's not like either of us has time to pick up other people.

That's not why y'all aren't sleeping with anyone else, and you know it.

"You and Wheeler have to give Bellamy Brooks another shot," Mom continues. "It's important you have boots on the ground here in Dallas. I mean that literally. Wheeler said these boutiques have tens of thousands of followers online."

My chest crumples. I don't know what I'm going to do about the ranch or Bellamy Brooks or the will.

I just know I need Cash. Now.

"Mom, I have to run."

"Wait, Mollie. We have a lot to discuss—"

"I'll call you tomorrow. Promise."

"Sweetheart—"

"*Mom.* I need to go."

"Are you all right?"

No. Yes. I don't know.

"I'll call you tomorrow," I repeat.

Then I say goodbye, hang up, and run out the door.

CHAPTER 28
The Longest Two Minutes
Mollie

Cash appears at the screen door as my footsteps thump across the cabin's front porch.

He pushes the door open. His brows snap together when he takes in my panicked expression. "Everything all right?"

He's still in his work clothes, although he's pulled his T-shirt out of his jeans. The hem rises as he reaches up to spear a hand through his hair, revealing a slice of thick, muscled stomach and side.

His eyes are pools of bright blue in the shade of the porch.

"I'm late," I blurt. Out of all the things I need to tell him, this seems like the most urgent.

"Late?" He steps out onto the porch, scrunching his forehead as he slips a hand inside my shirt. "Dinner's not for another twenty minutes. We got plenty of time for a shower."

Even now, sweating bullets and on the verge of a

panic attack, my body ignites at his touch. "No, Cash. My period is late."

He goes still. His expression morphs, but I can't read it.

"I'm really good about taking my birth control, and I haven't missed a pill or anything like that," I babble. "But I usually get my period by now, and there's no sign of it." I draw a shaky breath and look up at him, trying to figure out what he's thinking. "I'm pretty regular, so this is a little…yeah, scary."

Without a word, he steps forward and pulls me in for a tight, fierce hug.

And without a word, I wrap my arms around him. I bury my face in his big, broad chest and let the tears flow.

My stomachache lessens, then dissipates altogether.

I love—*love*—how safe I feel in this man's arms. There's a very real possibility that we're in very real trouble. But the way Cash is holding me, our embrace comfortable and familiar, makes me feel so much less alone in dealing with that trouble.

Come to think of it, I've never felt *less* lonely than I do when I'm with him. And the knowledge that Cash is here to face this with me is wonderfully affirming.

What if it felt like this all the time?

What if I had Cash by my side as I faced the rest of my life? Something tells me we'd make a really great team as we stared down life's challenges. Celebrated its joys.

Here, in his arms, I feel like I could get through anything as long as he was with me.

I feel mushy and vulnerable and *loved*.

I cry harder.

"Aw, honey, I'm sorry you're scared." He presses a kiss into my hair. "Talk to me."

"My doctor said the pill should be really effective. But obviously—"

"We don't use backup."

"Right." I truly have lost count of how many times Cash has come inside me in the past few weeks. Twenty? Fifty? Five hundred?

I also wonder if the way he, ahem, pushes his cum back inside me could lead to a higher chance of getting pregnant. I can't imagine it *didn't* help his sperm possibly find a rogue egg.

"Let's drive into town, then. Get you some tests."

I look up at him, puzzled by the calm, cool way he's handling this. "You don't seem upset."

"Should I be?" He tucks my hair behind my ear as he thumbs away my tears. The tenderness of his touch takes my breath away. "I don't mean to make you feel wrong for bein' scared. We obviously didn't plan this. But if I'm being honest…"

My heart beats hard and fast as I wait for him to finish that thought. Cash has been open about wanting a family of his own. So have I.

But it's way too soon, right, to have a baby together? I mean, yeah, Cash has practically moved me in with him. And he looks after me. And makes sure I'm fed and comfortable and happy. He asks about my work. Takes an interest in my opinions. He doesn't ever look at anyone else, and he only ever dances and drinks with me when we've been out at the Rattler.

I come first. Literally and figuratively.

Is Cash in love with me too?

Looking into his eyes, I see softness and concern.

I see interest. A little heat.

They're *alive*. Not tired or clouded over the way they were when I first met him. And isn't that love? Someone else making you feel thrilled you exist despite the hardship and the heartache life brings?

I'm gripped by the need to tell him about my conversation with Mom. How the stipulation has been struck down. But if I do that, I'm going to have to tell him how I feel. It's only fair he knows *why* I'm so torn over what to do next.

Will Cash want me to stay in Hartsville? Or will he make a fool of me for thinking I ever belonged here?

"Well," he says at last, "let's get the tests and go from there, okay?"

My heart turns over. I blink. "Okay."

"Whatever happens, Mollie, we'll be all right. I promise."

Because Cash is the kind of man who keeps his promises, I believe him.

———

On the ride into town, I text Patsy to tell her Cash and I won't be at supper. When she asks if we're okay, I tell her we're fine and that we'll see her at breakfast. My heart swells at her offer to wrap up some leftovers for us.

I'll leave them in the fridge for whenever y'all get hungry. Thinking of you two.

It's dusk by the time I climb back into Cash's truck with a Hope Pharmacy bag in my hand, a pair of plastic sticks tucked inside.

Cash climbs into the truck beside me. He tosses his

phone onto the dash. The timer he set inside the store for two minutes is counting down from one minute thirty-eight seconds.

One minute thirty-seven. Thirty-six.

My hand shakes as I take the tests out of the bag. I couldn't wait until we got home to take them, so I ducked into the restroom inside the pharmacy and peed on the two sticks that came in the package.

I set them on the seat between Cash and me. The little window where the result will appear—one line for not pregnant, two lines for pregnant—is currently stuck at one line. That line appears right after you pee on the stick. It's the second line you're looking for over the course of the two minutes. That one tells you you're pregnant.

Resting my elbow on the window ledge, I hold my hand to my mouth. My emotions are a tangled jumble inside a pressurized can that's just been shaken. I feel short of breath. On the verge of bursting at any moment.

I could be *pregnant*. With Cash Rivers's baby. If I am…

That could change everything. And nothing.

If I am pregnant and we decide to keep the baby, that would make my choice to stay or leave Hartsville very easy. Some fucked-up part of me longs for that, how black-and-white the situation would become.

But another—saner—part knows it's a decision I need to make outside of what happens in the next minute and three seconds. Would I love to be with Cash for the long haul and eventually have a family with him? Hell *yes*. But the timing has to be right, and I don't want to trap either of us in a life we're not ready for.

I don't want this to push us to make choices we shouldn't.

But goodness, does my heart beat faster at the idea of making a life—making babies—with Cash.

I need to tell him how I feel. I just have to wait another fifty-two seconds.

He reaches across the seat and puts a hand on my thigh. "Breathe, Mollie."

I force air into my lungs. "I'm trying."

"I'm not going anywhere, you hear?" He ducks his head so our gazes meet. "We'll handle this together. We don't have to make any decisions today."

I grab the hand he has on my leg and wrap my fingers around it. "Thank you for saying that. You're handling this like a fucking champ, Cash. Which I appreciate. I just…"

I'm brimming with feelings, and I don't know what to do with myself.

I need to tell you I'm in love with you, but I might be leaving, and I don't know what I should do.

I glance at his phone. Thirty seconds left.

I glance at the tests. No result yet.

My pulse pounds inside my temples.

"You ever have a scare before?" I ask.

He shakes his head. "You?"

"Nope." I look at him. "You're the only one who's ever—I don't know—made me a little reckless, I guess."

Cash lifts a brow. "You havin' second thoughts? About not using more protection?"

"No," I answer swiftly. "Not at all. I don't think it's any secret I'm addicted to you. To the sex we have."

One side of his mouth curls upward. "So you're using me to get quality dick."

I laugh. God*damn* it, leave it to this man to make me laugh in the middle of a very real crisis.

Is it a crisis, though?

"You're an all right dancer too. And your coffee is okay."

He chuckles. "Keep goin'. I like this game."

"Oh please. Last thing you need is an ego boost. You know how gorgeous and hardworking and sweet and selfless you are, Cash. I don't need to tell you that."

He lets his head fall back on the headrest and rolls it to the right so he can smile at me. "But you just did. So I'm gonna tell you how gorgeous and hardworking and caring and genuine you are, Mollie."

I look away, hoping he doesn't see how furiously I'm blushing. "You're just saying that because you're feeling guilty for possibly knocking me up."

"You think I feel guilty?"

His phone chimes, making me jump. I look down at the tests.

"One line means negative, right?" Cash asks, squeezing my hand.

"It does, yeah," I say.

Then I burst into tears. I'm swept up in a rush of emotion. Relief, exhaustion. A little bit of disappointment too, which takes me off guard.

Cash doesn't hesitate. He scoots over and pulls me into his lap. I curl up there, burying my face in his shirt, and I weep. He wraps his arms around me, holding me tightly against his chest.

"See?" He kisses the crown of my head. "It's okay, honey. We're okay."

We are okay. I'm not at all okay. I'm relieved and sad and happy and terrified.

My life may be in Dallas, but now my heart is in, well, Hartsville. Should've seen that one coming.

Cash wasn't upset when I told him I was late. As a matter of fact, the things he said almost made me think *he* wishes I was pregnant. Ordinarily, that'd raise my hackles. *Is this guy trying to tie me down? Hold me back? Keep me barefoot and pregnant in the kitchen?*

But I know Cash isn't that guy. He's got big dreams, and he respects the big dreams I have too.

I think he just wants a family.

I need to tell him. Now.

Sniffling, I sit up in Cash's lap. His blue eyes are full when they lock on mine. Full of concern and softness and something else.

Something that makes my breath catch.

"You said you don't feel guilty." I swallow the thump of terror in my throat. "About potentially getting me pregnant."

"I feel bad you were scared. But we're two consenting adults, having a lot of fun doing…stuff together."

I laugh, running my finger over the broken-in fabric of his T-shirt. "That stuff is great."

"Exactly. If something happened because we were enjoying that stuff a little too much…" He closes his mouth. Opens it. His eyes dart to the window.

Holy shit, Cash is *nervous*. About what?

What is *he* going to confess? I'm suddenly so anxious to know, I'm shaking.

"What if I was pregnant?" I ask softly.

His eyes return to mine. "I respect your timing, Mollie. I'd never push you to do something you weren't ready for. But if we did make a baby?" His Adam's apple bobs. "Honey, I'd marry the shit out of you. Not because it's the right thing to do but because I'm in love with you."

I blink, my eyes bulging. Maybe that's why they fill with tears all over again so quickly.

The timing couldn't be worse.

It couldn't be better.

"Cash," I breathe, because I can't formulate proper sentences now that my heart has beaten its way out of my body.

He takes my face in his hand, doing that thing where he wipes away my tears with the calloused pad of this thumb. "It's no secret I'm in love with you, Mollie. I've been—" He clears his throat. "I wanted to wait for the right moment to tell you. Not when we're naked or working or whatever. And that's all we seem to do these days. Be naked or work."

I fist his shirt in my hand. "That so bad?"

"I ain't complaining." He arcs his thumb over my cheek. "But I wanted this to feel special. I also don't want you to feel alone after a pregnancy scare. I told you not to worry, and now you know why I said that. I'm in, honey. I have no idea how you feel or where your head's at. But now you know what's goin' on in mine."

I can't.

I cannot *even* with this man.

I can only yank him to me and crush my mouth against his. Our teeth collide, and it hurts a little, but Cash only laughs, tilting his head so he can lick into my mouth with long, luxurious strokes of his tongue.

I have to tell him how I feel.

I *want* to tell him.

"I"—kiss—"love"—kiss—"you."

He smiles against my lips. "That's a fuckin' relief."

And now I have to tell him the other thing. The not-so-great thing.

My heart is throwing elbows inside my chest. The pressure is unbearable.

Cash deserves to know. Our relationship clearly isn't a flash in the pan for him. I don't want to lead him on if there isn't a way for us to be together.

If I'm ultimately going to end up in Dallas and he's going to be here, we can't do long-distance forever. And our lives in each of those places are so, *so* different. How could we possibly bring them together?

How can I possibly leave this man?

I break the kiss and lean my forehead against his. We're both breathing hard.

"I'm in love with you, Cash. But Dad's will—the stipulation keeping me on the ranch—it got struck down." I swallow. "I think—Cash, I have to go back to Dallas."

CHAPTER 29
Cowgirl Era
Cash

My heart sputters, then stops altogether.

I open my eyes and see Mollie looking at me. A thick rim of tears lines her bottom lashes. Her eyes toggle frantically between mine.

She's looking for something. What, I don't know.

But somehow, I know deep down that I can't give it to her.

Certainty maybe? Is she asking me to make the choice for her to stay or leave? Course I'll beg her to stay. Hell, I'm more than a little crushed those tests on the seat there didn't give us a different result.

I want Mollie to stay. I want her in my bed. In my life.

I want to put a baby in her.

But that ain't my call to make. Begging would only muddy the waters.

My chest feels tight. She's leaving. Or thinking about it. I knew this couldn't last forever. I knew this moment was coming.

Yet I'm unprepared for how fucking awful it feels. My body is hollowed out except for this weird, tinny reverberation that's like a kick to the chest.

Mollie is leaving.

"That's the call I was on." Mollie takes a sharp inhale through her nose. "Mom's lawyers have been trying to figure out a way around that stipulation since the reading of the will. They got a judge to strike it down."

"How?" It's an idiot question, but I don't know what to say.

Mollie shrugs. "I don't know. But her legal team means business, so…"

I wish I could be angry. Anger is clean. Easy.

Sadness isn't.

"So you gotta go back." I manage a tight smile.

"To sign the paperwork, yes."

"But for the long haul too."

Her eyes continue to search mine. "I do want to go back to Dallas. My mom, my friends…things for Bellamy Brooks are finally happening."

"And you've worked so hard for all that." I swallow. "You've built a life you should be proud of in Dallas."

"I am proud of it." She blinks, a tear rolling down her face. "But I'm also proud of the life I'm building here. I want to go, but I don't want to leave. In fact, I really, really want to stay."

My hands find her hips. I squeeze them and close my eyes. "Then stay, honey."

"But how do we make that work? I hate the idea of never being fully present in either place. The ranch is such a magical spot, and it deserves someone's full attention and devotion. It wouldn't be fair to half-ass it. It wouldn't be right." She wipes away a tear. "But God, I'm in love with it, and I don't want to just leave it all behind."

She's talking about the ranch.

She's also talking about me. Us. The spark between us that unexpectedly burst into a bonfire.

I run my thumb along the buttons on her shirt. She dresses like a real cowgirl now. Jeans, Ariat shirt, working boots.

I clear my throat. My voice is still hoarse with emotion when I say, "I want to make it crystal clear that I'd like you to stay on the ranch. I'd like that very much. But I also understand why you have to leave."

"I'm happy here." She takes my face in her hands. "Happier than I've been in a long, long time. But I'm also happy when I'm with my mom and my friends. I'm obsessed with the boots I'm making." Her lips feather over mine. "I'm more obsessed with you, though. You wouldn't consider—"

"Moving to Dallas?" I open my eyes. "You said it yourself. The people on this ranch are my everything. My family is here. My work is here. I'm not a city kinda guy."

Mollie scoffs. "One of the many things I love about you."

"Then don't try to turn me into something I'm not."

Her eyes flicker with hurt.

"I'm sorry," I say. "That came out wrong. I know you wouldn't ever try to change me."

"I wouldn't."

"I know. I'm sorry."

She takes a deep breath. "I appreciate the apology. Thank you."

343

"What I'm trying to say is we both deserve to chase our dreams. Yours are in Dallas, and mine are here. In Hartsville. Rivers Ranch *is* my dream. Making it into the place it was always meant to be. I want that more than anything. Or I used to want it more than anything." I swallow. "Now I want you."

She puts her hand over my heart. "But you also want to be around your family. Make them proud. Watch them start their own families."

Christ, this is fucking agony. I can barely breathe around the tightness in my throat.

"Yes."

Her eyes fill all over again as she nods her head. "I understand."

"But I don't wanna let you go." I squeeze her hips harder. "Even just to go sign that paperwork. I can't fuckin' stand the thought of you sleeping somewhere else. I'm worried…"

She looks at me. "You're worried about what?"

I glance down at my lap. "That you won't come back to me."

"I'm coming back, Cash." She tips up my chin with her thumb. "But if you're that worried, then you should come with me."

"To Dallas?"

"Yes."

I see her wheels turning as she straightens.

"It'd only be for a day or two. And I don't like the idea of sleeping without you either. Although I'm apparently about to get my period."

I hook my thumb into her belt loop. "You think that'll keep me away?"

344

"Somehow, I knew it wouldn't."

It hits me that a month ago, I would've unequivocally turned down Mollie's invitation. I hated her, for starters. And no way I could be gone an hour, much less a whole weekend. My brothers, Ella, the cowboys—everyone needed me, and I wasn't going to let them down.

Now, though, I am going to accept the invitation. I'd be letting myself down if I didn't. My brothers have proven they can hold their own while I'm gone. And I'm not gonna miss a chance to be with the girl who's turned my world upside down in all the best ways.

I am done missing out on the good shit.

"I'll come with you, sure." I give the loop a tug. "But then what? I know we're thinkin' ten steps ahead..."

"But we have to," she replies quietly, reading my thoughts. "It's the right thing to do."

It's right, because we're both in deep. We want to make this work long-term.

That confession, more than any others we've shared tonight, has my heart in a death grip.

It's not like I planned on falling in love with Mollie. We all like to think we have control over who we want, but I've learned over the past month that's not at all how it works.

I didn't want to fall, but I did. Knowing full well Mollie comes from a world that's totally different from mine.

I would've never opened myself up to that kind of slaughter if I could help it.

But now I have to figure out a way to keep Mollie in my life without either of us having to give up everything else that we love.

We have to figure that out. I guess I begin by taking John B's advice. I have fun with her. Make her laugh. Care for her.

And hope for the best.

Garrett, if you're listening, please help me out.

Mollie bites her lip, eyes fixed on my mouth. "I don't know what happens next, Cash. I think we take it one step at a time? Now we know how quickly things can change." She chuckles. "Maybe...I mean, who knows what can happen? I just want to be with you for as long as I can."

I glide my hand up her side and cup her nape in my palm. She's soft here, delicate, and her eyes go hazy when I draw my thumb down the column of her throat. "I'm yours, honey."

I do my best to prove that to her again and again that night.

Sweat drips into my eyes as I survey my work.

It took some rusty *Tetris* skills, but I think I nailed it. Mollie has spent the last two days figuring out what needed to come back to Dallas with her and narrowed it down to three suitcases, a laptop bag, a hatbox, and something she called a "weekender," which are now tucked neatly into the trunk of her Range Rover.

"Y'all are only going to Dallas for two nights, right?" Wyatt appears at my elbow, a brown paper bag in his arms.

I wipe my forehead on my sleeve. "Believe it or not, yes."

"Why we're surprised Mollie isn't a light packer, I don't know." Wyatt holds out the bag. "Patsy made

346

some snacks for y'all. Chocolate chip cookies and her homemade pimento cheese and crackers."

I scoff, even as my heart twists. "Of course she packed us snacks. I'll give her a call to thank her."

"You know Patsy. She doesn't want any of her people going hungry."

My brother watches me set the bag on the front console. As ridiculous as this car is, I'm looking forward to driving it. It has air-conditioning for one thing. Satellite radio with several country music channels for another.

And yeah, the idea of Mollie riding shotgun beside me, feet on the dash, long legs stretched out, doesn't suck either.

There's an awkward beat of silence between Wyatt and me as I close the door and wipe my hands. I filled him in on the broad strokes of my situation with Mollie. He knows we're more than friends. He knows she's no longer required to stay on the ranch to get her inheritance.

He doesn't know I'm a strung-out fucking wreck wondering if I'm gonna lose her after this weekend. Or maybe he does, and that's why he's out here right now seeing us off.

"So this is the first time you've been out of Hartsville in…how long?"

I glance at the New House's front door. Mollie is inside, finishing her makeup. "I've left plenty. The rodeo in Houston that one time. And the duck hunt outside Austin."

"That was fifteen years ago."

"So? Still counts."

More silence.

And then, from Wyatt, "She's the one, isn't she?"

I don't bother denying it. I just shove my hands into my pockets and watch the front door.

That's all the answer he needs.

"Don't forget Mom's ring is still in the safe," he continues. "If you wanted to give it to Mollie."

What would Mollie think of Mom's tiny diamond on its unassuming gold band? Would she laugh at it? Or would she love it?

"Putting a ring on her finger doesn't solve our problems." I glance at the Rover. Should I turn it on and get the AC going so Mollie doesn't get hot? It's warm out here. "Mollie's got a whole company in Dallas. And she's close with her mom."

Wyatt slowly nods. "Right. And you have two hundred fifty thousand acres of land at your disposal. Room enough for her company *and* whatever family y'all patch together."

I cut him a look. "Aubrey sure as hell ain't coming back to the ranch."

"Just sayin'." He holds up his hands. "You don't have to be nervous about meeting her people, you know."

"I'm not nervous."

He just laughs. "You're gonna be the fish out of water this time. And from what Garrett told us, Aubrey isn't going to take kindly to a cowboy. Least of all one who's dating her daughter."

"I'm not wearin' my hat." I smile at him.

He smiles back. "But you're bringing it with you. And you still got the Wranglers. And the farmer's tan. It's the mustache, though, that's the dead giveaway."

"Mollie likes it." I splay my thumb and forefinger across the hair on my upper lip. "It stays, no matter what her mama thinks."

"See? You're charming when you wanna be. You're treating Mollie right. You know what you want. Who you are. You work harder than anyone I know. If Aubrey ain't impressed…" Wyatt lets out a low whistle. "Who cares?"

"Mollie does." My heart lifts when I see the front door open. "Which means I do too."

Her face breaks into a smile when she sees Wyatt and me. She looks gorgeous in a long, checkered sundress that dances around her legs as she moves. She's wearing her jewelry and heels and a pair of enormous black sunglasses.

She'd look every inch the spoiled heiress if it weren't for *her* farmer's tan. Can't help but smile when I take in the lines on her chest and arms.

She's a city girl. But she's also a cowgirl now too. No way I can let her leave that part of her behind again. There's also no way I can ask her to abandon her life in Dallas.

"Just remember," Wyatt murmurs as he waves at Mollie, "where there's a will, there's a goddamn way."

I turn to stare at him, taken aback by the casual way he can read me like a book. Part of me is annoyed I'm that transparent. Another part likes the fact that my brother knows me so well.

I've broken my back to keep our family together. Nice to know my work's paid off. I know so many people who are estranged from their own families. Garrett. Mollie. It's rare—special—that not only do my brothers and I love each other, but we like each other too.

Which is exactly why I can't tear myself away from this place. But if I did get away more often—if, say, I had to accompany Mollie to Dallas a couple of times a month—my brothers would cover for me. They're not going anywhere.

I just have to show Mollie—and her mom too—that I'm willing to compromise so that my girl and I don't have to sacrifice our dreams to be together. We all deserve a happy ending.

I won't get mine unless Mollie's in it.

CHAPTER 30
Sex and the City
Mollie

I never thought my seven-hundred-square-foot condo was small until Cash Rivers walked into it.

Standing inside the kitchen in his Wranglers and Lucchese boots, he looks like a giant. A very handsome, very scruffy giant who I'm struggling not to climb like a tree right now.

He sets down our bags and looks around. "This is nice, Mollie."

"Thanks." I watch his face as his gaze moves over the open space of the kitchen and living room. "It's my cute little bachelorette pad."

"It's you." His eyes meet mine and he grins. "I like it."

The full feeling in my chest spills over. Of course Cash likes it. Of course he's not intimidated or put off by it. He's secure in who he is.

Makes me realize how insecure the other men in my life have been. Men like Palmer.

City lights are coming alive outside the windows.

The summer haze has cleared, and while I can't see any stars, the sky is wide open, dusky blue, edged with the pale orange of the sunset.

It's a pretty view. Granted, it doesn't compare with sunsets on the ranch. Few, if any, places do.

We went right to the office of Mom's legal team when we arrived in Dallas earlier this afternoon. Cash sat beside me for all three hours it took to go through everything and sign the necessary documents. The team doesn't typically work on Saturdays, but they made an exception for me.

I expected it to be more emotional than it was, but I kept my calm. By signing those documents, I basically acknowledged that I don't need to be anywhere near the ranch in order to get my inheritance. If I wanted to, I'd never have to go back to Hartsville ever again.

The stipulation made all this so much easier because it took that choice away from me. Now *I* have to decide what the future looks like. I don't want to sell the ranch. I can't imagine never seeing Patsy and Sally and John B and the Rivers boys again.

I can't imagine Cash being anyone else's foreman.

Lord, this man's rubbed off on me. He's possessive as hell, and now I am too.

What Mom will have to say about all this, I don't know. She had an event tonight with some friends, so we're meeting her tomorrow at our usual spot for lunch.

Mom was silent on the phone when I told her yesterday that Cash was coming with me to Dallas.

"Is he your boyfriend?" she asked at last.

"Yes. And I'd like you to meet him." I waited for my stomach to hurt, the way it always did when Mom got that tone. The one that let me know she was disappointed.

Yes, I was so nervous, I shook. But my stomachache didn't make an appearance.

"He's a cowboy. From your father's ranch," Mom said.

"He's our foreman, so he pretty much runs everything, yeah."

"Oh." More silence. "So what's y'all's plan, then? I imagine he doesn't want to leave Hartsville. None of them do."

I didn't know how to answer that. I knew it would freak Mom out if I told her the truth—that Cash and I don't know what our plans are yet except that we're in love and trying to figure out a way to make a life together.

"Let's take this one step at a time," I replied carefully. "Can you just promise to give him a chance? I know you don't like cowboys—"

"For good reason! I swear to God, Mollie, if I find out he's trying to tie you down to that place—"

"Cash isn't like that. Trust me, okay? I've never let you down."

Mom sighed. "I know, sweetheart. You have a good head on your shoulders. But I'd like to think I do too, and then your dad showed up, and we all know what happened then. Cowboys are selfish. They'll make you think they're in love—"

"Can you not talk about my dad like that?"

I could practically hear Mom blinking in surprise. "Goodness, Mollie, what's gotten into you? You're asking me to give this guy a chance, but I can already tell he's worked a number on you."

In bed, yes. And in life too, I guess, in all the best ways.

"If you're saying that he's helped open my eyes, then yes, that's true. But he's not pulling a fast one on me. You'd realize that if you met him. Remember you promised you'd do better?"

"Fine," Mom huffed. "I'll meet him. I have to run. See y'all tomorrow."

She'd hung up without saying goodbye. I haven't heard from her since.

Looking up at Cash, I wonder what he'll think of my mother. I told him my conversation with her didn't go well, but I spared him the details. He wasn't surprised. But he did admit to being nervous to meet her, which I thought was kinda cute.

"Should we christen my place or what?" I saunter across the kitchen and wrap my arms around his waist. "Your cabin's practically a holy site by now. We have some catching up to do here in Dallas."

Still grinning, he reaches down to grab my ass. "You do say God's name a lot when you're with me. 'Oh God, Cash.' 'God, that feels too good, Cash.' 'Oh my God, don't stop.'" His hand moves to the small of my back. "I hope you weren't plannin' on sleeping much while we're here."

I reach around to grab *his* ass. It feels as firm and delicious as it looks. "I've never been so happy to be so sleep-deprived in my life."

He leans down to kiss my mouth. I melt my hips into his, my body rising on a familiar tide of arousal. I reach out to tug his shirt out of his jeans, but Cash grabs my wrist.

354

"Isn't Wheeler comin' over?"

"Oh. Yeah. Wow. You're right. She'll be here"—I glance at the clock on the stove—"any minute. Sorry, you distracted me."

I turn back to Cash to see him smirk. "And I ain't even wearin' my hat."

I'm still smiling when I open the door for Wheeler ten minutes later.

"You're *back*!" she cries before pulling me in for a hug. "Oh my God, oh my God, oh my God, I'm so happy to see you! Look how tan you are! You look... happy, friend."

I've obviously told my best friend about Cash. Maybe that's why I blush so furiously—I assume she's hinting at the fact that I look good because I'm getting laid.

Really, why not accept the compliment? I *am* getting laid, and I *am* happy.

Really fucking happy.

"I've missed you," I say. "Gorgeous dress, as always."

Wheeler steps back and kicks up her foot, her dress falling back to reveal a pair of metallic-turquoise boots that are the cornerstone of our next collection.

I gasp. "Oh my God, they're here!"

"First pair off the assembly line," she says proudly. "Aren't they the tits?"

"I think I like you already." Cash emerges from the bedroom and holds out his hand. "Wheeler, I'm Cash. Pleasure."

Wheeler's eyes bulge as they move up, up, up. She's petite, barely five feet tall, and Cash towers over her.

She literally stares as she absently takes his hand. "Hey. Hi. Cash. Ha. Hello. Mollie told me about you, but..."

"Wheeler," I warn.

She turns her wide eyes to me. "What? You could've prepared me a little more. There are cowboys, and then there are *cowboys*."

"She's right," Cash says solemnly. "I'm the second kind."

I want to slap him and kiss him at the same time.

"Since when are you so cocky?" I ask, knowing full well what his answer will be.

One side of his mouth hitches up. "Since forever."

"Oh my." Wheeler puts her free hand on her chest. "I am *so* glad you came to visit us in Dallas, Cash."

"So you and Mollie go way back." Cash reaches for the huge tote bag she's got slung over her shoulder. "I'm dyin' to know what she was like in high school. She was a troublemaker, wasn't she?"

Wheeler is still staring as she lets him take her bag. "Good guess. She was feral."

"No, I wasn't!"

Wheeler leans in to whisper conspiratorially in Cash's ear, "She worked hard, but she played harder. I certainly wasn't the one who set our dorm room on fire."

"That was an accident." I follow them into the kitchen. "I still think someone else turned my straightener back on."

"It was a cigarette," Wheeler says. "It would've burned down the whole building if I didn't think to grab the fire extinguisher."

"Thank God Mollie has you," Cash says.

Wheeler smiles up at him. "Right? Lucky bitch."

She turns her head to give me a look over her shoulder. *Holy fuck*, she mouths.

My face hurts from smiling so hard. My eyes well as I watch the man I love and my best friend in the world lovingly talk shit about me as they get to know each other.

Despite being in a new place with someone he doesn't know, Cash is completely at ease. He's charming. Funny. A good listener. He asks intelligent questions and thoughtfully answers the ones Wheeler asks him about the ranch. My heart skips a beat when he brags about my cowgirl skills.

The only alcohol I have in the condo is a bottle of Opus One wine. I open it and pour us each a generous glass, marveling at how much life has changed since I opened the last bottle of this stuff with Palmer.

I'm in the same condo, opening the same brand of wine. But everything else is different. Not only does the man I'm with want to stay, but *I* want him to stay too, and I'd be crushed if he left.

The loneliness I'm only realizing now that I felt after Palmer would leave, the quiet, has been replaced by the happy chatter of dear friends and the anticipation of a night of really, really great sex.

"Love your boots, Wheeler," Cash is saying as I hand him his wine. "From the new collection, right?"

Wheeler eyes me over her glass. She keeps doing that—giving me these looks, a small smile on her lips.

"You're up-to-date on your Bellamy Brooks, I see." Wheeler turns back to Cash. "If we made men's boots, you'd be first on the list to model them."

"Would I have to take off my shirt?"

"Yes."

"Count me in." He grabs my leg when I try to sit in

357

the chair next to his. Without another word, he guides me onto his lap and puts his hand on my thigh. "Y'all have some real talent. The boots you make are beautiful."

Wheeler grins. "Coming from a cowboy, that's high praise. I have a few more pairs from our new collection in that bag." She nods at her tote on the counter. "Want to see?"

"Wheeler!" I jump up. "You should've said something."

She sips her wine before getting to her feet. "Excuse me for wanting to get to know your boyfriend first."

Cash chuckles. "Thank you kindly."

I flick on the overhead lights, and Wheeler sets the boots out, one at a time, on my kitchen counter. There's a pair of short chestnut-brown ones with star-shaped metallic gold cutouts that are breathtaking. Another knee-high pair is ivory, embroidered with pastel pink and orange flowers.

The midcalf pairs, though, are my favorite. They're like the ones Wheeler is wearing, only in different colors: silver, dark gray, lavender. Each pair is slightly different. The silver is metallic with classic Western embroidery that's so subtle, it's barely noticeable. The gray is python print with a rounded toe and *Long Live Cowgirls* sewn onto the shaft in candy-apple red.

The lavender boots steal the show, though. We named them the Madonna for a reason, and that reason is they absolutely rock. They're metallic, and the embroidery is done in dark shades of magenta and purple, which really pop against the lavender.

Picking up the boots, I marvel at how girlie and ridiculous and perfect they are.

"How'd I know you'd pick those up first?" Cash rises with a small grunt and saunters over to the kitchen. "Pretty. Just like you."

"You know, you don't have to lay it on so thick." I lean my head against his shoulder. "You're getting laid tonight regardless of how much you compliment me."

"Is that a subtle hint for me to chug this wine?" Wheeler holds up her glass.

Cash laughs. "Stay. And I mean it, Mollie. This is incredible work."

"Y'all are so cute, it's almost sick." Wheeler takes a long sip of her wine. "But yeah, this collection is fire."

I set down the lavender boots. "Should I add these to the closet?"

"The closet?" Cash asks.

Wheeler wags her eyebrows. "You haven't told him about the closet?"

"Now I need to see the closet." Cash's lips twitch.

Can you get a headache from smiling so much? I'm about to find out.

"Fine. I'll show you the closet."

I head toward the front door but hang a quick left. There's a single door tucked into a little nook back here. I open it and turn on the lights, then step aside to let Wheeler and Cash through.

"It's technically a second bedroom," I explain. "But we have enough boots to make it a closet-slash-unofficial office space."

He lets out a whistle when he takes in rack upon rack of neatly organized cowboy boots that line three walls. "That's a lot of boots, ladies."

"There's a copy of every pair we've ever made."

Wheeler bends down to drop the pair she's holding to the floor. "Plus some extras that didn't make the cut. Obviously, we warehouse most of our product when we're about to launch a collection. But this is a place to get creative." She motions to the corkboards that line the fourth wall. "We don't have a real office yet, so this is our spot to brainstorm."

"It helps seeing all the boots we've done," I add. "That way, we can riff on old designs without repeating them verbatim."

Cash looks at me, eyes twinkling. "Color me impressed. This is awesome."

"You're awesome." Wheeler nudges him with her elbow. "But that's beside the point. Where are we gonna put this new collection?" She twists her lips as she surveys the room.

We don't have much space in here. In fact, there's not a single empty spot on the boot racks.

"We'll get a real office." I reach over to adjust a stray bit of thread on a corkboard. "We can afford it now, I guess."

"Yeah." Cash is looking around the room. "You *could* do that…"

"Or?" Wheeler turns her attention to him. "You sound like you have an idea."

"I might." His eyes catch on mine before flicking back to the boots. "Sounds like y'all need more of a studio than an office. Because that's what y'all seem to enjoy most, right? The design part of all this?"

My heart flutters. Fuck this guy for paying such close attention to…well, everything.

"You're good," Wheeler says.

Cash laughs. "Something to consider. That's all."

That's all. *You only stole my heart, and now you're stealing my friend's too.*

I still don't know how Cash and I are going to make this work.

But I'm relatively certain I'll die on this hill. Because I don't think I'll be able to let this man go.

I practically fling myself at him the second Wheeler leaves. Chuckling, Cash stumbles backward, curling his arms around me as I suck on his neck.

"What's this about?"

"Thank you."

He presses his erection against me and reaches for the zipper at the back of my dress. "For what?"

"Loving my people."

"You love 'em, so I love 'em too." Cash pulls back to meet my eyes. "I'm only takin' notes from you, honey. You love my people well. So well, I think they're startin' to like you more than they like me."

I furrow my brow. "Of course they like me more. You're a grumpy asshole."

He leans in to nip at the corner of my lips. "That fuckin' mouth."

"It's a problem." I reach between us and cup his dick through his jeans. "What are you gonna do about it?"

"Oh, honey." His hands find my shoulders. He pushes me down. "I got some ideas."

Laughing, I sink to my knees as Cash rips open his zipper. "What kind of ideas?"

"Ideas that keep that sassy mouth busy. Open, honey."

"Only for you."

"That's right." His eyes go hazy when I reach up to pull his dick out of his pants. "Only me."

CHAPTER 31
Gold Rush
Cash

"I can't thank you enough, Wyatt." Keeping my voice low, I glance over my shoulder. "Those surveys were the missing piece of the puzzle."

"Tallulah came through too. Gonna be a big-ass project."

The door behind me is closed, but I can't be too careful. I'm in Bellamy Brooks's "closet," as far away from Mollie's bedroom as possible. It's early, a little past four, and she's dead asleep. I want her to get some rest before we meet her mom later today.

I move the mouse on my laptop over the PDF files Wyatt just sent over. "Yep."

"We'll need lots of money."

"Lucky for us, the ranch generates a lot of that."

"You ask her to marry you yet?"

"That's none of your goddamn business."

"Ah. So you're going to."

I look around the room. I'm at the small desk, which

is squeezed underneath Mollie and Wheeler's design boards. These aren't ideal working conditions, but then again, neither are the conditions at the office back at the ranch.

If I had to, I could make this work for however often Mollie and I would be back in Dallas. Especially if we're able to move some of this stuff to the studio I want to build her on the ranch. I also have an idea for a Bellamy Brooks storefront in downtown Hartsville, but I figure we'll take this one step at a time.

"It has to be special." I fall back in my chair. "I also want her mama to like me before I propose."

Wyatt lets out a low whistle. "Godspeed. How are you gonna convince a woman who hates cowboys to let her daughter date one?"

"I'm that good."

"Lord save us. You got your work cut out for you. Sure you don't want reinforcements?"

"I can't bum-rush Aubrey and Mollie like that. It'd be unfair. I know Mollie loves y'all, but I'm the one she's marrying. The one I hope she'll marry anyway."

Wyatt pauses. "Permission to be honest?"

"Like you need it."

"I get the feeling there's something you need to tell me."

"And what would that be?"

"I heard through the grapevine that y'all were spotted together at the pharmacy recently."

"Jesus Christ. Can't get away with anything in a small town, can I?"

"Nope."

Running a hand through my hair, I take a deep

breath. Our pregnancy scare made me realize a lot of things. That I'm ready to start a family of my own, for starters. And that getting married and having babies—it doesn't mean I'm abandoning the family I already have. Just means I'm growing it.

Really, it showed me I'm ready to put my happiness first. Mollie's too.

"We thought Mollie might be pregnant. She's not."

"But you want her to be."

I swallow. "I do, yeah. I'd like to marry her first, though. Do things in the right order."

"Y'all come back to the ranch engaged, then. If these sketches you and Tallulah are working on don't convince Mollie y'all can do this thing…" I can practically see my brother shaking his head. "I'm proud of you, brother. You're trying to make a change. A big one. I like this new you."

Aw shit, the sun's not even up yet, and I'm already getting all choked up. This is gonna be a long day. But hopefully a good one.

"Appreciate that," I reply gruffly. "I should get back to these sketches. Have a lot of work to get through before Mollie wakes up."

"Let me know how it goes, all right? Y'all best share the news as soon as it happens."

"Boundaries. I have them now. You should get some too."

Wyatt just laughs. "Good luck."

———

Reaching for the condo's front door, Mollie glances at me and frowns.

"You're not wearing your hat?"

I flip her car keys around my finger. "You said the restaurant was nice. Figured baseball hats were a no-go."

"Not your baseball hat." Mollie darts into the bedroom, emerging a second later with my hat in her hand. "This hat."

Heart skipping a beat, I look at the Stetson. Look up at her. "Aren't I trying to win your mama over, not scare her away?"

"You'll win her over. And you'll be wearing this hat while you do it."

I take the hat from her. "I'm confused. She hates cowboys, right?"

"She hates people who don't keep their promises."

"But the hat—it's gonna rub it in her face, the fact that I'm not at all what she wants for you."

Mollie takes the hat back and goes on her tiptoes to set it on my head. "Once she gets to know you, she'll realize you're exactly what she wants for me. I'm dating a cowboy. One who's a very good man. The sooner she accepts that, the sooner we can all move on from all these dumb assumptions we have about each other."

My heart's doing backflips now. Leave it to Mollie Luck to continually leave me speechless.

She's not trying to change me. To dress me up or smooth over the fact that I've got rough hands and a rougher past.

In fact, she's putting all that front and center.

Mollie doesn't have anything to hide. I'm not gonna hide either.

I smile, hard. Cup her chin in my hand and lean

down for another kiss. A pulse of lust hits me square between the legs. You'd think we hadn't fucked in the shower just now and made love in her cushy king-size bed before that. Never mind the head she gave me last night and the orgasm I gave her afterward as she held on to the headboard for dear life.

"How long you think lunch'll take?" I growl.

She laughs, her breath a warm gust against my cheek. "A couple of hours."

I glance down at her dress. "Glad you're not wearing pants. Will make the whole car thing a lot easier."

"What car thing?"

Smirking, I open the door. "You'll see. Let's go."

I swat her ass, and she laughs again.

I wanna hear that sound for the rest of my life. But her mama could very well cut that life short if I don't win her over today.

Pressing my hat onto my head, I follow Mollie to the elevator.

This ain't the first time I gotta cowboy up.

Sure as hell won't be the last.

———

The restaurant is *nice*.

It's the kind of place with white tablecloths and waiters wearing jackets. Well-heeled diners sip wine from enormous glasses and pick at elegant salads and perfectly blackened slabs of salmon.

We're still in Texas, though. I'd feel out of place in my nicest pair of jeans and white button-up if there wasn't a hat rack, crowded with all kinds of cowboy hats, beside the hostess stand.

I feel eyes on me as I take off my own hat and run a hand through my hair. Mollie's lips twitch.

"What?" I ask.

She glances across the restaurant. "I think Dallas likes you."

Looking around, I smile. I'm tall, so I'm used to getting some attention when I walk into places. But this is the kind of attention you have to laugh at. Otherwise, it'll make you blush.

Several people, men and women, openly stare as I hang my hat on the rack and follow Mollie and the hostess into the dining room.

"Long live cowboys," one woman says to her friend after I pass.

I chuckle.

"I think he heard you," the friend says.

"I hope he did. And I hope he hears that those Wranglers fit him real, *real* well."

I spot Aubrey well before we get to the table. She's blonder than Mollie, but they have the same nose and proud shoulders. Her gaze catches on her daughter first, then darts to me.

Aubrey purses her lips before pasting on a tight smile. "Hey, y'all."

She rises and pulls Mollie in for a hug.

"Mom! Hey! I hope you haven't been waiting long?"

"Not at all. I just wanted to make sure I wasn't late and ended up here a bit early. Traffic wasn't bad today." Aubrey's gaze is on me again. Her eyes go a little wide as she takes me in, boots to beard. "You must be Cash."

"Yes, ma'am. It's nice to finally meet you."

I extend my hand, and she takes it. In Hartsville, we

kiss our kin on the cheek. While Aubrey isn't technically family yet, I figure I have nothing—and everything—to lose.

So I lean in and peck Aubrey's cheek. Out of the corner of my eye, I see Mollie grin while her mom covers her cheek with her hand after I lean back.

"I'm Aubrey." Is that a pink flush I see working its way up her neck? "When Mollie told me you'd be joining us, it was a…surprise."

I pull out Mollie's chair. "I think we're all surprised I ended up here. Mollie and I didn't exactly get along when we first met."

"So I heard." Aubrey watches Mollie sit in the chair. I push her in, then reach for Aubrey's chair too. "I'm all right, thanks."

"Yes, ma'am."

The back of my neck burns as I sit opposite Aubrey. Unfolding her napkin, she's quiet as she settles it on her lap.

Yep. This is gonna be awkward. But I can't give up. I may not win Mollie's mom over today, but that doesn't mean she won't accept me eventually. I just have to show her I'll work my ass off to make her daughter happy.

Yeah, I don't have a ton of money. Not yet. And my family's kind of a mess. But I love them, and they love me. I take care of my own. I'll protect this woman till my last dying breath, and while I'm still alive, it'll be my mission to help her make her dreams come true.

I'm not here to take those dreams away. To dim Mollie's light. Luckily, I have proof of that in my back pocket.

"You look…tan." Aubrey's eyes flick over Mollie, lingering a beat too long on her face.

Mollie's grin is back. "Thank you. I've been spending a lot of time outside."

"Doing…"

"Stuff." Mollie turns that grin on me.

"Give yourself more credit. Ms. Brown, there's not much Mollie *isn't* doing on the ranch. She's lookin' mighty fine on horseback these days."

Aubrey does that thing where her lips twitch before she pulls them into what could be a sneer or a smile. "Is that so?"

"I remember loving it when I was little," Mollie replies, pushing at one of her forks with her first finger. "I still didn't expect to enjoy it as much as I do now."

"Right." Aubrey picks up her menu. "So what changed your tune about Mollie, Cash? Other than the fact that my daughter is about to inherit millions of dollars?"

"Jesus Christ, Mom." Mollie stares at her. "At least let us order our drinks before you make a scene."

Aubrey splays her fingers. "Why beat around the bush? I have a two thirty I need to make."

My chest twists at the pain that flickers across Mollie's face.

"Please don't be like this," she pleads. "If you're not going to give him a chance, we'll leave."

"And go where?" Aubrey leans across the table. "I've raised you your entire life, Mollie. I know you better than anyone. You belong in Dallas. You deserve opportunity and freedom and…" Her voice wobbles. "To be around like-minded people. Small towns are where dreams go to die."

"That's not right," Mollie replies thickly.

Aubrey shakes her head. "I'm not wrong."

Grabbing Mollie's hand, I give it a squeeze. "Mollie does belong in Dallas. Aubrey, you're not wrong about that."

That gives Aubrey pause. She blinks, looking at me. "Are you…are y'all moving in together? Into your condo?" She turns to look at Mollie, who looks at me, a confused look on her face.

I squeeze her hand again. *Stay with me.*

Mollie's throat works as she swallows. She squeezes back. *Okay.*

"Life in Dallas suits Mollie. I've seen that firsthand. Bellamy Brooks was born and bred in a city. And now that y'all are about to launch your biggest and, in my humble opinion, best collection yet—"

"You've seen it." Aubrey's words come out like an accusation, but I sense the question there.

I dip my head. "I have. It's incredible."

"It is. Which is exactly why Mollie needs to be here, in Dallas, to launch it. The publicity she and Wheeler will get from local boutiques alone—oh, hello." Aubrey glances at the server over her shoulder before looking at us. "Are we ready to order?"

I motion to Mollie. "You ready, honey?"

I don't miss the way she bites her lip. "I am. You?"

"Yes."

The girls order wine. When I suggest we make it a bottle since I'll be having some too, Aubrey's expression appears slightly less sour. But it's when Mollie orders her food after her mom requests a salad that things get really interesting.

She asks the server for a "tavern burger," which,

370

apparently, is a fancy cheeseburger with two patties, topped with some kind of special sauce. Yes to a side of fries, yes to cheddar cheese, yes to the sauce and the pickles and ketchup.

"I'll have the same," I say, handing my menu to the server.

Aubrey, though, narrows her eyes at her daughter. "Mollie, isn't that going to hurt your stomach? The gluten and the cheese—"

"They don't bother me anymore." Mollie adjusts the napkin on her lap. "As a matter of fact, I'm not sure they ever bothered me. I've been eating pretty much everything at the ranch, and I haven't had a stomachache in weeks."

Aubrey blinks. "Really?"

"Really. I think..." Mollie waves her hand. "Before I went to Hartsville, I think I knew on some level that I was unhappy, but I didn't see a way to change anything. I felt like I was doing life right, except my body was screaming at me that I wasn't."

"And now you think you are doing it right because your stomach doesn't hurt." Aubrey's expression is difficult to read.

Mollie looks at me. Looks down at her plate. "I love the ranch, Mom. I know that wasn't your experience, but living in Hartsville..." She looks at me again. "It's been healing? That sounds ridiculous, but it's true. I just feel *better* after being there. I feel good here too—don't get me wrong. I like both places. I think I need them both, which is the issue."

Our wine arrives. Aubrey takes a long, quiet pull from her glass.

I drink mine, gaze bouncing between Mollie and her mom. I have no fucking idea what's about to go down, but I have to keep the conversation from completely derailing.

"I've thought a lot about this," I say carefully. "Why Garrett put that stipulation in his will. He talked about y'all often."

Aubrey scoffs and rolls her eyes. "I'm sure he painted a lovely picture."

"He had a lot of regrets." I swallow. "I think he would've done things differently if he had another chance. I loved him, but he was stubborn as hell. I told him it wasn't too late to change things. To reach out and try again."

"He never listened," Aubrey replies.

"But Mollie does. I do. I'm listening. Getting to know your daughter—it's been one of the great joys of my life, and it's changed me for the better." I reach into my back pocket and pull out a single four-by-six-inch picture. "Talk about ridiculous things, but I think Garrett knew somehow that bringing Mollie back to Lucky Ranch would be good for us. For everyone. Like he's pulling strings from the grave, you know? What he couldn't pull off in life, he was going to do after he was gone."

I gently place the picture on the table. It's grainy, and I can't tell if it's faded from age or if the image was captured during a golden hour that softened the outlines of the three figures in it. Mollie, maybe four years old, is on a pony in between Garrett and Aubrey. The Colorado River is in the background. From the angle, I can tell it's close to the spot I showed Mollie on our first ride around the ranch.

Everyone is wearing cowboy hats and big smiles.

Aubrey looks at the picture and goes still. "Where did you get this?"

"Garrett left me a safety-deposit box in his will. Had no idea what was in it. When I opened the box, I found hundreds of photographs of y'all. He told Goody the pictures were one of his most prized possessions, so he wanted to keep them safe."

Mollie's hand goes to her mouth. "He left them to you?"

"At first, I thought it was a mistake. Now, though… now I think he might've given them to me for a reason."

Aubrey blinks. "He knew you'd share them with Mollie."

"He knew you'd show me I was always a cowgirl at heart." Mollie's voice is threadbare. "Because at heart, you're a good guy who's just a little rough around the edges."

I chuckle. "Something like that."

Aubrey's eyelashes continue to flutter as she points at the picture. "Is that—"

"The three of y'all. Look how cute you are." I tap my finger on little girl Mollie. "You look so happy up on that horse."

Aubrey swallows more wine. "Garrett gave her riding lessons a few times a week. She loved it."

Mollie turns to look at her mom. "I remember that. We'd do laps around the corral. Slow at first. When he let me trot, I couldn't stop giggling."

"You were so damn cute, Mollie." Aubrey's eyes crinkle, and she looks wistful—happy—for a full beat. "Still are."

"You look happy there too, Mom."

Aubrey blinks. "I was. In that moment anyway."

Mollie squeezes my hand. "Thank you. For sharing this with us."

"I have the rest in a bag at your apartment. But the spot where y'all are standing in this photo—the views of the river are incredible. It was one of Garrett's favorite places on the ranch. I took the liberty of doing a few mock-ups of a studio we could build there. Big windows, lots of light, and enough privacy so you and Wheeler feel comfortable doing your thing." I grab my phone and quickly scroll to images of the rough drawings I did this morning before continuing. "Bellamy Brooks has a studio here in Dallas. Figured it needs one in Hartsville too. If only because y'all are about to have a lot more inventory to show off and a lot more brainstorming to do for future collections. Y'all are inspired by the fashion here in Dallas, and now—maybe—the ranch could provide a comple- mentary kind of inspiration. Give y'all a new angle for your next collection while keeping your city roots intact."

I set my phone on the table and slide it over to Mollie.

My heart thumps as she stares at the phone for one beat. Two. She's holding her wine in her hand. She takes a sip. Blinks.

Then promptly bursts into tears, leaning her head on my shoulder.

My stomach bottoms out. I press a kiss to her temple. "Oh. Oh, Mollie, honey, I'm—"

"So fucking thoughtful," she manages as she picks up the phone and scrolls through the images. I like how she keeps her head on my shoulder. "And sweet. And wow, really good at renderings. When did you draw all this?"

I nearly have a heart attack when I see Aubrey dabbing at her eyes with her napkin.

"Earlier today. I know it's not the perfect solution to our problem, but it's a start. This will also give me a little more room to work here in Dallas when—if—we take some of the stock you have in the closet back to the ranch. We could put a big desk in the closet where we can all work with our laptops."

Aubrey scrunches her forehead. "You have a laptop?"

"Mom, he has a huge job overseeing a quarter of a million acres of land. Of course Cash has a laptop."

I nod. "I spend more time on it than I'd like, but such is life."

Aubrey sets down her wine. "If you have such a big job, how can you be away from the ranch?"

"I won't lie to you. It'll be an adjustment for everyone. But I've got four brothers who are doing a fine job holding down the fort while we're gone." I tip my chin at the phone. "Haven't heard from them once since we've been here."

Mollie gives me a watery smile. "Told you."

"You were right." I lean in to kiss her mouth. "Thanks for giving me the push I needed."

She nods, looking back down at my phone. "Maybe this is the push I needed. I mean…Cash, this could work." Her eyes light up as the pieces come together. "I'm pretty sure Wheeler would come out to the ranch if I told her you have four single brothers who live there. There's plenty of space for her in the New House. Now that I have access to my trust, I can hire some people to help out at Bellamy Brooks, which would free me up to help out on the ranch a couple of days a week. What do you think, Mom?"

Aubrey is quiet as she continues to sip her wine. "I'm not sure what I think. It's a lovely idea—"

"But it could work." Mollie blinks. "Holy shit, it could really work."

I swallow the thickness in my throat. "Why do you look so surprised?" I ask softly. "Did you not think we would figure this out?"

She's quiet for a beat. Mollie's eyes fill all over again. "Maybe I didn't think I deserved it. Being able to keep my life here *and* keep you. Feels like I'm getting away with something. Like I'm going to be punished for not doing things the way I've been taught they should be done."

"Making your dreams happen?" I ask. "That feels like a crime?"

Mollie's crying again. I don't miss how Aubrey reaches over and grabs her daughter's other hand.

"That's all I ever wanted for you, you know. For you to make your dreams come true." Aubrey sniffles. "I just don't want you to give up on the dreams you have here. You've worked so hard. Your boots are beautiful. I guess I assumed that if you ran off with a cowboy"—Aubrey cocks a brow in my direction—"you'd abandon all that. But now I'm starting to see I was wrong."

"I'm not abandoning my dreams, Mom. I'm just changing them. Making them bigger. My heart belongs to Bellamy Brooks and to Dallas, but it also belongs to Cash and the ranch and Hartsville. I hope you don't view that as some kind of betrayal, because it's not. It's just me, following my truth as I figure it out."

Aubrey closes her eyes. Her chin trembles.

A tear slips out of my own eye. Goddamn, being

around all this emotion is really getting me in my own feels.

"I won't lie to you, sweetheart. It hurts to hear you say that you might be leaving," Aubrey says at last. "But if you feel like this is the right move, then you have to make it. I knew in my gut life on a cattle ranch wasn't for me, but I tried to fight it because I loved your father so damn much. Don't fight what you know to be true."

Mollie stares at her mother. "You mean that? Seriously?"

"Seriously." Aubrey's eyes cut to me. "Don't waste time like I did trying to be someone you're not. What's all this money for if not to make you happy? Go be happy."

CHAPTER 32
Good-Luck Charms
Mollie

I'm scrolling through nineties country playlists on Spotify the next morning in the front seat of my car when Cash calls out from behind me.

"Hey, Mollie. I think your mom is here." He grunts as he lifts my largest suitcase into the trunk. "That her in the white Mercedes?"

I immediately whip around in the passenger seat to look out the windows. Yep, that's my mother. She's pulling into one of the parallel parking spots outside my building.

"That's her."

"You want me to run interference?" He meets my eyes in the rearview mirror.

"We'll be okay. I think. I hope."

Cash and I are on the opposite side of the street, just outside the building's front door. He's loading up the trunk while I figure out entertainment for our drive. Cash, being Cash, didn't so much as let me touch my luggage, much less load it into the trunk.

Having a boyfriend who's a filthy-mouthed cowboy in the sheets but an absolute gentleman in the streets sure as hell has its perks.

Watching Mom climb out of her sedan, my stomach dips. We left lunch on good enough terms yesterday. I feel like we had a breakthrough. At the very least, Mom understands where I'm coming from and why I'm making the choice to go back to the ranch today.

Still, when I called her this morning to tell her we were leaving after breakfast, I didn't expect her to offer to swing by.

I certainly didn't expect her to actually show up. It's a Sunday morning. While most people in her circle are at church or having brunch, Mom is usually working. Weekends are a real estate agent's bread and butter.

She's here, though. And I don't know if that's a good or a bad thing.

Looking both ways before crossing the street, she hurries over to us. I notice she has a white paper bag tucked underneath her arm.

"Mom! Hey." I push open the door and step out. Because it's early on a Sunday, the street is empty. "I'm glad you came by."

"Mornin', Ms. Brown." Cash straightens, hiking up his jeans. "How are you doing today?"

"Please, call me Aubrey. And I'm doing all right. How about yourself?"

"Just making sure Mollie has everything she needs." He gestures to the full trunk with a grin. "Turns out she needs a hell of a lot."

"I'm sure you've figured out by now that my daughter is a little high-maintenance."

I let out a bark of laughter. "Runs in the family."

"Guilty." Mom smiles.

I look at Cash. This is a good sign, right? The smile, the insistence he call her by her first name? She didn't say a word about that yesterday.

"Anyway"—Mom glances between us before she holds out the bag to me—"I'm glad I caught y'all. Here are some treats to bring back to the ranch with you. Figured y'all could use something to nibble on during the drive."

I take the bag, only now seeing the restaurant logo printed on its side. "My favorite. Wow. Thank you, Mom." I hold out an arm.

She pulls me in for a tight hug. "Just promise me you'll start answering your phone more often. I need to hear from you. Not every day, but more than once a week."

My eyes prickle with heat. I close them and nod. "I promise."

"I was up all night thinking about y'all."

"Mom—"

"It's all right, Mollie." She's still holding me. "I'm not going to ask when you'll be back in town—"

"Subtle," I say with a smile.

"But I want to be part of this." She finally lets me go and glances at Cash. "Part of y'all's life together. You're in your element when you're together—that much is clear. You're happy." Mom cups my cheek. "*He* makes you happy. Thank you, Cash, for taking such excellent care of my daughter. I've never seen her so lit up before."

My boyfriend's Adam's apple bobs. "That means a lot. Thank you. You have my word, I'll try my damnedest to make Mollie happy."

"I believe you," Mom replies.

I blink, genuinely shocked. "Wait, wait. *You* trust a *cowboy*?"

Mom's lips twitch. "No two people are alike. Same goes for cowboys."

"Amen to that." Cash touches his finger to the brim of his hat.

It's an obscenely beautiful, obscenely sexy gesture that has both Mom and me blushing like idiots.

"Well, y'all drive safe," Mom says.

Cash holds up that same finger. "Hang tight, Aubrey. I have something for you."

Turning to rummage through the back seat, he emerges a minute later with a Walgreens bag in his hand.

I smile at him. We were there for hours last night.

"What's this?" Mom asks, taking the bag from my boyfriend.

Cash curls an arm around my waist. "Copies of Garrett's pictures. Thought you might want them."

Staring into the bag, Mom blinks. I can tell by the way her chin quivers that she's trying not to cry.

I let the tears fall freely. "It was Cash's idea."

"That's"—Mom swallows, still looking down—"so thoughtful. Thank you."

Cash chuckles. "Of course. Can we hug it out now, or…?"

Mom laughs. "Yes. Yes, I'd like that."

Which is how the three of us end up hugging each other multiple times in the middle of the street on a Sunday morning.

Pulling back, I look at Mom. "Are you okay?"

"I'm okay. Really. I'll miss you tons, but I'll survive."

Cash is at my elbow now, his hand on the small of my back. "I know you're not Hartsville's biggest fan, Aubrey, but you're welcome to visit us on the ranch anytime. We'd love to have you."

Mom nods, her eyes bouncing between us. "Maybe one day. I'm excited to see what y'all do with the place."

Funny she mentions that. Ever since Cash surprised me with the plans he drew up for a studio by the river, I've been thinking nonstop about what else we could do with the ranch.

In particular, what else we could do with Rivers Ranch. Cash is doing everything he can to make my dreams come true. It's only fair I return the favor.

My heart is full as Mom pulls me in for one last hug.

My heart spills over when she pulls Cash in for one more hug too.

"See y'all soon." She smiles. "And send me updates on the studio. It's going to be beautiful."

———

"So Cash has four brothers."

I smile at Wheeler's not-so-subtle question as I guide the ATV away from the river and back toward the New House. "Yes."

"And they're all tall."

"Yes."

"And they have blue eyes."

"Yep."

"*And* they're cowboys."

"Wheeler, I just took you on a tour of my family's working cattle ranch. We saw cows, horses, snakes, and a freaking bald eagle. Not to mention the Colorado River. But all you can talk about is cowboys?"

Wheeler blinks. "Yes, cowboys are what interest me most. What's wrong with that?"

I laugh. "Nothing. They interest me too."

"Well, yeah." Wheeler grins at me as she tucks stray strands of her copper hair out of her eyes. "You're gonna marry one."

"I'm not asking Cash to marry me."

"No, you're just about to show him the branding we did for y'all's new ranch. The one you're going to run together."

"Exactly."

"He's gonna think you're asking him to marry you, Mollie. Friends don't combine ranches."

I lift a shoulder, like my heart isn't already thrumming inside my chest at the prospect of presenting my idea to Cash tonight over dinner. It's part of the reason why Wheeler drove down from Dallas this morning, two weeks after I signed the paperwork at Mom's lawyers' office. I need the moral support.

"If he wants to get married too, fine."

"Oh, stop it. You're dying to have that man's babies."

Grinning, I park the ATV by the back door. "I am."

Now that we're well into October, it gets dark early. The New House blazes with light, its windows glowing in the deepening twilight. I can see Patsy moving through the kitchen inside. The bittersweet smell of a fire fills my head at the same moment as my eyes catch on the smoke drifting up from the kitchen's chimney.

Home.

I'm finally, *finally* home.

My pulse seizes when I see Cash sidle up to the sink. He turns on the tap and slowly washes his hands, expression smoothed over as he works the soap into a lather. His hair is wet, slicked back from his face. He showered, then.

My body warms. In a couple of hours, probably less, we'll be alone together at the cabin. And when we're alone at the cabin, my clothes don't stand a chance. I can already smell his skin as he guides my shirt over my head and climbs over me in bed, settling his weight between my legs while he kisses my mouth, my neck. My breasts.

The way I crave this man is unlike any other urge I've had. I'll never get over it.

If tonight goes well, I'll never have to.

Taking a deep breath, I reach for the laptop case I tucked underneath the seat and glance at Wheeler. "You ready to meet the family?"

Because that's what these people are now. Part of my family. They know my history—my hopes—better than pretty much anyone besides Mom and Wheeler.

"I truly cannot wait." She rubs her hands together as she looks at the house. "Cowboys, here I come."

The second I push open the door, we're greeted by the smell of something good roasting in the oven and a cacophony of voices. It's like everyone knows I'm about to put my heart and my happiness on the line and they made sure they were at the table early.

All five Rivers boys are here. So are John B and Sally. And it appears Goody and Tallulah have stopped by for supper too.

Of course they have.

Wheeler grabs my arm as she takes in the tall cowboys at the table. "I think I'm going to like it here, Mollie."

"Mollie! Hey! This must be your friend you were telling me about. Welcome to the ranch, Wheeler." Patsy rounds the island, a bottle of white wine in one hand and a bottle of red in the other. "What can I pour y'all?"

"A tall glass of cowboy," I reply with a smirk.

Cash saunters over, wiping his hands on a kitchen towel. He's smirking too. "I'm right here, honey."

"I'd like one of those too, please." Wheeler's eyes still haven't left the table.

Cash laughs. "Here, let me introduce you to my brothers. I told them to be on their best behavior, but they don't listen to me, so apologies in advance."

I decide to wait until after dinner to make my announcement. Sitting in between Duke and Goody, I tuck into the most delicious pork tenderloin and mashed sweet potatoes and sip inky, dark red wine while we talk about everything and nothing.

Cash's foot finds mine underneath the table. His eyes dance with mischief. The man is forever finding ways to touch me. Tease me.

I love it.

Just like I love coming together this way every night for supper. Sharing a meal with the people I adore is the loveliest way to bookend the day. Growing up, Mom and I usually ate dinner together at a restaurant. But in boarding school and then at college, I never really found a great dinner crew. Wheeler had a lot of late afternoon and early evening classes in college, so she wasn't around a ton at that time of day.

Now I have found my crew, and it's kind of the best thing ever.

Goody gently elbows me as she cuts her pork. "I'm so glad you decided to stay on the ranch, Mollie."

I nod, sipping my wine. "Guess Dad's stipulation worked, huh?"

Goody raises a brow. "What do you mean?"

"Do you think Dad did it on purpose? Brought me back to the ranch because he knew I'd end up staying?"

Goody thinks on this for a minute, chewing, before she answers. "He remembered you loving the animals when you were little. He told me so many stories about how quickly you learned to ride. He was sad you didn't keep it up."

"He knew I'd never come back on my own." I'm ashamed to admit that, but no use hiding it now. "So he forced me to."

"He did." Goody wipes her mouth on her napkin. "I didn't always agree with Garrett, but he was ultimately a good man with a good heart. What he did came from a place of decency. He loved the land so much, Mollie. I think he didn't want you to miss out on that."

My throat feels tight as I finish my wine. A little liquid courage never hurt anyone, right? "Not gonna lie, I hated him at first for forcing me to come here."

"And now?" Goody glances at Cash, who's busy chatting up Wheeler.

I smile. "I don't hate him anymore."

I think I'll always have complicated feelings about my relationship with Dad. I'm sad I missed out on so much. I'm angry he let me. Yes, I had a part in that, but he was ultimately the adult in the room.

I'm angry at myself for adopting my mother's assumptions and prejudices as my own.

But all that anger—all the sadness and regret and pain—it makes this moment so much sweeter. I can appreciate life now in a way I never could before I came to the ranch.

I came *this close* to losing out on all this, but I didn't.

I came *this close* to washing my hands of the will and Dad and Cash, but I didn't.

Now here I am, about to propose joining forces with Cash.

I hope Dad would be proud. It's a huge risk, but I've learned those are the kind of risks you absolutely have to take if you want to create any kind of magic in your life.

What I have with Cash is magic.

Clearing my throat, I stand up. "Hey, y'all, if I could have your attention for a second, that'd be great."

Wyatt glances at me, his lips curling into a knowing smile. "I like the sound of this."

"What's up, honey?" Cash asks.

He's so shameless about calling me that in front of everyone these days. Even now, weeks after he started doing it, I feel myself smiling.

Wheeler holds up a fist. *You got this.*

I dig my laptop out of its protective sleeve. Opening it, I cradle it in the crook of my bent arm. "I've been working on a little something that I wanted to run by y'all. Well, specifically, I wanted to get Cash's opinion on it, but the rest of you are welcome to chime in too, since it involves everyone."

"She's starting a cult, isn't she?" Ryder asks Sawyer. "I've always wanted to be in one of those."

Sawyer nods. "She'd make a great leader. Very charismatic."

"Y'all, hush," Cash says.

I'm still smiling, but now I also feel like I'm going to cry. "As much as I appreciate the compliments, I'm not starting a cult. Yet. Instead, I'm starting a new ranch. Or would it be creating one? Combining one? Setting a new ranch up? I, um, didn't think that verbiage through."

Cash's eyes flicker. "Don't have to be perfect, Mollie."

"It just has to be with you," I blurt, then turn the laptop around so that he can see the horseshoe logo I designed on the screen. The ends of the horseshoe are pointed down, so the words *Lucky Rivers Ranch* are wrapped around the horseshoe's curve at the top. "You helped make plans for Bellamy Brooks. I want to help make plans for Rivers Ranch. Run it with me—your ranch and mine. Not as my foreman but as my partner. Total equals. We'll put everything together, pool our resources, and turn *our* ranch into the one you've always dreamed about."

The room goes dead quiet. Cash stares at the screen, his blue eyes wide as he looks and looks and *looks*.

My heart works its way up my throat. Oh boy. Maybe I misjudged this one. It's ballsy of me to suggest joining forces when Cash never expressed interest in any kind of partnership. I've way overstepped. Jesus, what was I—

"Lucky Rivers Ranch," Cash says at last.

I nod, sweat breaking out along my scalp as I bend my neck to look at the screen. "That's what I thought we'd call it. I'm not married to any of it, though."

"Good," Duke says. "Because the horseshoe—"

"Don't," Cash cuts him off.

I start to panic. "Don't what?"

Goody clears her throat.

"Someone tell me, please," I beg.

Wyatt glances at Cash. "That horseshoe, with the

ends facing down, it can, uh, sometimes be a symbol of bad luck. Like the horseshoe was full of good luck, but now you're letting it all out by putting it that way."

"Oh." My face burns as I look back at the screen. "Oh my God, how stupid of me—"

"It's perfect."

I look up at the decisive rumble of Cash's voice.

He's getting up.

He's rounding the table.

"Y'all aren't up on your horseshoe shit." His gaze is locked on mine as he approaches. "That kind of horseshoe can mean you're letting luck out. It can also mean you're letting luck rain down on anyone who passes underneath it."

Sawyer clicks his tongue. "Dang, that actually makes sense."

"It's perfect," Cash repeats. "My answer's yes, honey."

Then he takes my face in his hands and crushes his mouth against mine.

The room erupts in hoots and hollers. I try to break the kiss, pull away, but Cash holds me steady, giving me a long, deep kiss that's definitely inappropriate to share in front of others.

Cash, of course, doesn't care about that. Instead, he licks into my mouth and says, "On one condition."

"Name it."

His kiss deepens. Sucking on my bottom lip, he nicks it with his teeth, then pulls back. "Marry me."

My heart explodes. A starry, happy rush fills my skin, like my pulse has dissolved into a million tiny pinpricks of light.

Is this really happening?

How in the world did I get this lucky?

I can't believe this is actually happening. Not only have I met the love of my life. Now I get to marry him.

I smile, eyes welling with tears. "You proposing to me, cowboy?"

"Only because you proposed to me, cowgirl."

"It's a *hell yes* for me."

He grins. "It's a *hell yes* for me too."

The cowboys bang their boots on the floor. Sally wolf-whistles. John B starts to weep. And Cash just keeps on kissing me.

"One other thing," he says when he finally allows me to come up for air. "I think I like the sound of Lucky River Ranch better. You added a letter to your name— Luck became Lucky—so let's take one away from mine. Evens it out. Since we're equals and all."

Like I could say no to that.

"Yes," I breathe, going up on my toes to wrap my arms around his neck. "Yes. Yes. *Yes*, Cash."

We kiss. Then people are pulling us in for hugs. Patsy is crying. Wheeler is crying.

I'm crying.

But I know I'll be all right, because I'm home.

I end up in Cash's arms again, his lips finding mine for another searing kiss.

"Get a room," Wyatt says with a smile.

Sally shakes her head. "Champagne toast first. *Then* the room."

"I like the sound of that." I wipe my eyes.

Cash grins. "Cheers, y'all."

THE END

EPILOGUE
Wear the Hat
Cash

It's the kind of fall day I live for.

Blue skies, lots of sun. A breeze that's cool but not cold, refreshing in the best way.

Mollie's arm hangs out the pickup's passenger-side window. She's singing along to the Rascal Flatts song playing on the stereo, bopping her head to the beat. Her hair catches in the wind and blows around her face in a coppery-brown halo.

Tucking it behind her ear, she catches me looking at her and grins. "Eyes on the road, cowboy."

"Easier said than done when you're riding shotgun."

"Did I not take care of you already this morning? Twice?"

My body pulses at the memory of Mollie on her back in my bed and then on her knees in the shower.

"What can I say?" I lift my hand off her thigh. "I make the most of my days off."

Her lips twitch as she scoots across the bench to sit closer. "I could've slept in a *little* later."

"You were awake."

She'd rustled the sheets and sighed at half past six, so I did what any man waking up next to a beautiful woman would do. I kissed her neck and slipped a hand between her legs.

She laughed. I rolled on top of her, catching her leg with my arm so I could press her knee to her chest. Then I slipped inside her, the room quiet save for Mollie's moans.

I love how she wakes up wet. Always ready.

Always hungry.

"I was," she admits with a smile and puts a hand on my knee. "But I could've easily gone back to sleep."

"How about a nap later?"

"I'd love that."

Her eyes catch on mine. My stomach flips at the clear, liquid gleam in them. She's happy. Incandescently so.

It's the kind of happiness that fills my chest to bursting. I never thought I could feel this much, risk this much, and not stumble somehow. Not be let down or devastated.

But here we are, Mollie and me, taking a drive over to Rivers Ranch together after a glorious morning of sex and food and sun, contentment filling me from head to toe.

Here I am, indulging in hope and the promise of rest.

"You know, you've come so far, Cash," Mollie says, reading my thoughts. "Remember how I had to beg you to take a day off? Now you're taking whole weekends off, and you're *napping*."

"You didn't have to beg me."

She rolls her eyes, still smiling. "Keep telling yourself that. Maybe I just had to hate you for a little while to light that fire under your ass."

I laugh. "Lord, did you hate me."

"Pretty sure the feeling was mutual."

"You're too fucking beautiful to hate. Inside and out."

Her turn to laugh. "Glad you learned your lesson."

We pull into Rivers Ranch. I don't have to swerve to avoid any potholes or divots. When Mollie and I signed the papers that officially created Lucky River Ranch, we agreed that our first order of business would be to get all our roads in shape. That way, the crews we're hiring to help us with overhauling this side of the ranch won't have any trouble accessing it.

My pulse skips a beat, then another, as we drive across my family's land. I still have to pinch myself sometimes. It's happening.

The dreams I've had for this place—Mollie and I are making them come true.

I vividly remember driving down this same road after I first met Mollie that day at Goody's office downtown. The despondence I felt then—it was the lowest of lows. I saw no future for this land or for my family.

Funny how much can change and how quickly.

I park in front of the old hay barn. Mollie wanted to see it after I mentioned it as a possibility for Bellamy Brooks's future storage facility.

We walk hand in hand to the entrance, the air filled with the smell of recently cut grass. The sun is deliciously warm on my shoulders and back as I open the rickety door for Mollie.

I shamelessly check out her ass as she strolls inside the

barn, my dick taking note of just how good she looks in those jeans. Glancing over her shoulder, she catches me ogling her.

She slips a hand in her back pocket and smirks. "You're an animal."

"Yep." I pull the door closed behind me with a *thunk*. "Turned into one after I met you."

Mollie goes up on her tiptoes to press a kiss to my mouth after I walk over to her. "I'm not sorry."

"Neither am I." I slide my hand into her pocket behind hers. "So? What do you think?"

My girl tips up her chin as she looks around the barn. "It's a big space."

"It's a bit of a wreck now, but the bones are good. Y'all do need a bigger closet."

The edges of her eyes crinkle. "We do."

Bellamy Brooks's second collection hasn't launched yet, but the brand's gone semi-viral on social media, thanks to Mollie and Wheeler's kick-ass marketing campaign. They've fielded inquiries from some really big names in the retail space—one being a well-known Texas department store—so things are looking up.

"I'm proud of you, honey." I peck her lips.

"Thank you, cowboy."

I pluck the hat off my head and put it on hers. "Thank *you*, cowgirl, for sticking with me, even when I didn't deserve it."

"I heard something once." Mollie reaches up to touch my Stetson. "About what needs to happen when you wear a cowboy's hat."

I yank on her jeans, pulling her closer. "Oh yeah? What's that?"

"Something about…" She taps a finger against her lips as she pretends to think. "Hmm. I think it goes something like, *Wear the hat, ride the cowboy*."

My dick throbs. "Funny, I've heard the same thing."

"Here?" She glances up at the barn.

I grin. "Here."

"We do need to christen this side of the ranch."

Taking my hand out of her pocket, I reach around to unbutton her jeans and pull down the fly. "Which means you need to take these off."

She puts a hand on my chest. "But someone could catch us," she says with mock concern.

"Ride fast and ride hard, then. You know how."

Then I'm pulling down Mollie's jeans. She's giggling, tearing off her shirt. My hat goes flying, but she catches it and puts it back on her head.

Glancing at a nearby bale of hay—the renters we've had for the past year sometimes cut their own—and a horse blanket, my skin tightens.

Aw, yeah. This is gonna be fun.

I toss the blanket over the bale. Mollie's naked, save for my hat, so I grab her and lift her onto the bale too. "On your knees. There you go."

She pouts. "A repeat of the shower?"

"Give me more credit, honey." I wrap a hand around her neck and lean down to press a hard kiss to her mouth. "Trust me, you're gonna like this."

"I'd like it better if you were naked."

My blood jumps as Mollie looks at me from under the brim of my hat. Kneeling on the blanket, she looks fucking gorgeous: proud shoulders, full tits, thighs parted just enough to give me a glimpse of her pink pussy.

I'm shucking off my jeans and shirt before I know what's happening.

I'm getting on my own knees. Putting my hands on her thighs and guiding them wider. Leaning in, I suck one nipple into my mouth, then the other, Mollie's hands digging into my hair as she arches into my caress.

"How do I ride you?" She's panting, breathless. "When we're like this?"

"Patience, honey. You'll see."

I kiss my way down her belly, stopping to nip at each hip bone. I kiss her pubic hair.

Kiss her clit, giving it a quick, short stroke of tongue.

Mollie's hips jerk forward. "More. That. More of that, please."

"Yes, ma'am."

Then I'm turning around. I get on the ground so that my back is against the hay bale. I sit upright and tilt back my head so that Mollie's pussy hovers above me, right where I want her.

Leaning up, I lick her. A hard, long stroke of her slit that has her yelling my name.

"Someone's definitely going to hear us," I manage.

"I don't care. *More*."

I chuckle. "I'll do my part"—I suck on her clit— "and you do yours. Ride my mustache, honey. Like you mean it."

And, Lord, does she mean it. I place a hand on her hip and guide her movements against my mouth. She starts slow, little circles of her pelvis, but when I reach for my dick and start to jack myself off, her movements become frenzied, urgent, bigger.

I eat her pussy, and I tug on my dick. Mollie's cries

become louder, so loud that I know they'd hear us at my family's old house here on this side of the ranch. Luckily, our renters moved out last week, but there's always a chance someone will be nearby.

Not like I care.

"Let them hear you, cowgirl." I move my hand and thumb her pussy, spreading her wider so that I can nick at her clit with my teeth. "Don't hold back now."

I dip my tongue inside her entrance at the same time as I roll my thumb over her clit. She shouts my name, her legs shuddering, and I know she's coming, hard.

I come too, the orgasm ricocheting through me with the force of a nuclear blast. My hips buck. Cum leaks down my shaft and covers my hand.

"That's so hot." Mollie is panting. "You're so fucking hot, Cash."

When the rush recedes and Mollie sinks down onto my mouth, spent, I press one last kiss to her pussy. "Only you. You're the only one I want wearing that hat."

I can't see her face, but I know Mollie is smiling when she says, "Yes, *sir*."

———

We take our time getting dressed. I don't miss how Mollie keeps my hat on, refusing to give it back, even when we emerge into the sunshine a little while later.

I'm in the mood for a drive, so we take a long one, looping around this side of the ranch as we pepper each other with questions and ideas.

Lucky River Ranch is gonna be one hell of a destination once we're done with it.

We only head home—back to the cabin—when

Mollie's stomach starts to growl. It's suppertime, and I've got some pork chops I plan to make for us, along with the spicy ranch waters Mollie's grown to love.

It's a heavenly drive. Setting sun, cool air, George Strait on the stereo.

That is until we pull past the horse barn, and I see a knot of people gathered by the corral.

It's not dark yet, but I still have to squint to see who it is.

My stomach seizes as the scene takes shape before me. Wyatt is standing with his hands held up, his hat tipped back on his head. John B is aiming a rifle—Wyatt's Beretta, from the looks of it—at his chest.

There's shouting. A scream. Sally is at John B's side, her chest rising and falling.

"What the fuck?" I jam on the brakes.

Mollie's eyes go wide. "Careful, Cash."

"Stay here. I mean it, Mollie."

She looks at me, swallowing. Then she nods. "Holler if you need me."

I leave the truck running and hop out the door, stalking across the grass.

"I swear to God, John, it's not what you think," Wyatt says.

John B leans his cheek against the rifle. "You're lying, Wyatt."

"Dad, please, stop. This is ridiculous. Put the gun down." Sally's words are thick with emotion. "He's right—"

"What's going on here?" I ask.

Without looking away from Wyatt, John B replies, "This son of a bitch did my daughter dirty. That's what."

I stare at my brother. "Wyatt—"

"I can explain." His voice has a desperate edge to it.

Shit. That tells me all I need to know.

Shit, shit, *shit.*

Two Piña Coladas
Mollie

"All right, wife." **Cash nods at the bustling terminal. It** appears everyone in the greater Dallas-Fort Worth area has decided to travel today. "Do you want to get champagne before or after we hit up the store?"

As I meet his eyes, my stomach flutters. It keeps doing that, even while I was in the line for security just now. Not only am I jetting off on my honeymoon with my cowboy, but Bellamy Brooks is making its very first appearance in a major lifestyle magazine, *Elle.* The issue hits newsstands today. Its editorial team sent Wheeler and I several copies already, but I decided to wait until we got to the airport to buy one off the newsstand and look at the feature.

"Well, husband." I grab his hand. "I say we get the magazine first, and then we double up on the champagne after."

Cash grins, and everything inside me turns over. "Sounds like a plan."

His handsomeness still hits me like an arrow to the

chest. Today he looks especially delicious in boots, jeans, and a green-and-blue-checkered button-up that makes the color of his eyes pop. His hair is slicked back from his face; it's still a little wet from the shower, and it curls out at the ends.

His mustache is more prominent than usual. That's by request. I asked him to grow it out for our wedding and trim his scruff a bit more. It only seemed right, considering his mustache was practically its own character in the story of how Cash and I got together.

Doesn't hurt that a thicker mustache is, ahem, more fun to ride.

"You addicted to it or somethin'?" Cash asked earlier this morning.

I was still holding the headboard in a death grip, my body alive with the aftershocks of yet another seismic orgasm, when I simply replied, "Fuck yes. The 'stache stays, all right? Forever."

"Forever." He chuckled. "You got it, honey."

A pulse of longing slices through my center at the memory, drawing my nipples to hard, extremely painful points. My breath catches, and I resist the urge to put my hands on my breasts. *Ow.*

Cash, being Cash, picks right up on my discomfort. "You all right?"

"Yeah." I discreetly rub my elbows over my chest. "My boobs hurt a little. It's cold in here."

He cocks a teasing brow. "I can help with that. You got two boobs, and I got two hands."

"And here I thought you were gonna wait until we were on the plane to proposition me." Grinning, I go up on my toes to peck his lips.

He nips at the corner of my mouth. "I'm gonna do that too. But should you require my assistance beforehand—"

"Cool it, cowboy."

"I won't." His gaze flickers with heat. "Not when I'm with you."

I laugh. "That's what I like to hear. Let's go get this magazine, and then let's go on our honeymoon."

Our wedding took place two days ago on the ranch. It was perfect—exquisite, intimate, joyful—but not gonna lie, I've been more excited for our honeymoon. Cash and I are headed to Australia for ten days, where we plan to ride horses and enjoy lots of time naked in the private plunge pool at the villa we booked at a swanky five-star resort.

"Yes, ma'am." Grinning, he passes my tote bag to his left hand so he can use his right to grab my hand.

I twine our fingers. "I can carry that, you know."

"You're gonna need your strength, honey. We didn't buy those big-ass, first class seats for nothin'. C'mon, I see a newsstand place up ahead."

I smile when Cash gets checked out left and right as we make our way through the crowded terminal. His height already makes him stand out. Add in his thick, athletic build, the blue eyes, and that epic mustache, and you have one very tall glass of water.

My legs get this tingly, weightless feeling when Cash leads me into a store stocked with snacks, drinks, books, and a whole wall of magazines.

"There it is," I breathe, my eyes catching on the current issue of *Elle*. Mindy Kaling is on the cover, which seems fitting considering how obsessed I am with her. My girl crush on her started when she played Kelly in *The Office* and has continued as I devoured *The Mindy Project* and then *Sex Lives of College Girls*.

I can just make out the headline on the cover's top right corner: "Giddyup: Your Guide to the Season's Hottest Trend in Western Wear."

"That's you," Cash murmurs. "You're the hottest trend."

"Ha." Reaching for the magazine, I feel like I'm floating. "Cash, this is wild. I've been knocking on *Elle's* door for years, and now it's happening. My boots are in their freaking magazine."

Cash's eyes glimmer. "Proud of you, Mollie. Perseverance pays off."

"Did I teach you that?"

He laughs. "You've taught me a lot of things, cowgirl." Nodding at the magazine, he adds, "Let's see."

My fingers shake as I open it. I love the substantial weight of a magazine like *Elle*; it's satisfying to thumb through the glossy pages, stopping to admire a suede handbag in a bold shade of chartreuse, a vintage charm bracelet, a pair of metallic gold shorty cowboy boots.

My heart stumbles to a sudden stop in my chest. "Those are my boots. Holy shit, Cash, those are my boots!"

Cash reaches down to clutch the top of the magazine in his hand, flattening out the pages so we can get a better look. He lets out a low whistle. "Best looking boots I've ever seen."

I quickly scan the text on the page. *Are you a fan of* Yellowstone? *Add some Beth Dutton flair to your outfit with these cowgirl-approved looks.*

Underneath it are three outfits that are so creative and perfect and edgy that I literally squeal with delight. Our gold Marilyn boots are paired with a fringed leather midi skirt, a wide belt, and a denim button-up, all topped off with a brown Stetson hat I need to purchase immediately.

My eyes prick. Blinking, I read the page again and again, smiling harder each time until my face hurts.

I glance over my shoulder when I hear Cash sniffle.

"What?" His Adam's apple bobs. "I'm just so happy for you, honey. I know how hard you and Wheeler have worked for this. We have a lot to celebrate, yeah? A lot to be grateful for."

Leaning my head into his chest, I nod, letting the tears fall. "For so long, I wondered if I was wasting my time. Like, would any of this work out? Was I taking my life in the right direction? Everyone thought I was nuts for sticking with a boot company I couldn't really get off the ground."

He runs a hand up my arm. "And now that company is skyrocketing straight to the top."

"Both our companies are." I hook a finger in the *v* of his shirt. "Bellamy Brooks *and* Lucky River Ranch."

He smiles, the skin at the edges of his eyes crinkling. "Life is good."

My turn to swallow. "Really good."

Cash insists on buying every copy of *Elle* the store has. "So you can pass them out to everyone we meet in Australia," he says, handing over his credit card to the cashier. "We want you to be famous there too."

As promised, Cash makes good use of our lay-flat seats in first class. Out of all the things I'm proud of, hooking up thirty-six thousand feet over the Pacific Ocean without anyone being the wiser might be my crowning achievement.

"I think I pulled a hamstring," Cash grunts as we deplane in Sydney seventeen hours later.

I grin. "Worth it?"

"What do you think?" He presses a quick, hot kiss to my neck. "Yeah, honey. It was worth it."

I have to agree. I don't know if it was the thrill of getting off in a public space, the threat of getting caught, or the lingering excitement of having Bellamy Brooks boots featured in *Elle*, but my orgasm *rocked* me. Maybe that's why my boobs still hurt.

Or is it something else? My stomach does a backflip. Cash and I decided to pull the proverbial goalie a few weeks ago. While we're not actively trying to get pregnant—we thought it best to wait until after we were married to give it a real go—we're not *not* trying.

Holy shit, did Cash already knock me up?

I've been so busy with work and then the wedding that I haven't really noticed any symptoms—until now. My boobs really do hurt. I haven't had much of an appetite, which I blamed on all the excitement happening. I've been extra tired this week. And that champagne we had at the airport tasted weird.

Come to think of it, so did the coffee we just had before landing. Cash said it tasted fine, but I couldn't drink mine. I thought it was just bad airplane coffee.

Could it be something else, though?

We're pulling up to the resort when Cash looks at me and smiles.

"What?" I reach for my tote, but he beats me to it.

"Nothing." He shakes his head before opening his door. "You've just been smiling ever since we landed. Your"—he licks his lips—"*glow* doesn't usually last this long."

Oh God, I'm definitely pregnant, aren't I?

My stomach flips again. I wait for panic to set in. For the tears to start, happy, sad, whatever.

Instead, I feel...weirdly at peace.

Is it so weird, though? I've known I want to have a baby with Cash since we had that pregnancy scare back in the fall. His reaction was so calm, so positive. So *sure*.

He's my best friend. My biggest cheerleader. The best bathtub buddy. And now he's my husband.

It's not weird at all to feel thrilled by the prospect of him being our baby's father too.

We've already taken emergency pregnancy tests together once, and I'd rather not have a repeat of that whole experience. After we check in and bring our luggage to our villa—it's spectacular, with waterfront views and the biggest, cushiest-looking bed ever—I tell Cash I'm going to check out the cute little clothing store in the lobby.

"I'll meet you back up here in a bit?" I ask.

He's already unbuttoning his shirt. "Don't be too long. I been waiting a lifetime to skinny-dip with you, honey."

I smile. "I'll be quick."

Luckily, the store has a convenience section, complete with all kinds of medicine, bottled water, sunscreen, and—hallelujah—pregnancy tests.

Another stroke of luck: Cash is already naked in the plunge pool when I return to the room a few minutes later. I pee on the two sticks, set my timer, and quickly undress.

This time, the minutes pass like seconds. I smile, hard, when I see the results. Glancing in the mirror, I'm taken aback. Cash was right—I am glowing. My eyes are bright. Cheeks and chest are pink. And this smile won't quit.

I pad out to the pool. Cash emerges from under the water, eyes still closed as he reaches up to smooth back the hair from his face. He's facing away from me, so I can admire the way the muscles in his back and shoulders bunch as he moves. His skin glistens in the sun. I smile at his tan lines: his neck and forearms are a deep brown, but his back, biceps, and butt are bright white.

I descend the steps into the water. Hearing me, Cash glances over his shoulder, bending his knees so I can wrap my arms around his neck, my front pressed to his back.

"You feel good, honey." He reaches around to palm my ass.

"Actually, I've been feeling a little off." I hold up the pregnancy test. "Now I know why."

He goes still. Then he wraps his hand around my wrist, bringing the stick closer to his face.

My heart pounds in my chest as he looks. Looks some more. And then—

And then.

He's pulling me around to his front. He's taking my face in my hands, and he's kissing me. I can taste the salt of his tears on our lips. He's laughing and I'm crying, and I'm not sure I can withstand this amount of joy. I feel like I'm about to burst.

At last, he pulls back, resting his forehead on mine. "Finally," he says.

I chuckle. "What does that mean?"

"I've only been waiting to get this news since the first time you took one of these tests." He grabs the stick out of my hand and sets it on a concrete paver beside the pool.

"Happened fast," I say.

He grunts, hand slipping to my belly. "It's happening just when it should."

"Timing is everything."

"You." He kisses my mouth. "You're my everything. You and this baby."

I swallow the lump in my throat. "You're gonna be such a great daddy."

"And you're gonna be the best mom, honey. I can't wait." Smiling, he kisses me again before reaching between my legs. "I can't fucking wait to start the rest of our life together."

FOR MORE LUCKY RIVER RANCH AND RIVERS MEN,
READ THE FIRST CHAPTER IN WYATT'S STORY

CHAPTER 1
King of Hearts
Sally

PRESENT DAY
NOVEMBER

Checking out the cowboy across the bar, I have one thought
and one thought only—*Damn, I've missed this.*

Thick, tan, tattooed forearms rippling with muscle
and crisscrossed with large veins—check.

Stetson and a pair of broken-in Wranglers, which are
topped off with a clean white tee that stretches across his
broad chest and shows off his enormous biceps—check.

Scruffy, obscenely handsome smirk—*check.*

My heart flutters when he looks up from chatting
with the gorgeous blond at his elbow and turns that
smirk on me. This cowboy is the complete opposite of
the serious, seriously entitled guys I went to college and
veterinary school with, and I am *here* for it.

Maybe that's why I'm in the middle of the longest
sexual drought of my life. Up until this summer, I wasn't
hanging out with any cowboys.

The cowboys I grew up with are generous and
honest to a fault. They say what they mean, and they

don't play games. They certainly don't make you feel self-conscious, like you're asking for too much or you're not cute or cool enough. Having lived in a handful of different places over the course of my studies, I've learned how rare that kind of man is.

The cowboy across the bar holds up his first two fingers in his approximation of a wave. "Hey, Sunshine."

I manage a smile, my face burning. "Hey, Wyatt."

You'd think I'd be immune to my best friend's extreme hotness by now, even though I've been away from Hartsville more often than not over the past decade. He and I have been friends for—goodness—over twenty years now. Wyatt Rivers *should* be like a brother to me.

Only the raging crush I've had on him since the second I hit puberty makes my feelings for him anything but fraternal.

The supermodel type beside him hanging on his every word is exhibit A as to why I've never acted on those feelings. Wyatt is way, *way* out of my league. He was always Mr. Popularity, star of our high school baseball and football teams, while I was the nerd who played violin, had braces, and spent her free time assisting her dad, a veterinarian, with calls on ranches across the county.

Wyatt is also very much a free spirit. Or playboy, depending on who you ask.

He'd be the perfect hookup, if only he wasn't my best friend. I don't have time for a boyfriend; last week, I was offered my dream job in Northern, New York, so I'm not sticking around in Hartsville. But while I'm here, I'd like to be able to get out of my head and have some really great sex—work out some of the frustration I've felt lately about, well, everything.

My experience in that department has been lackluster at best.

I lost my virginity at twenty-one to my boyfriend at the time, and the sex was unexciting to say the least; I only orgasmed when I took care of it myself. He blamed me, saying he'd "be more into it" if I was adventurous and lost a few pounds.

The next guy I dated insisted I always went down on him, but he never returned the favor.

"I just don't love it" was his explanation, which made me feel like the grossest, unsexiest person alive.

Was my body *really* that much of a turn-off?

The last boyfriend I had—this was during my residency about a year ago—didn't seem interested in having sex with me at all. When we did hook up, it was always quick and to the point. I tried to be adventurous with him—tried to incorporate more playfulness, more foreplay—but he always said he was "too tired," thanks to the round-the-clock rigors of our program. Which I didn't entirely understand, because I was in the same program and I was tired too, but never too tired to have sex. His lukewarm reaction made me feel pretty shitty about myself.

Years of disappointing experiences have left me feeling anxious and excruciatingly self-conscious when I'm with men. I feel like I need to constantly watch what I say, what I wear, what I eat. If I could be a little less of *this*, a little of more *that*, maybe the magic would finally happen.

It hasn't, and now my confidence is hanging by a

thread. It's gotten to the point that I'm so self-conscious around guys, I end up overthinking myself out of a great time. I try so hard to be what I *think* a guy wants that I can barely talk to someone, much less hit on them. I don't enjoy sex, because I'm always in my head about whether *he's* enjoying it. At some point, I just gave up trying to date.

But now it's been almost a full year since I've done anything with a member of the opposite sex, and I feel like I'm coming out of my skin. A vibrator can only get you so far. I'm legitimately worried I've forgotten how to kiss someone. I know I've forgotten how to pick someone up.

Most of all, I've forgotten how to have *fun*.

I put on a smile when Tallulah—the Rattler's owner and bartender—hands me a spicy margarita on the rocks, the glass rimmed with just the right amount of Tajín.

"How'd you know I wanted—"

"The Tajín?" Tallulah glances over her shoulder at Wyatt. "Lover boy over there ordered it for you."

Rolling my eyes, I bite back a smile. "Of course he did. Here's my card. You can keep it open—"

"He took care of that too." She waves away my card. "C'mon, Sally. You've been back for months now. You oughta know that man isn't gonna let you pay for a damn thing while you're here."

And *this* is why I often wonder if my standards for men are just too high. Has Wyatt, with his forearms and his Stetsons and his generosity, ruined me for everyone else?

I've been living in New York for the past three years, where I did my residency in large animal surgery at

Northern University. Before that, I'd attended veterinary school in Chicago, and before that, I'd completed my undergraduate degree in Waco. Guys bought me drinks in those places, but they did it with the implied expectation that we'd have sex, or I'd at least go down on them. But of course my orgasm was an afterthought, if they thought about it at all.

Cowboys are a different breed. Makes me wonder what the hell I'm gonna do when I move back to New York at the end of December. When I completed my residency at the Northern University Hospital for Animals back in May, I applied for my dream job to be a surgeon there. Dad and I always talked about how great it would be to work at a university, where I could practice *and* teach, maybe even do the kind of research that would lead to breakthroughs in the field. In the meantime, I returned to Hartsville without the job offer to figure out my next steps.

I'd missed Texas like crazy over the years, so I didn't mind moving home, even if it meant living with my parents. I love my hometown. I also love the veterinary work I've gotten to do alongside Dad in the area.

But when my adviser called me earlier this week and offered me the job at Northern University, I immediately accepted it, even though the conversation gave me a stomachache. The pay is great, the position is prestigious, and it will set me up as one of the top equine surgeons in the nation. The job security alone is worth it. Never mind the real impact I can make there—from performing life-saving surgeries to teaching others how to provide top-notch veterinary care. Dad said it was his dream to be that kind of groundbreaking surgeon, but his grades weren't good enough to make it happen. It's one of his biggest regrets.

I start January 1. Which means I only have so many ladies' nights at the Rattler left. Only so many days to get my cowboy fix so I can go back to Northern University sated and steady, ready to live out my dreams.

In other words, getting this job offer has kicked my search for no-strings-attached fun with cowboys into high gear.

It's also brought my anxiety to new heights, but I think once I get cute guys in Wranglers out of my system, I'll be ready to move back to New York.

I'll finally feel excited about the next chapter in my life. Love is something I'm definitely looking for in the long term. When I think about my future, I always picture having a partner in life. Someone to help shoulder life's burdens and celebrate its joys. Someone to start a family with and grow old with.

In the meantime, though, I just need to blow off some steam.

"Thank you for the drink," I call over to Wyatt, even as I give him a pointed look.

He just shrugs, still smirking. "It's ladies' night. Cheers, Sally."

"Cheers."

It's a Tuesday night at the Rattler, Hartsville's one and only dive bar. It's our only bar, period, which is why there's already a crowd here at half past five.

The space, with its sticky floor and clapboard walls and ceiling, buzzes with conversation, country music pumping through the speakers. I know I'm biased, but the vibe in here is unlike anything I've experienced anywhere else. There's this energy in the air, this sense of anticipation, that makes you feel like you're about to have a damn good time.

Ladies' night has been a time-honored Tuesday night tradition at the Rattler for as long as I can remember. Tallulah marks the occasion with half-price tequila drinks.

I don't always make it out. Our days begin early; Dad has coffee going by four, and we're usually out the door not long after that, on our way to the first of many appointments and calls he'll get.

By the time supper rolls around at five p.m., I'm beat. But tonight, my libido won out over my exhaustion. I'm not going to scratch my fun-with-a-cowboy itch if all I do is work and sleep. And being around Wyatt more often than not—he's a cowboy on Lucky River Ranch, where Dad cares for the herd and the horses—has taken my sexual frustration to new heights.

Sipping my margarita, I watch Wyatt make the pretty blond laugh while simultaneously buying another girl—this one a redhead—a drink. He's smiling, a Shiner Bock in his hand, as a third girl approaches him. They clearly know each other. Wyatt smiles, says something that makes her giggle, and then wraps her in a tight, flirty hug, the kind that has her going up on her tiptoes to plaster her body against his.

To be fair, he is a tall guy—six two—with long legs and the kind of pecs that would make a Hollywood casting director cry. At five three, I basically have to leap into the air to give Wyatt a hug.

The woman holds him for a beat too long before stepping back, her hand lingering on his chest, his arm lingering around her waist.

415

He talks. She keeps giggling. The other two women wait patiently for him to return his attention to them at the bar.

Really, Wyatt got this sunshine thing all wrong. He's the one who's the sun. The rest of us just float in his orbit, waiting our turn to bask in his warmth and attention.

I watch in wonder as he seamlessly brings the third girl into his conversation with the first two. Now Wyatt is telling a story, and *all* the girls are giggling. The blond playfully slaps his shoulder, and he responds with a flirty nudge of his elbow.

The man is a master.

He's fun without being cheesy. Forward without being creepy. There's an ease to the way he casts his spell over these women, a confidence in his movements, that's epically, lethally sexy.

Wyatt is getting laid tonight, no question. Ignoring the twist of jealousy in my gut at the idea of him taking *any* of these women home, I force myself to look away.

Lucky for me, my friend Mollie—who also happens to be Mom and Dad's employer, as she's the owner of Lucky River Ranch—picks that moment to walk into the Rattler. Cash—her fiancée and Wyatt's older brother—is right behind her.

Like usual, Mollie is dressed to the nines in a miniskirt and metallic-purple cowboy boots.

And like usual, Cash drapes an arm over her shoulders, letting everyone in the bar know she's taken.

Smiling, I wave at them. You'd never know from the lovey-dovey way they act now that a few short months ago, they absolutely hated each other's guts. Amazing how quickly things can change.

"I'm sorry he's here." Mollie aims a smile at Cash. "I know it's supposed to be girls' night—"

"But somebody's gotta make sure no one bothers y'all." Cash's voice is gruff, but his eyes are soft as he looks down at Mollie.

When I decided earlier this afternoon that I'd find a second wind and give ladies' night a try, I asked Mollie to be my wingwoman. She landed a hot cowboy, so I figure I have something to learn from her. She and I have gotten close since I've been home. Plus, she's always down to have a good time.

"Pretty sure that's why Sally's here, Cash." Mollie tilts her head. "To get bothered by hot guys."

"I'll make sure they're the right kind of hot guys, then." Cash glances across the bar at Wyatt and shakes his head. "My brother sure as hell ain't one of 'em. Who's he talking to?"

Mollie squints. "Don't know. Flavors of the day, I guess."

"Of the hour, more like it," Cash murmurs.

I smile tightly at the oldest Rivers brother. "Please tell me you have some friends you can introduce me to."

Stepping away from Cash, Mollie loops her arm through mine as she surveys the crowd. "There're some *cute* ones here tonight."

"Hey," Cash says.

Mollie just waves him away. "Oh, please, you and I both know you're the cutest of them all. The grumpiest too, but that's neither here nor there."

She's not wrong. I love Cash dearly, but he definitely growls a lot.

I will say, he's been almost pleasant—pleasant for Cash anyway—ever since he and Mollie got together.

See? That's the power of good sex. Love too, I guess, but let's not put the cart before the horse.

I need a fuck that's not fictional, as rude as that sounds. I need to take advantage of being in such close proximity to so many gorgeous guys with big hands and bigger…hearts. All of a sudden, I have an end date for my stay in Texas, so it's time to make shit happen.

A gust of cool air hits the backs of my legs. I turn to see a broad-shouldered man in a cowboy hat and a striped button-up stride into the bar.

My stomach dips. It's Beck Wallace, a horse trainer who works on his family's ranch about twenty miles away.

He's really, really handsome. He's not as tall as the Rivers boys, but he's still tan, ripped, and wearing a Stetson. He's got a head full of thick, dark hair and a scruffy beard-mustache situation going on.

When he smiles at me, I feel sparks catch inside my skin.

I also feel myself already getting inside my head. *Do I play hard to get, or do I go right up and talk to him? Would he be into a girl with that kind of confidence? Or would he want a nice girl, one he got to chase?*

All these questions—along with my desire to put on the perfect performance—fill me with anxiety. Our interaction hasn't even happened yet, and I'm already dreading it.

I already feel…defeated and kinda dead inside.

Mollie pulls me closer. "Ask and you shall receive. C'mon. Let's go say hello."

Before I can respond, she's pulling me toward Beck.

He and I grew up running in the same circles, but

because his family's ranch is in a different town, we didn't go to the same school. We were only officially introduced a month or so ago, when Beck came to deliver a horse to Lucky River Ranch that Cash had purchased. I immediately developed a little crush on him.

Beck's a charming guy. He's also a rock star at his job. After I examined the horse Cash had bought, it was clear that Beck and his family bred some of the finest quarter horses this side of the Rockies.

I should not be this nervous to run into him. Then again, I'm nervous around all guys. Except Wyatt, of course. But he doesn't count. I think I've internalized the idea that because Wyatt is *so* much hotter than me, *so* much cooler, I don't have a shot in hell of ever catching his eye. Which means I can just be myself around him. I'm not at all self-conscious around him. I don't second-guess myself the way I am right now.

It helps that Wyatt and I grew up together. There's a level of comfort between us, of camaraderie, that I hope will never ever go away.

I manage a smile as Beck holds out an arm, clearly inviting me in for a hug.

"Hey, darlin'! How you been?"

A million thoughts whip through my head as I look up into his green eyes. *What did that blond do again with Wyatt? Do I press my boobs against Beck's chest? What if the boobs are too much? I feel like he'd be into boobs. What guy isn't? I don't want to give him the wrong idea, though. But wait, I actually do want to give him that idea. Isn't that why I'm here? I can't always be the nice girl—nice girls don't get laid. But if I don't play the nice girl, will he want to see me again?*

Mollie is looking at me expectantly.

"Hey there." My scalp prickles with heat as I try my best to mimic the blond's smooth, easy, flirty hug. I move forward, reaching up, and Beck immediately recoils.

"Ow."

I look down to see that I'm stepping on his foot. Both feet actually.

Great freaking start.

My face is on fire as I jump away. "Oh my God, I'm so sorry—"

"Don't sweat it. You're not doing the Rattler right if your boots don't get a little scuffed up from being knocked around."

"Amen." Mollie cuts me a look. "I hope that means we'll be seeing you on the dance floor, Beck? Sally gets a break tonight from being the star of the show." She nods to the empty stage on the other side of the bar.

My mom is the drummer for Frisky Whiskey, a local band that plays here every Friday night. When I'm in town, I moonlight as a backup singer and violinist.

"Hardly the star," I reply.

"I've seen you up there, doing your thing. You're great." Beck is still smiling at me—a good sign. "I don't have a musical bone in my body, so I'm always so impressed when people can sing or play an instrument."

I swallow, *thank you* on the tip of my tongue. But a bit of Tajín gets stuck in my throat. Suddenly, I'm choking, my eyes watering as I sip more tequila in an effort not to cough.

But oh, do I cough. Loud enough that I catch Wyatt looking up from his threesome—or it's a foursome, I guess, if you include him—and scrunching his brow while mouthing, *You okay?*

I hold up my thumb. "All good. Just went down the wrong pipe."

"You really all right?" Beck's eyebrows are pulled together. "I can get you some water if you need it."

I shake my head. "Water's the last thing I need."

"You sure?"

"Well, yeah." I suck down the dregs of my margarita, all the while wondering at what point interacting with men had become the opposite of fun. "I'm clearly a mess, so I probably need something a little stronger. You know, to, um…"

"Loosen up a little?" Mollie looks at me.

The sympathy in her eyes makes me wish the ground would open up and swallow me whole.

"Yes, that. Exactly. It's been a long day. I mean, we've all had long days, am I right? Because days here are long. And hard. Not that there's anything wrong with long and hard things. I just—oh. Oh wow, that…came out wrong. I was just trying to say that sometimes, I enjoy things *because* they're long and also hard—"

"How about we get you another margarita?" Mollie begins pulling me back toward the bar before offering Beck a smile. "We'll be right back."

Acknowledgments

This book would not exist without the help of my talented, gorgeous, hard-working, adorable, amazing, delightful, incredible, super smart team. I feel so, ★so★ lucky to have found each and every one of you, and I'm grateful for your support. Love y'all!

First up, I have to thank the ladies I work with day in and day out. Jodi and Meagan, y'all are my right hand gals, and you make what was once a lonely job one that I absolutely love. Thank you for putting up with my random voice messages, my rambling questions, and my general chaotic work-life mess. Could not adore you more!

To the ladies (and Charlie) at Valentine PR: I love, love, LOVE working with you! Nina, you're the smartest, most fun, most well-connected person I've ever met. Christine, Kelley, Valentine, Kim, Josette, and Sarah, I'm sorry I suck at answering emails. I can't forget to thank Tracy! I love you and I so appreciate you making the most beautiful PR boxes EVER for me.

To Najla Qamber and her team: y'all rock. Your work is second to none, and you make my job SO much easier. You always, always get the vibes right!

To my editors, Rachel, Joni, and Jovana: I am grammar's worst nightmare, but for some reason, you put up with me and fix all my mistakes. Y'all are the smartypants-es I need in my life.

Huge shout out to my alpha readers, Nina, Chasity and Meagan, and to my beautiful beta team: Catherine, Logan, and Logan (or Logan squared, whichever you prefer). Your feedback on early drafts of this book truly brought the story to the next level. THANK YOU!

To my Facebook Reader Group admins, Kenysha and Tara: thank you so very much for holding down the fort while I disappeared into my writing cave. Y'all rock.

To my fellow authors who have become dear friends. Marni, Lulu, Elizabeth, Maria, Monica, and Amy, y'all are such an inspiration, and I so appreciate your kindness!

To all the Instagram, Facebook, and TikTok girlies who have shown this book an overwhelming amount of love: thank you for helping spread the word about my books! I've loved getting to know each of y'all, and hope to squeeze you soon at a signing!

And most of all, to my readers: I get to live my dream every day because of you. I appreciate your support more than you'll ever know. Thank you from the bottom of my heart!

I also have to give a shout out to my little family. I've never worked harder in my life trying to balance my roles as mom and author, but I'm so grateful I have a whole world outside my work to get lost in. I love you!

About the Author

Jessica Peterson writes romance with heat, humor, and heart. Heroes with hot accents are her specialty. When she's not writing, she can be found bellying up to a bar in the south's best restaurants with her husband, Ben, reading books with her adorable daughter, Gracie, or snuggling up with her seventy-pound lap dog, Martha.

A Carolina girl at heart, she fantasizes about splitting her time between Charleston and Asheville, but currently lives in Charlotte, NC.